G P FRANCIS

PRIMED

PRIMED

Primed

A novel by G P Francis

1st Edition Trade Paperback

Publication date: March 2013

Published simultaneously in US, UK, Canada, China, India, Japan, Germany, France, Italy, Spain and Brazil by registered Canadian publisher Dissident Press, Unit 214 Harbourview, 550 Royal Avenue, New Westminster, BC, Canada V3L 5H9, website: http://gp4ancis.wix.com/dissidentpress

All rights reserved

ISBN: 978-0-9918678-1-3

Text copyright © 2013 by G P Francis

Cover art copyright © 2013 by G P Francis

Cover art contribution acknowledgements: Mr. Lightman; Victor Habbick; B Neptuno

No part of this book may be reproduced or transmitted in any form or by any means, electronic or mechanical, including photocopying, recording, or by any information storage and retrieval system, without permission in writing from the publisher. For information and usage or adaptation rights, contact Dissident Press

Dissident Press supports Socially Responsible Publishing through contributions to charitable crowdfunding causes. For more information, visit: http://igg.me/at/dogood

Primed is a work of fiction: any resemblance to persons living or dead is entirely coincidental.

PRIMED

DEDICATION

"Write to please just one person. If you open a window and make love to the world, so to speak, your story will get pneumonia." (Kurt Vonnegut, *Bagombo Snuff Box*, 1999)

For Grace

PRIMED

CONTENTS

Dedication — page 5

Preface — page 9

Chapter One: Operation Blast from the Past — page 10

Chapter Two: Operations Quick Rinse and Rolling Stone — page 16

Chapter Three: Operations Touchdown and Tread Water — page 35

Chapter Four: Operation Regroup — page 52

Chapter Five: Operation Revamp — page 60

Chapter Six: Operation Dog Hair — page 70

Chapter Seven: Operation Do-over — page 80

Chapter Eight: Operation First Impressions — page 87

Chapter Nine: Operation Tail Feather — page 113

Chapter Ten: Operation Scouring Pad   page 118

Chapter Eleven: Operation Target Practice   page 123

Chapter Twelve: Operation Bullseye   page 133

Chapter Thirteen: Operation Backflip   page 146

Chapter Fourteen: Operation Smokescreen   page 153

Chapter Fifteen: Operation Blonde Bombshell   page 159

Chapter Sixteen: Operation Wipe-out   page 169

Chapter Seventeen: Operation Thin Air   page 177

Chapter Eighteen: Operation Musketeers   page 213

Epilogue   page 225

Glossary   page 231

PRIMED

PREFACE

The setting for this novel actually began as a videogame I'd planned to produce. As it became increasingly complex and detailed the story and the characters really just grew into the space provided, insisting on being given form, much as in the theory that, given sufficient time, life will develop anywhere the correct conditions are met.

I'm fortunate to share this world with the most amazing sources of inspiration: friends, family, fellow writers and innovators who've shown me, through their own lives, how to persevere, to accomplish the goal no matter how gruelling the labour, and to follow ones heart to achieve ones greatest desires. I'll name them now to acknowledge their impact on my life, embarrass them and let you, the reader, know which reviews to ignore when you catch them online trying to praise my books!

Thanks to: Grace, for reading, editing, objectivity and insight, and for constantly asking me for the next chapter to read; the Francis clan of Anika, Zoe, Padmé, Barbara ('ello, Ma), Kirsten, Ian and Isabelle for putting up with me all my (or their) life; the Neptunos for welcoming me in; A Jabbar K; Kerry J; David Q; Chris O; Aidan and Lisa; Leslie and Aidan; Chris and Hiromi; Phillip T R; Frank and Kyoko; Richard, David & Mr M (Nam Myoho Renge Kyo); John C; Tony M; David A; Jakub K (aka James C); Mary S; Philip K D; Arthur C C; Kurt V; William G; J R R T; Sir Terry P; Daisaku I; Josei T; Tsunesaburo M; Mohandas G; Martin L K Jr; R Buckminster F; Nikola T; Wilhelm R; Carl J; Galileo G. My apologies to anyone I neglected to mention.

PRIMED

CHAPTER ONE: OPERATION BLAST FROM THE PAST

Fleeting sensations of light, dark, warmth, cold, unintelligible sounds, resolved to clearer experiences from childhood, but rushing through her mind so quickly it was impossible to distinguish individual events from the overall impression: a blur of increasingly familiar surroundings, within which the only constant seemed to be her own blossoming awareness. A stream of sensory impressions poured into her mind like water into a bucket, taking its shape, an entire, echoic vocabulary phonologically looping, cross-associating with iconic lightning-flashes: 'mommy', 'no', 'bottle', 'yes', 'what', 'that', 'flower', 'finger', 'kitty', 'doggy', 'potty', 'flyer'....

It was not a complete rerun of her life, more like a series of reminiscences, of events where novelty, strong emotions and associations had facilitated the encoding of vivid memories. Most welled up from her adolescence, flashing through levels of schooling to university, where fast-forward memories of partying began to outweigh those of studying.

Suddenly, she was in uniform. Basic training in the time it takes for a round of applause to die down. Then her surroundings were dramatically shifting – alien horizons, nights lit by multiple moons, sometimes days by multiple suns; jungles of fungi; deserts hot, cold; atmospheres breathable, toxic; gravities high, low; underwater; out in space, piloting fighters over gas giants, through asteroid fields; plummeting from an orbital drop ship; scrambling over rough terrain; through bombed-out ruins; all punctuated with bursts of weapons fire, explosions, blood and limbs flying as her companions were torn apart, sometimes her own body being torn apart, but always coming back, the same faces, laughing it off.

As if someone eyed 'play' everything suddenly returned to normal speed. She was scaling a foliate-lined ridge with her squad, carrying a rifle and a pack. A squad member reported to the group: "*.psy* uploads complete – switching back to offline protocols."

'Parker?' her own internal voice queried. It was an effort to remember his name, and her body didn't respond to her conscious desire to look around, ascertain her surroundings and the identities of her companions, making her aware that, as vivid as this was, she was outside the action, observing, remembering, or dreaming.

She remembered serving alongside him for over a year, ever since graduating out of Witch Head. 'Yes, it's Parker, the squad's Field Technician. He handles most of the squad's data streaming requirements.' Without her conscious volition, she watched herself dutifully issue eye-point instructions on her *arhud*, remotely shutting down the uplink from her field operations terminal, a small slab of nano-circuitry imbedded in her anti-ballistic helmet.

There was no familiarity about this scene, no sense of *déjà-vu*. It felt like she was streaming an avblog entry that she didn't remember making. Unable to affect the course of events as they unfolded, she allowed them to wash over her, dimly remembering similar experiences during previous revivals. 'Is that what this is?'

Along with her other team-mate, Keenan, and their squad commander, Major Harris, they climbed without another word, only their laboured breathing in the moon's thin atmosphere and the rattle of dislodged stones as they cascaded down the slope behind them breaking the silence.

Grasping at the slender, woody shoots of the parallel-evolved flora growing at the top of the ridge, trunks like young silver birches, crowned with globular clusters of dark purple-blue leaf analogues like gigantic, inverted bunches of grapes (UNE hadn't bothered sending xenobotanical surveyors to classify them; their interest in the system was purely as a staging and refuelling area for territorial expeditions above the solar plane on the beacon route out via Gleise 411), they pulled themselves up off the eroded, sandy face they had worked their way up, and into cover. Several seconds later, as they leant back on their packs, faces flushed, sucking in oxygen, the double boom of an atmospheric patrol passed over them.

"They triangulated that last transmission," Major Harris said to Parker, then, to the group "The third site's thirty metres along the ridge," slowly turning his head, presumably in the direction indicated on his arhud. "That way," he confirmed, with an instinctive, hastening hand gesture to fall out.

Peering up through the translucent canopy, squinting in the weak orange light of Groombridge 1618 as the night side of its massive, brown-banded, hydrogenous gas giant companion, Supiter, chased it high across this satellite's dusty brown sky, Parker muttered "I can't see 'em...."

"You wouldn't," her own mouth voiced, startling her a little, despite her immersion in the scene. "They'd be clocking over Mach twenty, air-spiking at high altitude. By the time we heard the booms, they'd've been well beyond visual, already."

Keenan eyed the skies, commenting in his Irish brogue "I can't see much of anyt'in'! Reckon they shoulda called this place '*Gloom*bridge.' D'ya t'ink they could've seen us climbin'?"

"Maybe. Depends on their lines of sight into the valley, how close we were to the floor when they passed. But probably, yes. They've got hi-mag' thermal imagers *and* satellite support," she informed him.

"It doesn't matter. We've got a job to do. As long as we get moving we'll be done before they can three-sixty," Harris advised them. They picked their way through the plant life across the top of the sedimentary escarpment they had found plateauing beyond the ridge, ducking under the occasional low-hanging globule. In less than a minute, Harris announced "We're here. Parker, scan it."

Parker drew a nanopoxy pole from his pack, and thrust it with all his body weight into the ground, activated its *SeizULFem* sensor bundle then focussed his attention on the ground around their feet. "I'm getting some readings – definitely a subterranean passageway. Vibrations... extrapolating movement. Yeah, it's heading this way, almost directly beneath us. Moving slowly, about thirty metres down. Nuke'll definitely chimney to the surface. Still wanna bother running?" He smiled around at the ring of colleagues.

"All the faster, for that news," said Keenan, fervently.

"Call it in, Parker," ordered Major Harris.

"Just let me finish these projections. Okay, I'm uploading!"

A moment later, Harris suddenly started. "Okay, they got it. Launch signal, let's move it, people!" They all knew they had about thirty seconds to get a hundred metres from where they were. Their mission support ship, *The Cassandra* – supposedly named after the daughter of a Conglomerate board member – awaited their signal in high orbit, equipped with a railgun to insert a two-phase hybrid armature into the atmosphere at a velocity that made it impossible to intercept.

The first phase, a tungsten-carbide, cone-tipped steel cylinder, bore a paramagnetic barium ferrate battery facilitating its acceleration during launch, linked to a secondary railgun running along the length of its core. In the instant before impact the battery would discharge to the railgun, driving the second phase from the protective cylinder back along its own trajectory path. The first phase would be further accelerated, restoring some of the kinetic energy lost to the atmosphere during its descent, striking the ground meteorically, displacing regolith and shattering the bedrock. The second phase, a more sophisticated tunneling device carrying an eighty kiloton thermonuclear device, would be rapidly decelerated to make a soft landing in the crater made by the impact of the first phase. It wouldn't detonate on impact, in fact not for a while, until it had burrowed through the lens of broken rock and shatter cones beneath the crater floor, as close as it could get to the subterranean, crawling command centre Parker had *XYZTed*.

The blast of displaced air from the hard-landing of the first phase would still knock everyone off their feet at a hundred metres out. The closer they were to the point of impact they'd be facing anything from internal haemorrhaging to ruptured organs, even complete soft tissue liquefaction.

They had talked about it earlier, in the ship's mess, whether to run or stay. Running would serve little rational purpose: the chances of surviving were infinitesimal, unless the final explosion was deep enough to be fully contained. Their intel' suggested it would not be, but there were so many variables involved in this operation. Sitting tight for the impact *would* be the easy way out, compared with a prolonged and tortuous death by exposure to radiation.

Keenan, who collected causes of death like badges of honour, had won the group's consensus, in the end: "Why are we even talkin' about it? Damn' right, I'm gonna run. Get out to a nice spot, then stop and admire the view. Fuck, I'll surf that ejecta like I'm back on the Nort' Shore, if I have to. I dunno about you 'guzzlers, but *I'm* not in this line of work 'cause I'm the type to go down easy, no matter *how* easy it might be to come back. I'm gonna hang on to life by the *scrote* - by the *last pube*, if I have to! Deat' already knows he's gonna have to shave my balls to get his bonies on *me*. T'ink about it; how many times do you t'ink we'll get a chance to bear witness to some'n' like this? It'll be spec-fucking-*tac*ular! *Fuck* the fallout, *and* the rads, if it comes to that: can't be worse than ships rations, anyway. What the fuck *is* this?" He had let the brown paste fall from his spoon in a dollop, making a small crater in the surface of the homogenous food-stuff in his bowl.

"You don't love life, Keenan, you're just too tight to bear the thought of the clone charge coming out of your wages," she'd told him. He had looked at her in silent contemplation, for a moment, so lost in thought that he even inadvertently spooned in and swallowed a mouthful of his brown paste without complaint.

"They're not charging for this one, are they?" He swivelled on his seat to address the squad leader. "Major Harris, this mission *is* covered by the A.O.D. clause, isn't it?"

So they ran. Even though they knew they were almost certainly going to die, one way or another, that 'Anticipated Operative Demise' was an accepted cost of carrying out the mission, autho'-stamped by corporate accountants. Not down the slope they had scaled: that wouldn't even exist by the time they were half way down it. They needed to stay high, and move radially from the point of impact. As one, they sprinted in the direction of their Extraction Point, parallel to the valley floor they had followed in. They didn't get far before a wall of flame erupted ahead of them, scorching wind and flaming debris making them drop for cover.

Keenan rolled over onto his back and, unclipping his chinstrap, let his helmet fall to the ground behind him. "Well, I guess we know if they saw us or not. *BOHICA*, everyone...."

Above the crackling flames and the sizzling and spitting of roasting leaf globules she heard her tactical advisory soft start to countdown in her mind, signaling the approach of the bunker buster.

It was too fast to see or hear, but she glanced up through the canopy, anyway, and sensed its deadly approach at a more primitive level than the eye or ear could discern, felt her skin prickle and tighten across her flesh in warning.

She heard and felt the impact an instant later, her whole body resonating like a beaten drum as she was double-smacked by the bucking ground and blast of air; clumps of regolith sprang up around her; clouds of soil, blown from the roots of plants, hung in the air as if some child had thrown a tantrum during a board game they were losing, and pounded on the board.

Adrenalin dragged the magic of the moment out, but soon the trick was over, and they were crashing back to the ground in a hail of shattered rocks, clods of earth and splintered vegetation.

Miraculously, her head was still in air, and she dared a look around as finer soil and dust settled. She wasn't buried, and nothing heavy had landed on top of her. But her ears were chiming, and her vision was blurred. She had the worst hangover she could remember. Not good signs. Her legs were barely responsive, and she concluded widespread damage to her nervous system.

Keenan had landed close by, buried up to the chest, motionless and unblinking as his upturned eyes and open mouth slowly filled with raining soil. One arm was propped up by a protruding rock so that his open hand reached up into the air in front of him. He looked peaceful.

Parker was nearby, lying mostly clear of the soil, perhaps thanks to his relatively slight build, but with a jagged boulder lying squarely across his lower back and legs. Pinned face down in the dirt, he was still moving, turning his face to the air. There was no sign of Harris.

She started crawling towards Parker, using her forearms, her task facilitated by the newly formed slope of ejecta she lay on. He was looking her way, his mouth moving. What was he saying? She got to within arm's length. He was still talking, but she still couldn't hear anything but an all pervading hum. She shook her head, wagged her finger by her ear. He smiled at her, and nodded weakly. His flesh had begun to swell and darken from cellular damage, but he forced his fingers to sign to her '*I hate this job.*' She nodded as strongly as she could in agreement, and he concluded '*I quit!*'

She signed back '*See you on the other side,*' and, seeing a tear form in the corner of Parker's eye she reached a purpled hand towards him to offer consolation. Parker's mouth moved again, indecipherably, then abruptly the ground beneath them vaporised in an instant of incomparable violence of white, heat and light....

CHAPTER TWO: OPERATIONS QUICK RINSE AND ROLLING STONE

Light. Painful light, piercing her eyes, stabbing her brain into reluctant wakefulness. Her arms were gripped and pulled; her head flopped back on a neck too weak to lift it, before it, too, was gripped and supported.

She felt herself lifted, as a viscous liquid sucked at her. Warm water sluiced away heavy clots that clung to her flesh, then something scraped across her skin, tangled up and immobilised her limbs, as she was jostled and pummelled, deposited roughly onto what felt like a bed of nails, raw, untrained nerve endings complaining and crying at their bitter treatment. Then an unwelcome, bruising pressure on the back of her hand, followed an instant later by a hot spike of fresh agony that jolted up her arm, through her brain, and prickling out through her scalp. She heard a wracking sob escape from her lips, as though someone else was crying out of her mouth. Reminded of speech, she tried to form her tongue around an intelligible complaint, but the effort involved left her settling for a disapproving grunt at her assailants, whoever they might be.

Soon, numbness began to spread from her impaled hand, and when it had soothed every part of her she felt comfortable enough to crack open one screwed-shut eye to investigate her surroundings.

This was not the Station Lab'. It looked like a basement. Bare concrete walls stained with patches of effervescence. Familiar equipment plugged into portable generators, unfamiliar technicians dressed casually, foregoing the familiar white coats which, for no good reason, reassured one of hygiene and professionalism. Feeling suddenly exhausted, she gave her eyes permission to draw closed: 'It seems safe enough; I'll open them again in a moment, just to be sure....'

∞

"Better?" Her eyes fluttered open, taking in her surroundings through the cotton-candy haze of the drugs in her system. A jumble of dream-like memories echoed in her mind. The question had come from an oval faced, crop-bearded man, with a Mediterranean complexion and streaks of gray in his otherwise black hair.

"Mmm." It was difficult to form words, she seemed to lack almost all incentive to do anything but lie there and breathe shallowly.

"Good. Good." The man sat at the side of her bed on a folding steel chair. As he moved, her head was sufficiently tempted to flop to that side. She noticed a raised rail beside her mattress, wondering idly if there were another to her left, but couldn't be bothered to turn her head all the way over to look. Too far. Check later.

"I'm Colonel Evagora. Are you thirsty? I can get you some water, if you like?" Barely curious, she allowed her tongue to explore her mouth. Everything felt very smooth and soft. Was that the drugs? She couldn't be sure, at this point. 'Not thirsty. Mouth dry, but not worth the effort to talk about it. Maybe later.' Her thoughts barely formed into words.

"No? Well, I suppose the I.V. is taking care of that." He directed his gaze above her to his right, where she guessed an I.V. drip fed through a tube into a vein in the back of her hand. Curiosity getting the better of her lethargy, she eventually turned her head for a better look. She took in more bare walls, a cracked and stained ceiling with antique, fluorescent light fixtures. A metal pole span into view near her left knee, suspending a bag of clear fluid from a hook.

'Ah, there it is,' she thought to herself. Following the line down from the tube, she noticed a digital feed clipped into the line, continuously administering drugs from three up-ended, quartztic cylinders atop the device. And, just to confirm all previous thoughts, she allowed her eyes to drop to her side, taking in the intravenous needle taped to the back of her curled hand, and, yes, the other raised bedrail.

"What'm I on?"

"Just an analgesic and an anxiolytic. We're easing those down. Which is why we're able to have this conversation. The third vial is your immune system restorative." For no apparent reason, he leant in towards her, and, giving her a conspiratorial look, false-whispered "Anti-bodies," as though he were slipping her a hip-flask of tequila instead of a tube of irradiated diseases. "What doesn't kill you makes you stronger...."

PRIMED

Suspecting a string of such trite comments in an attempt to put her at ease, and knowing that the opposite effect would be accomplished, she pushed through the receding haze in her brain to the present.

"Where are we? Thpis isn't thpe Station lab...." Her vocalisation was off: she'd tried to form a 'th' sound with her tongue against and just behind her teeth, but she missed: her tongue, probing forwards, kept going until it reached her lips, settling for the closest approximation it could get, a wet, plosive-sounding consonant, like one makes when spitting.

"No, this is a new facility. You've been assigned here for a new mission." She started to ask another question, but he silenced her with a raised hand. "No more questions, soldier: time to move out. The security of this facility *has* most likely been compromised. I'll explain the rest once we're mobile. Can you walk?"

He took her wrists, and she grasped his, both pulling as she sat up, the bedrail sliding away to the floor. She swung her legs over the edge of the mattress. They felt heavy, and her feet slapped the floor, loudly. She couldn't determine if this were due to her weak condition, the drugs affecting her strength, or the local gravity here, wherever *here* was, being higher than she was acclimatised to, or some combination. In any case, she found she could stand, if a little unsteadily. Evagora guided her hands to the walk-rail around her I.V. drip, making it clear that was about as much help as she could expect.

"There's about five minutes left on your I.S.R. Get dressed, take out the needle after the beep and meet me upstairs. I've got a few things to take care of before we leave." She nodded grimly, and started plucking at the civilian garments clearly intended for her on the back of a nearby chair. Once he was out of the room, she unfastened her bed clothes. Like her customary military garb, it auto-seamed up the sides, coming apart into a poncho-like, continuous pattern, so that she could remove it without having to pull her arm, along with its attached I.V. feed, out through the sleeve. The civilian clothes were not so equipped, however, and she would have to wait for the supply of anti-bodies to beep out before she could strip the needle out of the back of her hand to pull on a shirt.

Stiff-limbed, shivering, she painstakingly dressed, all the while becoming more conscious of her physical condition. She barely recognised her own body. It was, of course, lean, but much more so than she was used to: fresh clone bodies usually came with an optimal fat content, typically primed for endurance and survival activities, unless they'd been squelched out in a hurry, before the twelve week gestation cycle had run its course.

The poor condition of her muscles further testified to this eventuality: again, electrical stimulation of the major muscle groups and proper nutrition would build a clone body to fighting form, so an operative could hit the ground running, fresh out of the bell-shaped, fluid-filled vat that housed the clone during its gestation, once their *.psy* file was fully downloaded, of course.

Clone brains, already fully integrated with a duplicate of their donor's avtog interface, were preoccupied with a dream-speed stream of sensory data from their banked memory file, which, combined with full sensory suppression, prevented a clone from forming a rudimentary consciousness of its own. Without this precaution, revived operatives would recall *memories from the bell* belonging to the growing clone, clashing with their living timeline and jarring with their sense of identity. Despite the high level of neurological activity present in the brain of a gestating clone, this was always described in the donor literature as the donor's own mind, not the mind of the clone. The body was likened to the sacks of meat protein grown in nutri-vats.

O.A.C.I.'s private army taught its operatives a dualistic philosophy called *the Doctrine*, wherein the body was regarded as a tool and weapon for the warrior. The warrior was not the weapon, could be separated from the weapon, and a new weapon given to replace it. The warrior endured. The warrior was an entity of mind.

A properly indoctrinated O.A.C.I. operative could be capable of incredible acts of self-sacrifice and bravery in the face of the enemy, of enduring extreme interrogative techniques, and of ending their own life without a second thought, if to do so would secure or facilitate a military advantage. When fighting against the often numerically advantaged conventional forces of the United Nations of Earth, or taking on a genetically augmented, elite squad produced, somewhat controversially, by certain borderline rogue member states and Earth-loyal off-world colonies, the Doctrine could go a long way towards levelling the playing field.

She also recalled there'd been no feed mask when the technicians pulled her from the bell: she would have recalled the nauseating sensation and painful tug of the nutrient supply lines being drawn out of her throat and nostrils. A plastic clip on a severed and bloody protrusion from her navel indicated there must only have been an umbilical oxygen supply. Then she remembered her response to the ambient light, and the intense handling pain as she was drawn from the bell, cleaned and dried. The polysorb towels had felt like sandpaper across her thin skin. Her nerve endings must all have been freshly formed and prone to hyper-stimulation.

And, of course, she was completely hairless. She had no finger or toe nails, and soon discovered her speech difficulties had not been due to the drugs in her system, or at least not entirely: she also had no teeth.

All these factors pointed to an extremely premature end to her revival. She must have been pulled as soon as the genetic matrix set within the megaloblastocyst. Realising this, and contemplating the vaguely anthropomorphic cluster of stem cells that comprised her body until just a few hours ago, she felt sharply disconnected from her body, a wave of anxiety building from the pit of her stomach. Focussing on her hands, she comforted herself with The Doctrine: 'This is not *me*. Just a *tool*.' Not even a weapon, yet, more like an iron bar that needed to be forged and alloyed and folded and hammered and quenched and sharpened into a weapon. She mourned in advance the hours of physio' and exercise she'd have to consciously endure to recover her former condition, never mind the pain of the process, as she tested her short tendons during the struggle to get her socks and shoes on.

Apart from the physical difficulty, she also found it to be unexpectedly mentally challenging: when she came to lace her shoes, for a moment, she really didn't know how to do it. It seemed as though she had just gone through an avtog sim-torial, but this was her first time *actually* doing it herself. The sensation soon passed, and she turned her mind to the upcoming, wasted time spent grounded, when she could *and should* be out there, fighting the war. *Winning* the war.

The beeping of the dosimeter cut her thoughts short, and she moved as she was trained, as she was ordered. With a thumb on the insertion site, fingers on her palm, she drew out the needle from the back of her hand, pressing down on the tape to stem the bleeding. The accompanying, sickly pain paled in comparison to injuries she'd received throughout her military career, many of which had proved fatal, the worst of which not immediately so. She kept the pressure on for thirty seconds, then finished dressing, pulling on the t-shirt and hooded sweater provided.

The fleece-lined hood warmed her scalp when she pulled it up, and the act of covering her baldness, whilst, to her logical mind, arbitrary, nevertheless consoled whatever vestigial remnant of femininity she had cared to retain as part of her identity after all her years of training and field operations. She condemned her vanity as ridiculous, then noticed that, despite her adherence to medical procedure, her hand had started to bleed a little from the I.V. insertion site. She wordlessly scolded her body for its thin and fragile epidermis, its poor blood-clotting capability, and the technicians and her superiors for their decision to revive her in this condition. There would be other consequences, of course, to look forward to, both physical *and* mental. The strain on this fresh and fragile body was a lot to endure. But Command must have had its reasons, not least the need to vacate this facility A.S.A.P. So endure she must, it would seem.

Pushing through the swing door, she found a flight of metal stairs bolted to more bare concrete walls. Double doors at the top were fitted with frosted windows, past which she discerned a small group, moving and loading equipment, the muffled voice of Evagora issuing directions, urging haste. Gripping the banister, her knuckles whitening her pink flesh, she grunted in effort as she willed her reluctant body to climb, one step at a time. The first words she heard clearly when she half fell into the next room were: "...and prime the A.I. detonator. We may as well kill two birds with one stone. Or more, if possible."

∞

'Donuts – six a day for six weeks. That should help.' She continued to plan her physical recovery regime, concerned first and foremost with building up a healthy subcutaneous fat store, and stabilising her body's electrolyte levels. She had been offered a blanket, quite considerately, she thought, when she'd climbed into the passenger cab of the sub-orb' hauler at Evagora's insistence, but instead of using it for heat retention she had padded her torso against the restraint harness, which dug painfully through to her sparsely covered bones.

When Evagora strapped in facing her she didn't bother asking any of the thousands of questions someone in her situation might have. She was confident he would tell her everything she needed to know. Or, at least, everything *they* needed *her* to know. In the latter, she was not disappointed: "There's a lot I need to tell you, and not much time." He didn't bother with further platitudes, for which she was grateful. "By now you've probably surmised that you've been processed rather quickly."

"No shit!" She had never been much of a one for military formalities or adherence to intra-rank conversational conventions. But that was more a reflection on her operational capabilities than any insubordination. Operatives at her level were few in number, and treated each other as equals regardless of official rank. She intuitively sensed Evagora would grasp the distinction.

"Suffice to say that cloning conditions these days are less than ideal."

"'Deese days'?" She had given up trying to form a 'th' sound tergo-dentally, settling instead for a palatal 'd' or labial 'f,' depending on whether it was a soft or hard 'th.'

"Well, that brings me to my next point: you've been... *un-commissioned* for a little longer than you might be used to."

"'Un...?' *How* long?" Evagora had a reluctant look on his face, like a boyfriend about to break it off, worrying about her reaction. Those boyfriends had been right to worry, but since she didn't remember ever dating Evagora, who was way too old and not her type in any case, she guessed the answer would not be one she would receive well.

"Three years."

She bit back a string of further unconventional phrases that welled up, mindful of Evagora's warning that time was short. She settled for a concise, and genuinely uncomprehending, "*Why?*"

"The whole story?" She nodded, mutely. "Your unit's operational base was destroyed by an UNE bombardment three years ago. Everyone on station was killed." Evagora revealed his European origins with his pronunciation of the acronym for the United Nations of Earth: most anglophones would have said it like *YOON*, but he had used the teuto-francophonic *OON* variant.

Her mind swam with thoughts of her comrades, already trying to convince herself of their loss in the absence of her own experience of the event. Evagora hadn't said anything to indicate they were gone for good, but she was sufficiently pragmatic to come to that conclusion on her own. "We'd just called in da bunker buster at Groombridge...."

"Yes, that would be your last *memory*, but technically that wasn't your last *mission*. You were revived after Groombridge and during the attack on your base you and a fellow squad member mounted an extra-vehicular sabotage run against the deflector field generators on the UNE destroyer. As I said, the base was destroyed, but thanks to the two of you so was the UNE vessel. You were extracted by a company loss recon' ship sent to investigate the wreckage. You were both low on rebreathe-O, but alive.

"It turned out the UNE strike was one of many co-ordinated raids on corporate headquarters and operational facilities, which shut down our main supply lines at source, effectively putting an end to conventional military operations. We've continued with a series of hit-and-runs and resistance activities, but the equipment and supply losses severely restricted our re-cloning capabilities. As a result, these have been less ambitious than former operations.

"After a series of successful missions your colleague was transferred to train new recruits at Witch Head, while you came *here*, to A.C.P., about two years ago. Regrettably, your last loss of life occurred shortly afterwards, in the initial stages of the same UNE heightened security operation you were sent to investigate. Took most of us by surprise, I'm afraid."

"What? I don't remember –"

"No, you wouldn't. Our safe houses were raided, right across UNE's core jurisdictions; our mainframe was destroyed, along with all our *.psy* files; only a small group of operatives were able to upload to terminals before they died. We lost you, and many others."

'Oh, great, I'm on the losing side!' she internalised, but from the scarce intel' provided she discerned a glimmer of possibility, rationally downgraded from hope to protect it from the crush of disappointment: 'A crack-down in the core systems. But Witch Head's way out on the frontier...?'

"Sounds like Parker, landing a cushy training post." She speculated aloud. "D'you know if he's still alive?"

"I'm sorry, we're not usually given the luxury of operatives' names, here, but I don't doubt you know your squad members best. I *do* know that UNE ran down the Witch Head facility about a year ago, but it was impossible to sort through the propaganda to tell if they actually caught anyone, or our boys and girls pulled out in time. The only details I have are about you."

Evagora planted his elbows on his knees, leaning towards her as far as his restraints would permit. On closer inspection, she got the impression his grey-streaked hair was an affectation: his skin, though weathered, didn't look quite aged enough to support the salt-and-peppering. The backs of his hands, particularly, looked too fresh for the age he was trying to convey. This was common amongst senior operatives still participating in field operations, since their occasional revivals yielded mature clone bodies relatively unravaged by time, compared with their original bodies. An extended gestation cycle was often utilised to subject the cloned cell structures to free radicals, ozone and various toxins to induce an aged appearance, but Leonard guessed that option wasn't available; biologically, Evagora probably wasn't much more than a few months older than herself. "Last month, we received notice that a surviving core of O.A.C.I. technicians had been attempting to rebuild the *psy* database from scattered sources. One such source was a salvage operation, which retrieved a temporary memory cache from the wreckage of your old base. It turns out the cloning bells each hold one file at a time in a data storage buffer when it's downloading. Fortunately for us, and you, your *.psy* was the last file transferred to the recovered bell, and its buffer survived the mainframe's destruction. The Groombridge mission feed was in the grouped *.stm* file. That's why those are the last memories you have."

She had been taught and trained to understand that, from time to time, in less than ideal conditions, such things could happen; to look on it more as a case of amnesia brought about by injury in the line of duty. But it was still difficult to reconcile any sense of personal continuity with such revelations. Finally, frustrated by this challenge to her sense of manifestation (it was never pleasant to imagine oneself residing latently in a data file for any great length of time), by her poor physical condition and resulting discomfort and on behalf of her fallen comrades she allowed herself to express her anger. She could hold it in, she could hold any mere *feeling* in, but sometimes her controlling persona would agree with the voice of her emotional, animal self, and she would consciously lift the lid on the box she kept it in, let it out on a leash to stretch its legs before reeling it back in. "I would've fought dat wid free fucking years to fink about bringing me back you would have had time to grow me a body I could actually use out of da bell! Dis is a fucking dis*grace*! It's going to take me *monfs* to get *dis*," at which she waved her arms in a self-encompassing gesture, "to do anyfing harder dan a *shit*!"

Evagora absorbed her display placidly, giving her a moment to simmer down. With sympathy in his voice, if not in his choice of words, Evagora responded "I should think you'll find even going for a shit to be an uphill struggle, in your condition." She gave him a weakly sarcastic smile. "Your situation is not unique. Since your last... *recollection*," carefully selecting a euphemism less dehumanising than *data save point*, "the tide of the war has not been turning in our favour."

"It never did."

"Quite. In fact, right now, we're without a formal military." The shock of this news showed on her face. "The war for independence continues, but all remaining activists belong to guerrilla cells, like this one. Command is entirely underground, resistance style. UNE has completely overrun all our territories, shut down the central cloning facilities and liquidated most of our corporate sponsors. I told you earlier that we're behind enemy lines, but really there *are* no lines. Not anymore. We, and the other cells, continue to receive funding, weapons and supplies through clandestine methods from various surviving, sympathetic corporations. Our targets are military patrols and encampments, mostly planet-side. We don't have much of a navy left. You're highly trained in the use of explosives; sabotage; sniping; infiltration; assassination. These are our weapons of choice, now. You were special op's. Now we all are. We need you. We were lucky to get you back. In *any* condition. Wish we could've got your whole squad back, but... unfortunately we weren't able to retrieve their data. I'm sorry."

"Yeah. I figured." 'See you on the other side,' she thought to herself, as she allowed herself to mourn and honour their loss. "So, where do I start?"

Evagora reached inside his jacket, and pulled out a manila envelope, leaning towards her with his arm outstretched. It took some convincing body language on Evagora's part for her to realise that she should take the unfamiliar object. There was some writing scrawled indistinctly on its surface: *Angel Leonard, 35-2-08 Church Hill Block, 23:13:11 Godsgood City, Alpha Centauri Prime.*

As soon as she read the name, she knew it was not her own, just a new identity. But she became suddenly aware that she couldn't remember any *other* name – her *real* name – just as she hadn't remembered how to tie her shoelaces. Partial memory losses *were* a common side-effect of the revival process, usually correctable by an overwrite session or two with the techies. Except that task performance was a function of implicit memory, whereas autobiographical knowledge was part of explicit memory, with different encoding processes. She suppressed her unease with squaddy bravado.

"*Angel Leonard...* You write dis?"

"Yes."

"I'm surprised you remembered how."

Evagora permitted an affable chuckle. "I must admit, I was a little rusty, the first time. But we all had to get used to it, again. Avtog's still safe to use at civilian levels, but we can't use military encryptions for daily operations. Any time we exchange mission related data, we've gotta do it old-school style."

"You mean *kindergarten style!*"

Another chuckle. "If you like. Using crayons is a matter for personal preference. UNE's got nothing better to do than sit around monitoring avtog exchanges. We aim to give them something else to worry about, but we have to be careful about transmissions between operatives. No P2P avtogging. If you have an emergency, 'jack a civ's 'droid. Don't use it more than once."

She tilted the envelope, allowing its contents to slide into her other hand and lap. The bulkiest item was a blank, lined writing pad, coil bound with a cartoon-festooned child's pen inserted through the coil.

"Cute. Do you provide refills...?"

"Contact between operatives is kept minimal. If you run out, look around under E.C.E. supplies."

The other contents included a pair of plastic rectangles, the first a standard four-by-eight centimetre civilian handroid, translucent, flexible, covered in bright, corporate graphics, no more than a millimetre thick. As she turned it over in her hand, Evagora said "That's registered to your new identity. Use it for civilian purposes and purchases *only*. Keep it clean, *nothing* that might arouse suspicion." UNE militia would have all the access codes for civilian handroids, and monitoring algorithms would flag any suspicious communication, purchase history or online activity. By remotely accessing a flagged, active handroid-avtog interface, a Security Agent could gain access to whatever sensory experiences the monitored user was subjected to, even to their internal sub-vocalisations, their more coherent thoughts, colloquially referred to as *nens*, turning the suspect into a walking security camera and unwitting informant.

The second was a featureless, smoky-grey slab. She rolled it over in her hand. It had the same face dimensions as the civilian model, but was closer to a centimetre thick, rigid, and absorbed almost all the light that tried to pass through it.

"That's your field op's terminal. It came with your *.psy* file. It's already active and it's been recording your *.stm* feed since you were squelched. Keep it near you at all times in case we need to contact you on an encrypted link. You can use it for hacking and server manipulation without risking detection, but under current protocols don't activate its comlink within the city limits: the anti-terror D.A.I.s they're using now only need ten seconds to cross-reference your encoded signal with local militia chatter before figuring out yours doesn't belong. You'll have a squad of GUNEs up your *prōktos* in no time."

She understood Evagora's caution, drawing on her expertise in operating within enemy territory: UNESA's Security Agents, whether human or 'Dedicated Artificial Intelligences,' wouldn't be able to crack the encoder to monitor her sensory data streams, as they could with a civilian handroid. But once they figured out there was a military grade encoder operating that wasn't their own they *would* be able to triangulate her transmissions and scramble the *GUNEs*, a derogatory term widely used to describe *any* representative of the government of UNE, but especially with reference to federal police and militia. In this case, the GUNEs would be an anti-terrorist suppression squad of Colonial Marines spearheaded by a pair of Security Agent S.W.A.T. specialists, who in turn labelled Orion Arm Conglomerate for Independence operatives as 'Wackies.'

And that was the *least* pejorative slang used: blueberries – the majority of UNE peacekeepers drawn from Earth's poorer populations, named for their older-issue equipment including a blue beret – drew on superstitious and religious cultural traditions to cast aspersions on O.A.C.I. operatives in numerous languages, often translating to a core group of meanings: *living-dead*; *abominations*; *infidels*; *demons*.

By contrast, O.A.C.I. operatives favoured mocking terms for their opponents: the most frequently used distinction between blueberries and the state-of-the-art troops contributed by Earth's affluent nation-states and colonies was *Laurels* – again referring to the laurel-leaf-emblazoned blue beret – and *Hardys*. Together, the names evoked the slapstick comedic duo familiar to students of media history, from the early part of the togless entertainment era. A bookish PFC she went through basic training with, Era Veseli, had suggested an overly-analogous literary reference from the same period which was very apt, but too lengthy to be funny. It was lost on her fellow recruits.

S.O.P. in her situation was to keep encoded terminal use short, intermittent, and to keep moving as erratically as possible. Anyone with sniper training would grasp the defensive principles: take your shot; move to a new location; avoid detection.

"Anytime it's on, it'll automatically record your *.stm* feed. There's a compiler soft onboard that chunks the data into simulated *.psy* files, but once you step away from *in vivo* memory encoding there's almost no chance of being able to reliably retrieve the memories. It's useful for mission records and computer analysis, but that's about it. Using that format we can retrieve about eight waking hours of memories per second, but we should still check in from time to time and upload your real *.psy* file for authentic reproduction of your formed memories.

"Right now, your *.psy* backup includes all L.T.M.'s up to the bunker mission. If you get killed before you can upload a new *.psy* update then we can at least revert to that, and add on any simulated files from your op's terminal, assuming we can grow you another body. But then, of course, I'd probably have to tell you all this again, and I hate repeating myself," he delivered, deadpan.

"So, what'm I supposed to do?"

Evagora treated her to a half smile. "For now? Rest. Recover. Train. We'll drop you as close as we safely can to the port. Go to your residence. We'll contact you in a few weeks, see how you're doing. Leave your apartment every day for at least six hours – doesn't matter when. Try to be friendly to your neighbours, form contacts in the community, that sort of thing."

Stiffening, she informed him "I don't know what you read in my file, but you should know I don't do HUMINT." Although her Special Op's training had covered all aspects of military intelligence gathering, she found the level of deception and manipulation involved in human intelligence work particularly distasteful, routinely turning down such assignments.

Evagora gave her a steely stare, and reminded her, coldly, "Major, you'll do whatever is necessary to ensure the success of this operation." With a sigh, he thawed a little: "We understand you aren't experienced in long term undercover work, but I also know you're smart; resourceful. You'll pick it up. Besides, we're not asking you to derive information from people: just to avert suspicion. Short explanation is that new faces that hole up and keep to themselves make folk around here uncomfortable. There's a big ad' campaign, educating civ's how to spot spies and terrorists. You do *not* want your neighbours reporting you to the GUNEs for suspicious behaviour. The last I heard, they've got a tenth of the population in their files as active informants."

There was a long pause, as Evagora eyed her. Muscles in his jaw flexed. 'Here comes the bad news,' she thought.

"They also have complete files on all our own military personnel, present *and* former. To facilitate your mission, the technicians have introduced certain... *variations*... to your genetic sequence." The tone of his voice sounded more rehearsed than casual. Her eyes widened. Her hands fluttered to her face, trying to detect any differences. So far, she hadn't passed a single, accurately-reflective surface, and now suspected this was prearranged. The physical differences she *had* noticed she'd dismissed as an effect of the short gestation of her new body, differences she assumed would fade away as she regained body fat and muscle tone. This was *far* from what she had agreed to under the Indoctrinal Trust Pact: a fundamental violation of her contract with the O.A.C.I., the umbrella of corporations who funded and supplied the private army in which she served. Or, rather, *had* served in. Right now, it wasn't clear *whose* payroll she was on. Every previously trusted face that had ever promised her this would never happen flashed before her eyes, as she mentally re-filed them under '*liars.*'

"I know what you're thinking," Evagora paused thoughtfully, made a decision and continued without the rehearsed tone: "how you *feel*. We *all* do. Right?" He looked around the cab', and she instinctively followed suit: two technicians and a fellow operative met her eyes with grimly sympathetic faces: faces almost as new to them as they were to her, she realised. The last cell member, she guessed another operative from his affected disinterest, slouched against his restraint harness, his cap-concealed face downturned, as though dozing. "But it's necessary: the GUNE's have gait and facial recognition softs primed to pick each and every one of us out of any crowd. The changes are just enough to thwart the Security Agency's recog-rithms. Basically, they're cosmetic only: a set of inert sequences that reorder your genome, activating some genes, deactivating others. It's all still you, just different parts of you: mostly just reshuffling the deck, so to speak."

"Sounds like a line dey'd feed da grunts in da gene ferapy programs."

"Well, yes, it's a similar process to Project Super Trooper. UNE seized our cloning technology, now we're using some of their own against them."

"So now I'll show up as genetically augmented? Dat's *not* very low profile."

"They won't be able to detect any augmentation: our genetic manipulation technology is still *decades* ahead of anything UNE has – the benefits of years of privately funded research, away from the influence of religious book-thumpers back on Earth and their pocket politicians." Evagora's eyes flickered as he reined in his rhetoric. "But you *do* need to make a conscious effort to retrain yourself, to avoid certain old habits. Most transit centres have gait recognition, and if you're ever taken in for questioning you can be sure that you'll be constantly monitored for distinctive mannerisms as long as you're in a cell or an interrogation room."

"What kind of mannerisms? I assume you're not talking about my current speech impediment, 'cause a set of dentures would clear dis right up."

"Hard to say. Everyone has something different, something they do sub-consciously in stressful situations. Nail biting, foot tapping, drumming fingers. For you, probably some kind of fiddling with your hair. You don't have a single strand, but you've tucked the hem of your hood behind your ear at least three times since you strapped in. Try to figure out any distinctive postures or body movements you might have, and then *stop* them, at least where you might be seen. Until you do, stay away from transit centres – no hov'trains, no malls, avoid the main block atria. Get your groceries in local level stores. The address we selected for you will help you stay out of the security spot light. Pasqualé can help you, if you need it." The female technician waved a *victory* hand signal at her, to identify herself. "She's our SPITS specialist."

Pasqualé weighed in: "Eighteen months ago, UNE stormed the headquarters of Helicorp, the largest genetic intellectual property-based company in the quadrant. Helicorp were singlehandedly responsible for all our bio-tech' superiority and their deep storage contained the genetic records of every O.A.C.I. operative ever submitted during basic training, compromising every active service person with unaltered D.N.A. So, you see, we had to change your sequence. Your old one was a death sentence just waiting to be signed at the next genescreen.

"But that's all based on centuries-old tech'. As far as SPITS goes, we can only make an edu-guess as to how it works. We know UNE obtained our *.psy* files during the 'war crimes' trial of Neuromemetic Industries; we think they're using a next-gen' D.A.I. to sift the neural data for strongly reinforced somatic tendencies, which emerge *in vivo* as a set of unconsciously choreographed body movements. If anyone enacts one of the identifiable choreographies, it flags the linked identity to the Security Agents for further surveillance and confirmation. They call it 'SPITS: Subversive Personnel Identifiable Traits System.' The system is based here, in Godsgood, together with a hardstore of the *.psy* files. So far, that's about all we know, for sure. Within a month of SPITS coming online, UNESA picked up every O.A.C.I. operative that passed through a major transit centre throughout the core systems, despite heavy disguises, cosmetic surgery, gait modification. Like Evagora said, the only ones left are those that were able to kill themselves before the UNESA techs could dry-clean us.

"The earliest of us re-cloned were able to figure out how SPITS spotted us, and set the protocol for genetic alteration. Shortly after that all our labs were raided, shut down. We tried to set up new ones, but it was never long before they found each one. We haven't figured out how, yet, but since not all of us are accounted for we suspect that a number of our former comrades were unable to terminate before the dry-cleaners got to them, and that they're now helping the S.A.s to profile us, figure out our next move, the next likely location for a cloning lab, and so on. We've been able to stay one step ahead, but only one. The lab you were at earlier? That's our only current technical facility. We've left a little surprise there for our UNESA friends, when they come a-calling, as we're sure they will, and we can only hope that their pet traitors are on site with them. It'll be a while before we can get the next site operating securely.

"Our primary mission objective *will* be to eliminate the UNESA informants; limit the intel' available to the Security Agency so that we can operate with greater latitude. But first, we have to conceal our equipment and sleep our cell until this latest security shit-storm passes. Yours might be the last revival attempt we can make for the foreseeable future. Try not to get yourself killed, at least until further notice."

The other technician, a young man with gangly limbs and curly blonde hair, chimed in: "We don't know for sure if there's a traitor. Plus, that's a strong word for someone who's been dry-cleaned: you wouldn't end up with a whole lot of choice about what you did, once the tech's had finished washing your brains out. SPITS *could* just be better than any of us give it credit for."

"Kochansky's right. We don't know exactly how the GUNEs are having so much success against us. In any case, we need to lay low for a while, build up the credibility of our new civilian identities." Evagora's eyes slid right, along with a tiny tilt of his head to that side. An almost imperceptible nod followed, and she deduced he was streaming. "Okay, we're going to set you down here. Turns out there's a lot of GUNE activity, ahead, and we don't want to run the risk of *any* footage of you getting out of this vehicle. Martinez is our infiltrator," pointing out the disinterested operative across the cab. With the brim of his cap pulled low, he'd kept his head down, face towards the cabin's door porthole the whole time, so she hadn't had a good look at his face. Even under scrutiny, she couldn't make out any recognisable features or ethnicity, and doubted she could recognise him if she met him again – certainly couldn't pick him out of a line-up. He was good, a natural. But she needed to know who he was, who she could trust.

"Martinez? I'm Leonard. Apparently." He broke his low-profile posture to make eye contact.

"Welcome back, Leonard. I am apparently Martinez." His voice was soft, with a faint Latin accent he was probably faking.

"There's an un-networked terminal safeguarding access to archived spaceport files. Martinez'll hard-plant footage to simulate your arrival. We'll send Kochansky to you to record it in a few weeks, when you've got some more meat on your bones. Until then, keep your head down. Literally: we don't want any sec'cam' footage of you looking like you just crawled out of a cloning bell, do we?" He pulled an autoseal bag from his jacket pocket. "This should help, for now, at least." He tossed it to her, and she caught its uneven load with a muted rattle. Inside, she found a bottle marked *multi-vitamins*, a short-haired wig, a pair of polyurethane driving gloves, a surgical mask, sunglasses and a set of dentures.

One other item stuck to the bag lining. It was a transparent dermal patch, the standard issue *Blue Option* for an operative to use in the event of capture. Only a thin film of carrageenan encapsulated the poison-saturated, skin lacerating wad of nano-filament within. One good hand clap or slap against exposed skin would deliver a twice-lethal dose of organic toxin to the bloodstream. Histotoxic hypoxia was a widely favoured cause of death amongst most operatives, due to the rapidly induced loss of consciousness, coma preventing any possible interrogation, and certain brain death; a modern spin on the old spy-staple *cyanide capsule*, with the advantage being that, in a pinch, a captured agent could also use the patch to kill one other person, be they friend or foe, since the wad cut in both directions when crushed. Being comprised entirely from organic molecules undetectable to chemical sensors, and being almost invisible when worn, made the patch easy to pass through all but the most rigorous security checks. You just had to be careful to wear it somewhere where it wouldn't get patted by a hapless security guard.

She knew some operatives who liked to hold them in their mouth; behind a lip; under the tongue; against a cheek. They could use their tongue to move the patch around, avoiding its detection in the event of a mouth cavity search, with that muscle being strong enough to crush the patch against the teeth or hard palate, in the event of discovery. Jaw muscle strength and a sturdy set of teeth were adequate to prevent the patch being taken by force, unless the search was robotic. The kappa variant of the gel coating was not soluble in the mouth at body temperatures, but would be digested if swallowed, with the same lethal effect somewhat delayed.

She slipped in the dentures, biting down on the horseshoe-shaped, adhesive foam pads, feeling them conform to her gums. "Now *that's* what I'm talking about," she said, relishing the sound enabled by the ceramic incisors against the tip of her tongue. Briefly wishing she'd had a tog clip of that sensation whilst toothless, she left the other items in the bag, for now. "Next time you squelch me out early, how about popping a set of these on my bedside table from the start. It would have been nice, that's all I'm saying."

"I'll take your request into consideration." Evagora pointed at the contents of her lap. "You'll need the pills especially for nail, tooth and hair growth. You've been bio-engineered to respond to the elevated nutrient levels with increased anabolism. They'll help with other processes, too: bone mineralisation; muscle building; I understand you can even speed injury recovery, but it's not well tested. Take six with every meal until you're fully restored. The Security Agency like to interview recent arrivals as they pass their residency visa milestones. You'll want to look the part, by then.

"We've also taken the liberty of providing you with a set of avlog entries. They're suspicion-averting, and you can use them to fill in the blanks: back story; travel itinerary. Once you get secure, check it out. Good luck, Major. We'll be in touch."

With a familiar, rubbery bounce, the hauler got as close to the ground as it would ever get, unless it sprung a dark energy leak from between its Casimir plates, and the cab hatch popped open with a blast of hot air from outside. She slipped out of her restraints, leaving the blanket on the seat, slapped on the wig, pinning it with the arms of the sunglasses and the elastic straps of the face mask, sucking on the dentures to firmly seat them before pulling it up to cover her nose and mouth, and pulled on her gloves. Suitably shielded from prying eyes, she worked her way as quickly as she dared down the narrow steps of the disembarking ladder.

The other operative from the cab followed her down and set a metre-and-a-half long cylindrical hovertrunk on its flat base beside her. He was lean, but well muscled, shorn black hair on his dark-skinned scalp.

"Llank..." Her dentures, slipping loose from her palate, created a welsh-sounding consonant in place of the intended 'th,' like a soft 'ch,' as air escaped unintentionally between the top of her dentures and the roof of her mouth. Reaching under the mask with her thumb, she pushed the plate back up into her mouth, once again feeling the gel form on to her gums. "*Thank* you."

"Victor. You're welcome." With one foot and hand on the ladder, he half turned his head back towards her. "I was the last one, before you. It..." his spare hand made a circular, waving gesture, encompassing his face, and maybe more: "...takes some getting used to. But it's better than being dead. As far as I know." He cracked a bright grin. "Take care... *Angel*." She nodded her grateful assent.

As soon as he was back in the cab, the ladder auto-folded into its recess in the hauler's hull as the hatch closed. The freight vehicle bobbed up like a cork in water as its Casimir plates contracted nanometrically with a throbbing, pitch-climbing whine, compressing and exciting the store of dark energy between them, sending fat, electrostatic, blue-white bolts leaping between the plates and the ground before its side-mounted turbo-fans powered it away on stubby stabiliser wings. She watched it go, until it was lost in the aerial traffic.

'Major?' She wondered when that particular promotion had taken place. 'Must have been posthumous', she concluded. Despite all the training, it was still very unsettling to be confronted with evidence of personal death and missing time.

She seized and yanked the tether on the hovertrunk Victor had left for her. It bobbed a step-height into the air, whining and sparking in miniature imitation of the departed hauler.

CHAPTER THREE: OPERATIONS TOUCHDOWN AND TREAD WATER

From the flat tower top, bordered with drop-off zones for flyers, she could see across the honeycomb layout of the city. She stood atop one amongst thousands of sixty storey mixed-use towers a hundred metres across, on the southern outskirts of the 'C' shaped central business district wrapped around the spaceport and its attendant warehouse and shipping district. An artificial sinkhole to the north, formed by the sudden end of the business district as skyscrapers abruptly gave way to open freight storage lots and low level structures, marked its position.

Together with five other mirrored-sided towers, variously topped with running tracks, outdoor play areas, landscaped parks and the occasional lido, it ringed a taller, central mega block, crowned by an off-centre commercial spire. To the south, the city skyline descended in a series of uneven terraces towards low rise residences in the suburban residential districts. To the west, the hexagonal grid pattern repeated its way around to the far side of the port in a sweeping arc extending to the northern horizon. To the east, white light from the risen primary glittered off the surface of a massive body of water, and scattered between the reflective buildings, making the lower city sparkle like a cut diamond. The even curve of the lake's cliff-like shores suggested an impact crater or super-volcanic origin. The caldera formation extended beyond the planet's own surface curvature, the structure of its raised rim occasionally burnished by flashes of silver where water had eroded through the surrounding levee to pour down the embankment then meander across the plain that seemed to make up the rest of the surface of the planet in a series of horseshoes and oxbows. Green avenues of vegetation tracked the streams until they dried out, leaving flat streaks of salt on the arid plain.

At the centre of the tower, a seamless glass wall with an overhang feature protected pedestrians from a forty metre drop, involuntarily or otherwise, down a wide, central atrium. A central shaft with six elevators, linked to the building's rim by a series of platforms and walkways spanning the central hollow at intervals, ran all the way down to the building's lobby level. Rooftop walkways traversed the voids between tower tops with larger conduits connecting the mid-levels, together joining the cluster of seven towers into a super block. Distant blocks displayed the same pattern, some with even larger multi-storey conduits, horizontal buildings in their own right, linking super blocks in a radial network.

With her hovertrunk bobbing along behind her, she worked her way along the lightly-surveilled rooftop walkways, avoiding the closer scrutiny present at mega blocks and high traffic conduits, shuffling stiffly for half an hour before resolving to activate her new civilian handroid. Safer to wait and relocate in case, at some point in the future, some overly-industrious Security Agent should cross-reference her handroid's GP/t with the hauler's black box, and put her at the drop-off point at the same time as a by-then-known terrorist driven vehicle. Worst case scenario. 'What do I have on the bright side?' She wondered about this for a while, until her painfully blistering feet supplied her train of thought with a direction: 'At least I won't have to worry about gait recognition for a while.'

She caught herself too late with this careless, stray thought. '*Exactly* the kind of nenning I need to avoid,' she chided herself for making such a rookie mistake: keyword nen chatter like that could flag comdropping D.A.I.'s, attracting the unwanted attention of the Security Agency or local police.

Like most streamers, she had to impose self-control over the random, coherent thoughts she might have during a P2P com. The same neural pathways activated during both proper vocal and internal speech, with high neural conformity and perceptional cleavage between sender and receiver. Where avtog *did* excel was in the rapid telegraphy of internal visual and vocal concepts. However, divergent neural pathway activations in the roughly third-of-a-second volitional process of vocal inhibition did not translate between streamers, since the sender's character, shaped by events and tendencies to which the receiver was not privy, came to bear.

Simulated propriety softs *usually* succeeded in screening out the five percent of violent and/or sexual nens that involuntary associative recollection processes triggered, but could not be guaranteed. The wisdom of *entirely* trusting a computer to decide what was socially appropriate was questionable. When not willing to risk propriety soft failure, a segment of conversation could be edited for inappropriate or unintended thoughts before telegraphy as a clip. This made for more formal, stilting conversations, but was still broadly acceptable, especially in workplace coms where sexual harassment or bullying litigation often resulted, earning the tongue-in-cheek classification of *communiquétion*, with the connotation of *a formal dispatch of information suitable for the public*.

Firewalls were only effective against private access attempts, since UNE legislated Security Agency access to all civilian encryption codes. And a hibernated handroid, whilst a good defence against regular comdropping, offered no protection from a nen screen, which interfaced directly with any *Encephalic Avtog Nano-plant* within reception range, an irrefusable connection allowing S.A.s direct access to nens. The only good thing about nen screens is that they were usually short ranged, operating only within certain government buildings, transit centres and police flight path blockades.

Her Special Op's training had included nen discipline exercises, indispensable for field operatives, involving meditative practices enabling an operative to pass through nen screens without telegraphing echoic/iconic triggers to threat assessment algorithms.

'Here we go, *Through the Looking Glass.*' Applying her thumbprint to the surface of the handroid, she cringed inwardly as the system initialised, transmitting her G-PIP across the network. The cityscape around her filled from ground to sky with lurid LANverts and public infocasts, traffic signals, flight paths and landing zones, all devoid of physical presence, mass, as if rendered from sculpted shards of shattered rainbows, a mosaic of light. Simultaneously, her mind was lapped by a wave of pervasive, aural babble that no mere ear-plugging could block out.

Lacking UNESA's mandate for thought-policing, the world of commerce found its own way through firewalls: under the guise of *user-pertinent content*, LANverts broadcast strictly pre-approved, licensed commercials on short-ranged public information frequencies that were encoded to bypass a handroid's firewall settings and pop-up blockers, the legal argument being that simply by entering a commercial district, mall or store vicinity you were permitting the relevant stream. Whilst arguing that LANverts were less intrusive than nen screens, since they were only broadcast via active handroids, not connecting directly to E.A.N.s, advertising corporations congratulated themselves on knowing *exactly* what their targets were thinking, because they had supplied the thought.

The system was pioneered by emergency services and flight path maintenance crews to quickly broadcast local system changes. This allowed civilians to navigate around traffic accidents, crime scenes or repair efforts as they came within range of their *buoy-casts*. Keeping data off the main network reduced public perception of repair work extent and emergency service activity, keeping gawkers away from scenes of crimes and accidents, and elevating the perception of civic efficiency, safety and security. Even sirens and lights were buoy-cast.

Calling up the Opacity Slider, she eye-slid the *Base Sensory* stream signal strength down to a third – a practice widely and jocularly described as *cutting the B.S.*, allowing a streamer to function in the real world without distraction impairment induced by virtual sensory hyper-stimulation – bringing the audio-visual barrage into tolerable limits, then took a moment to calibrate depth perception, establish privacy settings and customise use preferences: themes, com tones, pop-up blocking, sleep cycle and mailbox settings, allowing her to define the terms and times of her interaction with incoming streams and connection requests.

Next, she set reception protocols to add sensory tags; a discernible taste of mint accompanying any gustatory stream; the scent of lemon on the olfactory stream. Synaesthetic effects could also be useful; she selected a pink light accompanying virtual sounds; an audible chime accompanying virtual imagery; the feel of wet sand between the toes to accompany virtually sourced smells or tastes.

A growing breed of streamers preferred complete immersion, blurring the boundary between realities perceived directly by the sense organs and those induced technologically. Those few who cared to offer a philosophical account for this trend described it as an acceptance of the evolution of human perception, a full embrace of the melding and extension of mind into the network they had created to fully realise individual and societal potential. She preferred to know where her senses ended and augmented reality began.

Finally, satisfied with her firewall settings, she called up a map of the city. In her mind's eye, a three dimensional, scale image showing central Godsgood's hexagonal layout sprang into existence before her, pinpointing her own location, and, after a quick, nenned input, the location of the address on her envelope. Adjusting the map for optimal spatial awareness, she returned to the task of navigating through her real world environment.

The only available walkways at this level lead directly towards the port, connecting superblocks together into a serviceable transit network for pedestrians. Each named block was located on a three-way numbered intersection.

The hauler had been heading towards the spaceport, presumably the point of heightened security. This made sense: she was supposed to have arrived at the port, and made her way from there to her apartment building. 'Could even have taken an autocab. No matter. First day in a new city, I decided to walk. The S.A.s can make of that what they want.'

Her route followed a set of conduits following a slaloming, north-westerly transit line, intersecting the edge of the warehouse and shipping district several blocks from here. It wouldn't be possible to avoid surveillance cameras any more.

She had never been to Alpha Centauri Prime before. Well, not in her living memory. Its close proximity to Earth had lead to it being the first extra-solar system to be surveyed for habitable planets, and the first to be colonised. It also happened to be one of the most Earth-like planets she had ever been to: a yellow dwarf, main sequence star, only a little larger and hotter than Sol, shone down through a blue sky.

She called up a wikitog, turned down the video, tactile, olfactory and gustatory components to zero and kept the audio component for the sense of company and a study course as she headed in the direction of her new apartment.

"Alpha Centauri Prime: just like Earth – only *bigger*!"

The stream sounded like a tourist-board sponsored av'vert. Fortunately, the wikitog continued with a more easily tolerated narrator, sounding more like a travblog entry, had it not been for the real-time data.

"Godsgood City, Alpha Centauri Prime. From your current location, at this time of the twenty-six point eight hour day, and four hundred and eighty three day orbital period with a triennial leap year, the system's secondary star, *Alpha Centauri β*, hangs a quarter of the way above the eastern horizon, visible to the unaided eye as a small, yellow-orange disk."

The clearly enunciated female speaker seemed very interested in her own information, a trick used by kindergarten teachers to capture the attention of young children. She found the trick still effective on her, as she almost involuntarily sought out the object described. In any case, the interactive guide waited until she eye-pointed the right region of sky before continuing. "On its own, it's almost a match for Sol, and has its own set of gravitationally bound planets, including the cold but habitable and industrialised rocky planet, *Seconde*."

Here, she guessed the video stream would have included images from space, and perhaps a capital city fly-over, possibly even a tactile stream of ambient surface temperature for bare hands and face. She would have welcomed that, and regretted turning down the tactile element of the sense-stream, as her face mask and gloves were trapping body heat and sweat uncomfortably. But it would have been a momentary respite, at best.

After a sufficient interval to stream such impressions, the audio continued: "However, this secondary star never approaches much closer than nine A.U.'s to A.C.P., and even then roughly only every ninety years: the amount of thermal gain to ground supplied to A.C.P. even at its peak is around two point five watt hours per square metre at equatorial ground level, barely exceeding the human sensory threshold. *Proxima*, Sol's nearest stellar neighbour, and the final, tertiary star gravitationally bound to the Alpha Centauri stellar system, is currently obscured during the day by Raleigh scattering in A.C.P.'s humid atmosphere. At other times of year, both *Alpha Centauri β* and *Alpha Centauri Proxima* may be observed at night time from the surface of Alpha Centauri Prime, although, to the unaided eye, *Proxima* is a reddish-orange star only a little brighter and larger than its celestial neighbours, at the best of times, much as Mars would appear during its closest approaches to Earth.

"Pioneering survey expeditions arrived here with the advent of jump gate technology in twenty-one forty-three, the culmination of the eighty-five year mission of the unmanned, nuclear pulse propelled gate carrier, *The Centaur*. They found an Earth-like planet that had escaped remote detection due, amongst other reasons, to an orbit that did not transit across the face of its orbited star, from Earth's viewing angle. Highly active super volcanic regions close to the small, polar ice caps cycle life-essential nutrients in the absence of tectonic activity, leaving the tropical and equatorial belt unscathed by the periodic upheavals.

"Unlike Earth, A.C.P. has no oceans, with a higher percentage of exposed land area than Earth. However, a significant portion of the felsic surface rock is broken down to a submerged layer of sima rock-types by the many lower latitude ice-comet impact craters extant from an earlier, highly active impact period. Many are still partially filled with the deuterium-rich melt-water they contributed to A.C.P.'s hydrosphere, often salinised by dissolved minerals from their bedrock. Between the polar lava flows, and the equatorial ice bombardment period, most indigenous life on A.C.P. was endangered at the time of human occupation.

"Large scale colonisation only really commenced when the jump gate was opened to public use in twenty-one fifty-one, enabling instantaneous transit between Alpha Centauri and Sol. A.C.P. quickly became home to the largest human population outside the solar system.

"During *The Centaur's* prolonged mission, further advances in space transit technology meant the spread of humanity through the Local Bubble lagged only a few decades behind, first with the development of the light speed equivalent skip drive, and the recent nova gate programme which has lead to the unprecedentedly rapid development of a sprawling network of viable jump gates across the entire Orion Arm. The region of space now opened to exploration is so vast it's estimated it'll take humanity another thousand years to fully explore, let alone colonise it.

"Perhaps because of its long colonial history and close proximity to Earth, A.C.P. remains a staunchly Earth-loyal colony." Leonard knew this to be the case: Primers gained the somewhat derogatory distinction amongst O.A.C.I. loyalists of being *more terran than terrans themselves.*

"Godsgood City, capital city of A.C.P., sprang up around the initially established spaceport, which lies on the equatorial, western shore of A.C.P.'s largest salt lake, the *New Red Sea.* Early settlers took advantage of the planet's rotation to launch orbital payloads over the lake for improved safety, prior to the completion of the space elevator.

"Since its completion, most orbital conveyances today take place via the space-port's orbital lifters, a regulated series of freight containers and passenger compartments in constant motion between the port and the tethered, geostationary orbiting docking ring. The system is named *Jacob's Ladder*, in keeping with A.C.P.'s often biblical place-naming tradition, or just *the Ladder*, by its frequenters."

She stopped walking and looked out through the clear-sided walkway tube. She had reached the closest towers to the port, the innermost ring of mixed use blocks surrounding its attendant warehouses and open cargo lots. The simple, one-way travelator she had taken provided an excellent view, where other walkways had been enclosed, or even lined with vending stalls. She could see the Ladder, or rather the series of freight and passenger containers that moved vertically along it. Matching visual data processed in her occipital lobe to its library of cityscape images, the wikitog continued.

"Although it provides an excellent view of the containers entering and exiting orbit, the actual framework of The Ladder is not visible from this viewpoint. The award-winning design pairs orbital and surface *SpinnerET* devices inspired by Earth's web-spinning spiders, overcoming the operational danger of catastrophic failure over time brought about by material fatigue. Each terminal of the Ladder dissolves the bio-chemical adhesive strands applied to incoming containers and re-spins the material onto outgoing containers, always applying sufficient webbing to safely support and convey the combined payload to the next terminal.

"With careful balancing of ascending and descending payloads, and the SpinnerETs locking and unlocking chemical energy in the organic webbing, the Ladder achieves a high level of efficiency, with a relatively small, sustainable energy input required to guarantee the Ladder's continuous operation long into the foreseeable future."

What she took for a plume of smoke or steam rising from the roof of a warehouse north of the Ladder caught her eye as the moving travelator beneath her feet shifted her perspective. The plume resolved under focus into a translucent figure. With slow deliberation, the spectral image turned towards her, flexing expansive wings in an awe-inspiring, silent spread, locking eyes across two kilometres of city, and following her along the walkway until a mega block commercial spire broke the line of sight. The wikitog rose to the challenge: "*Metatron*, archangel and voice of God in the Judaeo-Christian-Islamic tradition, was the inspiration for this iconic, and, at the time of its activation in twenty-one fifty-five, controversial piece of virtual statuary currently celebrating its fortieth year of operation. Historically, the district surrounding the port was occupied by low-rise warehouses and shipping concerns. Shortly after the opening of the Alpha Centauri-Sol jump gate, Christian fundamentalists came to view A.C.P. as something of a promised land, a haven for those uncomfortable with the rise of unchristian beliefs on Earth. The extensive involvement of such immigrants in the founding and early development of Godsgood City is evident in the faith-based names attributed to the city itself and many of the districts, buildings and transit routes therein.

"By twenty-one fifty-three, the *Alpha Omega Evangelicals* sect had a firmly established membership-base, founding their church on the edge of the warehouse district, due north of the port, to make the site more accessible to newly arriving immigrants. To further facilitate the influx of new members, generous contributions were taken from the congregation to purchase a large LANcasting array and the domain rights for an ambitious display: in the airspace of the converted warehouse, and with a broadcast range of close to five kilometres, extending across the warehouse district and some way into the central business district, especially to the north, the commissioned installation depicted the three hundred metre tall titular seraphim floating above the roof of the church's converted warehouse building, the medium's default image translucency lending naturally to the suggestion of the figure's insubstantiality. Its designers aimed to *claim the city for God*, and so matched the height of the top of Metatron's head, at three-hundred and forty-three metres above ground level, with that of

Earth's *Eiffel Tower*, hoping to generate the same strength of association between the city and its virtual structure as that Parisian landmark achieved. The necessity of low building height in the shipping district continues to preserve a viewing space around The Metatron to this day.

"The initial installation carried both audio and video streams with *Public Information Broadcast* protocols; however, controversy arose with regard to the unprecedented scale of the visual image and the audio content at that time, which, whilst in keeping with the church's evangelical mandate, and, given that the P.I.B. protocol did not afford viewers the option to firewall the stream, was considered to be sensorily overwhelming, intrusive and offensive to those adhering to more widely-held spiritual belief systems.

"Like many modern store front displays, LANverts, traffic control systems and other public info-casts, *the Metatron* installation matches an onlooker's G-PIP address with perspective recognition softs to preserve the impression of the broadcast image occupying the same geo-spatial location, regardless of the viewer's distance or viewing angle. Any eye-point landing on the real space occupied by the statue triggers an animation of Metatron turning to meet the onlooker with *a gaze scripted to pierce to their very soul*. The original accompanying audio comprised a *personalised message from God* in a suitably awe-inspiring and booming voice scripted to sound within the very head of the listener: '<Username>, God Knows You, God Loves You, God Forgives You Your Sins. Repent Now, And Praise The Lord, Your Creator And Saviour!' Since usernames must be unique across the entire network, whereas given names do not, many people continue to view their username as being more an expression of their true identity than that given to them at birth, adding to the impact of *The Message*.

"Soon after its installation, the church was beset by protests and web pickets. An intense legal battle culminated in the issuing of a court order to mute the virtual statuary, but passersby were still saddled with the sight of the Archangel's penetrating gaze following them about the city. Over time, and with the waning popularity and influence of the Alpha Omega Evangelicals, public perception has eroded any negative association with the sect and claimed the statue as civic property, an inseparable and indispensable landmark, a patron saint or protecting guardian of the city, watching over the port and all passing through it. At least in this regard, its creators achieved success."

By the time the encyclopaedia entry was finished, she had been carried away from the edge of the warehouse district, back amongst the forest of skyscrapers, and *The Metatron*, courtesy of her active perspective recognition softs eliminating its image in acknowledgement of intervening real-world objects, was out of sight. Still, she imagined the titan's judging gaze following her, the concrete and steel of this world as transparent to its otherworldly eyes as its body was to hers. The thought made her shudder involuntarily. At the next elevator shaft she waited in line and took the first car she could squeeze herself and her floating luggage into straight to the lobby.

Once she reached ground level, she found the lobby was an open space, continuous with the triangular plazas outside. The tower architecturally floated on a set of pillars, with a hov-X course, complete with park hits off to the sides, weaving around them. A handful of hovers practiced tricks to the disinterest of milling pedestrians. She eyed their boards nostalgically, misspent youth recalled.

Permitted graffiti coloured almost every surface. She had to push her way through a throng of teenagers, a roughly even gender mix, who were hurling verbal abuse and the occasional quartztic bottle at a second group, retaliating in kind, milling around beyond the impassable steel barred turnstiles and four metre fence enclosing the perimeter of the block's grounds.

The turnstile exit she took prevented entry to any of the gathered youths outside. Access to the premises via the separate entryways was restricted to residents via handroid analysis, similar to the auto-purchase systems in retail outlets which ensured customers were automatically charged at the exit for any items they took from the store. Unless the person entering was a resident, or had been given a temporary, level-restricted access code to visit a resident, the revolving doors would not turn. Insults and bottles didn't need a code to bypass the horizontal bars, of course, and the resident group sensibly remained within their enclosure, rather than risk exiting two-by-two into the hostile crowd pressing around the exit point, despite their bold addresses.

Once amongst them, she found they weren't as hostile as their taunts claimed. Perhaps her isolation amongst them was unthreatening, or the presence of her hovertrunk, which had to come through the turnstile behind her, identified her as a non-resident of the block, or at worst an ex-resident, on her way out. Whatever the reason, the teens on both sides reduced their catcalls and missile hurling as she passed through them, neither sure if she was on one side or the other. She felt all eyes upon her, but not threatened. They moved aside to let her through, but as she cleared the group a pair of boys peeled off and followed her across the plaza.

"Hey, girlie, you look hungry. Why don't you come here, let me give you something to eat?" His companion giggled, high pitched. She ignored them, and kept walking. "Yeah, good comeback, bitch!" The volume of his reproaches diminished below her range of hearing, as he and his partner lost interest, soon returning their attention to the baiting of the block residents, where more *kudos* was to be earned than harassing a lone woman with her luggage.

She would have no more success in trying to re-enter that block than the group of antagonists she'd just passed. Nor any other block, she realised, apart from her own. Once you're out, you stay out, unless you have somewhere to get in again, legitimately. She realised she would need an alibi, after all, for allegedly getting from the spaceport to the rooftop she had been dropped at: a faked autocab-ride, or a neighbourly lift from a fellow traveller? She could figure it out later.

A surprising amount of natural light filtered into the plazas through the offset blocks, bounced from the various mirrored facets and curves curtaining every tower. City planners had sought to reduce vehicle collision risks, supply utilities and transit routes more efficiently, and eliminate the perpetual ground-level twilight suffered by older cites with classical block layouts, believing that a little extra daylight could help to reduce urban crime rates and improve public well-being. It clearly wasn't enough to eliminate all social problems, however.

Between the blocks, the occasional rough sleeper asked her for UNO's, a fairly futile request since most people rarely handled solid currency, these days. More often, they'd ask for a gel-o'tine, a more viable currency on the street. Without a residential address, they were trapped out here, she realised. The block security systems excluded them, and there was nothing out here for them. Every facility was inside the blocks. They were physically prevented from interacting with anyone holed up inside the blocks, and it was clearly a rare and perplexing event for a resident to exit at street level, especially alone. That being said, people seemed harmless enough. At least to a highly trained and seasoned veteran commando such as herself. She indulged in a self-satisfied smile, confident in her ability to handle any situation this world might throw at her.

None of the pedestrianised plazas between the towering city-blocks had navigable names at ground level. Only the aerial walkways were named for the blocks they traversed. In a city like this, though, it was only necessary to know your destination.

High above, the air traffic was thick with private flyers and autocabs flitting between rooftops, following pre-designated flight paths that never dipped below the height of the towers. Foot traffic, too, was thin on the ground, the majority of pedestrians using the faster inter-block travelators, or the mid-level hover-trains for longer trips.

Looking up from ground level, Leonard could only guess at the summits of the commercial spires. There was little air traffic at that altitude, limited to corporate fliers and their private landing pads only, probably. The elevation of the commercial structures over residences painted a clear picture of the perceived importance of business in A.C.P. society. The visual effect was a clearly differentiated, two-tiered society.

With only a few more blocks to hobble to her new apartment block, she diligently deactivated her handroid so that her subsequent musings could be kept private from comdropping. By the sound of things, with the current heightened security level in the Solar system, Alpha Centauri was the closest she was going to get to Earth, for a while at least. If she was *ever* going to get there, she'd need to establish a credible and clean-living identity here for five years or more, with a legitimate work history, community contacts, network of friends, if not family members. When her body was sufficiently recovered, and all glaring evidence of cloning had subsided, she would need to register with and visit a local doctor. UNESA would review every Solar system visa application, and check all cited references for validity at a direct person-to-person confirmation level. The biggest problem would be the personal interview at the High Commission. She had been trained to acquit herself well during standard verassessments, but SPITS sounded an order of magnitude tougher to beat. Anyway, she didn't know if her tour of duty would lead to Earth. It sounded like her unit had its hands full right here on A.C.P., at least for a while.

Twenty minutes later, she was at the base of Church Hill block. Once around the perimeter confirmed that all entrances were video monitored, so with her most neutral posture and effected stillness, hooded head lowered, she selected the largest and busiest lobby entrance to come home to. 'May as well make them work to pick me out,' she reasoned. The elevators were cam'd, as well. She rode to her own floor directly, without so much as twitching a single muscle. With other passengers entering and exiting, the ride took about ten minutes. She consciously neglected to look for cameras in the hallways, leading to her apartment, aware that this was something a person fearful of scrutiny would do, and she should not be such a person if her identity was to be credible to the authorities. She felt the other riders eyeing her hovertrunk, putting it in context with her gloves and surgical mask, one by one concluding 'recent spaceport arrival' before losing interest, a thought no doubt sitting more agreeably than 'I'm stuck in an elevator with a potential bio-hazard!' which was probably the first impression she was giving. She also realised that this was not the best time to make small-talk, nor attract attention to her appearance and speech impediment: the dentures made a big difference, but still felt unfamiliar in her mouth, her vocalisations unpracticed. Social networking would just have to wait.

This was her first day in a new city. UNESA might take a while to get around to it, but she knew sooner or later they'd process footage on all new arrivals. It's what she would do, if she were responsible for locating security threats: laborious, but thorough. When panning for gold, you needed to sort a lot of gravel. So instead she followed Evagora's advice, and literally kept her head down, affecting the same self-conscious stillness and pained shuffle she had adopted to cross the lobby. With a little block layout consultation via her reactivated handroid, she was able to trace a route to her apartment door avoiding high traffic areas.

Her handroid unlocked the door, and she stepped in to an oven of a room. The whole tower was subdivided, vertically, into six sections, numbered clockwise from the north. Hexagons within hexagons. The layout ensured that every facet of the building, and therefore every unit, received at least some direct sunlight, but section two faced the rising primary directly, and the vacant suite's inactive environmental control unit had allowed a lot of thermal gain through the outer wall's window. Officially taking up residence when she unlocked the door, the air conditioning system suddenly stuttered to life, with the goal of satisfying its default settings. She tugged the hovertrunk in through the door before closing and locking it. When she released the tether, it reeled automatically into the body of the trunk, and with a series of warning beeps and a dying whine the trunk settled gently to the ground and deactivated.

She quickly explored the E-CU menu, prompting the control unit to close a set of anodised shutters beyond the internal glazing before heading into the wetcube, a one-piece ceramic enclosure beside her apartment door, opposite the kitchen. She ran the cold tap into the plugged sink, filling it between scooping cupped handfuls to her mouth to quench her thirst.

Scraping the damp hair piece from her head, dropping it to the small counter around the sink, she began to splash her face, scalp and neck, lowering her head, allowing the water to trickle from her nose, and to run down her forearms, soaking into the sleeves of her hoodie where she had rolled them to her elbows. She finally worked up the resolve to look at her reflection in the cabinet mirror.

Despite the cooling effect of the water, her face was still very pink, many of the blood vessels visible through her skin. Forgetting the fact that she was bald, and that her face was painfully thin, she looked into her own eyes and sobbed when she didn't recognise them. It was like looking at her sister, if she had one: a much younger sister, with the lean proportions of a lanky teenager. She could tell that the person in the mirror was closely related to her, with similar features. But they were just not quite her own.

Tightening her lips, she returned, dripping, to the hovertrunk by the door. Without bothering to reactivate the hover function, she tipped the top towards her and dragged the trunk across the smooth, ceramic floor to the middle of the living room, lay it flat and opened it.

The contents were completely and bizarrely normal. Just a few sets of climate appropriate clothing and footwear, bedding, a minimal bag of toiletries, including a basic first aid kit, some make-up and false finger nails, a multi-tool with a folding blade, and a set of cooking and eating utensils. Apart from the multi-tool, which she knew she could still kill with, if necessary, and the kitchen knives, there were no concealed weapons, no spy gadgets. Just the things she needed for now, to fulfil the earliest stages of her current mission: rest; recover; train. Snatching up the bed sheet, she shuffled to the foldout bed, wrestling with the mechanism to convert it from a sofa. Satisfied, she slumped onto its foam surface, dragging the sheet over the top of her, kicking her shoes off and out of the bed. 'Rest.'

∞

When she woke, it was still dark outside, still early on the next morning, according to avtog. Her socks were bloodied in patches, so she peeled them off carefully and patched up the burst blisters she found with her first aid kit. Gelatinous nanodaids autosealed on to her injuries, administering a topical pain-blocker and activating nano-tech' healing accelerators.

Anaesthetised and padded, she braved the cold, hard floor to peep out through the blinds. The sky was clear, with just a hint of light bouncing around between the neighbouring blocks. There was too much light pollution in the city to see the stars, but she took some comfort in the knowledge that, this close to Sol, the constellations she had grown up under during her childhood on Earth were almost exactly the same.

Centaurus, being a southern constellation, was not one she was familiar with from her Cascadian childhood star gazing.

Sitting down on the edge of the bed, she called up *Angel Leonard's* fabricated avlog, and began to work her way through the entries chronologically, gradually sliding up to scan at about five times the entry speed. According to the immersive recordings, *Angel* had inherited a modest sum upon the death of her last surviving relative, her great aunt, who had taken her in and raised her when her parents died during her early childhood. With no remaining family and nothing to lose, she'd left her home in Upsilon Andromedae – still considered a UNE core system despite numerous protests and almost constant industrial action by the workforce – for A.C.P. with high hopes for a career in the entertainment industry as an avtog actor. This would provide good cover for her physical fitness regime – actors were expected to be in excellent shape – for being otherwise unemployed, and for coming and going at various times of day and night.

According to the 'logs, shortly before her flight she had fallen severely ill with a vicious gastro-intestinal infection, recovering only just in time to clear quarantine conditions. The disease left her physically weakened and fatigued, and resulted in substantial weight and even hair loss, such was the shock to her system. The spread of humanity through the stars had provided their accompanying micro-organisms with wonderful new opportunities to mutate and sometimes achieve plague-like potencies: isolated populations, exposure to radiations, extra-terrestrial toxins and compounds sometimes yielded unanticipated results, not even accounting for the effects of hitherto unknown microbes from alien worlds. It was inevitable that some would slip through the standard quarantine protocols and evade the environmental surveys, laying low for decades in some as-yet unexplored niche in the ecosystem.

The 'log linked to a public avblog, intended as Angel's record of her climb to fame from obscurity, recorded for posterity for the billions of fans she imagined she would one day have. So far, there were a few entries convincingly depicting her journey. The technician falsifying the record must have accessed port departures and in-transit footage to have pulled it off, as the surroundings and people would have to be real, and in real time, to endure UNESA scrutiny and cross-examination.

Adding on to the 'blog also had the potential to serve as a rehearsal tool for Leonard, get her used to maintaining a sensory diary – a common practice from adolescence for many people, but her youthful interests had been more visceral and physically inclined – and conveying herself as a real actor would do in a commercial production. Whilst the 'log entries were restricted to av streams, the 'blog was full-sensory, in keeping with the avtog industry's favoured format.

The nausea conveyed by the 'blog entries during her illness was utterly convincing, considering that the whole diary was constructed from code, perhaps implementing sensory capture to prevent uncanny valley detection. Whoever had done this was *really* good. Was this Kochansky's work? If so, she would have to congratulate him.

After experiencing the last entry, in which Angel was in flight, approaching A.C.P.'s orbital docking ring, about to embark on a new chapter in her life, she sat for a moment, absorbing her surroundings, rolling the character of Angel over in her mind. 'Now it's my turn to be an actor.'

Eyeing the record icon in her avblog, she began to speak: "Well, here I am, in my new apartment on Alpha Centauri Prime! I was totally krunked by the time I got here – I'm still not fully recovered from the gut-bug – so I completely flaked as soon as I got through the door. But it's an early start on a brand new day, and for the first time in a long time I feel *hungry*! I'm gonna see what's to eat from the level store down the hall, and check in with *you*, my many adoring fans, after breakfast." 'Stop.' Like all the most convincing lies, most of this statement had been true. She would have to start gently, build up a repertoire of safe-to-eat foodstuffs – her own gastro-intestinal system was previously unused, entirely devoid of friendly bacteria, so she would certainly spend the next few days with symptoms similar to those that Angel had, until she could properly digest what she ate.

She picked out some comfortable slip-on shoes for her first excursion, although by now she couldn't feel any pain in her feet. She recovered her hair piece from the bathroom, regretted not washing it, as it was now quite matted with dried sweat, but slipped it on as convincingly as she could in the cabinet mirror, and pulled up her hood to cover the majority of her bad hair day. 'Avtog actor in wardrobe malfunction,' she headlined to herself, before braving the hallway outside her apartment.

The level store was within a hundred metres, for which she was grateful, and generously stocked with basics. She grabbed a bag of V-nanos, cartons of peanut butter and soy milk, soft-crusted bread, powdered oatmeal, and as many cans and packets of beans and soup as she thought she could carry, which turned out to be eight.

Carting these back to her apartment in a hemp grocery bag, she locked herself in and hoisted the bag onto the glowing quartztic dining counter beside the kitchen.

Seating herself on one of two stools, she pulled out the V-nanos and lay them beside the bag. Selecting and peeling one V-nano, she managed to eat about half of the fruit-like, engineered foodstuff before a wave of nausea and stomach cramping assailed her, her body struggling to adapt to the processes of ingestion. With one hand over her mouth, and another cradling her belly, she crawled into bed again, dragged the sheet up to her chin, closing her eyes.

'Rest. Recover.'

CHAPTER FOUR: OPERATION REGROUP

It had taken eight meals for her digestive tract to accept ingested food without complaint. Her body had been like a spirited horse refusing a rider. Most of the mushy meals had stayed down, but those hadn't stayed in for long: stomach cramps and diarrhea had been frequent dining companions. Now, one week after her revival, she was still painfully thin. Subcutaneous fat was starting to build, her skin losing the baby pink hue, fading towards white. A full set of teeth had also erupted painfully from her gums. Two day later, they started to fall out, causing her to wonder if something had gone wrong with the cloning procedure, until the next day when a second set became evident, and she realised she was simply losing her milk teeth.

She was in the process of moving onto firmer foods. A fuzz of hair presented from her scalp, and she could make out the beginnings of eyebrows and lashes, reducing the need to pencil in such features when venturing outside. She had glued on the thoughtfully-provided false nails, but guessed that beneath their glossy surfaces, her own fingernails had begun to emerge, if her budding toenails were any indicator. Her teeth were still a little short, but she had already disposed of her dentures and could, with relief, properly form all consonant sounds again. With disciplined self-awareness, she affected convincingly shy smiles without revealing her teeth. The first time she brushed them, she had the same unnerving sensation that she had in the cloning lab when she tried to tie her shoe laces: that this was a task she had never attempted before, only ever seen done in a sim-torial. Her fine-motor skills were degraded, and she had to make a conscious effort to move the brush around in her mouth to effectively clean the enamelled surfaces. She had found this to be the case with many simple self-care tasks.

Her best friend, to date, was the Gambian level store owner with whom she had a long conversation – mostly in French – about whether he could order-in certain food supplements she wanted. He had argued convincingly and persistently *no*, but had offered her several reasonable alternatives. Of course, she wasn't able to tell him why she couldn't yet venture into the main shopping areas of the mega block, because of the heavy surveillance.

She mentally filed their budding relationship under 'businesslike: must try harder.' As for the specialist supplements, powdered body-building compounds, she had received an obscure communiqué from Kochansky, in which he claimed to be a family friend working in the avtog industry. He had promised his grandfather on Seconde, an old 'friend' of Angel's great aunt, to check in on her, make sure she was settling in, and to help her network for acting gigs. He mentioned he'd be bringing some groceries and some good old fashioned home cooking with him. She hoped he'd know to bring the compounds. At this point in her recovery, she needed high nutritional density to offset the small volumes of food she could handle at a time.

In the straight-to-inbox message he'd sent, he also suggested that 'maybe they could go out somewhere – she should wear the same outfit she had on the last time he saw her.'

The tone she had pre-selected for telecom' requests chimed in her left ear, or at least so the neural scaffolding in the sensory portions of her brain led her to believe, by inducing the same pattern of electro-chemical signals between synapses that *actual* hearing would have created.

"Hello?"

"Hello, Angel?"

"Aaron?" She allowed a note of excitement to enter her voice. She didn't need to fake it, just temper the genuine desire for company she craved, especially with someone she could relax and be herself around. But she was still sufficiently cautious to avoid self-identifying to a potential threat source.

"Yeah. Can you sanction me?"

She transmitted the single-use access code that would allow her visitor to reach her hallway section. With the size of the block, and the foot traffic within it, it would still be about five minutes before she would hear his knock on the door. She didn't have avtog access to the hallway security camera live-feed. Even with her modest hacking skills, she could easily obtain it, but on her civilian avtog this would leave a distinctly abnormal data print, after which the next knock on her door would not be from a friendly.

PRIMED

The apartment lacked a distinct, enclosed hall or even entry way: the apartment door opened inwards to a little over ninety degrees before coming to a stop that prevented it from banging into the corner of the kitchen countertop, where it overhung a waste disposal unit. This layout would make it undesirable for most civilians, who liked to hang up their keys and coats, leave their shoes, or whatever, and then not have to look at them, but it suited her perfectly: the lack of a restrictive corridor behind the main entry point left her manoeuvring room, should she need it.

Snatching up the un-seasonably heavy coat that she had found in her hovertrunk, she hung it over the back of one of the two padded vinyl bar stools at her dining counter, lifted a chair silently and set it down facing the door. She slid a long bladed chef's knife and a long handled spatula from a wall-mounted, magnetic stowage rail, then, from the chair's footrail, clambered noiselessly onto the engineered quartztic countertop to crouch beside the door.

Once in position, she tested the distance to the chair with her foot, easily reaching the top of it without fully extending her leg, testing the chair by tipping it back on its back two legs, its rubberised feet preventing it from slipping across the seamless, ceramic floor. Satisfied, she stabilised her crouch, on the balls of both feet, and waited.

Several minutes passed before the anticipated *da da-da-da don*. She waited a few seconds more, then, extending her spatula-bearing hand tentatively across the doorway, she flapped its large, silicone head across the spyhole, and held it there for a few seconds. After letting it fall from the spyhole, nothing untoward happened. Again, she waited a few seconds and, again, covered the spyhole with the spatula. Letting it fall a second time, and waiting a second time, during which, again, nothing happened, she slipped down from the counter, leaving the spatula, but retaining the knife held underhand, its blade flat against her forearm. This time, she pressed her own fragile, vulnerable eye to the small circle in the middle of her door, and was presented with a fish-eye image of the hallway outside her apartment, with the disproportionately magnified head of Kochansky looking down the hall. She tried to follow his gaze, but couldn't see anything. She inspected his hands, and saw that he was carrying a grocery bag in each. As she watched, he bent to set the bags down, and, standing up empty-handed, raised one hand to knock again. He paused when he heard her disengage the bolting mechanisms, which she did by feel, keeping her eye on the spyhole. Kochansky bent to pick up the bags again, and when she opened the door he waited politely in the hallway for her to beckon him in.

She dragged the barstool aside to let him pass her, which he regarded with a quizzically raised eyebrow. Once inside, she closed and re-bolted the door, several metal bars passing from one side of the door frame, which was securely bolted to the concrete wall, through the body of the door to latch on the opposite side of the frame.

Kochansky hoisted up the bags with his skinny arms, depositing them heavily on the edge of the counter closest to the entrance, and started to unload the contents for her to inspect. She immediately resisted the temptation to do so, returning her attention to the spyhole. A man and woman were walking towards her door, talking casually. As they drew close, her fingers tightened on the handle of the kitchen knife, and she instinctively held her breath. She scrutinised their hands for any sudden, arming movements, but they passed the door without incident, and moved off down the hallway, out of sight. Reluctantly peeling herself away from the door, she picked up the spatula and put it and the knife back on the magnetic rail. Kochansky watched calmly.

"Everything okay?"

"I hope so. What'd you bring?"

"Well, really, some groceries, and some softs to record raw footage for your spaceport arrival. We don't want to leave it too long before depositing the file in the port database. We're not sure how long it'll take for the S.A.s to review the footage, but we don't want to take too many chances. The chocolate bar is from Victor. He's a real sweetheart. And he paid me to tell you that, by the way," he added, matter-of-factly. She laughed easily, genuinely, for the first time in company since the day of her revival. It felt good. Human.

She inspected some of the groceries, including a stack of frozen ready-meals, and with relief found a tub of powdered protein shake and another of a rapid weight-gain formula. Out of the corner of her eye, she saw a look of awkwardness, embarrassment, flit across Kochansky's face, casting his eyes to the floor and dipping his head as she turned the weight gain formula tub to read the label. 'Never mention a woman's weight, huh?' Lifting the tubs from the counter, one in either hand she faced him squarely: "Better than chocolate. Thanks."

Kochansky relaxed, visibly, head-bobbing a *you're welcome*.

"I have to report to Evagora on your physical condition. Any concerns?" For a brief moment she wasn't sure if he meant health concerns or concerns about him reporting on her to Evagora. She guessed health.

"No, under the circumstances, as well as can be expected. I'll be happy to start training, get a bit more meat on these bones!" Kochansky chose not to comment. 'Cautious around women, in general, or just powerful ones? Maybe I'm more intimidating than I realise.'

"Are those all the same clothes you wore in the hauler?"

"Yep. We're not really going out anywhere, are we?"

Kochansky laughed. "No, I'm afraid not," he said, "I just need to get some footage to simulate your arrival at the port. Do you mind if I set up?"

"No, go ahead. Anything I can do?"

"Uh..." Kochansky cast his eyes around the spartan apartment. "...you could slide that koffee table against the wall. We need some open space." He backed towards the far windows, then into the corner, focussing his gaze on the floor, moving his head like a painter trying to establish perspective, hands out in front of him as though he were holding a large box by its sides. After checking around his feet and behind him for adequate room, he made a dropping gesture. "Okay, if I can just get that chair over here while I paste up some markers for you."

She retrieved the barstool from near the entrance, and carried it over to where Kochansky had been standing, while he paced a winding route across the floor, leading towards the corner, and then around and behind the stool's position. "We can simulate the security camera footage of your movements through the port, but they store avtog footage from the customs officers for all non-residents and new arrivals. We could fake that, too, but you know as well as I do that it wouldn't look quite right."

As he spoke, he adjusted the height of the stool a couple of times, until certain his eye level was correct, and then said "Okay, go stand at the end of the line. We've found a section of footage from the port where there's a big enough gap in all frames for an extra person in the queue. That's going to be you. There's a couple of points where it's a bit tight, so I'll give you a stop and walk light: we'll need prompt responses to keep you from overlapping the people in front and behind you. When the stop light's on just try to keep your arms down by your sides – no fidgeting. I'm sure you'll have no problem. I mean, you don't look like you would fidget. Okay, here's the light." He raised his hand, palm out, to above his right shoulder. When he lowered his hand, he slipped it under his buttocks, along with his other hand, and carefully placed his heels on the foot rail of the bar stool, even though he could easily have reached the floor with them, with his long legs.

Her arhud blinked a video stream request, which she accepted. Promptly, a round, red light, about ten centimetres across, winked into existence where Kochansky's hand had been, and the room filled with ghostly figures in a frozen tableau, thirty-five Ladder passengers with their carry-ons, queuing for Customs and Immigration. "And here's a script for our conversation. I'm gonna start the footage now. Stay in the line, watch for the lights. I'll speak to you in a minute."

Shortly, the red light turned green, and she dutifully shuffled along closely behind the abruptly animated, translucent figure before her until it turned red again just a moment later. She reviewed the script. It was just a few lines, she didn't even need to scroll it across her field of vision, it was all visible in one go. The red light stayed red for a few minutes, then blinked green again for just two scuffing steps. This continued for nearly an hour, as she worked her way across the room, from side to side and back again, gradually drawing nearer to the front of the illusory line up. She resisted the urge to look at the figures behind her, trusting that she was avoiding contact. Turning around in the queue would cause real-world responses from those around her – natural, instinctive attempts to make or avoid eye contact, according to social conventions, that would be visible to any Security Agent reviewing the footage. But, since she was not in the real-world queue, these pre-recorded figures would not respond to her in any way, making her look out of place. Finally she closed on Kochansky, who spoke: "I can help the next person." She approached his chair, stopping just in front of a virtual line he had pasted to indicate the front edge of a counter. "Please state your name, and the purpose and duration of your visit."

"Angel Leonard. I'm here on a two year working visa."

"Oh? What line of work are you in?"

"The entertainment industry."

"Do you have an employment position?"

"No, but I'll be auditioning as soon as possible."

"And where will you be staying?"

"I've rented an apartment in Church Hill."

PRIMED

After a pause of a few seconds, Kochansky said "Everything seems to be in order. If you change address, be sure to notify us within five days. Welcome to Godsgood City, Alpha Centauri Prime, we hope you have a pleasant stay."

"Thank you."

The script indicated that she should follow the virtual guide line around and behind Kochansky. He took a few seconds to make sure the following footage fitted properly, then stood and turned to her. "Okay, I just need to upload your simulated *.psy* cache. A weeks' worth of *.stm*s – that'll take about fifteen to twenty seconds, depending on how much sleep you've been getting." His eyebrows fluttered in a micro-expression she couldn't quite pin down: it was either out of concern for her health, about which he felt awkward, or a discomfort resulting from his invasion of her privacy, that he would know from the upload completion time whether she was sleepless or untroubled. She set her op's terminal to its weakest LANcasting setting, equivalent to the same-room signal strength that usually connected an E.A.N. to a handroid, and opened a port for Kochansky to access the device's flexi-drive. He nodded a little, confirming the port's accessibility on his arhud. "I just have to stay in LANtact range until that's finished, but otherwise that's it for now. I'll run the footage by Pasqualé: she'll make sure there's nothing in there that might alert SPITS. If there's a problem, she'll let you know."

"Actually, there might be a problem, already. When I was walking here from the hauler, I realised there's no way I could've made it to the rooftops without a ride: my 'droid only cleared me for ground-level entry to my *own* building."

"Of course. Don't sweat it, we took care of that on the day. For future reference, you took an autocab from the port, and made a mid-flight request for a premature drop off. Pick a reason, I dunno, to take in the ambience of a new city?"

"Sounds just like me. Can I go through a mall, yet? I need some equipment for training."

"Uh... better wait for Pasqualé to clear you on that. SPITS has a way of seeing things we don't even know we're doing, some mannerisms we're not even conscious of, but they identify us like a kiss from Judas, she says. We've contended with face and gait recognition for decades, but this is something else. None of us want to fuck with it. If you get a chance, ask the other oper's for their *How I Got Caught* stories. They'll give you a good idea what to expect. In the meantime, I'll be your *gopher*: av' me a list of anything you need, and I'll drop it off to you as soon as I can. Okay?"

"Okay, thanks." Kochansky bobbed his head again, and made for the door. As his hand reached for the door handle, she stopped him.

"Wait: what's *your* SPITS tell?"

"*Tell*? Like in poker?"

"Ah-huh."

"Huh, I never thought of it like that. Well, Pasqualé showed me a whole bunch. I'm not very good at hiding them, either. There's the walk, of course. Everyone has the walk, that's like Security Agent one-oh-one stuff. Other than that, I'm mostly good, standing, except for this thing I do where I shift my weight onto one foot, and put my other foot on top of it. Done it since I was a kid, I guess. But when I sit down, all hell breaks loose – postural indicators, for starters, plus I practically have to sit on my hands in a public place, fold my arms, cross my legs. Basically, I need something like a straight-jacket to stop me drumming my fingers on tables, counters, any flat surface. And I tap my feet, too. Makes my whole leg pump. Pasqualé calls me *Thumper*. Total give-aways, apparently."

"Did you have a drum kit, when you were a kid?"

"Now that's creepy. Pasqualé asked me the same question. Yeah, I even played in a band in high school. We never got out of my garage, but we had dreams. No talent, mind, but *dreams!*"

She laughed. "Yeah, we all had dreams, before the war."

"You'd be surprised, Leonard, there're still a few dreamers left in our ranks. Send me that list. I'll see you again soon."

"Thanks again." Again, the *you're welcome* head wobble as he went out the door. 'Another SPITS tell?' She wondered if he knew about that one, or Pasqualé, for that matter. She made a mental note to ask her, when she got some face time.

CHAPTER FIVE: OPERATION REVAMP

Kochansky was back within a couple of days, bringing some equipment for her to train. She ran through the same routine with the spatula and the bar stool with the heavy coat behind the door before she braved the spy hole. She was surprised to see Pasqualé on the other side of the door, wearing a black, silicone flike-suit and carrying a crash helmet. Kochansky was there, too, but stood to the side with his hand on a hovertrunk. She opened the door for them, and Pasqualé hurried into the room, gripping and moving the chair quietly off to the side so that Kochansky could pass through with the hovertrunk.

"Good evening, Leonard. What's with the chair, again? You're not too short to reach the spy hole, are you?"

Pasqualé appraised him for a moment, before answering on Leonard's behalf: "No, you dick, it's to simulate her body behind the door." Kochansky looked blank for a second. "Allah, preserve us from techies." she muttered. "The spy hole went dark three times before she opened the door. I'm guessing only the last time was from you looking through the spy hole yourself, right?" Leonard nodded reluctantly. She made a mental note to add at least two more passes of the spatula before looking. It's not that she didn't trust Pasqualé, or Kochansky or any of the other members of her cell, just that she had seen and heard about enough missions turned sour to know that trust only went so far towards saving your ass when operations got *FUBAR*.

Kochansky put it together. He wasn't stupid, just a technician. His training hadn't included the same level of self-defence and subterfuge as hers, or perhaps even Pasqualé's. No doubt there were things he could do with a handroid that would leave her speechless, and him wondering how she couldn't know that and still survive.

"Okay. I guess that explains some of these equipment requests, then." He sank the hovertrunk, and laid it horizontally, as she had, before cracking it open. "Now, where is it...?" He started pulling out equipment: wrist and ankle weights; a weighted waistcoat; a pair of lightly padded, open-fingered boxing gloves, for mixed martial arts; foot, shin, knee and elbow pads. "Okay, here it is. Here. This was Victor's idea, he thought you might like it" He passed her a featureless, white cardboard box, just about the size a small piece of jewellery might come in. "Don't worry, it's not a proposal. Open it."

    Inside was a small device, about the size and shape of an engagement ring, to be sure, but with a lens where a finger would go. "Spycam?"

    "Yeah, but look." He reached out for the device, which she returned to him. He walked back to the door as he talked. "It has a light admitter, audio in *and* out, and a LANterface you can access from up to a couple o' hundred metres away. What is this, the thirty-fifth floor, right? Yeah, you should be able to access the camera from the plaza outside, or from the roof. He quickly glanced through the spy hole before opening the door, and in a quick movement tooled the original lens out of the door into his palm. He pulled out the activation tag on the spycam, a small strip of clear plastic that had insulated the battery connection, wiped the device down with a small lens cloth, and inserted it into the hole in the door, before closing and locking the door again. "Search for the device. You can use your handroid, but set up for a passive LANnection only, so it won't run through the network."

    She accessed her handroid connection settings, a series of activation windows popping up on her arhud. She made her selections and closed them with eye-points. Some streamers still preferred virtual simulations of physical human interface devices, such as keyboards or touchable screens. These were still useful for certain vocational tasks and games, but nenned commands and eye-point were the established norm. If she ever suspected nens were under scrutiny, she could think just as well in sign-language, which usually slipped under the security radar. Typically, Security Agents would be focussed on the audio-visual streams for nen monitoring, missing the more subtle tactile and kinetic impressions user-generated by a signer. Individual agents were encouraged to develop their own personal avtog command dialects, with military sign language as a starting point, to render their avtog interactions indecipherable to enemy counter intelligence agents – even if they registered the tactile stream, they could not determine the meaning of the command, since intent was one of the few facets of mind that avtog was incapable of discerning. In this respect, it fell short of what might be considered true telepathy: streamers were assured at least of that level of privacy. Unless intent was clearly nenned, or a deducible emotional state led to predictable actions, it was impossible for a nen screener or comdropper to determine a telegrapher's objective or impending course of action.

She quickly located the device. "Got it."

"Okay, here's the security access code." Kochansky made a gesture with his right hand. From where he stood by the door, he flicked a small, luminous data-stream request window, like a thrown playing card. It span across the room, suddenly stopping about a metre and a half in front of her. She accepted the request, and a set of code started scrolling through the window that opened.

"That's... a lot of code."

Kochansky smiled. "Yeah, military grade encryption makes for pretty dull reading."

"Quite. I'll just copy and paste, if it's all the same to you?"

"Be my guest. Don't forget to clear the copy cache from your handroid, though."

"You know, I *can* wipe my *own* ass, thank you!"

"Sorry, I didn't mean to be patronising. Just being thorough."

"No offence taken. I was just being thorough, too." She gave him her best, wicked half smile, baring her left canine. Kochansky actually blushed.

She entered the code, overwrote the cache contents to prevent Security Agents from finding it, and accessed the camera. Her whole perception instantly shifted to the lens. The full opacity setting and perspective blocker softs blinded her real vision. She left it like that; she could always change it later, if she wanted to. She enjoyed the clarity of the image, and the scale, filling her full field of vision, allowed a much more detailed view of the hallway outside. She would be able to get a better look at any passersby or visitors, their expressions, body language, hand movements and contents. Along the bottom of the image were five black mini-screens, and three toggle icons marked 'Spk,' 'A' and 'LA'.

"What're these togglicons?"

"Uh... *Light Admitter*," she heard Kochansky say. She could tell he hadn't moved from the door. "White is on, black is off, obviously. When it's on, ambient light is allowed to pass through to the other side of the spyhole, but toggling it off activates the L.C.D. shutter, cutting off the light. Not quite as low tech' as a spatula...." She could hear the smile in his voice.

"Alright, alright: so I improvised."

"You can still look through the lens from this side like a regular spyhole. The other two are for the in and out audio streams. Uh, as in a microphone and a speaker. You can talk through the door even if you're not in the room. Wanna try it?"

Pasqualé had moved quietly, but now she was clinking glasses out of a kitchen cabinet. Scrolling down the opacity on the video feed, she saw Pasqualé in the kitchen with three glasses on the counter, and a gigantic bottle of alcohol. She was pouring. She toggled the speaker button, and experimentally tried a coherent thought: '<bang bang bang> Police! Open up!'

The device on the door instantly sounded out a convincing triple knocking sound, followed by "Police! Open up," much like the voice she imagined, which was unlike her own, male, gravelly.

The sudden noise startled Kochansky, who actually looked through the device into the hallway. "What!?" He turned and looked back at the women in the room with him. Pasqualé was shaking her shoulders in silent laughter. "Cool! I didn't know it could do that."

"In the hands of an expert...." Pasqualé volunteered. She handed a full glass of clear liquid to Kochansky. Leonard gave her a theatrical bow, and accepted another proffered glass.

"You might want to borrow the spatula, though, before sticking your head to the door like that. Leonard's caution might seem excessive, to you, but that right there is the kind of rookie move that'd get your head blown clean off by any GUNEs out there."

"Talking about head moves," she said to Pasqualé, sniffing at her glass, "does he know about his *you're welcome* thing?"

Pasqualé smiled slyly, glancing at Kochansky as she replied. "Yeah, we caught that one, eventually. He only does it around hot chicks, 'though, right, Kochansky? We had to run a few," as she grabbed and hoisted her breasts, lewdly "*augmented* role-play sessions to ferret that out, didn't we, sweetheart?"

"Yeah, that's right. Oh, and – fuck *you*, Pasqualé." His voice was still playful, mildly embarrassed at worst.

'Not a squaddy, obviously, but a good sport at least,' she concluded. She knew she was gauging the characters and capabilities of her colleagues, expanding the necessary limits of trust, and cautioned herself to stay emotionally detached, reserved. She wasn't here to make friends, no matter how much comfort that would bring. It would be easier if she didn't find them so likable.

"Oh, now, we've been over that, Kochansky – we wouldn't want to complicate our relationship, now, would we?" She blew him a kiss.

Leonard appreciated how close her team members were. It was a good sign when operatives could tease each other to this extent. Morale was high. Tensions were dissipated. Bonds were strengthened. If it came down to it, lives would be put on the line to save each other, even *without* the promise of revival.

She checked her train of thought. "Okay, break it up, bitches. Don't make me hose you down. Any news on a new cloning facility?"

Pasqualé sobered instantly. Business before pleasure. "Nothing, yet. The one we squelched you out of was busted, what," she looked towards Kochansky for confirmation, "thirty hours after we cleared out?" Kochansky nodded his agreement. "D'you see it in the news?" Leonard shook her head. "Well, they described it as an electrical fire in a disused industrial building, so it's hardly surprising. But less disturbing to the civ's than *a resistance A.I. bomb which took out a whole team of UNE Security Agents.*" She looked pleased by this result, proud. She raised her drink: "*Salute!*" and took a long slug from the tall glass.

Kochansky joined her with a conservative sip. A military strike against a military target. Probably better than they were used to. "*L'chaim.*" Grim faced and toasting the lives of his fallen enemies, clearly Kochansky didn't get any joy out of it, but he did his duty as needed.

"*Slàinte mhòr.*" Dutifully, she tested her drink, conscious of her fragile condition and the fact that this body had never actually been subjected to alcohol before. The antiseptic smell reached her just before the burning sting lit the thin skin of her lips and the inside of her mouth. 'Vodka.' Pasqualé had just given her a full tumbler of neat vodka. She contemplated the mechanism by which she was able to recognise something that, technically, she had never really tasted before. "Thanks,

Pasqualé. It's... been a while." Within a few seconds, she felt her face warm from vasodilation as the alcohol hit her bloodstream.

"Hey, don't thank *me*. Officially, this is the bottle you picked up in duty-free on your way here. It's about time we had a house-warming!"

"You know," said Kochansky, "it actually took a while longer than we expected for the GUNEs to raid the lab. It could be that we're getting better at evading them – or their intel's not so hot, any more," Kochansky suggested. "We're still sticking to the plan: no new facility, yet, nothing for them to raid, everyone lying low. Hopefully they'll think we all went off-world."

"*Or* their intel' is *better* than we suspect, and they planned the last slow response to lull us into a false sense of security, make us sloppy, so they can wipe us all out in one go," suggested Pasqualé.

"How about some optimism, Pasqualé? I hear it's good for morale."

"May *be*, but then again, I know too many dead optimists. And I bet your left nut that Ms. Leonard here does, too. Plus, being dead is *not* good for morale."

"No doubt, but in the future I'd appreciate it if you bet with your *own* nuts."

Leonard wondered how long the pair would continue in this vein, cutting in with a warning: "Guys, I'd better take it easy on this stuff; I'm still –"

"Oh, no-no-no-no-*no*! Drink up. Doctor's orders, Leonard."

"Yeah, sorry, that's actually true," sympathised Kochansky, "You were so well behaved during our little avtog shoot the other day that Pasqualé here couldn't read any mannerisms from the footage. I mean, that's good, right? Nothing for SPITS to pick up on."

"Yes, yes, she was very prim and proper, under ideal, stress-free conditions. But now we have to *mess things up* a little. Break through your self control, see what floats up."

"So the vodka...?"

"Reduces inhibitions? Yep." Pasqualé took another long sip of her drink.

PRIMED

"If you're monitoring me, then shouldn't you be staying sober?"

"Now, where would be the fun in that? Besides, you wouldn't want to drink this whole bottle on your own, would you?" Lips pursed, Leonard shook her head at the two litre bottle Pasqualé was cradling like a baby.

Kochansky wandered over to the hovertrunk, peering inside. "How about I put this together while you ladies get better acquainted. This could be a long night."

Taking a long pull from her glass, her stomach complaining with an indigestive burn, Leonard asked "What is it?"

Kochansky had opened the top of another box that had been packed in the bottom section of the hovertrunk, and lifted out a translucent silicone-covered skull. It had rudimentary features, smoothed and softened, but still looked convincingly anthropomorphic. With considerable excitement, raising the skull like a trophy, Kochansky replied: "Sparbot!"

Assembling the android domestic aid – a sturdy model well suited to adaptation to an A.I. punch bag and combat training resource – took all their combined efforts. Somehow, Pasqualé managed to turn it into a drinking game, by confiscating the manual, and insisting they take turns, with failed attempts to functionally combine components followed by downing two fingers of vodka. Kochansky, initially sure his technical expertise would enable him to build the 'bot blindfolded, and with either a desire to impress his female companions or a degree of chivalry seldom evident, these days, tackled the most difficult assembly tasks first: the tactile feedback piezo-electric fibers, the android analog of a nervous system.

Because Pasqualé was merciless in her definition of 'failed attempts,' each time Kochansky missed threading the fine, slippery, plasticrystal strands into their corresponding sockets he was obligated to drink the stipulated dose. The rapid impact of the alcohol on his slender frame dramatically impaired his ability to perform the same task again, and after several such incidents he decried a positive feedback loop, and seized the two largest components he could find to stick together. Leonard and Pasqualé quickly found the same task to be dauntingly difficult, and relaxed the rules for themselves whilst Kochansky was distracted with a thigh segment.

"That's funny, Kochansky, I never took you for a leg man." Pasqualé quipped.

Finally, all drunk and sweating, they had completed the 'bot. It resembled a high-school laboratory prop, a white nanopoxy skeleton, covered by a translucent cladding of elastomer, mimicking the tactile properties of human tissue. Pasqualé lifted it up from under its arms, as it flopped rag doll-like, staggering drunkenly back against a partitioning wall between apartments.

"Fuck *me*! It's like wrestling an alligator! Turn it on!"

Kochansky reached out his right hand, typed a command on a virtual keyboard only he could see, then hit 'enter' with a flourish. The training device sprang to standing, leaving Pasqualé to slide to the floor, off balance. She sat there with her legs splayed, cackling.

"Now what," Leonard asked.

"Now you beat seven shades of robotic shit out of it!" cried Kochansky. Having long since abandoned his glass, he made a hilarious display of winding up for a comical punch, landing a surprisingly firm uppercut on the jaw of the android, considering his slender build and the amount he had to drink. The android rose up on its toes, and took two swift steps backwards before recovering its poise and balance, its head snapping quickly back into position.

"Whoa!" exclaimed Pasqualé, as the droid came to a skidding stop between her legs. She lifted her right knee to her chin, and, twisting her whole body sideways as she pivoted onto her left knee, left palm pressed to the floor, she forcefully drove the heel of her foot horizontally into the pit at the back of the android's knee. Its leg buckled at the joint, and the whole device dropped towards the floor, but after a split second it converted its movement into a forward step with its other leg, making a lunge-like manoeuvre, and returned to standing. The servomotors in its skeletal joints, muffled by its fleshy exterior, were scarcely audible. Leonard made a note to set her avtog to eliminate the sound completely from her perception, for training purposes, along with any un-realistic advantage she might gain as a result of hearing its movements.

Leonard stepped up to the device, toe to toe, staring into its disturbingly human-looking eyes. "Show us some moves, Leonard," urged Pasqualé, still on the floor. Laying her hand on the cheek of the device, she found it cool; fleshy; unresponsive. It made unblinking eye-contact. She gave it a little slap.

"You and I are gonna have a lot of fun, you bad boy. But not now. Not like this. You deserve better." Better than she could offer, right now, still weak and skinny, and half-cut.

Kochansky stepped up beside her. "Well, if you're sure, I can show you some of the augments and uploads I've put together for you."

"Yes. Please." She felt flushed, a little wobbly on her feet, but her head felt clear. Kochansky had put a lot of effort into this equipment for her, and she could see its potential.

"Okay, basic augments: anatomical." Her avtog lit up vibrantly coloured, but accurately positioned and shaped, vital organs represented within the android's fleshy cladding as if she could clearly see through it. "Skinned." Here, the surface of the android seemed to morph through a selection of different skin tones and facial features. "Clothed." Again, a selection of outfits: civilian; uniformed; lab-coated; military garb. "And... armoured." The android assumed the outward appearance of a UNE peacekeeper's anti-ballistic exo-skeleton. Reaching for its arm, avtog presented the tactile sensation of a smooth, hard surface, but with a conscious squeeze, her hand passed through it to the soft, silicone-covered limb within the illusion. "There are pros and cons, of course," said Kochansky, defensively making excuses for the loss of immersiveness. "With a purely avtog sparring partner, you wouldn't lose the tactile impression of the surface, but you also wouldn't be working against any real mass. No impact, no opponent weight, or resistance. Only your own muscles to simulate oppositional forces, or, worse, just imagined ones. That'd be fine for a game, but I thought you'd prefer a more reality-based training program."

"You were right. Kochansky?"

"Mm-hmm?" Kochansky was still engrossed with transferring his training softs to Leonard's handroid.

"It's better than chocolate." Kochansky took a second to acknowledge her gratitude, but when he did it was with his *you're welcome* head bob. Pasqualé had stood up by this time, and had joined them to inspect the android and Kochansky's upgrades. When she saw his SPITS tell she wasted no time in palm-smacking him across the back of his head.

"Ow! What the fuck, Pasqualé? I hope you were aiming for the 'droid!"

"Aversion therapy, dick-weed. You look like *un piccione del Piazza del Duomo!*" She caricatured his head-bob, adding a wide, avian-eyed look, and sucked-in cheeks to complete her impression of a Milanese pigeon pecking for breadcrumbs. Kochansky stared at her, dumbstruck, in horror. "Good comeback, Kochansky."

They set aside any further hostilities when they heard Major 'Angel Leonard' emptying her mostly vodka-filled stomach contents into her toilet. She had hurried to the wetcube when she first felt the wave of nausea rise and, having divested herself of further intoxicants, she felt considerably better. She rinsed out her mouth from the sink's faucet, and found herself again splashing cold water on her face, neck, wrists. She appraised herself in the mirror. The face she saw was starting to look a little more familiar with each passing day, though it would never be the one she truly identified as her own. There were no childhood photos of *this* face, except for those that might be faked to avert suspicion. The stubble of her hair was reassuring, though, indicative of growth, recovery. 'Hello, again, Angel Leonard. It looks like we're stuck with each other.'

Emerging from the 'cube with a fresh towel around her neck, patting herself dry, she met the concerned faces of her colleagues.

"I'm starving. Let's eat."

PRIMED

CHAPTER SIX: OPERATION DOG HAIR

When she awoke, Kochansky was making a sizzling breakfast, using every kitchen implement she owned. Pasqualé was 'togging at the dining counter. She vaguely remembered Pasqualé getting out of the sofa bed they'd shared last night, but had no idea how long ago that had been. Kochansky had gallantly slept in a sleeping bag on the floor.

"Ugh. What time is it?"

From the kitchen, Kochansky called back "Let's be generous, and call it 'almost time for brunch,' shall we? How do you feel about veggs Benedict?"

"*Big* fan. Third album sucked shit, though."

Kochansky started dishing up onto three of her four plates, a process involving transferring sliced sham and delicate, poached veggs by spatula to toasted English muffins, and spoonings of Hollandaise sauce between every stage. These were joined by baked beans, fried mushrooms and tofurkey sausages.

Leonard had shuffled over to the counter to sit beside Pasqualé. "So *that's* what a spatula's for."

"*In the hands of an expert.* Koffee?"

She nodded enthusiastically at his offer. He poured three cups from a filter jug, sliding two onto the counter before Leonard and Pasqualé.

"Kochansky, will you marry me?" Pasqualé emerged from her trance to locate the koffee, the tantalising aroma penetrating the depths of her immersion.

"I already did, last night. Beautiful service. Don't you remember? I'm hurt. Really. Truly." He slid their plates in front of them, and started forking his own plateful into his mouth at the kitchen counter across from them, slouching forward, on one elbow.

Her first forkful exploded with flavour in her mouth, her parotid glands pumping serous saliva with a sudden, sharp pain, cutting through the vodka fur – lemon juice, mustard, salt and pepper in the sauce, crisply fried, smoky sham, barely contained on a toasted English muffin base.

"Oh, oh, *oh*.... Congratulations, Pasqualé, he's a real catch. Kochansky, it's really too bad you're already spoken for: this is fantastic!"

"Two offers in one meal. That's a personal record. Now I just need to get a girl to stay until breakfast...."

"I'm pretty much done reviewing the footage from last night," Pasqualé informed Leonard, "and it looks like Evagora was right. I guess he didn't sleep his way to the top after all."

"I hope that's not going to end up online, later?"

"Not unless we want the GUNEs kicking your door in. It's the hair, Leonard. Even when you don't have any. Listen, one of the best defences we've come up with against SPITS is a spin-off from the short clone gestation cycle. With a fully gestated clone, over a twelve week cycle, we would have run and re-run your long term memory files continuously. Thousands of passes, reinforcing the neural pathways laid down in your previous life. The brain architecture comes out pretty close to what you had before, so you end up with all the same tendencies, muscle memory retention. You also get all the old kinks and quirks into the system from the previous set-up, and those are what SPITS homes in on. When you were revived, like most of us, there was only a single pass. You get all the same memories, but not ingrained to the same depth."

"Is that why I had to think twice before tying my shoe laces; brushing my teeth?"

"Exactly. That's the low level of motor learning from a single neural inscription pass. Real muscle memory takes multiple passes to establish. Effectively, you have to re-learn everything, practically from scratch, and in doing so you learn it slightly differently. Definitely different enough to fool any gait recognition softs. Different enough to thwart SPITS, in most cases. Sometimes, even just one inscription pass is enough to convey an especially ingrained mannerism."

"Is that what happened with Kochansky?"

"Ah!" Pasqualé turned to survey the gangly looking technician. "Not quite. Kochansky's a special case, aren't you, Kochansky?" He returned her look with a tight-lipped glance then turned to look out the window. "Kochansky here has been with us the longest, in his present incarnation. He was the first revivee after the SPITS arrests, and it was him who figured out the protocols for the rest of the revivals. So, he had a standard, multiple-pass inscription: he's a bundle of ticks and twitches, always was, and is again."

"I'm right here," said Kochansky, with mock indignation.

"So how does he get past SPITS?"

"Guys?" Kochansky waved his arm comically between them.

"Okay, why don't you tell the Major, here, how you manage to avoid capture by SPITS?"

"Well, I'm glad you asked! It's a funny story. I used to be much bigger than I am now. I mean, maybe six inches taller, and *fat. Really* fat. So, when I was last revived, the technicians weren't sure about SPITS, yet, how it operated. They thought it was just an advanced gait and facial recognition system. So the majority of changes made were to my genetic sequence, not to the neural inscription technique. With a drastic overhaul, the changes to my build and height have sufficiently altered my gait and posture so that SPITS doesn't recognise them. As for the other mannerisms, like I said before, I just have to be mindful. Avoid certain situations in public places."

"So why don't we use that method for everyone? Isn't full skill retention worth a few cosmetic changes?"

"To be honest, neither process is foolproof, as far as we've been able to figure out. It's worked well for Kochansky, 'cause *his* operative skill set is tech' based, not so much physical. He needs to remember all that stuff to duplicate it. The skills that are valuable to *you*, though, are more physically based, so a full set of physical skills in a physically different body, even with slight differences, wouldn't be the big advantage you would imagine: you'd have to *un*learn, and then *re*learn everything, 'cause all your body awareness would be of a body with slightly different proportions. At the level I imagine you *normally* operate at, it would be a major hindrance: you'd constantly be at odds with your own instincts and body positioning. It's actually an advantage to start with a clean slate, work up from scratch."

"It's true. After nearly three years, I still sometimes fumble, knock stuff over. I'm *way* more clumsy than I used to be. Plus there are other...

disadvantages. I... find it hard to believe I'm the same person I was before. It's... disturbing. I have a different name, face, body. But I remember the same things. When I'm sleeping, I dream I have my old face, but I wake up and it's like I've been body-snatched. Sometimes I can't help but wonder if the UNErs are right about us: I don't feel like a real person, just something our techies stuck together in a lab." Kochansky shook his head, looking very distressed. "Sorry, guys. Sorry. Fuck it." He ducked his head down to his koffee, and drank in silence.

Leonard couldn't think of a single encouraging thing to say. She felt the same way, but *most* of her physical differences would pass, with time, except for a relatively minor decrease in facial resemblance.

Pasqualé cleared her throat. Her eyes were wet and her nose reddened. No matter how much she tore off Kochansky, when it came down to the bone she really felt for him. "I'm sorry, Kochansky. It was just bad luck, brother. It'll come good in the end, though, you'll see. Me, I squelched outta the bell looking just like my kid sister, and since I was always jealous of her looks I thought I got a pretty good deal." She was back to the bluster. She turned to Leonard, and away from the awkward topic. "Based on what I recorded last night, you came through the neural inscription process pretty clean. But there is something hard-wired into your unconscious mind, must be something you started doing as a child, and did a lot, 'cause it re-emerged even with just a single pass. Lemme see...." Pasqualé's eyes flickered about her arhud for a few seconds, then: "Okay, let's see if I can show you this."

Scooping the best-for-last, oversized forkful from her plate into her mouth, Leonard relished the sensation of the poached vegg yolk popping in her mouth, stickily coating her tongue and teeth with the rich delicacy. She opened Pasqualé's stream, set to display as a virtual screen about a metre in front of her. It showed a slow motion montage of five clips from the previous night. Time after time, she had made a sweeping gesture with her right hand across her temple and behind her ear, only the ring finger of that hand contacting her skin, her other fingers poised the same way each time. This had absolutely no effect on the fine stubble protruding from her scalp, but evoked memories of her previous life: a lock of hair which, since childhood, had always fallen across her eyes and which, time and time again, she had swept up and tucked behind her ear only to have it slip free again and obscure her vision.

"You see that?"

"Yes. I can't believe *that* stuck, but I can't remember my own name." After an awkward silence ensued, she glanced away from the montage: Pasqualé was looking at her, sidelong. "You know, my original one?"

"Seriously?"

"Yeah, seriously. I think I remember everything else, but not that. Have you heard of that happening, before?"

"Yeah, I have: Victor said the same thing. He's been active for six months, still can't remember. Evagora thinks it'll come back, in time. All the memories were run during inscription, so we know the data is in there, somewhere. Probably just needs a jog, some kind of associative experience to remind you where you stored it."

"Maybe it's just like when you can't remember your own IPA, you know, 'cause you never av' yourself?" Kochansky chimed in. "It's an identity thing, right? We don't think of ourselves by name, it's just what other people call us. Like, I'm just 'me' to me. If that makes any sense...?"

"About as much sense as anything: we've been walking around with our brains full of wires for three generations, but the *mind* is still full of mysteries."

"Can't you just tell me?" Leonard looked from Pasqualé to Kochansky. They both returned her imploring look with pity in their eyes.

"Sorry, kiddo, we don't know it, either. As far as I know, you're really *Angel Leonard*. To be honest, we're all probably safer that way anyway. If you *do* remember, please don't tell me: it'd just be one more thing I'd have to keep from nenning." Pasqualé visibly shrugged off her sympathy like dust, snapping back to business: "Now, about this tell: if SPITS is gonna spot *some*thing, I'll bet my *own* nuts," as she threw Kochansky a conciliatory nod "this'll be it. Early in the footage, there was just one instance, but once you'd had a few drinks you were doing it roughly every twenty minutes, give or take. Now, the alcohol just lowers your inhibition level, lets the *real* you *through*. I use it to simulate the effects of distraction and stress during field op's. If it shows when you're drunk, it'll show when you're intent on some task or other, under operational stress. I'm not saying there aren't any other indicators that SPITS might pick up on, but this is the one you should focus on eliminating right now, before you can be of any use to our cell. Until you do, you won't last twenty minutes under standard Security Agency surveillance conditions. And that means anywhere outside your level."

"How do I stop myself from doing something I don't even realise I'm doing?"

"Well, we can help you with that. We've found aversion therapy to be effective. Put this..." said Pasqualé, as she lifted her left hand, pinching air. A small stream request appeared between them, which she offered to Leonard. "...into your avtog buffer. It's a small enough file, you won't need to keep it on your handroid, just in case it gets searched."

Leonard pinched the proferred end of the luminous rectangle, accepting the file transfer as Pasqualé released it. It faded out of existence as it transferred to the data storage buffer in her cerebral avtog interface.

"How do I use it?" she asked, as she glanced over the code. It seemed to be a motion recogniser, mostly indistinguishable from the type of code she'd used to program her op's terminal to recognise her unique sign language commands.

"Avtog can't read intent, but since your tell is involuntary that won't be an issue. Instead of trying to recognise when you're going to do it, the softs use motor cortex neural pathway activation cues – specifically, the pattern that co-ordinates the movement of your right hand to your right temple. Any time your brain initiates that motion, the softs will activate. Watch out for any conscious movements you might make along those lines, I dunno, like putting on sunglasses right handed, stuff like that. The softs won't know the difference in intent, and it'll activate anyway. Try it."

Leonard experimentally lifted her hand towards the side of her head. Her hand had barely started to move, when a sensation of dizziness, heat and a prickling of her skin started to build. With her hand still thirty centimetres from her ear, her stomach convulsed, and a recently swallowed chunk of fried tofu paid a second visit to her mouth. Lowering her hand, the overwhelming wave of nausea quickly subsided, leaving her with only a chunk of brunch as a reminder. She swallowed it back down.

"That wasn't just the hangover, was it?"

"Nope. I shouldn't think it'll take long to cure you of your SPITS tell. Maybe a week, to be safe? The unconscious mind responds pretty quickly to Pavlovian conditioning. Let me know if it's not enough. We could always throw in some pain simulation: blinding headaches, burning hands, that kind of thing."

"That sounds *super awesome*! Thanks a lot."

"Any time."

"Pasqualé, we'd better motor. I've got that *thing* to take care of...."

"Right." Pasqualé clapped a hand on Leonard's shoulder. "Welcome to A.C.P., Leonard. Let's talk soon."

Kochansky moved into the main room, grabbed his light jacket, and was about to stuff the packaging back into the hovertrunk.

"Kochansky, would you mind if I kept the hovertrunk? I'll clean up the mess, again, don't worry." Kochansky stood, surveying the boxes and component wrappings they had strewn about during their assembly of the android.

"Well, okay, sure. What do you want with the trunk? You already have one, don't you?"

"I do, but I have a little project in mind." This piqued his curiosity, and he studied her carefully. He opened his mouth, about to inquire further, when Pasqualé took his hand and lead him to the door.

"Leave the lady to her tinkering, Kochansky. I'm sure you guys can nerd it up next time. There's that *thing* to take care of, remember?"

"Right. Thanks for having us, Leonard. Are you sure you don't want me to clean up in the kitchen? I think I dirtied everything you own."

"That's okay. It was totally worth it."

"What about the spatula? I could give it a quick wipe: you might need it in case anyone calls around...?"

"Ho, ho. Get out, you jerk."

He grinned, wolfishly, at her, threw her a quick salute, and then they were gone. For practice, she switched her perception to the new spycam in her door, watched them head off down the hallway. She was surprised to see that Pasqualé grabbed him around the waist, and Kochansky threw his arm over her shoulders as they walked. Were they actually lovers, or was it just an act for the hall cam's? Not that it mattered to her either way, but relationships other than professional were frowned upon in the O.A.C.I. military: loyalty between lovers might exceed loyalty to the cause, resulting in compromised operatives unable to carry out their mission because of a threat to their lover.

The blank peripheral screens could pick up footage from other streaming security cams, buoycasting directly to her nano-plant. The encryption was unregistered, illegal, but short range, so unless its active signal was triangulated there was little risk of the authorities locating it, or her as its user.

She skipped the screens through a layout model of the hundreds of streams from lobbies, moorinas, hallways, malls, stairwells and external cameras around her apartment building within transmission range of the device. She saw her colleagues leave the building separately, Pasqualé crossing to the mega block moorina to pick up her flike, Kochansky taking an aerial walkway to the neighbouring Walmberg Block. She followed Kochansky to the far end of the walkway before he passed out of range. All the way, he maintained a controlled posture, and kept his hands in his pockets. Controlling his SPITS tells. She would have to learn to do the same.

Deactivating her spycam, she crossed to her wetcube. Cabinet lighting activated as she slid the door open, and she stood once more in front of the mirror, staring herself in the eyes. She lifted her right hand from the cool surface of the sink, slowly bringing it up to the side of her head. In the mirror, her lips and eyes tightened, reddening along with her face. Veins began to show, and her throat started to bob with swallowing movements. Her hand, as it rose, began to shake uncontrollably.

As her ring finger brushed her temple, she doubled over, almost striking her head on the sink faucet, and with a violent heave of her abdomen, emptied her stomach contents into the sink. She slid down the smooth wall, sank to the floor, clinging to the edge of the sink, sucking in air.

'A week of this? That's just great. This assignment just keeps getting better and better.'

As she picked off one of the false nails that had broken at some point during their drunken assembly of her new android sparring partner, inspecting the new growth of her own, real fingernail beneath, her breathing returned to normal and the aversion therapy soft-induced nausea ebbed away. Something remained, though, in the pit of her stomach; a residual knot of discomfort at the limit of her awareness. Maybe it *was* just the after-effects of the aversion, or the residual effects of her body's first vodka-drinking binge.

Or perhaps, for the first time, she had the growing feeling she would have preferred not to have been revived for this assignment: if they were really so close to defeat then what was the point in putting herself through all this? Why go on struggling against the inevitable, against annihilation? Why not just sit this one out, let someone else put in the effort? In fact, wouldn't they be able to do the job better without her?

Of course, she'd heard this kind of talk before from other veterans, those described as having been *up against the void* one time too many. The payroll psy-techs were still trying to rationalise the phenomenon as the consequence of psychological strain from repeated revivals, or the cumulative effect of multiple death experiences. The cases never matched the criteria for diagnosing Post-traumatic stress. There was so little definitive data that they were still a long way from any new classification.

She thought for a moment of the vacant, slack expressions she'd seen pass across the faces of voiders, like clouds across the moon, the lights in their eyes flickering out as though they were already in that other state, residing, latent between lives, going through the motions until their next termination.

Rookies were warned to stay away from the voiders. They sapped morale. And they were sloppy in the field, literally careless, getting themselves and those around them killed through inaction at mission-critical moments. If that happened, there'd be no psy-tech auto-stamp on their file for another revival. They were *retired from active service*. They were never retired *before* getting a bunch of rookies killed, no matter how great the concern for their well being. They were simply removed from the success-critical missions, put in with the freshly recruited operatives to serve one last time as cannon fodder. Such a front-line death was regarded by the novices as an informal initiation, a *blooding*, but for the voiders it was more of a swan song.

There were no *living* retired clones that she knew of. No golden handshake from O.A.C.I. brass. No discharge, honourable or otherwise. Nor were there any official funerals, no acknowledgement of sacrifice, no shots fired by an honour guard over the grave. As an Operative you were either *In Service* or *Not In Service*. The nature of death, rendered temporary and non-final by the revival process, remained ambiguous with regard to those comrades who were deselected for subsequent revival. The Doctrine's assertion, that at some point there was always the possibility that the Conglomerate would find a renewed purpose for them, bring them back again for a *Last Hurrah*, offered little comfort or opportunities for mourning or closure. Instead of their death, or even their life, being honoured, voiders shuffled off quietly in to limbo, with no warriors' resting place known.

Perhaps it was simply a natural human response to fill gaps in a belief system with speculation, but if you asked the Greeneyes – the self-styled elite clique whose Doctrinal fanaticism was channelled into dedication to battle-readiness, savagery and transcendence of physical limitations on the battlefield – about the voiders they would tell you with flushed faces and gleaming eyes that this was already *Valhalla*, Odin's hall of the honoured dead, where the souls of warriors picked from the battlefields fought to the death each day and were restored each night to the feast hall in training for *Ragnarok*, when their destiny would be fulfilled as they issued forth to fight their final battle against the mighty wolf that would swallow the sun, enemy of the gods, *Fenrir*. Voiders were those souls who failed to make the grade, deemed inadequate, too constrained by mortal limitations to face the supernatural foes unleashed against the words of men and gods in the *Final Battle*. As such, their fate was to join *Hel* in *Nifleheim*, in her realm of the dishonoured dead, those dead from sickness or old age, for an eternity in mist and cold.

Maybe the passion of the Greeneyes was a natural antidote, a self-protective response to the apathy and withdrawal from the world of the living that she'd seen happen to the voiders. Neither path seemed a sane response to the situation, though – there had to be a middle way. Shaking the thought from her head, Leonard asserted, aloud, from the floor of the wetcube, with only herself and her mirrored reflection for an audience: "I'm no Greeneye. And I'm *definitely* not a *voider*."

CHAPTER SEVEN: OPERATION DO-OVER

The first three days had been gruelling. Along with a new diet and exercise regime, hand-to-hand combat training with her new android sparring partner, she had thrown herself into the nano-tech project she had conceived, dismantling the two hovertrunks, and repacking the electronics to make the end product more compact. The task required focus and concentration, and hunching over the cylindrical devices on the floor she had found that, to begin with, her SPITS tell had manifested frequently. The first couple of times she had almost thrown up into the hovertrunk cavity she was working on, and hastened to the wetcube to minimise the mess. Each time she reached the toilet the nausea subsided, and she was able to resume work.

A few days later, Kochansky had dropped by with a plasma pencil, a double tube of epoxy resin and two miniature LANlink components she'd requested, similar to the one used by her spycam.

With his technical knowledge, he was able to deduce the nature of the device she was working on and, after a brief quizzing and a quick trip to the block mall, returned with a round backpack she could modify to carry the completed project unobtrusively.

As she sat back from her task, her hand started the motion to her temple, getting half way to its target before she dry-heaved, her cheeks puffing out as they caught the air pumped into her mouth by her convulsing diaphragm, accompanied by an audible *whugh*.

"So, how are you getting on with your SPITS tell, then?" Kochansky inquired, in feigned innocence.

"Great. Just great. Remember to thank Pasqualé for making my life even more of a living hell." Kochansky's eyes smiled, and he couldn't restrain another wolfish grin. "Actually, it's not too bad, now. The first day I started taking these," as she gestured at the disembowelled hovertrunks, "apart it felt like I was taking my *own* guts out, too. Just like Pasqualé said, pretty much every twenty minutes or so, I was swiping away at some lock of hair I don't even have, anymore. Yesterday, though, not so often. And today I think that's only the second time. Well on target for quitting the junk, I think."

"Good. We need you up and about as soon as possible. Can't keep you cooped up in here much longer." He eyed her progress. She had removed both sets of Casimir plates from the pair of trunks, and was cutting down their frames to repack the plates into disk-thin cylindrical stacks. She could see him straining to resist the temptation to offer his help.

"Okay, I'll be in touch. Now get outta here before you say something chivalrous we'll both regret. I wanna see this project through."

"I understand totally. I might just have to go and make some for myself – that looks like a lot of fun. Maybe we could have a race?" He moved for the door.

"Thanks for the gear. And the bag."

With a self-consciously stiffened neck, he replied from the open doorway: "You're welcome." He was working on his SPITS tell too, it seemed. Maybe Pasqualé had even tailored some aversion softs for him. "I wanna see those things when you're finished. Maybe even try them out? After you, of course."

"You're on." Having secured her word on the matter, he let the door close behind him.

'Time for a stretch.' Dragging the sheet on which she had laid all her materials under the side table between the sofa bed and window to clear some floor space, she called up a menu on her arhud. 'Marcus,' she nenned. She had christened and skinned the android after her least favourite ex-boyfriend from high-school. The one who had slept with her best friend, when she was drunk. As in *asleep* drunk. She had kicked his ass back then, but after all these years she found it was something she just never got tired of. Plus who said she couldn't combine combat training with therapy?

Marcus, from his resting spot, cross legged in the corner under the dining counter where it met the dividing wall, rolled forward onto its skeletal hands and knees and assumed the opaque visage she'd programmed for it, as it moved, then sprang upright, feet shoulder-width apart, in a smooth motion resembling the last half of a burpee. It swayed almost imperceptibly, rhythmically, a minute, circular rocking from heel to ball of foot, matched by knees circling horizontally above, the constant motion serving to maintain the android's balance in constant readiness for prompted movement.

"Centre room, Marcus," she commanded, and Marcus responded by taking three strides to the middle of the room. It hadn't actually heard her, but had responded to the signal her avtog device generated when she heard *herself* speak.

Leonard quickly surveyed the available floor space. With the sofa bed and other furniture against the left wall, a roughly four by four-and-a-half metre area devoid of obstacles seemed adequate for an exchange of single blows, but restrictive for follow-up combos.

The day before, she had already pushed her knuckles, feet, knees and elbows to their limits with Marcus in punch bag mode. Today she would allow her body to heal and strengthen, switch her training to cardio', balance, speed, agility.

'Martial Art Style: *Capoeira*.' Marcus responded to her inner-voice command, dropping into a low crouch, elbows raised outwards, bringing its arms almost parallel to the floor and taking swinging steps from side to side, the second foot landing in line, a step's length behind the first. While the feet made a four-beat rhythm, the upper torso and arms swivelled to a six-beat. Marcus' footfalls made soft, scuffing thuds as it moved.

'Select sparring parameters,' she nenned: 'player attacks first, alternate defence and attack roles, *esquivas* only, mimic player attack pattern only.' With these parameters, Marcus wouldn't throw any surprise moves her way. It wouldn't do for her to take any injurious blows at this point. She was steadily gaining weight and muscle mass, but had a long way to go to reach combat readiness. It would also be hard to cover-up or explain any visible bruising during one of her occasional local excursions. She had made enough small-talk connections with neighbours and level business owners for them to remember her by sight, and recall a detail such as a black-eye if questioned by the militia.

'Spar,' she instructed, determined to start things slowly, gradually build up speed, completing a four-step *ginga* before launching a simple straight punch aiming for Marcus' mid-face area, a contemporary *asfixiante*, rather than the throat-crushing move that may have spawned its name in traditional *Capoeira*. Marcus dodged the line of the punch by adding an extra lean of its torso and neck as it continued to sidestep rhythmically. Her fist shot past the side of the android's head, where she snapped her punch and withdrew to await the android's reversal.

Four steps later, Marcus launched the same punch at her face, and she copied his defensive dodge, the established rhythm helping her predict and evade the blow. She completed another four-step *ginga*, right leg behind her left, then, bringing her back leg up, chambered her knee to her chest and pumped her heel at Marcus' sternum, a straight push-kick known in *capoeira* as a *bênção*. The training droid responded by curling into a balled-up duck beneath her leg, buttocks almost touching the floor, continuing its sideways motion as it rose back to the default, higher crouching position.

She recovered her footing, planting her right foot forward to the right of her original position, then landing her left behind it.

Four steps later, Marcus returned her kick. Although it only matched the speed of her kick, performing at well below its maximum operating speed, and she knew well enough from the rhythm of the *ginga* when it was coming, she only just managed to duck beneath the extended foot of the android.

'Better take it slow,' she reflected, as she slid sideways and rose back to the basic stance. She still had to concentrate to move the way she wanted. Nothing happened on instinct, right now. In a real combat situation, she wouldn't have time to think about her next move: she'd have to be moving as soon as her opponent telegraphed the attack. From what she'd learned about her last cloning, her body hadn't been programmed to the full extent she was accustomed to. She would have to be the programmer. She'd done it before, in the first place. She just had to do it again. 'Repetition.' Four syllables. Four beats. Four steps. She repeated the word like a mantra as she swung her body through the *ginga*, continuing the sequence of simple attacks and defences with her silent companion.

The soft scuffing and planting of their bare feet created a percussive music. Before long, the simplicity of the movements became second nature, as she had hoped, and she doubled the tempo of her attack: *one, punch, three, punch*, immediately followed by Marcus, *one, punch, three, punch*, then her own *one, kick, three, kick*, with Marcus repeating *one, kick, three, kick*.

Her heart rate had roughly doubled, too, and she began to time and consciously deepen her breathing, controlling her blood's oxygenation, resisting the instinct to breathe quickly and shallowly. Around ten minutes later, again feeling confident, she doubled the tempo again, creating a flowing sequence of attack, dodge and counter-attack, still slower and more stylised than a real fight, but engrossing in its own way: as the minutes slid by, the music of their feet, the repetition of movement, her focussed breathing and the climbing hammer of her heart in her ears, combined to establish a state of mental relaxation, whilst her body continued the sequence of movements without her conscious attention.

Her visual perception slipped away, and in its place she was running through the events of her former life, her former body, until she was once again scaling the ridge with her unit, tracking a mobile, subterranean enemy command centre for an orbital nuclear armature strike.

Again, she experienced the shockwave of the armature's impact hurling her, her comrades, the very ground itself into the air, the boundaries between air, ground, people and plants blurred and confused in the disruption to the established order. Again, she was crawling towards Parker, trapped and crushed under the boulder, again she was reaching for him, and again the ground erupted with white heat and light, bringing all to oblivion.

She felt the ripple travelling up her arm before she registered the sensation of contact against her last three knuckles. Her vivid recollection faded, replaced by real-world perception. She saw her own right arm extended, fist held vertically and cocked upwards from the wrist. Marcus was already toppling back from its impact, its heels serving as fulcra, buttocks dropping the short distance to the floor before rolling onto its back, and rocking there, frozen-limbed. She was drenched with sweat, her own limbs felt leaden, her arm gratefully dropping to her side as she collected her wits to comprehend the situation.

On her arhud, her heartbeat indicator was quickly dropping from a hundred-and-thirty beats per minute, and a series of text messages from Marcus indicated a chronology of unheeded warnings indicating low battery power, imminent hibernation, and finally: *entering reserve power conservation safety mode.* The latter explained Marcus' frozen limbs: the 'droid was programmed to use its last reserves of power to seize up, minimise the risk of injuring nearby humans by falling on them, for example. A truly powerless 'droid would be as limp-limbed as a sleeping human. Presumably, she had punched it in the head shortly after this. Her chronometer suggested that over two hours had passed since she had activated Marcus, which was typical for its battery charge, considering the activity level.

Reluctantly, her legs bore her to the wetcube, where she recovered a towel and padded back with it around her shoulders, drying her face and scalp. The short crop of hair there did little to stem the flow of beaded sweat, which sprang from her head and ran, stinging, into her eyes.

When she attempted to dry the right side of her head right handed, her aversion softs reminded her that this was not enjoyable: the queasiness quickly discouraged the attempt, and she resorted to a left-handed technique which was much more agreeable.

'Marcus.' After a few seconds, the rigid body of the android softened, and slowly it rocked to a cross legged posture on the floor. 'Recharge point and hibernate.' Wordlessly, Marcus executed a minimalist sideways roll back to his corner under the dining counter, arriving cross legged and becoming motionless again. On her arhud, she received its command text confirmation: *Recharge; Hibernate.*

"That's the best suggestion you've made all day." She took a long pull of isotonic from a quartztic bottle, mopping her brow again. It continued to pump out sweat as her heart rate fell towards resting, trying to cool her down. The room was hot, humid. She crossed the floor to Marcus' alcove, where she pulled a roller-door across from the wall to cover the android, then headed to the opposite side of the room, as she nenned a command to the environmental control unit: 'E-CU, open shutters.' On whispering motors, the anodised slats between the widely-spaced double-glazing split along almost invisible seams, pivoting ninety degrees into the room to reveal the cityscape beyond. A.C.P.'s bright primary had already passed overhead, sinking beyond the far side of her block. The summer sky was clear. The external windows, being a passive part of the block's climate control system, were beyond her ability to open. Beyond her volition, her right hand released its grip on the towel about her neck, and began the familiar climb to sweep away a non-existent lock of hair. It didn't get more than ten centimetres into its journey before the first hint of rising nausea alerted her to its mutinous intent. Like a groundhog frightened by its own shadow, her hand dropped, persuaded of the folly of its attempt. Instead, she felt the shimmering air beside the nearest trombe shutter panel. The exposed, smoky black face radiated enough heat to fry a slab of tofu on. The opposite face, the side that surfaced her apartment, when the shutters were closed, was cool to the touch, damp with condensation from her own exertion. Each glazed shutter panel housed a dark, liquid crystal coolant layer that efficiently absorbed infra-red and visible spectrum emissions, conveying the acquired thermal energy to a heat exchanger above the window, and electrical energy generated by a photovoltaic effect induced by ultraviolet frequencies to the building's electrical storage system. Although it did yield a pleasant enough view of this side of Godsgood City, opening the shutters did nothing to cool the room. In fact, it had quite the opposite effect, radiating gained heat into the room whilst reducing the overall efficiency of the passive energy collection system.

'E-CU, close trombe shutters.' Wordlessly, the E-CU complied with her request, darkening the room. She took another long pull from her bottle then headed for a cool shower in her wetcube, rinsing off the sweat and salt of her activity, and carefully, consciously avoiding the right side of her head with her right hand, crossing her wrists as she scrubbed at her hair. Once she felt sufficiently cooled and refreshed, she deactivated the shower and grabbed a clean towel from the rack.

She dried the right side of her head with her left hand only, without even having to think about it, on this occasion. By this time, the E-CU had lowered the main room temperature to a stipulated chill. Her feet and the ceramic floor were slightly damp; the walls were bedewed with condensation. She could hear the E-CU's labouring, mechanical efforts to extract humidity from the air, and despite the coolness, felt her skin begin to bead with sweat again, as if in sympathy.

She snatched a frosty beer bottle from the chiller in the kitchen, and flopped on to the sofa bed, resolving not to move again until she stopped sweating. Flipping through avtog menus, she selected an immersive wildlife documentary recorded from the perspective of a local celebrity biologist.

Surrounded by the exotic chirrups of alien wildlife, and the sweet aroma of the flowering, bamboo-like forests, she soon drifted off to sleep as the biologist narrated his surroundings in a soothing bass rumble.

CHAPTER EIGHT: OPERATION FIRST IMPRESSIONS

One month. That was how long it took the Security Agency to review recent arrivals. Too long to stay for a holiday, pushing it for visiting relatives, unless they were your parents, and you were unemployed. Probably going to stay for a while longer, if you'd lasted that long. The interview was set for two weeks time. They hadn't bothered to ask if she was busy, if another time would suit her better. Just:

From: Alpha Centauri Prime Customs and Immigration

Ref: R58973J584M

Angel Leonard,

Under Section 96, Subsections 5.2 and 5.5 of the United Nations of Earth Extra-Solar System Colonial Territories Security Article 2408.23 you are hereby required to be in attendance at our offices by 08:30 Tuesday 27th June 2421. Please report to reception upon arrival and be prepared to submit your personal computelecom device for inspection. Do not wear any make-up, hair-piece or other device that augments or otherwise alters your physical appearance on this occasion. Be prepared to declare and

submit any prosthetic device considered essential to mobility at reception.

Security Agent 9P47H1

on behalf of Alpha Centauri Prime Customs and Immigration Bureau

and the United Nations of Earth Security Agency

When her handroid received it, her arhud blinking an anachronistic envelope icon to alert her to the new message, she quickly scanned it and concluded it was the kind of message that an A.I. data processor would send automatically, entirely devoid of human consideration, when certain data sets coincided.

'Too bad for anyone with false legs, by the sound of it.' She guessed that prosthetics would be separately scanned and returned, or replaced with known-to-be-safe, in-house devices for security purposes whilst within the building. It would not be like UNE to make anyone but their known, sworn enemies crawl across the ground with no legs. Dredged up by their attached chain of association, a rush of images welled into her consciousness, vying recollections of herself and her comrades-in-arms clawing their path through churned mud and blood, trailing mangled legs or mere stumps as UNE artillery continued to rain down around them.

Except for the rookies, the faces she saw were usually still grimly determined, pushing on to complete their mission objective despite the sudden misfortune. These were, after all, children of the Doctrine, confident that their limbs would be restored to them in their next life, that their loss was just a temporary setback, a hindrance.

Back in the mess hall, once they had crawled back out of their life-restoring cloning bells, and reunited with their squaddies, they would all laugh about it:

"...and then you just kept on fuckin' crawlin', like you were still gonna fuckin' get to the fuckin' E.P! But all the time, the blood was just pissin' outta yer knees, an' yer face was like *I don't need my fuckin' legs, anyway, I had plenty of practice crawlin' when I was a baby, and every Friday night since I could get served*, but you just kept goin' slower an' slower 'til you just flopped forward into the fuckin' mud, like face fuckin' first, mind!"

"Yeah? Well the joke was on you, ya Welsh cunt, 'cause there *was* no fuckin' E.P., an' you were just as dead as me three hundred metres later, so fuck you!"

Idly, detached, she wondered if her own face had shown the same determination when it had been her turn to crawl, or if others saw another expression written there. She couldn't remember feeling afraid, nor even feeling pain. But had she felt them at the time, had those feelings been omitted, edited out by some lab tech' before her revival? She never would have thought so, before: the bond of trust was once so deep, the promise by the Conglomerate that their individuality would be preserved was held sacred by both parties, that they would be restored to life in their entirety, both body and mind, for better or worse. But this time, this life, it was different: that promise now seemed *expedient*. This time, with the changed fortune of the Conglomerate, they had done something to that promise to better suit their new purposes and methods. 'Maybe not broken, but perhaps bent, or dented? Maybe *tarnished*?' She still hadn't quite decided the full extent of the damage to that promise. With the same grim determination she had read on the faces she had recalled, she pushed such thoughts from her mind, telling herself 'Such things are sometimes clearer in retrospect. This can be figured out later. Mission first.'

The offices were located at the spaceport. Since she had never been to the port, in person, she acquainted herself with the layout from avtog walk-throughs obtained from Kochansky, running the simulation of her arrival at the port in real-time, so she could convey the correct amount of familiarity.

The edited footage included her one-hour line-up at the immigration desk prior to the brief interview that Kochansky had conducted in her apartment. Whilst not the most riveting footage she had viewed, she was able to appreciate the quality and seamlessness of Kochansky's work. Most was security camera simulation, yielding only a video feed. Except for the colour, it reminded her of the monochromatic silent movies she had learned about from an avtog documentary about the history of sense-streaming, predating even togless movies. The rest was Kochansky's avtog feed from the viewpoint of the immigration officer that interviewed her.

She caught sight of herself a few times in the line as it switched left and right across his field of vision, but was never the object of his scrutiny. Nor had she done anything to deserve it. Her image had been 'shopped a little, she guessed, since she didn't remember looking quite that good so fresh out of the cloning bell. Certainly, the wig and the dentures did not look obvious in the final edit.

After a once-over, she knew enough to answer questions about where she was supposed to have been, and little enough to genuinely be ignorant of parts of the port she had not visited, for example, the departure area, in case they asked. The footage showed that after disembarking from the passenger compartment she had proceeded to the public washrooms, spending several minutes in there, presumably freshening herself up, perhaps still feeling weak and nauseous from the illness she was supposed to have suffered from prior to travel. From there she had proceeded directly to the immigration desk line-up, placing her close to the back of the queue.

The only person behind her was a single, young male, probably too distracted by his excessive immersion in avtog to closely follow the progress of the queue ahead of him. This must have allowed Kochansky to paste in her meeting with the desk officer near, but not at, the end of his recording for that compartment's passengers. Last place was often the only available slot for a falsified entry, without overwriting the physical presence of another passenger, unless the desk officer had a long gap between passengers in the line. This rarely happened, as the line served to bottle-neck arriving immigrants, supplying a constant feed of arrivees for the officer to question.

Kochansky had done a fine job ensuring she wasn't the last person, who would no doubt be gone over with an exceedingly fine-toothed comb. And possibly some silicone gloves. The poor young man wouldn't be permitted any avtog immersion to alleviate discomfort during interrogation.

Confident by this time that her SPITS tell was aversion-trained out of her, she spent the time leading up to the interview concentrating on re-honing her operational skill set, optimising body fat and muscle composition for survival, strength, speed and endurance, and avoiding training injury.

A variety of immersive games utilised real-world physics and were often used even in conventional military training sim-grams to help cadets grasp and develop basic skills: loading and handling weapons, aiming and firing guns with kick-back, and so on. Many had optional avatar set-ups, so you could play in a virtual version of your own body, rather than the typical role-play skins provided within the context of the game.

The only discernible difference between such games and live training exercises lay in the amount of actual, physical exercise, which was entirely absent in a virtual environment. Any fatigue a player felt due to in-game exertion was simulated. For a fully immersive gaming environment, players selected physical immobilisation during game-play. This allowed a full range of virtual activity – running, jumping, fighting – with no danger of actual injury to the player through collision with real-world objects.

To achieve an almost complete paralysis the nano-plant scaffolding surrounding the player's neural pathways detected movement initiation precursors in the brain via pick-up filaments, conveyed the activity to the CPU, which ran a feedback response of electromagnetic cancellation interference in the pre- and primary motor cortices of the brain along induction filaments. This left only residual micro-movements in the real world, almost imperceptible muscular flutterings, with the movement being fully simulated in the virtual environment complete with an induced sense-stream to provide the brain with sufficient feedback to convince the player they really had moved.

This allowed her to skill-train without any risk of injury, pushing her virtual self to its limits. Balanced with a proper diet and exercise regime, her training system was complete.

Marcus still provided high-impact skeletal conditioning opportunities, every time it absorbed her blows. The sparring robot also served as her real-world touchstone, a tool for calibration and confirmation of the effectiveness of her virtual training environment, helping her determine if it was measuring up to reality, blow by blow.

Pasqualé had recommended a set of skin-callousing practices designed to roughen, thicken and visibly age her skin, including U.V. exposure and chemical skin treatments, but also repetitive exercises such as daily and gloveless hand-scrubbing of her apartment floor with a small brush, on hands and knees. These activities quickly wore out her false finger nails, and she was relieved to find her own nails had grown in completely beneath. Toenails, teeth, head and body hair were also fully developed, and she was able to discontinue the mineral and vitamin supplements she had been taking to accelerate their growth. She wouldn't miss the six pills at every meal.

A quick filing took the fresh growth edge off her nails. Pasqualé's prescribed, nightly tooth grinding exercise and thrice-daily swilling of a set of harsh chemical mouthwashes aged her teeth. She also paid a visit to the level dentist for the X-ray data and new dental record they generated as a standard process for new patients, which Kochansky promptly hacked and used to create a false trail of dental records extending back into her imaginary past. She knew the aging had been successful when the dentist suggested she should book another appointment to fill a couple of cavities.

With just two days to go before the appointed interview, she dropped in to an upper level hair salon a neighbour had recommended for a trim and style befitting an ambitious avtog actor, leaving her hair a little on the short and unfashionable side, but disposing of the natural round hair tips that would reveal an improbably complete head of fresh hair growth: forensic evidence, for those who knew what to look for, indicative of her status as a recently created clone.

She took the stylist's advice on hair colouring techniques. He sounded like he knew what he was doing, so she gave him free reign, but to her his terminology was as incomprehensible as her own O.A.C.I. sign language would have been to him. The result he showed her was surprisingly pleasing, though: for the first time, she looked at her mirror image with a sense of ownership, finally feeling as though she could settle with it. The skin aging processes and gained body mass had finally made her look more like the woman she remembered being, reducing her sense of alienation from her own body. Maybe Victor had been right: it just took some getting used to.

When her stylist was finished, she asked him: "How old do you think I look? I mean, really, don't try to be kind – I need an honest opinion."

"Girlfriend, dat's de only kind Ah have! An' you is a stone cold killer. Wit' your looks, an' my styles, you should be puttin' it on de avtog circuit, y'know what Ah'm sayin'?"

"Anton, you are *full* of shit. *How old* do I look?"

Anton sucked his teeth at her for maligning his professional integrity. "Well, jus' fuh bein' a *bitch*, Ah'm gunna add five years, an' tell ya dat ya look *twenty-eight*!"

She smiled as she walked out of the salon, heading back to her apartment. She'd been thirty-two when her squad concluded the bunker buster mission. Of course she hadn't aged a bit in the three years she'd spent *dead*, but that nevertheless put her official age at thirty-five. Taking Anton's five year penalty for bad behaviour off, he'd guessed she was twenty-three – still young enough to make a career in avtog acting, and a considerable improvement over her initial post-pubescent looks, just two months ago. Part of the miracle of cloning.

She'd become used to the concept of life beyond death through the Doctrine: O.A.C.I. cloning technology had always imbued operatives with a sense of invulnerability, but for the first time she actually felt the touch of immortality. She had become younger, her body had been renewed, remolded. There was no reason why someone like her, if given unlimited access to cloning facilities and technicians, couldn't live forever. Her bodies would age and die, but her consciousness would have continuity, from one body to the next.

'Okay, cool it with the god complex. Who would be interested in paying for you to live forever?' She chided herself in the second person quite frequently, without being able to identify who was doing the telling-off and who was on the receiving end. Even with the aid of the contractually-obligatory therapy sessions she had been required to *share* in, during debriefings, she had never arrived at a satisfactory conclusion.

She also recalled her therapist advising her that self-deprecating thought processes and nenning to an imaginary second person were neither indicative of, nor conducive to, a good state of mental health. But then, nor was serving in a private army where her duties included killing anyone designated as a target, regardless of apparent friend or foe status, and repeatedly dying and being restored to life by illicit technologies that, despite the most thorough indoctrination, undermined any sense of self, on orders that sometimes required her to take her own life. If there ever was a vector for mental health degradation, she would eye-point the whole cloned warrior lifestyle over a tendency towards mild, self-administered wrist slapping and dissociation.

Despite that, she had a firm grasp of who *she* was; an officer in the O.A.C.I. military, or whatever remained of it. This put things clearly in perspective: her life was of value to her employers only until they were drummed out of business by UNE, along with all the other financial backers and sponsors of the Independence movement, or the conflict ended by some other means. An O.A.C.I. victory? That seemed a remote possibility, under the current circumstances, but she'd seen seemingly hopeless situations turned around before, with good intelligence, strategy and implementation. Either way, an end to the war would be an end to her value.

Now she found herself wondering: 'if the war was called off today, how long would I have left to live?' During O.A.C.I. induction, no-one had mentioned what the average life-expectancy of a clone body was. No-one in her training group had imagined dying of old age or sickness when they enlisted. Everyone was young, and stupid. Never imagined they'd be dying a hundred different ways during the coming war. Youthful perception was often clouded with its own sense of immortality, a sense that for some reason they would be the lucky one that nothing bad happened to, a belief in their manifest destiny to succeed, to rise to the top of the pile, that they could do anything if they just tried hard enough. '*Optimism*, that's it. *Youthful optimism.*'

She remembered how veterans were always ragging on the rookies, telling them campfire horror stories about the engagements they'd been in, the atrocities they had born witness to. And those they had instigated. At the time, she'd thought they were just trying to mind-fuck for kicks, like it was some college hazing ritual, a cycle of abuse: vet's had done it to them when they were rookies, so now they were doing it to the new class. But after a few years of action, she'd become the vet' herself.

PRIMED

She was garrisoned in the Witch Head Nebula, near Rigel, amongst the OACIst dust cloud rigs they were defending from acts of piracy. The local riggers were mostly after diamond dust for industrial applications, but netted a fair amount of metals, too. The rigging rights were franchised from a big mining company that owned and placed the platforms, and controlled the access rights. She'd forgotten this particular company's name. There were so many sponsors behind the Orion Arm Conglomerate, some big, some small. The usual deal, she understood, was to withhold the corporate taxes demanded by UNERA, and pay them instead to the Conglomerate Holding Fund. Depending on who you talked to, this system was regarded as anything from a protection racket to that of a *de facto* government. Most of the time nobody cared who was paying their wages, as long as they got paid. UNE propaganda painted the OACIst private army as greedy mercenaries, selling out humanity's future to the highest bidder, devoid of morals and conscience. The standard OACIst rebuttal was 'So what? You're just pissed 'cause we're not buying the crap *you're* selling!' In the early days of the conflict, there were many people on both sides who saw through the UNE propaganda to the thinly-veiled, corporate-driven agenda.

Everyone talked about it back then, how people should be free to decide for themselves how to live and be governed. But a few months after the aggressions started, after the memorably vicious UNE militia suppression of Independentist-sympathetic demonstrations and so-called riots on Earth, and after publicly-visible misfortunes befell certain notably outspoken members of the free press and celebrity proponents of Independence, you never really heard anyone talking that way, anymore. Not in public, at least. And the media quickly took a staunchly UNE-supportive stance, with broad hints that Independence was not a socially desirable, or even viable goal, and that anyone who declared it to be so was simply naive, immature, ignorant of the way things *needed* to function in a civilised galaxy. To be pitied, ostracised, and above all *reported to the relevant authorities.*

The public were told what the public thought by a trusted source – beloved avtog – so it became the civic responsibility of the individual to align their thoughts with the public, if they wished to consider themselves a member of that public. After all, *If you're not with us, you're against us!* Such phrases were abruptly yelled in avtog chatrooms and forums by anonymous participants, who would hang around long enough to vehemently defend their polarised perspective, whilst defaming or threatening to report any who disagreed with them, before disappearing again, leaving a disconcerted group of chatters and avtweeters to guardedly pick up the conversational thread, each wondering exactly who else was listening in, and what was actually safe to say, anymore.

Witch Head was a rare, quiet posting in her career, with a large contingent of rookies being broken in gently after basic training. The isolated, low strategic importance of the system was utilised to the advantage of O.A.C.I. by establishing their Special Op's advanced training facility there, without a low risk of UNE engagement in the vicinity. Of course, she was selected by virtue of her remarkable service record up to that date to participate in the course. According to her training officer, her performance definitively identified her *vastly superior calibre*.

The base C.O. had requested that she and the other vet's in the programme take the trouble to show the rookies the ropes. It was at this point that she realised the hazing had another, nobler intent entirely. As a rookie, she'd misread it, thought it was malicious: disillusioned, over-the-hill grunts passed over for promotion, unable to tolerate the existence of bright hopefuls who knew they would be their commanding officers in a few short years. Kick a rookie while you can. But it was actually an attempt to pass on the only benefit of experience that could be conveyed; that their whole view of life was fundamentally flawed, and about to devastatingly collapse; that with a conscious effort they could change their erroneous perspective now and spare themselves suffering later.

Optimists were fundamentally unprepared to deal with the failure, disappointment, loss, despair, hopelessness and horror that war inevitably brings. But that was how the schools turned them out, year after year, young men and women blinded to reality by the brightness of their own vision of the future. Of course, no rookie ever took any notice of a veteran. She hadn't. Optimists were doomed to find out the hard way, through trial and error. The errors started with dismissing the advice of seniors who, it turned out, really did know better, after all. But what fresh-faced twenty-something, grad' certificate in hand, and the whole galaxy laid out before them like an all-you-can-eat buffet, would want to accept *that* view-point.

In the end, it didn't matter whether one philosophy was right, or another. Right and wrong had no place in the equation of survival. The only thing of importance was what was effective, what *worked*. Optimism simply didn't work. The O.A.C.I. psych' wards were full of shell-shocked optimists, not a one of which could wrap their head around the universe's simple and impartial refutation of their closely-held beliefs: *good things happen to good people*; *the universe, or whatever deity, is on the side of the righteous*. One word played over and over like avtog reruns in the minds of soldiers in the wards: *why?* The question would never be answered as long as they clung to their opinion that it was the universe that was somehow wrong, while their belief system was correct. Those that stayed out of the psych' wards did so because they allowed the universe to grind the erroneous out of them, incident by incident, accepting the teachings it provided, not trying to cling to their fabricated perspective in the face of all contrary evidence. What was left of the process of living by trial and error was a simple calculation: omitting the errors, only the trials remain.

If the war had taught her anything, it was the importance of grounding oneself. There was a place for hope and confidence in one's ability to succeed. In fact, not much would be attempted without them. But taking all necessary steps to be prepared for the universe to throw a sooner-or-later inevitable curve ball, to adapt and respond in the moment when hopes and preconceived outcomes were thwarted; to put all effort and focus into success in the smallest of tasks, yet remain undefeated by failures, moving on with renewed effort to the next task. For this, realism, not optimism, was required and worlds of difference lay between the two. These were not behavioural skills they taught explicitly in the Doctrine, but they were vital tools in the sanity maintenance kit of any long-term survivor and achiever. And that's all a veteran *was*, all that set them apart from a rookie. She thought of it as the most fundamental enactment of scientific process; the empirical observation of life, the universe and everything. Clearly, bad things sometimes happen to good people, and good things to bad. Clearly, the righteous are not filled with a mystical force allowing them to survive against all adversity, but are rather just as likely to fall to a sniper, or a land mine, or to bleed out from a wound, or succumb to a fatal infection as the unrighteous. The universe made no distinction, no moral judgement.

After a long, dispassionate inquiry into the operating protocols of the universe, the best she could deduce was this: shit happens. And then, some other shit happens because of it, and so on. Cause and effect. That's all. The only way to achieve a desired result was to take all necessary steps to achieve it. No *Manifest Destiny*, no *Might of Right*.

She had wandered from the salon to the elevators in a reverie, completely distracted, without for a moment considering that she was in the middle of a warzone. As she waited for a car she reminded herself 'This is *not* my home.' She was grateful for the aversion treatment that had eliminated her habitual hair swiping.

She had counted eight security cameras between her apartment door and the salon on her way there, and must have walked past five of those retracing her route back to the elevator shafts, with no conscious recollection of having done so. It revealed a level of dangerous obliviousness to her surroundings she'd been trained to think of as *White Alert*, below the watchful, mindful state of *Yellow Alert* that an operative should maintain at almost every waking moment. That meant she was unfocused, not on her most guarded behaviour as she passed them.

Her drill sergeant told her during basic training she thought too much – it was *not* appropriate behaviour for a soldier. Of course, her high intelligence and observational skills had set her aside from the rank-and-file, which was the how, and the why, of her ending up as a Special Operative. But her sergeant was of course referring to her daydreaming tendencies, moments when she would slip out of conscious, present-mindfulness, where her internal reality became more vivid to her than the stimuli of the real world. Great for formulating creative solutions to strategic problems. Also great for getting your ass shot off in the field. There was a time and a place for it, she used to know that. Was this another skill that had deteriorated due to the rapid ingraining process employed during this revival? Was her former present-mindedness an ability she had cultivated, and she was now behaving more like her raw, untrained former self, before the years of practiced self-discipline?

Most of the residential level cameras were low level security rated and lower resolution devices, but at least one was on a main thoroughfare and intersection, with the nearby salon belonging to a small group of commercial units that would probably qualify as a strip mall – the type of nexus uplink that would be routinely monitored by the Security Agency, or at least by D.A.I.'s, running standard facial and gait recognition softs. Maybe even by SPITS. This time, at least, she felt her mind begin to slip out of focus from the now, as she began to speculate on the nature of SPITS, before snapping herself back to attention. 'Huh. *Definitely* rusty.'

If her handroid had been active, she was sure that her nen chatter could have been picked up by eavesdropping Security Agents. Coherent thoughts and visualisations could be broadcast as vividly as real sounds and sights. D.A.I.'s were programmed and trained to hone in on certain words, phrases, images, and would quickly flag these for the personal attention of a supervising Security Agent. On or off, the devices still transmitted four dimensional data to the network, recorded as the device's GP/t, standing for either *Global* or *Galactic Positioning over time*, even though different systems recorded interstellar handroid locations. UNE made it a legal requirement to carry a handroid in public, using the GP/t data generated to facilitate law enforcement. Video footage from urban security cameras could be cross-referenced with handroid G-PIP addresses to visually identify carriers, and, by an admittedly arduous process of elimination, determine the presence of anyone trying to 'ghost' through a metropolitan area without the legally required device.

Of course, she had her handroid on to pay for the haircut, but had at least deactivated it before stepping out of the salon. '*This* time,' she chided herself. She would have to get a handle on her roving mind's eye before undertaking any major excursions, *especially* before heading in to the Spaceport complex. Since the first declaration of martial law in the colonies, all major transit centres and governmental buildings operated auto-link servers, which bypassed handroid firewalls, connecting automatically to all avtog devices within their reception range, using a government controlled, emergency override channel routinely monitored locally by Security Agents, enabling a rapid response to any perceived threat.

At the time of its implementation, civil rights spokespeople complained about the unprecedented violation of privacy, but UNE didn't qualify the complaint with an official response. Instead, there was a widespread public condemnation of such 'unpatriotic' attitudes from the usual sources: chat show hosts; newscasters; minor celebrities. The campaign reinforced such notions as only the guilty had anything to fear, and the loyalists should do anything they could to stamp out the smouldering embers of terror in their communities. Weeks of rhetoric finally out-shouted considered debate, the public-minded liberals once again backing down from a seemingly strong, contrary, public opinion, questioning their own motives for trying to defend people who eschewed their defence, welcomed and embraced the dissolution of their individual freedom, deferring to the noble ideal of civic duty. The topic was quickly added to the growing list of subjects considered impolite to raise in public, a matter of political opinion best kept to oneself.

Daydreaming was too broad a cognitive process to treat with one of Pasqualé's aversion therapy softs. She'd also become averse to creative thinking, imagination. The military hadn't succeeded in squeezing it out of her, so she must have learned to control it herself. Now, she'd just have to learn to do so again. In two days.

∞

Pasqualé and Kochansky paid her a 'social call' the next morning, essentially for a last minute briefing to prepare her for her interview the next day. She was enjoying the physical presence of her team mates, an unavoidable necessity to talk freely about operational matters, with all handroids off. Under normal conditions, insofar as anything could be referred to as normal, anymore, a social call would be carried out via avtog, consisting of a conference call to their friends, connecting practically instantly. People only rarely got together in person, mainly because they rarely had enough time for other people, these days, or rather enough *corresponding* free time, with the prevalence of shift work and the freedom to move not only around the surface of a planet, occupying different time zones, but also to different worlds and moons, or space stations, where the concept of a twenty-four hour clock had no relevance. The chances were that when you had free time to make a social call your nearest and dearest would be either working or sleeping. Often narrow windows allowed people spread across the human-occupied quadrant of the galaxy to communicate directly. But avtog made it possible to share your experiences with others, nonetheless, and arguably more directly and completely than the natural exchange could allow: by invitation, social network members could check out each others' avblog entries whenever they had their own free time.

Avblogging was a popular, almost ubiquitous procedure wherein the 'blogger' would upload a sometimes edited, sometimes raw, sense-stream from their own daily experiences and share with their participating community. Sights, sounds, smells, tastes, touch and nens could be conveyed in the avblog entries, and re-experienced by anyone with permission to access them. Avtog conveyed the data exactly as the user intended, and was the most accurate way in which anyone could convey their thoughts to another. Of course, the person receiving such a stream would still have to interpret the data within their own brain, where subtle differences in neural architecture and the conforming scaffolding of their own avtog device could introduce a varying degree of divergent perception from the way the blogger perceived phenomena at the time of recording. Additionally, the blog entry would stimulate different emotional and associational responses in the accessor, according to their own life experiences and personality, so there would always remain a subjective element to communication between individuals.

There was a relatively new school of artists, frequently those who described themselves as *Artistes*, who would only permit their works to be shared with the public in the form of an avblog, in an attempt to *most closely conserve the purity of the Artistes intent*. Of course, there was also the popular entertainment form of avblogging, where contracted actors working for broadcasting networks would conduct themselves according to scripted behaviour, or unscripted in the case of the more cheaply produced reality avblogs, which relied on following characters who appealed to mass accessing because of pre-existing celebritism, unique outlook on life or unusual and interesting lifestyles and occupations. This was the career towards which Angel Leonard aspired, according to the official record of her fabricated existence.

"We could rig a third-person intervener, it would be like watching your thoughts on a screen, like an old togless movie." This was Kochansky's suggestion, when she presented them with her concerns about her incontinent imagination. "There's plenty of room in an E.A.N. buffer for a simple feedback program like that."

"So she could use the feedback to regulate and diminish the occurrence?" Pasqualé weighed in. "Negative feedback instead of aversion? It could work, I suppose, but we're kind of running out of time. I think you'll just have to be extra fucking careful, Leonard. There's no way around it, at this point."

"Yeah, that's what I figured. It'll be okay. I'd already kind of settled on a nentra - a pink iced donut. If I catch myself wandering, I'll snap back to the donut: it should drown out any nenning, and give any monitoring S.A.s something else to chew on. Virtually, anyway."

"Stream it," Kochansky directed, holding up his handroid in plain view to everyone, so they could see him activating it.

"Yeah, I'll try a bite, too, seeing as it's calorie free." Pasqualé also held up her handroid, the established protocol in their cell to alert other operatives that they were connecting to the network, and that there was a heightened risk their sense-stream could be monitored by Security Agents. In other words, be careful what you said. The protocol required the acknowledgement and agreement of everyone present. Leonard held her own handroid up, and they synchronised their activation of the interface devices.

Navigating through the broadcast settings, Leonard sent invitations to Kochansky and Pasqualé. When she received confirmation that they had both accepted, that they were both tapping in, in real time, to her own experience of her surroundings, she hit them with *The Donut*, an intense imagination episode she had practiced, consisting of the most vivid impression she could muster of a pink, iced donut, starting with the greasy feel of the deep-fried batter underside against her fingertips, the bright pink, glossy icing rising to fill her field of vision before slipping beneath her eyes, tension and strain in her jaw muscles as she opened her mouth wide to bite, the smell of the fried batter and moist, sugary coating reaching her nostrils, the unique feel of the icing when it met her top incisors, its air-crisped outer layer yielding to a softer, plastic layer beneath, and her lower jaw closing, teeth entering the spongy matter beneath, her tongue pressing against it, feeling and tasting the frying oil, the sweetened, starchy dough, its aerated structure compacting under pressure into a stodgy morsel, her top lip kissing against the crackled glaze of the surface of the icing as her jaws snipped through it, working with her tongue to pull the bite away from the remaining mass of the donut, the hint of vanilla and cloying sweetness mingling and mounting as she chewed again and again, her tongue churning it in with her saliva. She allowed the visualisation to slip away as she opened her own eyes.

Across from her, Kochansky and Pasqualé sat motionless, their eyes still closed, Kochansky frowning with concentration, as if trying to sustain the vision, Pasqualé with her lips slightly parted, and eyebrows raised in a rapturous expression. She smacked her lips together a few times before opening her eyes slowly, as if waking.

"I just had the most wonderful dream...." she joked.

"Shut up!" snapped Kochansky, with his eyes frowned shut, then after a moment: "I can still taste the vanilla. And what's that – nutmeg?"

"And you're worrying about your ability to focus? I could have sworn I was actually eating it!"

"Well, when I *remember* to focus, there doesn't seem to be a problem. It's when I forget that my mind starts to wander."

"Then don't fucking *forget!*" Pasqualé aimed a palm-smack at the side of Leonard's head, which she instinctively angled away from, Pasqualé pawing empty air. "They're going to empty your pockets, confiscate your handroid to run scans on the softs, and LANnect their nenscreen directly to your E.A.N. They *will* be listening to your thoughts, and watching your visualisations. If they so much as sniff a subversive concept they'll be crawling up your ass with a bug. You *should* be *afraid*. Use that fear to stay sharp, and don't fuck up. That's all there is. You'll be fine. We'll wait for you to call us when you get out. Okay?" Leonard nodded.

Kochansky asked "D'you wanna go through the arrivals footage or building blueprints, again?"

"No, I don't want to seem *too* familiar with the layout."

After Kochansky completed the routine upload of her op's terminal's latest simulated *.psy* chunks, he and Pasqualé bid her and each other goodbye. Leonard again monitored their departures to the reception range limit of her security camera-hacking spy hole device, scouring the crowds around them both for any indication of a tail. Even in the absence of tangible proof, the physical presence of a shadowing agent, she found the ease with which she had kept track of them using the simple block security systems did little to reassure her that UNESA were not following them likewise.

∞

The next morning, she took an autocab and joined a line of about thirty people waiting in an enclosed block atrium for the doors to the customs offices to open. She'd passed by the door to reach the back of the queue, giving her a chance to survey the line. Most would be genuine travellers called in, like herself, but she guessed that at least one would be a planted Security Agent, already linked into the local security network to feed footage of the queue. She was aware that she was already within range of the port and customs LAN, and her cerebral transceiver was already compromised by the local server. She had to be on best behaviour.

As she walked along the line, she casually scanned faces. When she recognised a face from the immigration footage she had been inserted into by Kochansky, she made eye contact and gave a nod of recognition, or a smile. Most people nodded or smiled back. Of course none of them had ever seen her before, but since she behaved as if she knew them, etiquette dictated that they should, out of politeness, pretend to know her, too, in case they *did* know her, and had simply forgotten who she was. It was easy to establish a basic, sensory alibi in this way. Security would probably have their hands full processing audio-visual streams, at this point, and would not be too concerned with coherent thoughts of *who's that girl?* from the line, which could just as easily be caused by poor recollection as genuine non-recognition.

The last person in the line was an elderly gentleman she recalled seeing in Kochansky's arrivals footage. Perfect. Drawing behind him, she remarked "Same line, different day. How's your stay?" He was delighted to have someone so vivacious to talk to, and, as she had surmised from the crust of shaving foam extant behind his ears from his morning shave, had uncorrected eyesight and possibly slipping mental faculties. By the time the office doors were opened by an oversized security guard, half an hour later than the time she had been asked to arrive, she had learned all about it from her new dialogue partner, Bruce Michelczyk, a retired mining engineer from Seconde. He was here to help out his youngest of three daughters, who had just had her first baby. In engaging in active conversation, her nenning was almost entirely limited to the subject matter.

As they chatted, a few more civilians lined up behind her. By the time Bruce was told to step through the dark doorway with a small group of people in front, she was quite sure he believed he *remembered* her from The Ladder passenger car, as it carried them down from the orbital docking ring.

About two minutes later, the security guard, who she decided to nickname 'Burly,' briefly peered into the interior then motioned her and four other people to enter. Beyond the small, unlit entryway, a second set of doors opened into a small reception room. Arhud instructions lit up around her field of vision, an abrupt reminder that she was connected to the port security server. Glowing texts directed her to activate and unlock her handroid, advance to the unmanned reception window, which looked thick enough to withstand a grenade, and place the device into a pull-out steel drawer in the wall, along with any other metallic objects on her person. In the room beyond the window, two staff members were talking inaudibly to each other, showing no interest in speaking to her, while a third was removing the contents of another steel draw, which had travelled along a conveyor to the far end of the room. Having completed this task, she was instructed to pass through a body scanner to her left. She entered the quartztic cylinder, which sealed behind her. Scrolling text ordered her to place her feet and hands on marked locations on the floor and walls of the scanner, to look directly into the camera, and state her full name and address. As soon as she finished speaking, the camera flashed brightly, stabbing painfully at her eyes, and a blast of air swept around her as the scanner frisked her. By the time her vision recovered, the scanner had completed its examination, and, finding nothing dangerous on her person, the far side of the cylinder slid open, and she was prompted to step through into the waiting room.

Another guard stood at attention beside a double doorway, successfully looking unapproachable. He stood in such close proximity to the only water cooler that it would be necessary to enter his personal space to obtain a drink. She could not imagine him moving aside to make the task less intimidating. She immediately nicknamed him 'Surly.'

Rows of sparsely padded seats were already mostly taken by all the people she had seen in the line-up outside. Some talked quietly amongst themselves, groups of family members or friends, but most sat quietly, looking around at their fellow detainees, or for some source of sensory stimulation in the absence of their familiar handroids.

Solid walls denied even so much as an outside view, and the room was lit with cheap, outdated fluorescents. One flickered on intermittently, jarringly. Along with the aged vinyl and steel seating, the room was best described as antiquated, industrial, cold and uncomfortable. She worked hard to avoid making any analysis or judgement about the crude psychology that had spawned this unsettling environment, keeping her mind busy by counting and recounting chairs; people; stains on the floor and walls. She also tried to predict the flickering of the light, but it seemed to be governed by entirely random processes.

It took another half an hour before the first person received their silent summons. She noticed him start suddenly in his seat, before standing and heading to the door beside Surly. Surly eyed him suspiciously over folded arms as he approached, but allowed him to pass through the door without challenge.

Emboldened, a lightly built young man made the trip to the cooler. Surly eyed him with equal suspicion. The young man wrestled for a moment with the conical cup protruding from the underside of the cooler's cup holder: the angle of the cone, the slickness of the cup's surface and the force with which the cup holder gripped it by its rim looked like it would add up to a Herculean task, but after bobbing his head around the height of Surly's nearby crotch, he was at last able to see the required technique was to twist, and triumphantly filled his trophy from the quartztic flask above. As he walked back to his seat with his tiny cone of water, the cooler abruptly sucked in pressure-equalising air, making a loud, angry, boiling sound in the hushed room. He actually jumped at the noise, spilling a little of his hard-won water and adding another stain to the floor for her to recount.

After twenty minutes, she knew by heart every discolouration in the room, and had carefully studied every detail of every individual unobtrusively. There was no new subject matter. Her nen discipline training had taught her the nature of mind was to generate thought after thought, forming prior memory associations with sensory stimuli. In the absence of external stimulation, the mind would turn inward, tending towards reminiscence. She was aware of the need to break the monotony, to give her brain new material if it was to avoid delving into her unconscious library of encoded memories. There resided a variety of experiences that she would rather not share with nen screening Security Agents. Only a change of scenery would suppress the associated memory-churning nature of the mind, but she was part of a captive audience. The only available option was to go to the wetcube.

It was occupied. Several more minutes passed, during which she studied every detail of the surface of the 'cube, and every sound emanating from within, before the sliding door was opened, and a thickly built man emerged, with an apologetic look on his face when he saw her at the door. Judging by the sounds she'd heard, it wasn't just the wait he was apologetic about. She allowed the door to close, permitting the 'cube to initiate its auto-clean routine. A staccato rattle, like the sound of rain on the roof of a flyer, broke out inside the 'cube as its high pressure jets hosed down the interior, followed by a noise like a revving flike as an airblade dried the surfaces. After a total of thirty seconds the 'cube pinged her notification that it was ready for use and the door unlocked. Passing through the sliding door and closing it behind her, she was relieved to find the process had completely cleared the stench from the previous occupant.

She avoided looking in the mirror: that could provoke all kinds of flag-triggering trains of thought. Instead she sat on the toilet, and studied the wetcube interior.

There were few variations in the designs of public wetcubes. Positions of sink and toilet were optimised for facility and space conservation. Walls and furniture blended smoothly and seamlessly together, with no sharp corners that might harbour micro-organisms, nor sharp edges, reducing the risk and severity of potential fall injuries. The floor grate was invariably comprised of the same interlocking panels of hydrophobic material. Beneath the grate, the same greywater and antiseptic detergent mix that had sluiced the walls would be used for the next toilet flush cycle. After lingering over these details for as long as she could, she stood and turned to wash her hands in the small sink. Proximity sensors were used to dispense warm water and soap appropriately. When she lathered her hands, the sweet, stimulating aroma of cinnamon hit her nose, a surprisingly luxurious and user-friendly touch, given the oppressiveness of the waiting room outside. An oversight, perhaps, on the part of the room's psychitechts? She rolled her hands over each other in the lather, fully exploring the sensations, nourishing her mind with input to keep it planted in the moment. Only when it started to dry on her hands did she rinse off the soap, dry her hands on the airblade and exit.

The weight of the atmosphere in the waiting room hit her anew. Behind her, the wetcube door closed, and it loudly recommenced its auto-clean cycle. From then on, every few minutes, she would cup her hands together over her face, and inhale the lingering scent of cinnamon.

Several other people were summoned through the double doors over the next half hour, until finally it was her turn. The text popped up in front of her, and was accompanied by a chiming sound and a synthetic voice reading of the same text in her head:

PRIMED

'ANGEL LEONARD, proceed through the highlighted doorway'

From her feet, glowing arrows tracked towards the double doors, and a highlighting glow pulsed around its frame. As she started to move, Surly's eyes swivelled to appraise her. She meant to make eye contact, offer a confident and comfortable smile, but Surly did not give her the opportunity, since he spent the interval staring unashamedly at her breasts. She realised he had probably been streaming all the body scan images, and was mentally matching her denuded scan image to her clothed body. She felt a flash of irritation, but also knew that avtog actors had to be comfortable with the attention their bodies gained from others. To suppress her reaction and prevent any out-of-place nenning that could raise questions and suspicions amongst monitoring Security Agents, she started to imagine *The Donut*, allowing the nentra to slip once she was through the doorway, and had put Surly's ogling from her mind.

A short corridor lead past unmarked doors to a flight of stairs, glowing arrows indicating she should climb. At the top, she found another short corridor, and was guided to the third door on the left. Like all the doors she had seen, it was black, unmarked and windowless. Her instructions told her to wait. After a couple of minutes, during which she carefully inspected her surroundings, the door was abruptly opened. A woman in her mid-forties, about her own height, scrutinised her from the doorway. Short, greying brown curls tightly framed her angular face. Her navy suit was practically UNESA uniform, missing only the trademark blue, laurel-wreath embroidered cap. 'And *Curly*.' An instant after this nen, the Security Agent self-consciously patted at her hair. A coincidence, or was she accessing live streams from her subject? Drawing on her training, she subdued the instinct to render her observations coherently, in her mind's voice, deflecting it into her personal sign dialect to obscure her query from prying minds.

"Miss Leonard, I'm Agent Dunn." She proffered a bony hand, but when Leonard took it to shake the agent flipped her hand palm up, and used her other hand to examine the quality of skin there. It was an effort to suppress the almost automatic, self-trained response to pull away, resist the movement or retaliate with a counter-grapple, a kinetic menu of a dozen moves presented by her unconscious in a flash, for her dining pleasure. Fortunately, the flurry of neural pathway activation, when inhibited from motor cortices, did not telegraph coherently to the agent.

She stepped into the room. The interior was a little more comfortable than most interrogation rooms she had been in. A resin desk divided the middle of the room, a filing cabinet stood against one wall. It was unlikely that there were any actual, physical files inside it: just dressing for the room, somewhere to put the potted plant, something extra-terrestrial and low-maintenance looking; something to hang a neutral picture over, a view of the port and Ladder from the surface of the landlocked sea that lay to the east. There was nothing personal here, nothing that belonged to her interrogator. Not even a mug on the desk. She stood and waited to be told what to do next, like a good little citizen.

"Please sit down, Miss Leonard." The security agent used her open palm to indicate the nearest chair, the same design as those in the waiting room, which would place her with her back to the door. She took her seat with what she contrived to be a grateful looking smile.

Behind her back, the agent took three clicking steps to the filing cabinet, grated open a drawer. With a scraping turn and two more clicks she was beside her, holding a ten centimetre stick with a fibrous bud on the end.

"Before we proceed, I just need to make sure we have the right person." The waxy lips pressed together into a thin line, which might have been described generously as a smile. The cheek swab twitched urgently in the agent's hand.

"Of course." She opened her mouth, and the agent deftly darted the end of the stick into her mouth, swiping the inside of her right cheek. Spinning around with another scrape, and clicking back to the filing cabinet, she heard the agent make some adjustments in the metal drawer before grating it closed again.

Clicking past her, the agent stood behind the far chair, an altogether more comfortable looking model than her own, leaning on her elbows against its high back. Then she just stood there, looking at her. After an awkward moment, a humming whir sounded from within the drawer behind her, and as if prompted by the sound the agent began to speak.

"How is the job search going, Miss Leonard?"

"Uh... not going at all, just yet. I'm still recovering from my illness. Once I'm back at a hundred percent, I'll find an agent to get me some work."

"Ah, yes, of course. Is the G.I. infection still active?"

"No, I was cleared from quarantine. But the after effects have been hard to shake off."

"In what way?"

"Um - nausea, fatigue, dizziness, blurred vision. Stuff like that."

"Not to mention weight, and even some hair loss, isn't that right?"

She nodded, mutely.

"I can see how that would be a problem for someone in your - pro*fession*," as she uncurled her fingers from her upturned palm, as though holding the chosen word there, weighing it to decide if it was appropriate. Abruptly, she let her hand fall, as though the word had failed its weight test.

"Do you mind?" The agent clicked back behind her. Being a rhetorical question, she didn't wait for permission: thin fingers lifted a sward of hair near the back of her neck, and a puff of warm air from the agent's nostrils instructed her skin that she had leant in closely to inspect it. The fingers slid upwards, letting strands of hair slip slowly through their grasp. They froze for a moment before a pin sharp pain signalled from the root of a plucked strand.

"Please forgive me." It was an order, not a request. "We are required to be thorough." The agent finally found her way into her seat, leaning comfortably in its padded back, the strand of stolen hair pinched and waving in her right hand.

"I understand."

"Good. That is an unusual symptom, Miss Leonard, hair loss. It makes us very... *curious*." The agent peered at the hair minutely, tapping the tip with the index finger of her left hand. From the ceiling a recessed spotlight brightened, illuminating the agent's hands.

"My doctor told me it was *viral alopecia*. It's not common, but some of the new strains coming in from the frontiers can have that effect."

"Fascinating. Do you know much about micro-biology, Miss Leonard?"

"No, not really. That's just what my doctor said."

"Doctor Maneesh." Again, it was a statement of known fact, not a question. "We do like to meet our new residents, Miss Leonard. It's important to know who's moving in to the neighbourhood, don't you think?"

"Yes, of course."

"You certainly are a very agreeable young lady. I look forward to 'togging your streams. When you do feel ready to start work, of course. We have a very active avtog industry on A.C.P. I'm sure you'll be very successful, here."

"Thank you. I'm very excited."

"Well, the swab scanner confirms your identity." The device in the filing cabinet had fallen silent. "The port administrators would just like you to complete a questionnaire about your arrival experience, if it's not too much trouble."

"Actually, if we're done I'd really like to go. May I?"

"Oh, come now, Miss Leonard, it's just a few questions. Helps them improve the port for future visitors. You *do* want to help out, don't you, Miss Leonard? Do your bit? As a new resident?" Leonard got the distinct impression from the agent's manner that this was not at all optional.

"Yes, of course."

"Excellent." The agent's eyes widened, fixing closely on her like a cat on a mouse, as she flashed a toothy grin devoid of mirth. "Then; was the arrival area organised properly? By which I mean did you have any difficulty locating facilities, or finding where you needed to go?"

"Er – no, it seemed fine."

The agent leaned in closer. "And; would you say the port was clean when you arrived?"

"Yes, it seemed *very* clean."

"How about the washroom? I'd like you to think very carefully, now, Miss Leonard. Was the washroom clean, when you used it?"

The simulated port walkthrough footage she'd seen had been from the perspective of the low-res security cameras there. Her visit to the washroom had been included to correctly place her in the customs queue, but of course there were no cameras in the washrooms, which would have been cleaned according to a recorded schedule, signed and timed by the member of staff responsible. This agent could conceivably have access to port maintenance records. The notion made her feel uneasy about where this line of questioning was going, and she had to make extra effort to remain centred. Having been told to think carefully, she made a show of increasing her eye movements, as one does when searching through long term memory instead of thinking on the spot. "Yeees, I *think* so."

"You don't seem very sure, Miss Leonard." The agent shook her head in exaggerated disapproval. "Perhaps your memory just needs a little jog. Now, try to remember. You used the washroom when you arrived. I'm sure you know why you needed to do that - it's a long descent time from orbit, and you were probably still feeling a little weak and ill from your virus, right?"

"Mm-hm."

"Well, whatever you did in there, I'm sure you washed your hands when you were finished: *first rule of decontamination.* So, you used warm water from the faucet to wet your hands then you reached for the soap dispenser. Was there soap, or was it empty?"

"There was soap," she said, again adding an eye movement for extra believability.

"Good. And did you like the smell of the soap?" When Leonard didn't respond immediately, the agent continued to pitch the question: "Our maintenance crew is always trying to improve a traveller's experience. You might be surprised, but small details can make a big difference. Did you like the smell, or do you think they should change it?"

"It smelled fine."

"*Fine?* I'm sure they'll be pleased to hear that. And; do you remember which smell was in use, that day? Just to be certain they know which smell you found... *agreeable*? They do say that our sense of smell is most closely linked to memory, and we would like our visitors to find their experience here memorable." Under the agent's unwavering gaze, Leonard eventually blinked. The minute motion served as a visual indicator of the awkward length of her silence. "Surely you haven't forgotten the smell of the soap...?"

This was it. The *wheat from the chaff* question. Her unease peaked. She accepted the rising wave of fear, concentrated on it without analysing it; used it to fight the strong urge to pursue her own speculation about whether the soap was one that was changed regularly to catch people out, or if it was just the question that was designed to provoke a give-away thought process, a panicked burst of nenning that was certainly being monitored for, and which would strongly indicate her deception. Gripping her mind as firmly as she could, allowing the welling tide of fear of capture to infiltrate every part of her consciousness, pinning her in the moment like a butterfly in a display case, she gave an answer that would either liberate or incarcerate her.

"Cinnamon." Beyond volition her heart raced in her chest, a primitive, adrenal response. She could feel it flutter, as though trying to break free.

The agent stared at her in silence for a long moment before asking "You seem nervous, Miss Leonard: is there something you should tell me?"

"Sorry, I'm still feeling quite ill. Coming here today has been very draining. I'm just worried that I might be about to throw up in your office." If the agent was streaming her tactile, the fear-induced knot in her gut, increased heart rate and perspiration could easily be re-construed as pre-emetic indicators. She visualised suddenly hurling her stomach contents across the desk, and all over that navy suit. The agent's eyes bulged almost immediately.

After an instant of consideration, the agent sprang to her feet, pushing her rolling chair backwards.

"I'm terribly sorry to have detained you for so long, in your condition, Miss Leonard." She was already helping her to stand and guiding her towards the door with one hand on her elbow, the other reaching for the handle. "As I said, we *are* required to be thorough, but I think we have everything we need, for now. If we have any other questions, we'll be sure to contact you. Please notify us if you relocate."

She was already back in the hallway, the agent swiftly closing the door behind her. Her arhud highlighted a door to her right, opposite the way she had arrived here. It unlocked and slid open as she approached, revealing a descending stairwell and corridor which brought her around to a window on the far side of the reception area. Through the window, across the room and out through the other side, she could see the door she had entered the building by. The door had been closed, locked: interrogations

PRIMED

were concluded for the day. Her arhud indicated she should open the metal drawer in the wall beside the window. Inside she found her handroid. As she activated the device, the highlighted door at the end of the corridor opened, admitting natural light framing the bulky form of Burly. He rolled up beside her, banging on the window. In one hand he gripped a half eaten, sugar glazed donut. Icing sugar stuck to the corners of his mouth. On his other hand, he balanced an open box, revealing eleven other assorted donuts and pastries.

"Who ordered the pink one?" he barked through the intercom.

Suppressing a smile, she casually made for the exit.

CHAPTER NINE: OPERATION TAIL FEATHER

Pasqualé handed her the cardboard folder. She'd taken another autocab back from the port authority offices, and met up with her on the roof of the first full height tower bordering the shipping district, well beyond the reception range of the port authority complex. Now they followed the westerly radial route of unmonitored rooftop walkways in the rough direction of Church Hill, their handroids on standby.

"Congratulations on passing the UNESA interview. Now that you're considered a legit' resident, I've got you some new orders from on high."

She flopped open the unfamiliar object. There was a hand written cover letter from Evagora, which she had to struggle to read: there was so much variation in the appearance of each letter. As she scanned through the contents, she murmured to Pasqualé "Thanks, but I'm not altogether sure I *did* pass. The S.A. hit me with a question about the soap in the washrooms in the arrival lounge. I guessed an answer."

"What did he ask you?"

"She," Leonard corrected. "The smell of the soap."

Pasqualé sucked through her teeth. "Shit. Those fuckers get tricksier every day. What'd you say?"

"Cinnamon. That's what was in the 'cube in the waiting room. I figured they probably had the same supplies and maintenance team servicing the whole complex. And I couldn't think too hard about it while they were monitoring my nens."

"You're probably right. Kochansky's the only one among us that actually arrived here via the port. And you, of course, but you wouldn't remember that. The rest of us are home grown. And they could easily have changed the soap since then. Maybe even a different scent every day, like a code they can use to catch out anyone trying to fake port arrival."

"Yeah, I wondered about that. I think she was bluffing, 'though, just trying to get me to slip up."

"Martinez would know. I'll check with him, to be on the safe side. In the meantime, make a few random excursions before running your mission, and be extra vigilant for tails. But don't lose any sleep. It's not S.A. style to let a suspect walk. Sure, they could follow you, stake out your apartment, stream you from your 'droid, bring down everyone you make contact with, but that's *really* labour intensive. They could get all the same info' out of you in a couple of hours of dry cleaning. I say they wouldn't have let you go unless they didn't have any suspicions."

The folder also held a printed city map, hand marked with weapons caches, safe houses and drop points. There was also a scrawled inventory of weapons, explosives, equipment and ammunition to go with it, cross-referenced, as far as she could tell.

"That's everything we've got. Welcome to the club."

"I thought I was already *in* the club."

Pasqualé gave her a wry smile. "Sorry, kiddo, it's all *need-to-know*."

"And I need to know now, because...?"

"We're going active. Evagora's controller has confirmed the SPITS program *is* being fed by former O.A.C.I. operatives, and that they're right here in Godsgood. Our primary objective is to locate and eliminate the traitors, deny their intel' to SPITS to get ourselves some breathing room. Then we can re-establish a cloning facility, and resume full scale operations."

Having flipped through the whole folder, there was no sign of any target intel'. Pasqualé *had* said *locate* and eliminate.

"This is a city of thirty million people. Don't we have anything to go on?"

"Well, that's the rub. Evagora's suggestion is that we just need to put ourselves in their shoes. Imagine what you would do, if you were working for the GUNE's. Where would you live, where would you shop, what would you eat, who would you talk to. Look for patterns. You've had the same training as them. This is exactly how they've been getting the jump on *us*. We just use their own techniques against them."

"Look for patterns amongst thirty million suspects? That's not a technique, that's bullshit! How many are we looking for?"

"We don't know."

"Well, how many of us are working on this?"

"Field operatives only. That means you, Victor, Martinez and Evagora. Me an' Kochansky'll provide technical support."

Leonard pinched her lips between her teeth, mirroring the mental act of shutting down a purposeless string of invective. She knew her orders, knew the mission: trawling through billions of transactions and communications logs for indicators that meant nothing in isolation, but when connected with certain other indicators would start to build up a profile, creating a not-so-shortlist of potential suspects warranting closer investigation. It sounded just like a Security Agent job description. Counter intelligence was her least favourite discipline. She released her lips with a pursed puff, resigning herself to the onerous task.

Pasqualé cut in to her self-control process: "I parked my flike at the meg', there." She gestured with her chin towards the looming commercial spire of the superblock's central tower. "D'you wanna ride, or are you gonna head for the mid-levels?"

They had reached the radial turn-off. To reach Church Hill from this block, she would have to descend to mid-level walkways, which meant increased surveillance, or ground level, which would be slow going.

"Thanks, but I think I'll walk. Another time, though? Let me know what Martinez says, will you?"

"Sure. Anything to put your mind at rest. See you, then, Leonard."

When she waved goodbye, she showed Pasqualé her palmed handroid. A flicker of acknowledgement in her eyes, Pasqualé slipped a hand into her jacket pocket, presumably reaching for her own device as she turned to leave.

Activating her handroid, she watched Pasqualé as she worked her way around the rooftop to the mega block connector, leaning against the block atrium's suicide-prevention railings. 'Time for an avblog update.' She nentitled the entry 'Walking home from the port,' and began to stream: "I just got my official welcome to Godsgood City, today. Here it is: my new home. Looks like I'm here to stay." She turned around, taking in the panorama for the benefit of her imagined 'blog followers. She also took the opportunity to scan the faces of other pedestrians as they walked by her, "These are my new neighbours, then," subtly and indecipherably sign-flagging those that seemed to go the same route as Pasqualé, and those that seemed to make a stop in the distance.

'Publish project.' She hibernated the handroid. Her blog entry would look innocent. If UNESA *already* suspected her, and were monitoring her handroid, it might further arouse their suspicion, but not actually furnish further proof. Avtog could cut both ways: with her blog made public, anyone could stream the contents, and the S.A.s would lose their exclusive access to her sense-stream. Pasqualé could just as easily use it surreptitiously to check for her own tails.

Of course, any S.A. worth their e-badge would be operating as a team: the first tail would walk on by and keep going, stopping at the limit of visibility to monitor her, with their partner hanging back out of sight, probably with a parked vehicle, until she started moving again. To avoid getting made, the second agent would pick up the tail, with the first falling back, picking up the flyer. If she made a couple of stops, they'd repeat the manoeuvre, and she might see a familiar face again. Unless there were more than two agents in the team. With luck, the team would split to keep tabs on Pasqualé, too. But an operative depending on luck was a dead operative.

After her panoramic survey, she strode quickly back to the walkway she had just crossed with Pasqualé. By tucking her chin to her collar bones as she walked, pretending interest in her pocket contents as she rummaged first to one side then the other, she was able to look almost directly behind herself, over her cheekbones. To an onlooker, she seemed to be peering down. It was an old fliker's trick, perfect for scoping blind spots around the rider before manoeuvring. In this case, she was looking for any tell-tale direction-switchers in the scant rooftop foot traffic, and anyone suddenly hurrying where they had been idling before. As long as she stuck to the top decks, S.A.s would need to continue with old school surveillance methods. Once below, they could rely on block camera feeds. She would lose any tails, along with any chance she had of making them.

So far, there was no sign of a tail. In retracing her steps, she would probably be walking directly towards the rear guard agent, who would now take point. But she had a plan. Two blocks around the meg', a series of running trails wound through landscaped gardens, spanning the void to its neighbouring block in a creative feat of engineering, and doubled back in a scribbled figure-of-eight. As she approached the entrance, she roused her handroid for another 'blog entry: 'time for a workout.' Of *course* her fans would be interested in pounding around some muddy tracks with her.

She broke fast for a hundred metres, but instead of following the trail across the void she hurdled a hedge meant to divide two parallel tracks and doubled back, scanning the handful of faces that passed her on the adjacent course. As she drew close to the entrance, she abruptly dropped into a crouch, adjusting her footwear to fit more tightly, using the forward tilt of her head to again check behind her, relying on peripheral vision. Two runners were coming up behind her, but their outfit colours didn't match those she'd seen going the other way. So, none of them had hopped over and turned around as she had. Once they were passed, she stood and jogged along behind them, confirming with better focus that these were not the Security Agents she was looking for.

Her handroid registered her results: she completed a sixteen kilometre circuit, alternately sprinting and running, in fifty-four minutes and forty two point two seconds. She had thrown in several reversals at random intervals, explicable as exercises in an agility building circuit-training programme, and each time saw only fellow runners that did not resemble the people around her when she had parted with Pasqualé.

She nenned a quick closing entry: 'Considering A.C.P.'s one point two g's, I'm pretty pleased with this time. In case any of you are interested in joining me, I'll try this again in forty-eight hours, see if I can beat it', then hibernated her handroid, slipping it into its solitary, purpose-built pocket on her thigh.

Still breathing evenly, but deeply, she cooled down with a slow walk back to her apartment, taking the rooftops to her radial turn-off, then after a final survey of her fellow pedestrians, delved down amongst the mid-levels.

The travelators made the rest of the journey short, and she took the luxury of standing still on several of the inter-blocks, giving her slightly wobbly legs a break. Feeling safe in her disconnection from avtog, she nenned to herself: 'No signs of any tail. But then, they *do* know where I live....'

CHAPTER TEN: OPERATION SCOURING PAD

With only Marcus for company, she spent the next fortnight working through a mountain of SIGINT data. Occasional forays for food, and exercise beyond that she could obtain from sparring with the customised robotic butler broke the monotony. But monotony was the norm.

Taking cues from her instructions to imagine herself in the position of the target she sought, she made a series of trivial assumptions to whittle down the dataset to a more manageable sized portion to start with. If this set proved fruitless, she would move onto other sets that did not meet her ideal conditions. She assumed that, given the choice of living environment, she would choose a detached, ground level dwelling rather than her current superblock accommodation: the one way in and out always made her feel hemmed in, reduced the possibilities of escape if the GUNEs came to take her down, whereas a ground level dwelling had multiple exit possibilities. So, her starting set included only residents in the low-rise suburbs, rather than the tower district. Immediately, this narrowed her search down to ten million from the initial thirty million inhabitants. Again, based on her own preferences, she eliminated the third directly to the west of the tower district. She liked sunlight, and sunrises. Liked to get outside to exercise at dawn, part of her military discipline. Wouldn't want to be in the shadow of these towers. Six million. North or south segment? Godsgood was equatorial, for the benefits of orbital launching over the eastern waters. She was a northern girl, liked the way the clouds turned, and the way water span down a plughole north of the line. So, north. Three million. And then extraction criteria: if it became necessary for her survival, she would want to be able to get off-planet as quickly as possible, avoiding any handroid activation. That meant walking. She'd want to live close to the port, if not for The Ladder then for a private launcher, a safer strategy, less under UNESA control. One million. And finally, for her daily exercise regime, including running, she'd prefer to be close to a set of trails: inclined treadmills, block walkways or even outdoor running tracks were no substitute for the uneven surfaces of real trails. The closer to battlefield conditions, the better. Frequent directional changes, obstacles, uneven stride lengths and footfall heights.

Peering at the printed map, she popped the lid from a red gel pen, and arranging the still-unfamiliar object carefully in a three-fingered grip, she outlined a small section of blocks that fit her criteria, around Jordan Fleet Park. A quick avtog search revealed that many watercourses radiating out from the crater lake on the city's eastern side were diverted beneath the city via a system of underground, concrete channels, often feeding into automated desalination and treatment plants for the city's potable water supply. Excess water was directed along a large bore pipe, emerging from beneath the tower district into an artificial basin, around which lay Jordan Fleet Park, with a system of running and riding trails, wet and dry obstacle courses, artificial ski slopes, indoor and outdoor bouldering and rock-climbing walls, zip-lines, a saltwater lido and the largest indoor recreational facility north of the city centre. The whole park was irrigated to support a tract of terrestrial arboriculture, a little piece of the home world amongst the stars. Lying within the city limits, the park wasn't bound by the conservation zoning applied to A.C.P.'s tropical belt of crater lakes, oases for the planet's recovering ecosystem. She estimated the residential population to be around a hundred and twenty thousand.

Accessing civilian handroid usage data at this level was restricted to UNESA and local police divisions, so she had to submit the subset to Evagora, via Pasquale, who flike-couriered back with a P2P LAN file, avoiding transmission over the network.

"Why are you focussing on this area?" Pasqualé asked.

"Gotta start somewhere. I decided if I could live anywhere in this city, I'd live there. Maybe our defectors think the same."

"Hmm. Maybe." She sounded dubious. It was a long shot, probably the first of many, but the best edu-guess she could make. "Kochansky had to hack the local sheriff's office to get this data. He *says* they didn't even know he was in their system, but he took a big risk. I hope it's worth it."

Even though it was a mere skeleton of handroid usage, devoid of any avtog stream element, consisting simply of logs of GP/t, stream durations and sources, telecommunication records and financial transactions, it was still an enormous amount of data compiled over the previous two year period. She targeted this subset with her basic SIGINT algorithms, which kicked back eleven hundred residents demonstrating the cross-referenced traits she had filtered for. Morning exercise routines and dietary patterns such as any serious athlete would evidence, but together with regular blocs of time invested in playing certain avtog games, which were often used as substitutes for real-world military training exercises: generally the habits of a service person keeping a low profile. Substance abuse and/or addiction, diagnoses of psychiatric disorders, disinterest in online referendum participation and other symptoms of social disconnection were statistically, significantly co-morbid amongst veterans, but could not be considered reliable indicators in their own right. Case by case, everyone dealt with traumatic battlefield experiences in their own way. She couldn't be too specific, and risk ruling out a real suspect in pursuit of a non-existent archetype.

By this point, the science portion was over. The remaining process was more of an art form, where hunches and gut feelings, more than statistics, would guide the way. She went through the list alphabetically, imagining herself in a day in the life of each person, dividing the *presumed innocents* from the *warrants further investigations*. As she drew towards the end of the list, she resigned herself to a second pass; and a third; and a fourth, if necessary.

Until she came to *Penelope Watson*. She felt the name resonate within her, like an antique crystal glass in harmony with an operatic voice.

Pen had been her friend at Uni'. They had studied together, partied together. After graduation, the rush into basic training to meet the conditions of her corporate study programme sponsor, and the abrupt plunge into the war, had driven a wedge between her and her former life. She never spoke to her again. Just a few years later, she heard from a mutual friend that Pen was terminally ill with lymphoma. It had been misdiagnosed and treated as glandular fever, and by the time her doctor realised the error she had only six weeks left to live.

Pen's family and closest friends rallied around, and decided that it would be best not to tell her the truth, to let her live out her remaining days without knowing that they were to be her last. Leonard had not understood this decision at all, would not have wanted this for herself if she were in this situation. She wanted to visit her friend in the hospital, even would have gone AWOL to do it, but she was urged to stay away, warned her sudden reappearance might make Pen suspicious that her illness was more severe than people were letting on? So, she respected the family's wishes, and learned soon afterwards that her friend had died.

Perhaps because she never got to say the goodbye she wanted, Pen was often in her thoughts. The assignment they had worked most closely on together, where they had really cemented their friendship, was a lecture hall presentation on the works of Sir Arthur Conan Doyle. Pen used a deerstalker and pipe to portray Sherlock Holmes. Leonard – although, of course, she hadn't been *Angel Leonard* back then – had cobbled together a passable John Watson outfit with some steampunk cosplay accessories.

'That's funny. I still don't remember my real name. Why doesn't that bother me?' Was it really just a side effect of the single pass inscription, or had her memories been selectively edited, perhaps for enhanced security purposes: if she didn't remember her former identity, she would have no polygraphable reaction to a security agent calling her by it during interrogation. It *could* help to establish her innocence in such a situation. But wouldn't Evagora, or Pasqualé, or *someone*, have told her if they'd done that to her memories? She had to boil it down to the essential point, present herself with the coherent question, albeit reluctantly: 'Do I trust them? *Should* I trust them?' Her desire to belong, to feel companionship, led her to hope 'yes', but her training reminded her it was prudent to assume 'no'. It was an impossible question, and useless to pore over. 'Maybe it just doesn't bother me because I'm a pro', and I have a job to do, and I'm so used to having a dozen pseudonyms that it just really isn't important...?' She let the topic slip away unresolved into her nen-stream, leaving it to her unconscious to churn over as her focus returned to the assigned mission.

Objectively, *Penelope Watson* was just an obscure association with her own compromised autobiographical memory set. 'But what are you doing on my list?' Yet another unresolved question, strumming at the wires of her instincts, that indefinable gut feeling which she knew could not be trusted, but also could not be ignored. 'Establish facts, evidence to support hunch.' Somewhere inside her lurked a detective, and she resented it.

Combing through the pertinent data reconfirmed Ms. Watson met all her correlated search criteria: an early riser; a daily trail-runner; a healthy eater with menu-planning consistent with a disciplined, utilitarian diet; an otherwise spartan lifestyle, with occasional and calendared purchases of frivolous items, conforming to social gift-giving expectations; basic grooming, no spa sessions or interest in cosmetic products; routine blocs of fps, hth and flightsim gameplay. Extended periods of GP/t at her home address suggested a work-from-homer, with no distinct workplace indicated. Low rate of telecoms, same handful of P2P communications over and over again indicated a small and barely maintained social network. No discernible family member contact. A loner; awkward, isolated, alienated.

Then she found an odd I.P.A. out. Despite its length, she recognised the address code. It had been repeatedly drilled into her L.T.M. during training, and frequently used in the field: a proxy server hacked by Special Op's to bounce packaged com encryptions to Witch Head's training centre. The server also fulfilled a number of entirely innocent functions, which is what made it such a good bounce board. But it *was* a coincidence, or more, to see it referenced here on her list of suspects. But what to do? Stick with the system, review the data, tighten the list? Or follow her gut?

CHAPTER ELEVEN: OPERATION TARGET PRACTICE

The interview with the avtog agent had gone about as well as could be expected. She'd recorded the whole thing for posterity. And as an excellent alibi, which was her reason for requesting it in the first place. The agent was a phony, claiming on his site to connect actors with the best studios for work on A.C.P., by which he meant the best sex-industry studios. The type of acting he arranged castings for was only for the burgeoning adult entertainment aspect of the business. He'd explained the industry to her as though she was as young and naive as she appeared, and she'd gone along with the whole process for the sake of demonstrating to the satisfaction of the authorities that she was a legitimate actor looking for gainful employment until he raised the anticipated subject: "How do you feel about *anal*?"

If nothing else, the guy was professional: she'd fully expected the build-up to that question to have included asking her to undress, let him touch her breasts, maybe even for a blowjob, but instead he'd offered her an un-drugged beverage and seated her comfortably in his office/den. His demeanor was protective, even apologetic, as he explained that today's 'toggers expected a high level of performance from professional actors. There was a high degree of competition from amateur avbloggers and semi-pro's using product placement agreements with corporate sponsors to fund their broadcasts. He actually called it the *Curse of Reality Avblogs*, and her an *actress*, an incredibly old-fashioned, gender-based contradistinction between vocational titles.

She was grateful for his conduct, and despite declining his services she awarded him a *+1* and a *like* when she posted the whole interview on her avblog.

The other reason she liked him was because his live-work unit was a stone's throw from Jordan Fleet Park, and she now had a legitimate reason to have cabbed it to this area. It was too late in the day to expect to run into Ms. Watson, but not too late to take in the ambience, scope out the park and establish potential sniping locations and extraction points. If Ms. Watson was what she suspected, the park might be the best place to fulfill her mission objectives. Who knew what kind of security her UNE controllers would lay on around her residence?

It also helped her get inside her target's head. She had two years of Watson's morning run routes from her handroid's GP/t data. There were no two identical data sets. Watson tended to mix up her routes, throw in reversals and off trail diversions, just as she would have done, herself. An operative trait. Most civilians would run a repetitive route, even if they bothered with reversals. The only exceptions were freerunning/parkour enthusiasts. She selected one that looked especially challenging, the route ranging all over the expansive park for over an hour. 'Let's see what you can do on a *good* day.'

As she approached the route's starting point, she used the data to generate a ghost image as a running partner, a featureless, translucent anthropomorph centred on the GP/t of the hibernated handroid Watson had carried during this run. She would follow the ghost, make sure she could easily keep up, get the measure of her target. This entrance, most frequently used, was under a tree-lined avenue. It was a secure choice: if she were making a hit in the park, given the unpredictable course of her target, a known entry/exit point would be the ideal site to establish a kill zone, if it weren't for the cover provided by the trees. Instead, she might have to follow Watson for a while to determine a likely route for that day, based on known precedents, then break off to find the ideal sniping point for that route, maybe even get well ahead of the target to do so.

She adjusted the ghost's position relative to that of its data-yielding handroid, bringing its feet level with the ground by assuming a left thigh adhesion point for the device. With all settings and software running in her cerebral buffer, together with a map of the park and facility details, she was able to deactivate her handroid and work offline, free from UNE comdropping.

Once initiated, the ghost broke into a slow jog beneath the trees. Leonard matched speed, hanging back to an inconspicuous distance, as though she were really following a live target.

Where the cover broke into a clearing populated by kite flyers, ball kickers, sunbathers and frisbee throwers, the image accelerated sharply into a sprint, weaving across the width of the park and made a hit off a bench, springing onto the cast alumalloy arm at one side, leaping across to the far arm and catching some air before dropping. Here, it sank into the ground up to its knees before bobbing up and resuming a level run. The real runner must have landed and dropped into a shoulder roll, absorbing the landing energy across all four limbs and back before smoothly rising to her feet. The ghost could only convey the height of the handroid transceiver during the manoeuvre: GP/t data did not include subject orientation, so it couldn't anticipate any acrobatics; access to an activated handroid's pitch, roll and yaw sensors, or to a user's avtog streams was necessary to derive that extent of information.

It looked like Watson *was* a *traceur*, or, as the porn-tog agent this morning might have said, based on his apparent, anachronistic penchant for genderising nouns, a *traceuse*. But was she also an operative?

Since the bench was currently occupied by an elderly gentleman with a 'togged out expression on his face, she did not duplicate the ghost's *passement*, but maintained a steady distance behind it.

A hundred metres ahead, the trail made a right turn before a tree lined embankment. Instead of turning with the path, the ghost ran straight into the trees and up the steep slope.

She broke into the shade of the trees at a sprint, almost tripping before her eyes adjusted to the dim light beneath the canopy. Weaving between the trees, slapping their trunks as she passed to maintain balance and propel her forward, she followed the course laid down by her quarry while reviewing the overhead map on her arhud. The embankment looked like a man-made levy to contain the course of the Jordan Fleet, which emerged from its underground channel to the east. The path she had left looped around the eastern end of the levy to the outer boundary of the park on that side, bridging the buried watercourse close to where it disgorged, and ran around the far side of a similar earthwork to the north.

She followed the ghost over the crest and down to the waterway, where it peeled off to the right. The ground was soft, boggy, sucking at her feet as she ran. Her programmed target stayed close to the treeline, where gnarled roots bound the soil, and drew out some of the moisture. She followed suit, appreciating the need to run along the slight slope and cope with the irregular surface presented by the roots. She was forced to continuously adapt her stride length with each footfall. She also appreciated how the harder surface made tracking footprints more difficult than the softer soil of the bank, just a few feet away.

After a kilometre, an ache in her right *soleus* reminded her that she was still not acclimatised to run this kind of trail in this body. Most of her workouts had, by necessity, been in or close to home, with the built environment offering only regular running surfaces. Even her rooftop trails were considerably more manicured than this.

PRIMED

Ahead, a concrete wall came into view through the canopy. According to the map, she was close to where the overflow issued from beneath the city. As she drew closer, she was surprised to see the simulated data projection motionless in mid air. Water cascaded from a wide concrete pipe covered by a metal grille, thick, closely spaced bars running vertically across the front of the outlet. By default, the anthropomorphic expression of the GP/t data was facing still in its direction of travel. She stopped and watched it carefully. Occasionally, it would flick around, switching direction backwards and forwards. It was not likely that the person whose GP/t yielded the data for the ghost was actually standing in the water, randomly moving backwards and forwards. People had purpose, an unmonitorable intent. Whatever Watson had been doing at the time the data was recorded, it probably had something to do with the pipe.

She closed on the scene, climbing up onto the curved concrete top, dropped to her knees and, grasping the rim of the pipe, lowered her head down to look inside. Of course it was dark. She couldn't see anything of interest. Assuming there was even anything still here to see: this data was almost a year old. Bracing herself with her legs around the top of the pipe, she hung over the edge and extended her arm in through the grille as far as she could, and began feeling around the inside of the pipe: concrete; concrete; more concrete; and then, something smooth. Not polished, but vitreous, slightly raised and rippled. Feeling across the bump, she located a raised, sharp edge, which flexed a little, when pushed. Tracing its other side, she pinched it and twisted the protrusion: it bent a little way before snapping, and she quickly withdrew the fragment into tree-dappled daylight for inspection.

It was grey, much the same shade as the concrete, but as her fingers had detected, definitely some form of plastic. One side was curved, with a rippled, glossy surface, but the other was flat, with a matte surface that looked like something had been stuck to it, giving it its shape, but then pulled away, stressing the adhesive face of the material. A thermoset plastic adhesive, thixotropic, maybe epoxy, urethane or polyester resin. It didn't even matter what type of plastic it was. Something had been stuck to the concrete, and later removed, snapped out of its adhesive setting. By Watson? She couldn't know. But Watson had lingered here for some reason, at some point.

The ghost had moved off, completing its crossing of the fleet and making off down the far bank. Dropping her discovery into the water, she gave pursuit.

Assuming Watson *had* removed something from the pipe, perhaps something she herself had stored there at an earlier time, or something she had been instructed to recover that had been left for her by someone else, this would fit the description of a field drop-point, a concealed location for the indirect exchange of information or equipment. Or it could have been an innocent repair job on the concrete by a city technician. She had to avoid making assumptions on limited information.

Sticking close to the trees, again, this time heading west on the north side of the water, placed the same strain on the same leg: she still had her breath, and her thighs felt no burn of accumulating lactic acid, but unconditioned muscles ached from the unusual demands placed on them. She struggled to close on the ghost image up ahead, being careful to avoid injury. After another kilometre, it cut back into the trees and up to the top of the northern embankment. The pain in Leonard's leg subsided as she did the same. From the ridge, she squinted down at the receding image as it wove through the trees.

Skidding and slipping down the slope, bumping into tree trunks as she went, she finally stumbled to the bottom. Turning left onto the pathway, still under tree cover, she spotted her quarry approaching a bend in the trail ahead, and she hastened after it, pushing herself faster and faster as she saw it slipping further ahead. The trail was sporadically crossed by felled trees, creating hurdles and duck-unders, and sets of boulders creating obstacles and opportunities for hits. The map indicated it was a freerunning trail, leading to the more traditional *parcours du combattant* on the lake side of the large rec' building.

She was aware that the trail was gradually working its way back up to the ridge of the embankment, taking another winding two kilometres to do so. A raised wooden structure came into view, with a cleared line of trees beyond it. Without her arhud to inform her, she would have misjudged it to be a viewpoint. It was best reached by a dynamic *lache*, a running jump across a ditch onto a steel monkey bar followed by a rapid pull-up and arm-jump to reach a second, higher bar, with enough momentum to swing across to the platform.

Far from being a place to stop and enjoy the scenery, the platform was actually a zip-line launch point. Continuing her momentum, she grabbed for the bar. Its smart-harness auto-seamed around her wrists, and she hurled herself off the platform. The ghost was already well away. She could see it magically running through thin air beneath the cable before her, the simple software comically matching the projection's leg movements with its horizontal speed. Since this was far in excess of normal running speed, the ghost's legs blurringly whirred in the air like a hummingbird's wings.

She quickly gathered speed in the high gravity, swinging her legs in a pumping motion to enhance her acceleration. Once at top speed, she tucked her knees up to her chest, pulling on the bar to angle her body and reduce air friction.

A second bar whipped by her on an upward journey, dragged by a return line on a pulley system: the half way point. Between her knees, she couldn't discern any gain against her simulated opponent. It was off the line and running at a human speed again.

Feeling the strain in her arms and torso, she was relieved to hit the perpendicular brake line near the bottom, the elasticated rope smoothly slowing the overhead bar to a safer speed as the harness released her wrists. She forced her fingers to uncurl, relinquishing their vice-like grip on the bar, dropped and shoulder rolled onto and across the foam crash pad, coming up onto her feet on the solid ground beyond, back to running.

A few seconds later she broke into the open, squinting in the bright light from the primary. Off to the right, a modular structure housed the park's indoor sports and recreation facilities. To the left, reflected light sparkled back from the rippling surface of Jordan Fleet Lake. Between them, as her eyes adjusted, the structures of the outdoor obstacle course swam into focus. The ghost was already a few obstacles in. With a snort of annoyance, she picked up her pace, feeling that she was pushing her limits.

Reaching the first obstacle, she grabbed for the rope that swung her over a ditch, drawing a second rope back to the swing-off behind her, and raised her feet to land as high as possible on the cargo net at the other side. Pumping herself up the net, she got a firm under and overhand grip on the horizontal beam at the top as soon as she could reach it, and using mostly upper body strength swung her body up and around to clear the beam and reverse face with minimum energy expenditure.

The descent was much easier, allowing the springing action of the netting to raise each foot as she took her load off it, transferring it each time to the lower foot.

Spinning around at the base, she faced a short sprint to a steeply sloped travelator belt. She correctly guessed that it would start to move under her weight, so used the same strategy to get as high a start as possible on the obstacle, making a single legged jump up the slope, then pumped her legs quickly to reach the three-metre-high top before the belt could overcome its inertia and get up to match her speed.

From the top of the ramp, a zig-zagging horizontal beam of three ten metre, straight sections traversed a full height drop into muddy water. Measuring her shortened strides to enable her to make an inside-foot step across the obtuse angle formed as the beams changed direction, she was able to smooth off the switches, curve her path a little each time to help her maintain speed and balance.

Monkey bars followed, with another mat drop and roll back to ground level to face an elevated, horizontal cargo net presenting the options of a slow, muddy crawl beneath, or a focussed, tire-hopping type run across the top. Not knowing, at this point, what Watson had done – the ghost was nowhere in sight – she opted for the quicker and cleaner high road, leading to a climbing wall, with three difficulty routes. Crossing the deep padding at its foot, she chose the hardest, with an upper section overhang returning strain to her upper body.

A narrow, descending beam stopped short before a set of offset stepping stones rising out of more mud to variable heights, weaving their way to the far side. Overhead bars provided a variety of brachiating options to skip some of the stones, making a more direct route, which she took.

Beyond the mud, a set of six boards at alternating forty-five degree angles, with increasing spacing between them, necessitated a running, jumping, accelerating movement to traverse, where she finished to ground with a shoulder roll. This brought her to the last obstacle: a decent run up lead to an upward curving ramp, looking better suited to a skate park.

After her third footfall the surface reached vertical, offering little further opportunity to gain upward momentum, so she sprang up, stretching to grab the lip of the ramp where it curved into an overhang above her. But the high local gravity and her own instincts betrayed her: the lip had seemed obtainable, her outstretched fingers poised to clamp down so she could haul herself up to the platform above. Instead, the great mass of the planet beneath her feet pulled her back a little more than she had anticipated, so that only her fingertip brushed against the top of the curve, not enough contact to make the grab, before she tumbled back to the ramp, swiveling to prevent the steep slope from twisting her ankle, and she was forced to brake-run off the end of its lower curve.

'Shit! I'm *still* not used to this gravity.' Her retraining to date had not included much real-world jumping. Evidently, the basketball sim's she'd been playing, even with the local gravity correction, were a poor substitute. Resolving to amend that oversight, she checked for the ghost's location on her map, and found that it was already engaged in a leisurely run around the lake. Converting the data to her arhud enabled a luminous pointer for the ghost's real-world position, and an indicator that the ghost was over eight-hundred metres away.

"*Shit!*" for a moment, she couldn't decide whether to finish the course, or catch up with the ghost. 'This isn't a real tailing situation', she reminded herself, as she eyed the last obstacle.

This time, she kicked off her third step up the curving ramp with a little extra force, accounting for the higher gravity, and was able to snag the lip of the overhead platform with one hand. Grunting with the effort, she managed to get her second hand up in a wide grip, and heaved herself up until she could turn her arms elbow-up, right then left, extending them beneath her to bring her thighs against the lip, then, lifting one hand, swung her hips around to sit on the platform.

She got a good view of the lake, noting the ghost pointer at nine-hundred-something metres, before dropping and rolling across the thick padding behind the obstacle. Dusting herself down as she broke into a trot, she set her face in an expression of grim determination. She hit the trail leading to the lakeside, and pushed her pace. The distance between her and the ghost climbed even faster, as she was running in the opposite direction until she rounded the northern shore, and started along the same southern trail it was on. By then, it was already sixteen-hundred metres ahead. 'Four laps. Close it.'

There were still about ten kilometres left on the route data she was following, with only twenty-five minutes. Recalling her purpose, she knew she needed to catch the ghost before the end of the run if she stood a chance of making a clean kill, under real-world conditions. A quick calculation – she still preferred the mental exercise, even though her buffer toolkit softs could have done it for her – indicated that she would need to gain over one metre per second just to catch up. After reviewing the data for a few seconds, she saw that she was barely exceeding the speed of the ghost: the total run distance was falling by six point seven metres per second, but the distance to target only dropped one metre every three seconds.

Breathing deeply, she pushed herself to run at eight metres per second, satisfied only when she saw the distance to target dropping every second. She swept past other runners on the lake trail in both directions, barely registering their presence.

Ten minutes later, the gruelling pace was taking its toll. Her face was moist with perspiration, the charcoal-grey fabric of her wicking garments even more so. Her breathing was still even, and her legs still felt strong, but her right calf and ankle were sore where the unusual demands of the course had strained them earlier. Soon afterwards, she had to fight the instinct to adjust her gait to improve her comfort: it would feel better, she knew, if she favoured the left leg, landed on and pushed off a little more softly with her right, but it would also reduce the speed and efficiency of her running. Before too long her left leg would tire and she would exhaust herself before the end of the route. So she pushed on through the pain, feeling it but not relenting to it, practicing present-mindedness, focus on the moment to avoid anticipation of the pain of her next step. Her world contracted to a focal point as the Doctrine kicked in: '...just a tool.'

When the trail peeled away from the edge of the lake, it rose to a level, straight path, heading back to the exit. She was finally in sight of the ghost, and all her focus shifted to that point. Ahead, she could see the tree-lined avenue, and beyond, under shade, the gateway out. A pulse of light and a chiming sound snapped her back to wider awareness, the pain in her right leg intruding with it: she saw from the data there were only four hundred metres left, explaining the *last lap* warnings, and that she was eighty metres behind the ghost. With a start, she boosted into a final lap sprint, where a runner would put in every joule they had left to win. Ahead, she could see the ghost was doing the same, its synchronised footfalls giving a good indicator of the data-provider's ground speed. Immediately, she realised that she didn't have very many joules of her own left: the roughness of the trails, the head start she'd given the ghost after investigating the outfall pipe, her fumble on the final obstacle, had given the ghost a lot of ground. She was forced to admit that Penelope Watson was in excellent condition, possibly better than her own, all things considered. She wasn't going to catch her. Not today.

The tight pain message from her *soleus* finally acknowledged, she slowed her pace until she drew level with a vacant bench. She sat down, bringing her right leg up onto her lap to massage the overworked muscle, and let her target slip away, blinking out of existence when it reached the gateway, and the route data countdown hit zero.

She washed down a handful of recovery pills from a ziplock bag with a protein drink in her quartztic hipflask, and looked back along the route, over the lake. She'd chosen it because it had been an atypical run, longer than the suspect's usual courses, perhaps accounted for by Watson's detour to the outfall pipe. Reviewing the route data over only the last few months showed that Watson's recent runs were more regular: usually the same route, little variation in start and completion times. 'Getting complacent? Or tame?'

She could stake out the entrance before Watson's usual arrival, and instead of following after her sighting she could run the route in reverse, set up a kill zone from the trees by the lake and wait for Watson to reach it from the other direction. But she still wasn't sure who she was dealing with. A handful of people in the city could match this fitness level without it denoting military training. The fastest distance runner she'd ever competed against had been sixty-four years old at the event. Leonard – 'no, *not* Leonard: what *was* my name?' – was only twenty, still at university, before joining up with her sponsor's private army, and already at peak fitness. But she'd still lost.

She had to be sure. She had to look her in the eyes. Maybe even get a confession. That would change her mission parameters from a relatively simple assassination to those of abduction, interrogation; and murder, assuming Watson's guilt. But what if she was innocent? Wouldn't she have to kill her, anyway, to prevent her from identifying her to the S.A.s? If so, why bother with the extra risk of bringing her in for questioning, why not just shoot her in the head and be done with it? She thought about her not-so-short list of suspects, and realised that if she were that indiscriminate, if she killed Watson on the light weight of the evidence she *really* had, then she would have to do the same to everyone on that list. No. She had to be sure. These were civilians. Certainly, every one of them would turn her in to UNESA if they knew what she was, but that didn't make them the enemy. *They* weren't pointing the guns at her, UNE was.

CHAPTER TWELVE: OPERATION BULLSEYE

According to her GP/t, Watson rarely left this neighbourhood, which lay south east of Jordan Fleet Park. Out here, the hexagonal layout broke down into a rectangular grid, air traffic flying freely above the low-lying buildings within the safely projected flight paths designated by the centralised traffic control system. Her purchasing history identified the nearby *ICA Maxi* as her preferred, local grocery store.

Out in the suburbs, people still often shopped centrally for food. Level stores in the towers still provided go-to locations for small purchases, but most block inhabitants received deliveries of larger, weekly orders, brought to inter-block service-locks by hoverbarges.

Vending stalls, like those found along the inter-blocks, were usually over-the-counter or hole-in-the-wall service only, the goods inside too densely stored to admit customers for perusal. She'd even seen a barber's shop, complete with a traditional, candy-striped virtual pole, where the customers sat in a chair out in the walkway during opening hours, and the barber leant out through a hatch. Hoverdolly-pushing couriers made steady tips shuttling provisions to nearby block customers, scuffling with the barge-boys over the rougher turfs.

From her investigation so far she had Watson's home address, G-PIP and visual likeness. Picking up her tail from the Watson residence six blocks from the Maxi, whilst a tempting shortcut, was excessively risky. If Watson was UNESA's pet informant, there was every possibility that the vicinity was covered by a nen screen, with at least a D.A.I. watchdog to mind the fort. Possibly a live agent or an entire team, depending on exactly how valuable she was to the Agency. That left her with the park and the Maxi as known haunts, public places away from nen screens, out in the open where she could easily identify a security detail, if Watson brought one.

The park was where she exercised, and she already knew Watson was in excellent physical condition. But there she was an athlete, and there was little more to learn from observing her in that setting. Leonard wanted to see Watson interact with people, how she connected or refrained from connecting with her fellow human beings.

The Maxi was a perfect venue to maintain close, prolonged observation. She could even push it as far as making Watson's acquaintance, with careful timing. The only difficulty was in maintaining a stakeout without arousing suspicion. She had no business in the neighbourhood, no excuse to do anything other than pass by. Her GP/t would provide a record of her in the vicinity for the extended period necessary to make visual contact. If she took a flyer to the moorings, a natural hide and base of operations for comfort and protection from the elements – A.C.P.'s incident primarylight was the biggest concern, but the equatorial region did experience a daily downpour, like its terrestrial cousin – she would have to operate with an active handroid to get flight path permission. She could try ghosting, illegally leave her handroid at home, take a cab and pay with UNOs, but all cabs had av recorders. She could easily get arrested for ghosting and vagrancy, carrying only the cash in her pocket with no electronic payment means. But even if she made it to the store, she'd have to stand around outside in the open for anything up to forty-eight hours – many of Watson's shopping habits were quite routine, but the day of the week and time of day did tend to vary within a two day window, with the occasional statistical outlier – or wander around inside the store at intervals for respite, where she'd be caught on security cameras.

Realistically, she could not run the mission as Angel Leonard without being identified by UNESA. The only logical solution was to run it as someone else. *'jack a civ's droid*, Evagora had told her. Their flyer would be pretty handy, too.

∞

It wasn't too hard to find the right mark. She went for the corporate look, wore a red bobbed wig and whitened her complexion, applying heavy green eye shadow and matching lipstick. She eschewed the entry-level worker's pencil skirt in favour of a seniority-suggesting, dark grey pin-striped *pantalons femme*. They offered more mobility, and better concealed practical shoes she could actually run in. Her apparent youth made it difficult to pull off the look convincingly, but the covered legs were becoming far more common throughout corporate structures where Islamic sensibilities held sway.

She took a promenade around the local meg' mooring bays early on Monday morning. She found a latest-model *AgustaWestland AW3181P*, all sleek curves in a chassis almost completely comprised of a wrap around, reactolite quartztic windshield. The vacant vehicle security tinting rendered the quartztic an opaque black. It was moored in a V.I.P. visitor bay reserved for BHP Billiton, UNE's largest mining company, buoycasting its rental company comsite. She copied its latent VIN and kicked out one of its landing lights.

She then rode the elevator to the commercial spire's main lobby and approached the security desk. The heavy-set duty guard looked her up and down as she exited the elevator, and continued to watch her peripherally as she approached.

"How can I help you, Miss?"

"Actually, I was just on my way out when I saw someone smash into a moored flyer in the bays, and just take off. I thought I should come back and report it."

The eyebrows twitched upwards in a micro-expression of surprise on the guard's otherwise serenely immutable face. "Did you get their license code?"

"No, they were gone so fast." 'And I'm just a girl who can't be expected to notice such details, which is why we count on attentive guards like you,' she nenned, placing herself firmly in character: "But I think the owner might want to check the damage, it looked pretty bad." She fed him the AW's latent VIN from her arhud, and watched the guard's face blanch when he established its ownership on his own arhud database display.

"Oh, *merde*.... Thank you, Miss, I'll inform the owner right away. Excuse me." His eyes glazed as he commed the BHP Billiton receptionist.

She excused him, and herself, returned to the elevator, and went back to the mooring bay, waiting in sight of the damaged flyer until the enraged renter arrived to inspect the damage. He was in his fifties, powerful body turning to fat, grey and thinning hair, a ruddy complexion, wearing an expensive suit and shoes. A flash of gold at his wrist revealed he actually wore a watch, an affectation requiring that it be a watch worth wearing for reasons other than telling time, since it was easier to check an arhud chronometer display. He looked like the kind of man who had an assistant to take care of problems like this, but this was his *flyer*. This was personal.

He spotted the smashed landing light on approach, cursing loudly. Muttering to himself and shaking his head, he made a circuit of his vehicle, to see if there was any further damage. Satisfied he had the measure of the situation, he made a similar tour of the adjacent flyers, looking for tell-tale damage to their exteriors that might identify the offender. She was at the limit of visual scene confirmation, but she could still make out the veins standing out in his neck and temples. He showed so many indicators of hypertension she worried he might not live long enough to complete her objectives, but she started to move anyway, waiting for his triangulatable transmission. It lit up on her arhud as he commed the rental company, and she circled his position to *XYZT* him.

That's when she 'jacked his handroid. Using her op's terminal she was already hacking the rental company comsite and local network server traffic. She knew the com he was going to make, and with line of sight was able to place his uplink signal, connecting the com trail to match up his device's G-PIP. It was a hacker's comdrop, success depending on the initial con to get an observed streamer to connect to a known com.

Streaming the back-and-forth communiqétions between the irate renter, Michael McMahon, and the rental company, GigaHertz, she dumped his C.I.N., autho-stamp, Netransact account number and password from his negligently undeleted eye-point and nen history cache, everything she needed to duplicate his virtual identity on her own handroid. The only other data she needed was his rental account number, which he revealed when prompted by the service agent. From the content of the communiquétion, she gathered the agreement between GigaHertz and their client was to send a courier with an undamaged replacement vehicle to make a seamless exchange within two business days.

With his com concluded, she switched direction through the bays, intersecting his return to the elevator. As she passed behind him she re-designated his G-PIP, activating his original code on her own terminal.

Most systems wouldn't query a new G-PIP, which could be system-designated simply by activating a new handroid or switching between server providers. Only secure transaction requests tied to a registered G-PIP would require confirmation of the new code. As long as he wasn't banking or conducting stock market trades personally, he wouldn't even get this small indicator that something was amiss. She was counting on him having *people* to take care of financial matters for him, while he concerned himself solely with his business, or not thinking a G-PIP registration request was a sign of anything more serious than a routine security check or reception problem.

She partitioned her op's terminal's flexi-drive to run Angel's handroid as a virtual device, complete with G-PIP and GP/t transmission, then transferred the McMahon data to the blank handroid. Wryly, she designated the replica *McMandroid*.

She continued walking, heading back towards the tower-top trail runs. About an hour later she placed a comcall to the flyer rental company.

"GigaHertz Flyer Rentals, my name is Emily, how may we help you?"

"Good morning, Emily, I'm calling on behalf of Mr. Michael McMahon: he has a rental account with you, *bgvd8f7gh*. He called in some collision damage to your office, earlier this morning?"

"Yes, that's right. And you are...?"

"Petra Stravinsky, his P.A. Mr. McMahon has an important function to attend this evening, and re*quires* arrival by private flyer – there will be valet parking. Mr McMahon feels the damage to the landing light would be a source of embarrassment, more than an inconvenience, under the circumstances."

"Yes, Ms. Stravinsky, I understand: it's important to keep up appearances. If you would like to bring in the vehicle sooner than the arranged courier exchange, we would be happy help."

"I'm sorry, Emily, Mr. McMahon needs the vehicle all day, and there's no way I could make an exchange and deliver the replacement flyer with sufficient time. Under the circumstances, Mr. McMahon has requested a second vehicle be added to the account until the end of the week, where there should be an opportunity to bring in the damaged flyer."

"A second vehicle? I'm not sure if our policy –"

"Of course, Mr. McMahon is happy to pay the extra rental fee for the overlap. He's far too busy at the moment to be concerned with such trivial matters. I have his autho-stamp."

"That will be fine, Ms. Stravinsky. We have a number of vehicles on the lot that might be suitable – why don't you come down and make an appropriate selection."

"Call me Petra. I'll be there shortly, Emily, thank you."

PRIMED

The flyer rental franchise was in the shipping district, close enough to the spaceport to pick up a steady flow of arriving customers, but far enough to lie outside the nen screens. The LANvert above the mooring lot was an av looped stream portraying the flyers of their fleet in action. Certainly half the things they showed the vehicles doing would breach the rental agreement if a re-enactment were attempted.

Emily was not actually at the site. She probably did reception for a dozen or more service desks working from home. Instead, she had logged the pickup details with the location's work orders, covered by a solitary, overworked mechanic who didn't spare her a second glance when McMahon's G-PIP and rental account number cleared her through the sec-cube entryway into the open-air flyer lot. To avoid attracting his attention through indecision, she quickly navigated through the rental confirmation windows to select an available flyer based more on function than appearance.

Multiple doors and a large storage compartment may have spoiled the flyer's chances of sporty minimalism, but the *DASA EC668* made no such compromise on performance or reliability, with a centuries-long heritage of battle-tested German engineering in its stable. The EC668 boasted the most rapid vertical acceleration in its class, thanks to cutting-edge refinements in the nanometric contraction medium between its four sets of Casimir plates. Its looks went the opposite direction to the AgustaWestland, with little more than a tank-slit quartztic window and a comparatively boxy alumalloy fairing designed for impact protection over visibility.

With the process completed, the key codes were transferred to McMandroid. The flyer door pivoted out like a beetle's carapace, and she slipped in to its padded interior. Initiating the propulsion, as always, triggered all the vehicle's safety operations automatically: the door hissed shut, landing lights activated, and the restraint straps extended an interlocking 'X' over her torso, contracting to pin her to the flight seat. Traffic control constructs sprang up around her vehicle, defining her safe unmooring zone and projecting a linking light-tunnel to the nearest Tri-way. External stereoscopic cameras yielded all-round visibility through her arhud, the vehicle's default perspective recognition softs rendering the alumalloy double hull as clear as glass, only the subtlest visual indication of its presence extant.

'Please state your destination.' The flyer's AI sounded in her mind, emulating a soothing, female, European voice. Calling up the vehicle's operation menus, Leonard selected *Manual*.

'You have disengaged your autopilot.'

'Duh!' Leonard continued scouring the technical menus as the flight-attendant voice continued its pre-flight script.

'To reactivate your autopilot at any time during flight, simply nen *autopilot*. Alpha Centauri Prime Central Traffic Control System's regulations require pre-designated flight paths to be submitted by – You have selected *Test drive mode*. Please drive carefully, and enjoy the features and comfort of the EC668.'

Not trusting her memories of prior flight experience, she chose a control interface familiar to her from favoured flight sims: a cyclic, yaw-pedals, left hand throttle and CP collective. Setting the collective modestly, the rising-pitched whine and crackling of the plates barely audible through the well sound-proofed chassis, she made an inconspicuous VTO from the mooring point and throttled towards the Tri-way.

∞

The Maxi was a typical structure for its type: rooftop mooring bays, alumalloy beam construction with a suspended quartztic facade. As usual, only its LANvertised store front display distinguished it from competing supermarkets: a time-honoured red and white logo circling the air-space perimeter, cast from the sweeping beam of an archaic, whitewashed lighthouse. It guided shoppers to groceries instead of sailors to safety. This was the Scandinavian quarter, and such imagery evoked the region's rugged, crenellated coastline: pure rhetoric, plucking at the faded weft of its catchment market's cultural tapestry.

Compared to her apartment level, it was a quiet neighbourhood: very little foot traffic during mid-shifts, and only occasional flyovers outside the three shift-change rush-hours. A commuter belt, where residents travelled in to the block-festooned city centre or shipping district, or performed tertiary or quaternary sector tasks, often on a freelance or self-employed basis, from the comfort of their homes.

She moored the DASA atop the Maxi, and hibernated the McMandroid. It would still broadcast McMahon's GP/t, but she was confident there'd be no flags to alert either McMahon or the Security Agency.

She'd set out from her apartment as soon as her op's terminal notified her of Watson's GP/t movement towards the store. Right now it was hosting a virtual version of Angel's handroid from her kitchen countertop, complete with a goose-chase of simulated GP/t that had *Angel* making daily dawn excursions to Jordan Fleet Park, but she assumed Watson was still inside picking up supplies.

Leaving the op's terminal behind did blind her GP/t tracking capability, but it was an essential part of her extraction plan: at the first sign of GUNEs she would ditch the flyer, purge the flexi-drive McMandroid partition and ghost it to the park on foot. Once there, she could use the park's terrain and cover to hide until dawn then nonchalantly re-initialise Angel's original handroid G-PIP, which would signal her op's terminal to synch' the GP/ts and deactivate. Back on the network as *Angel Leonard*, with at least an electronic alibi. She could get Kochansky's help to fabricate more; she just had to throw the S.A.s off her scent long enough for Kochansky to complete the false e-trail.

She was still in her light corporate disguise. She mentally rechecked her preparedness before exiting the vehicle – the rain was just starting to spot her blouse, falling as it did every day at the end of the afternoon around the planet's equatorial belt – and heading for the store entrance, choosing the stairwell over the elevator, which was sure to contain a security camera. There was one in the stairwell, too, of course, but watching her footing gave her an excellent excuse to cast her eyes downward, cheating any facial recogrithms UNESA's D.A.I.s might run on the footage. Keeping a distance from the rest of the cameras in the store, given their typical low resolution, would achieve the same result.

She grabbed the plastic handle of a store basket by the entrance. It had a cheap, wheeled design, no hover capability. Looking around for Watson, occasionally putting an item into her basket for the sake of appearances, she noted that many of the other shoppers had brought their own domestic hover-dolleys for larger loads.

She finally spotted her in an unlikely setting. Watson was in the children's supplies section. She also tugged a wheeled basket, already filled with the usual nutritious selections, but was in the process of balancing a box of diapers across its top. A box of diapers did not exactly fit the former OACI operative profile Leonard had imagined. 'What's she doing? Buying them for a friend?'

She followed Watson back towards the exit, assuming she'd autopay on departure, but instead she stopped a store assistant. 'There were close to a million OACI operatives, with *were* being the operative word. I must've met about a thousand....' She hadn't recognised Watson from her online avatar, but now, here in the flesh, there *was* something familiar about her. The store assistant was nodding in agreement to something Watson had said, and they moved towards the vacant customer service desk. Pretending interest in the ingredients printed on a ready-meal box, Leonard maintained a close watch.

Watson was pulling a small wad of paper out of her jacket pocket, handing some to the assistant. Leonard didn't want to activate McMandroid just to identify them. Instead, she began walking towards them, still gripping the ready-meal to avert her eyes to, in case they looked her way. They were laughing about something together, the assistant handing back a piece of paper: '...too many?' Watson held it up, thanking the assistant audibly, now that Leonard was closer.

They were coupons. Colonial issued coupons, part of a pro-natal policy to encourage rapid population growth away from the Sol system. Leonard had seen them before on other planets. Colonial administrative offices issue them to low income and single parent families. All children's food, clothing, medicine and hygiene expenses were covered by the coupons, which were non-transferrable and still bore the stigma of being anachronistically corporeal – paper-based – just to add to the daily shame-load of the lower socio-economic classes. 'Not for a friend. She has a kid!' Watson was just a single mother, working from home as much as possible to take care of her child, getting respite when she could and taking care of her health, perhaps a little fanatically, under the given circumstances. No active operative, traitorous or otherwise, would have a child in the field. Leonard switched her focus to the exit elevator, lengthening her stride. This whole Watson investigation had taken her off track, there was a whole list of suspects she'd need to get back to, and no time to waste.

From the corner of her eye, she detected the motion. If it hadn't been for the residual effects of the aversion therapy program then perhaps she wouldn't have noticed, but the clutching sensation in her gut was too familiar to ignore. Time distended as her focus snapped back to Watson. Her hand was there, at the side of her head, right ring finger brushing back a strand of hair that had strayed from behind her ear. The sympathetic response in her pre-motor cortex, an evolved ability allowing us to learn by mimicking others, tripped her acquired associative response. Her stride faltered, and her head swam. The assistant looked at her in concern.

"Are you feeling OK, Miss?" She waved away his concern, and continued into the elevator, covering her lowered head with her hand for the benefit of continued anonymity. As the doors slid shut, she heard the muffled voice of the assistant: "Maybe it was just the makeup, but I'd swear she just turned green...."

PRIMED

A.C.P.'s daily deluge was in full swing, the Maxi's rooftop dancing like the skin of a beaten drum in the downpour. She crossed the bays to her flyer, nenning the storage hatch open, and started to load the sodden items from her basket inside. The skin-warm water crept up her calves, soaking higher into the fabric as the rain bounced back up off the ground, drenching her from the bottom up despite her standing under the cover of the flyer's extended hatch.

Practicing present-mindedness, clamping down on her emotions with all her nen discipline, she concentrated on storing the items she had autopurchased optimally, distributing the items evenly to balance the load in the vehicle. As she worked methodically, an over-recycled cardboard carton of veggs disintegrated in her hands, turning to mush under the equatorial deluge, refusing to conform to her expectation of orderliness. The veggs dropped into the storage compartment, soft-skinned balls rolling around chaotically under the fluid dynamic influence of their cores.

It was more than she could take. Hot, angry tears escaped, flying from her cheeks as she violently threw the rest of the items from her basket into the compartment and slammed the hatch. Turning her face to the rain, a strangled, guttural sobbing roar tore between her clenched teeth as she slid down the wet hull of the flyer into a balled-up crouch, letting the rain complete its work.

She didn't know how long she stayed like that. Her mind was completely turned in on itself, forcing inwards like the walls of a pressure-cooker, trying to keep the steam inside. At first, she thought it was her own internal monologue, part of the maelstrom of nen roiling within her mind, beyond her capacity to process. But the second time, she correctly placed the sound outside, her ears working in stereo to process the minute time difference between it reaching the nearest ear, then the furthest. A voice. Her own voice. No. *Her* voice.

"I said *are you okay?*"

Leonard looked up at the woman standing over her. The darkened sky revealed little detail, and the sweeping beam of the LANvert, while luminous in its own right, was not a real source of light, offered no reflection or clarity. She sensibly held an umbrella, was using it to cover Leonard to little effect, as the rain falling around her was still bouncing back up and splashing her, anyway, but she appreciated the gesture. The hair was a different colour. The mouth and nose a different shape. Certainly the eyelids were stretched, somewhat, from what she remembered, but the eyes themselves and the hand where it gripped the umbrella were the same.

"Sorry. Yeah. Just having a bad day. You ever have a bad day?" Leonard's synapses were still fizzing, sputtering along disused neural pathways to establish a connection. She could feel the knowledge, just beyond the reach of her conscious mind. A word. A name.

Watson shrugged. "Yeah, sure." She looked edgy. Leonard *was* staring at her. "Ooo*okaaay*. I'm going to go, now."

"Sorry, I'm being weird. Blood sugar. Listen, thanks for checking on me, most people don't bother, you know?"

"No problem. Take care of yourself."

"Thanks! You too." Watson turned on her heel, began to walk away, but her head was tilted down: the same old fliker's trick. Leonard waited until she saw the chin bob up out of sight before springing with all her might. She needed to plant her foot once in the water collecting on the mooring bays too quickly to drain away. Just one step to close the gap. To her credit, at the splash, Watson started to turn, raising her right elbow and shoulder, tucking her head under their cover, but it was too late: Leonard stretched out her foot, landing hard on the back of Watson's leading right knee, reversing the turn. She coiled her right arm under Watson's right armpit, around the raised defence, gripping Watson's collar at the back of her neck with her right hand as the rest of her body drove into her back. They were already falling. She kept her left arm low across her body, and as Watson's left reached backwards for a belt grab, defying the powerful instinct to reach for the ground to break her fall, Leonard swept it away with the outside of her forearm, and snaked through and up for a second collar grip.

Watson managed to skip her left foot forwards, saving her right patella when it hit the bay surface, turning the face-plant into a sideways roll. They both hit the ground along their right sides, Watson's head and neck protected by her raised right arm. Leonard turned her face up, and pressed her cheek to the back of her hands to prevent her head from striking the ground over her right shoulder, and the ensuing whiplash injury to her neck.

Watson was working her legs to regain control, trying to get them under her. Leonard spread her right leg, pushing the ground with her knee to turn them both face up, and kicked out with her left leg against Watson's heels as she tried to make a bridge. This made the impact of her pelvis, when she used the advantage of gravity to drive it down into Leonard's abdomen, just tolerable, but still she felt the wind rush out of her.

Locking her fingers together, she pressed in and down with all her upper body strength, got her legs wide enough to get her heels over Watson's thighs, pulling them back and in to control the dangerous limbs, locking knee over knee.

Together, they struggled with every reserve of energy. Watson's convulsive attempts to break free met Leonard's steady application of constraining pressure, both snorting for breath. It seemed like it would go on forever, but Leonard knew it couldn't. Eventually, the convulsions weakened, slowed, stopped, and Watson went limp.

She didn't release her right away. She counted to thirty in her head, still pressing on her neck, her arm muscles burning from the continued effort, before unlocking her stiff fingers, and pushing Watson's unconscious body off to her side.

With difficulty, she sat up, looking around for witnesses. None. A cluster of moored flyers around them had provided good cover, and the customers in the store had lingered to wait out the downpour. It was already easing off. She'd have to work quickly.

Her body leaden, she struggled to her feet and nenned the flyer hatches open. Dragging and lifting Watson in to the storage compartment took the last of her strength, and she lay on top of her for a moment to recover, until Watson's stirrings prompted her into further action. Using the supplies in the compartment, she gagged the woman with a sock in her mouth and bound her wrists to her ankles behind her back with polypropylene packing cord, putting a constricting loop around her neck for good measure. She could always knock herself out again, if she insisted on trying to break free.

Some of the errant veggs had popped, making a mess of Watson's coat and hair. Leonard stared at her again, struggling to accept the enormity of the ramifications. Her eyes started to flicker open, consciousness returning. Leonard slammed the hatch door: she wasn't ready to look into them again. Not yet. She slid into the pilot's seat, sealing her door. In the darkened and silenced interior her lips fluttered with the word that had taken form in her mind. She was afraid to say it aloud, but compelled, as if speaking it was the only act capable of making it real.

"Marion."

CHAPTER THIRTEEN: OPERATION BACKFLIP

"I'm sorry for the discomfort; I didn't think you'd come if I just asked nicely." Watson turned her head to look at her captor, her lips pinched together in anger, now that the improvised sock gag was out. "You look like you have something to say. That's good. That's all I want. Go ahead and say it, you can tell me *any*thing."

"Let me go!" The bound woman's voice was thick with emotion, hoarse with bruising on her trachea. She lay in shadow in the DASA's storage compartment. Taking advantage of the few minutes it took for her to regain consciousness, Leonard had moored-up on a relatively quiet level in the nearby Leopold I Super Block, on the outskirts of the tower district.

"I will. I just need some answers, first. About these." Leonard hoisted the pack of diapers onto a headrest on the flyer's rear seat row for Watson to see. The captive woman's eyes flickered with conflicting emotions, settling in to realisation.

"You're not UNESA...?"

"No, Ma'am. How about *you*?"

Watson shook her head, eyes narrowing distrustfully. "Bullshit. You *are* UNESA. So you got a few fashion tips and a makeover, but that doesn't change who you are inside."

"Lady, you have no idea who I am inside." She shook the diaper box again. "Where's the kid?" Watson's lips tightened again, their thin line promising that nothing in the galaxy could make her answer that question.

"Okay, I get it: protective Mom. Let me rephrase. I just mean are they safe? Is there someone taking care of them? The father?" Watson gave her nothing but the same unwavering, venomous stare.

"Fuck! Why would you have a *kid*? That doesn't make any fucking sense! If they dry-cleaned you, I could understand: you wouldn't even remember who you were, right? But then you'd be no further use to them, couldn't predict our movements. And I know they didn't dry-clean you, or you couldn't have put up *half* the fight when I took you down. If it were me, I mean, in your situation, I would never... *never*...." She stared at Watson in muted incomprehension. 'Who would knowingly bring a child to war? Unless they weren't *in* a war, not on *either* side?'

"Listen, I don't want to waste your time. It sounds to me like you have a lot of problems. And I really have *no fucking idea* what you're talking about. And I'm not just saying that to fuck with your mind, 'cause you really don't look like the kind of person who'd appreciate it. So if you're going to kill me then just fucking get on with it. If not, then let me go, and we can both get on with our own business."

"That's very civil of you, Marion." There was just the barest flicker in Watson's eyes. If they hadn't been her own, she couldn't have recognised it. "But you're right. I do have a lot of problems. I was sent to kill you, so that could solve one of them. But the thing is, I thought you were already dead. And I need to understand why... *how* you're still alive. If you tell me the truth," Watson started to shake her head, closing her eyes, showing that she already didn't believe what Leonard was about to say, "*look at me!* Look me in the eyes. *If* you tell me the truth, I'll let you live. For now. You can go home, see your kid. We'll talk about whether that's a permanent offer next time we meet."

"That's not much of a deal."

"I know, but it's sincere." Again, Watson averted her eyes. "I know you *want* to trust me. I want to trust you, too. But we can't, can we?" Watson shook her head. "So let's forget about trust, and just tell the truth. I'll go first. I was revived in a basement here on A.C.P. about four months ago. I was given a new name and residence, and precious little else, by my C.O. I was ordered to stay undercover, recover from the early squelch-out, and clear the UNESA security check. After that, I was ordered to find traitors supplying insider intel' to UNE. I ran a few recogrithms, and your name came up on a list. I dug a little deeper, and now I know you were O.A.C.I. I know who you were. And here's another problem I have: if you were providing intel' to UNESA on O.A.C.I. protocols, helping them catch us, then you would never have a child, never give anyone that kind of leverage over you. Never put your child in that *danger*."

"You know that, do you?"

"Yes. I believe I do. And now, I think it's your turn."

"Pfff." Watson snorted, derisively. "Even if that *is* true, there's nothing in what you said that would make me believe you. It's just a story any S.A. could make up."

"Okay." Leonard nodded, acknowledging the fact. It was a sterile statement that revealed nothing, incriminated no-one, practically a *communiquétion*. If she wanted Watson to talk, she would have to stick her neck out and risk UNESA chopping her head off. But at this point, she doubted Watson *was* working with UNESA. And that's what scared her.

"Okay, you're right. All bones and no meat. Just remember you asked for the main course." Watson gave her a sidelong look. "My C.O. told me I'd been out of action for a while, that they'd only recently recovered my *.psy* file and DNA from a salvage operation. You know about UNE seizing the HQ hardstores, I take it?" Nothing to read from Watson. "I'll take that as a *yes*. Anyway, I was pretty surprised to find out it was three years later than my last memory. Even more surprised to find the tech's had shuffled up my genetic sequence, changed my face so the facial recogrithms and gene screens wouldn't ID me. Even put in some *augmentations* to speed up my recovery from the short gestation." Watson looked at her sharply. "Something to say? Go ahead."

"I was just thinking... surely a gene screen would pick up the augmentations. I mean, from what I've heard about the Super Soldier program."

Leonard found it hard to suppress a smile. "Yeah, I thought almost exactly the same thing. My C.O. said they had it covered. I've just got one other problem to share with you, and then it's *definitely* your turn. My last memory, before I was revived, was from a mission *.stm* feed. It ended the usual way, of course, specifically getting vaporised by an underground nuke we called down from orbit." Watson lifted her head from the floor of the storage compartment to watch Leonard more carefully, eyes widening from their distrustful slits for the first time since she'd recovered consciousness. At last she had her interest. "From *The Cassandra*. My C.O. then was Major Harris. Corporals Parker and Keenan were with me. Ring any bells?"

Watson was studying her face intently, looking for something familiar to support Leonard's statement. Leonard guessed she saw what *she* had seen in the wetcube mirror that first time, a face that could have belonged to a sister she'd never had. After a long moment of silence, Watson relaxed her stare, allowed her head to drop back into the goop of veggs. "You tell a very interesting story, but that's just *name, rank and serial number* material. Anyone could get that from mission records."

"After the hard lander – before the nuke went off – I managed to crawl to Parker. We were both deafened by the air blast, but we managed to say something to each other in sign language before we got disintegrated." She waited for Watson to look at her again before signing 'See you on the other side' to her. It was an obscure dialect they'd learned at Witch Head, but a dedicated S.A. could have learned it in an attempt to gain an O.A.C.I. operative's trust. It wouldn't be enough on its own to fool a Special Operative, though, especially not this one. The content was the key. The only source of that information was the *.stm* feed from the mission.

After another long stare, Watson deduced "You streamed the feed."

"Only in the bell. Right after the *.psy* file download. We could compare childhood memories all day, if you like, but I think you have better places to be. It's your call."

"*If* you're telling me the truth – if you're *me* – then we have another problem."

'*We* have a problem: she believes me!' Leonard concluded.

"I'm still alive because I quit. Went AWOL. I'm not supplying intel' to UNESA. I'm hiding from them. You wouldn't know, but two years ago they started bringing us down, all the operatives. UNE overran our territories, and everyone behind the new lines just started disappearing."

"I heard about it. *SPITS*. The S.A.s developed a next generation recogrithm, a D.A.I. or something, that identifies operatives from behavioural tendencies and mannerisms."

"No. They didn't. They probably tried, but their tech's aren't nearly as good as they pretend, always been held back by book-thumping constituents and their fawning politicians. It's all just propaganda. SPITS doesn't exist! At least not in the way you imagine. Now shut the fuck up, it's my turn. When it started, when people around me started vanishing, I knew it was the S.A.s. The few of us that were left guessed the same thing, there was a traitor. Someone was turning us in, or feeding intel' to UNESA. O.A.C.I. teaches two scenarios for when they find an operative: take the *Blue Option*, and get revived in a safer locale; or get caught and

PRIMED

dry-cleaned. *My* problem was that I couldn't let either of these things happen. I hadn't told anyone, but I was three months pregnant. The baby would have died with me, or the S.A.s would've taken her, keeping me in captivity to do what you suggested, betray O.A.C.I. Or just dry-cleaned me, and taken the baby into custody. Anyway, I would have lost her. When it came to it, I just couldn't let that happen. So I dropped under the radar, lost myself among the 'civs, became a single mom. Pretty good cover, I thought. S.A.s have probably been looking for me ever since, but just couldn't pick me out of the numbers. Until you came along. No need to ask how *you* made me, where their whole bureau failed: talk about *set a thief to catch a thief*."

Leonard was hanging on every word. The gap in her life was being filled in, although as she had discovered, it wasn't really her life. Or, at least, not hers *alone*. She stared uncomprehendingly at Watson, willing her to go on.

"Shit, you still don't get it, do you?" Leonard blinked, her head bobbing back from where she had thrust it forwards, intent on Watson's revelation.

'Get what?'

"It's *you. You're* SPITS. You and all your basement buddies." Watson turned away in disgust, resigning herself to the consequences. "Whether you know it or not, you're working for UNESA. Maybe your C.O.'s an S.A., or maybe his contact. Whatever you've told them about me will help them track me down. I'm as good as dead, anyway. You may as well kill me now."

Leonard gave them each enough credit to bypass the denial stage. Quietly, she responded: "I didn't tell them anything. I asked for GP/t data for the neighborhood, but that's all."

"How many were on your list? After you ran the algorithms?"

"Just over a thousand. It was your name that tipped me off – 'cause of Pen. That and the Witch Head bounce-board, but I didn't spot that until after I got your name. No-one else could make that link."

Watson tutted softly, and murmured more to herself than Leonard "It doesn't matter. They'll go through everyone on the list with a nen screen, one by one. It's just a matter of time...."

"Long enough, though. Long enough to change your identity again, get you and your daughter off world, maybe. Somewhere they'll *never* find you."

"Yeah. Long enough. Are you *really* going to let me go?"

"Yes. There's a war going on, and this is no place for a child. Get her out of here. You hear me? Keep her safe!"

"Yeah, I hear you." Her jaw started to work, a visible sign of conflicting impulses to speak and remain silent. "Her second birthday's in two months. Her name's *Michaela*. 'Cause of the city, you know, I'm not much for the *Big Books*, myself. Of course, you'd know that."

"Michaela. *Gift of God*. Do me a favour, pick some names randomly, this time. I don't want *me*, or whoever comes after me, to be able to find you again."

"Okay." There was a long pause as the women stared at each other. Leonard didn't know what else to say. "It was Josh. The father. In case you ever see him again. I tried to reach him at Witch Head, after Michaela was born. I thought he should know. I heard about the UNE raid - I don't even know if he's still alive. Uh, just tell him if you see him, okay?"

"Josh? Corporal Parker? Seriously?"

"Yeah, Josh Parker – what the fuck? He's a good guy!"

"I guess you guys went through some shit together after Groombridge. I'd never have guessed. But, sure, he's a good guy. If I see him, I'll let him know." She stared at Watson for a long moment. "I'm going to let you go, now, but if I were you I think I'd still try to kill me. Nothing personal, right? So I'm not going to untie you. You'll have to do that yourself. Gotta problem with that?"

"'ve I gotta choice?"

Leonard climbed out of the flyer into Leopold I's mooring complex. The DASA's hull opacity and sound proofing had given her all the privacy she'd needed for the interrogation. It was mid-shift, and pretty quiet. A handful of people were moving to and from their flyers on this level, but none close enough to see anything suspicious. She placed Watson's inactive handroid and her own multitool with the blade pulled out on the ground at the back of a flyer moored three bays away then walked to the back of her flyer, nenning the door open. She'd moored with the storage hatch to the interior wall, and was able to roll Watson out and lower her to the ground without any witnesses.

"Three bays that way. Good luck."

"You too. Give 'em hell, Tiger."

Nodding grimly, Leonard skipped around to the open flyer's door and nenned it shut. The DASA's external cameras showed Watson was already crawling towards the blade. As soon as she was fully concealed behind the adjacent vehicle, she started the flyer moving, angling the cyclic forwards as she notched up the CP collective, balancing the two to maintain the same height as she nosed forward out of the side of the structure.

"Goodbye, Marion." Watson had more right to retain the name than she did. Neither of them were *original*, by any stretch of the imagination, but Watson had held the name for longer, even accounting for the time she'd spent as *Penelope*.

'Time to ditch the flyer and purge McMandroid' she confirmed with herself. She studied her image in the inverted passenger cabin interior cam stream. "Looks like you and me are stuck with each other, Angel."

CHAPTER FOURTEEN: OPERATION SMOKESCREEN

She made sure to use the device Kochansky had installed in the door when Pasqualé called, sliding the opacity down so she could still see well enough to move around the apartment. She picked up her image on the elevator cam as she made her way down from the roof. She was wearing the fliker outfit again, probably moored her flike at the central meg'. While she was waiting for her to reach the right level, she slipped two slices of bread into the griller, and set the device to full. Within a few minutes smoke wisped at first then poured from between the cooking plates, triggering the apartment's smoke alarm. The E-CU kicked in automatically, an extractor fan noisily sucking out the occluded air. She nenned it to stay on until deactivated.

Switching to the spy-hole cam, she spotted Pasqualé rounding the corner from the elevator walkway, and patiently waited for her to reach the door to be sure she was alone. Hearing the alarm, she came up short, almost turning back with uncertainty. Leonard whipped open the door and stuck her head into the hallway.

"Sorry, I just burned some toast – come on in." Picking up a polysorb kitchen cloth, Leonard flapped it energetically around the smoke detector, propping the door open with her foot until Pasqualé relieved her. After a few seconds the smoke triggering the detector dispersed, silencing the alarm. Only then did Pasqualé enter, the door gliding shut automatically behind her. Leonard walked over to the far window, placing her hands on the seamless quartztic. "Too bad these things don't just open." Drawn in by the need to hear Leonard over the extractor fan, Pasqualé followed Leonard to stand in the middle of the room.

"So, what, Special Op's training doesn't cover basic meal prep'?"

"Never was my strong point. We should get Kochansky over here to cook for us."

"Amen, sister. So, how's it going with the *search by neighbourhood* technique – d'you need another batch of data?"

"Actually... no. I found one."

"Dumb luck!" said Pasqualé, in a tone of incredulity. "Well, what the fuck? You need help bringing 'em down? I could get Victor to you, if you need a partner."

"No, that's okay. I already interrogated her. I let her go."

"You *what*?" Pasqualé's head was tilted forwards as her jaw dropped, an expression more of outrage than surprise. This was going just as Leonard had predicted. Pasqualé was afraid Leonard had placed the whole team in danger by identifying herself to a UNESA informant she'd allowed to live. That right now, GUNEs could be surrounding the apartment, cornering them here, closing in to seize and dry-clean them.

"I said *I let her go*. She wasn't an informant, just an operative in hiding, inactive. AWOL. So I let her go."

"Fuck, Leonard, did *she* tell you that? Of *course* she told you she wasn't an informant, she was trying to save her skin! Wow – I never took you for a sucker, but I guess we can *all* make mistakes. The important thing to consider is it's not too late to set it right. Finish the job."

"I can't do that."

"Then give me her name and address, I'll get Victor on the case."

Still looking out through the window, her back to Pasqualé, Leonard gave her final answer, a simple, quiet "No."

"I can't... *Evagora* wouldn't allow this. You *have* to tell me." There was a long pause, then she repeated "*Tell* me. Now." The noise from the fan concealed any sound of movement Pasqualé may have made, but the fresh menace in her voice suggested something suitably menacing had arrived in her hand to back it up. Turning only her head, Leonard caught sight of the stubby pistol in Pasqualé's hand as she warily edged backwards to increase the distance between them. She probably knew quite well what an operative like Leonard was capable of doing to a person with a pistol at such close range. Unfortunately for Pasqualé, not well enough.

"Hey, how come I didn't get a gun? So much for *welcome to the club*."

"Sorry, kiddo. Issued only as needed."

"And what did *you* need one for?"

Pasqualé shrugged nonchalantly. "You never know when a girl might need to – *aaah*!" She cried out in surprise and pain as Marcus struck the radial nerve on her gun arm with robotic force and precision, and swept the pistol out of her limp fingers with inhuman fluidity. The white noise of the extractor had deafened Pasqualé to the sound of the android's muffled, whirring servomotors.

Passing the handgun to Leonard, Marcus rolled back into the charging spot under the counter from which it had emerged. Leonard nenned the E-CU to deactivate the extractor, rattling to silence.

"Thank you, Marcus." Hefting the grip, she inspected the weapon, a Heckler and Kock forty-five compact tactical. "Hmm. Now I *really* feel like I'm in the club." She spotted the threading on the barrel. "You got a suppressor for this?"

Clutching her paralysed arm, Pasqualé eyed her in mute fury. Leonard let the end of the barrel swing towards Pasqualé's centre of mass, making her question more compelling. With a roll of her eyes and an exasperated puff, Pasqualé used her functioning left hand to open her fliker jacket, and slowly, awkwardly, withdraw the knurled cylinder from her inside breast pocket between her thumb and forefinger.

"Great. I'll take it as a good sign that you didn't come here with it already assembled. You may as well take a seat. It'll be a while before you can fly again with that arm there." She motioned Pasqualé to the sofa bed on the side wall, flipping the gun barrel. Without taking her eyes off Leonard, Pasqualé reluctantly followed the instruction. Once seated, she began kneading sensation back into her arm. Leonard moved to stand between Pasqualé and the door.

"I'm going to tell you something that you will not want to believe. I know this, because I didn't want to believe it when I heard it. If I hadn't trusted the source, I *wouldn't* have believed it. I realise that you can't give me that same degree of trust, but I'm going to need you to believe me anyway, because if you don't I'm going to have to kill you. And I don't want to do that. I kinda like you."

"I'm all fucking ears, Leonard."

"Good." Leonard took a deep breath. She'd rehearsed a speech just as carefully as she'd set the trap for Pasqualé, but now the importance of convincing her friend of the truth, the consequence of failure, made her doubt her script. "Do you trust Evagora?"

Pasqualé gave her a bored look. "Of course: he's our C.O. He's got *all* our backs. Just tell him you fucked up, we'll get all this sorted –"

"Shut up, Pasqualé." The woman's mouth clamped. "This goes beyond that. Do you know his contact?" Pasqualé looked at her quizzically. "Where he gets the *.psy* files and DNA?"

Pasqualé gave the question genuine thought for a moment. "We have an operative undercover in UNESA. I don't know who he is. I don't think Evagora even knows. He has to keep his identity a secret, for his own safety. They use a system of drops to pass material and messages."

"Sounds like a sweet setup. It also sounds like a crock of shit! What if the contact's just a regular Security Agent, and we're taking our orders from him?"

Batting her eyelids rapidly, as if that micro=gesture alone could waft the unsubstantiated proposition away, Pasqualé shook her head as she relaxed into the sofa. "That's crazy. Why would UNESA activate a group of enemy operatives in one of their biggest population centres? That's just asking for trouble."

"Not really. They know who we are, what we look like, where we live. They could pick us up in a snap, if they wanted to. It's a pretty short leash, when you think about it, an illusion of freedom."

"Okay, let's play this out to its logical conclusion, then you give me the gun and we go to Evagora together; why the fuck would they bother?"

"Because *we* are the SPITS program. They're not using a next gen' artificial intelligence to track *us* down, they're using our own *.psy* files. We're tracking *ourselves* down." Pasqualé's eyes were screwed shut, her head making motions of steady refutation. If she didn't stop soon, she'd have to put a bullet in there. "We all wondered why O.A.C.I. would betray the Indoctrinal Trust Pact, why they would suddenly start tampering with our DNA. They wouldn't. They *didn't*. *UNE* did." There was nothing left to tell her but the truth. "It was *me* Pasqualé. I found my*self*. She didn't get caught, or killed, two years ago by SPITS. She changed her face and went off the radar. She's still alive! Catching her, killing her, was *my* mission. SPITS's mission. *Subversive Personnel Identifiable Traits System*: it's a sick joke, Pasqualé. I found her because I knew how she would think, what name she'd choose for a false identity, where she'd live, what fucking brand of deodorant she buys – *I* identified her traits!"

Pasqualé's eyes were open, now, her brow furrowed in thought. "Identical twins...." she murmured to herself, then with growing certainty to Leonard, "Identical twin studies: siblings separated at birth, leading separate lives into adulthood. There's a greater-than-statisitically-significant trend towards similarities between the siblings in later life: marrying people with the same name, having the same number of kids with the same names; moving to the same town; working in the same field...." Pasqualé nodded, slowly. "It's possible, taking advantage of psycho-genetics and high cleavage rates between synaptic networks. Add in common life experiences...."

"Whatever gives you a techie hard-on, Pasqualé. At least you know what I'm talking about.

"I figure UNE have all the angles covered: if we kill our targets without realising who they are, all they have to do is kill us, too, wouldn't even see them coming. Or they keep us around to carry on doing their dirty work.

"On the other hand, If we realise who the target is, don't kill them," she emphasised her case with a self-identifying thumb gesture, "they can count on the operative running back to their team in confusion with some improbable story about recognising the target, the rest of the team assuming the recognition is just based on knowing them from the service, which just confirms they're viable, and finishing the job. There's enough amnesia to leave the operative never quite sure they were right about the target. Worst case scenario, the whole team believes the operative, and the C.O. runs back to the contact with a bunch of flagging questions, and out of nowhere a battalion of GUNEs wipe them out. Blame any collateral damage on the Wackies. Good excuse to maintain martial law. And it certainly wouldn't be the first time in human history that a secret police force had an agent in every terrorist cell, and allowed them to continue operating. Or manipulated events to steer political power into their ranks...?"

"Picking targets and making sure only the innocent get hurt, keep their own interests unaffected, or even furthered. Let's say for the sake of argument you're right. What do we do?"

"It's a safe bet that Evagora, Martinez and Victor are out there looking for the original versions of themselves, right now, without realising it. We do what you said. I give you the gun and we go to Evagora together. Except that in *my* version of the plan, you have my back. Right?"

Pasqualé stared hard at Leonard, swallowing nervously. "Right. Wait, what difference does that make? You said the S.A.s had all the angles covered. Assuming they've been running this scam for two years, mopping up our boys and girls this whole time, what gives us a better-than-normal chance of getting out of this?"

"'Cause this time, my friend, they fucked with the wrong clones." It was pure bravado, and Pasqualé laughed out loud before covering her mouth with her good hand.

"Seriously, you have a plan, right?"

"Yes. I have a plan. But we have to work together. How's your arm doing?"

Pasqualé flexed it experimentally. "Good enough to fly. Need a ride?"

CHAPTER FIFTEEN: OPERATION BLONDE BOMBSHELL

Leonard felt the sickening draw of the syringe as it tugged at the inside of her artery. Once her blood filled the barrel Pasqualé placed a polysorb ball on the insertion site, slid out the needle and motioned Leonard to apply pressure to the ball. Pasqualé unscrewed the barrel from the needle head, discharging the needle into a sharps bin. She set the barrel in a wire frame stand beside her and assembled a second needle and quartztic barrel.

"Next!" Her military nursing background showed in her bedside manner.

It had been her idea, probably a calculated gamble when they realised Evagora wasn't convinced of Leonard's claims. Her offer of scientific proof had been most persuasive, in the end. Evagora ordered everyone to set goose chases on their op's terminals and ghost together to provide the blood samples she requested, setting up camp in a public storage container in the shipping district, rented under a 'jacked ID. They had a portable generator inside. Kochansky stuck adhesive fluorescent panels up on the corrugated steel ceiling and set up folding chairs and a table, flopping an inductive charging mat down on top so they could power their handroids and Pasqualé's lab equipment, which she'd brought in a suitably nondescript briefcase.

Flexing her arm to facilitate blood coagulation, speed the healing of the puncture, Leonard remarked "And I thought that last basement we had was pretty classy. It just gets better and better. What's our next safe house gonna be, a packing crate?"

"Aah! Wait 'til I'm not looking, Pasqualé. You *know* I don't like watching them go in." Victor was providing Pasqualé's next sample.

"Oh, sorry, baby, did I *scare* you?" she crooned.

"Jesus, fuck, just get it over with." Pasqualé began withdrawing his blood. "I don't see why you couldn't just take a cheek swab, like they do at gene screens."

"Press!" she stood up brusquely, detaching the needle from the full barrel. "Hmm, that's a great idea, Victor. I *never* thought of that." She treated him to her chirpiest brand of sarcasm, posing with her index finger pointed into her cheek for full effect. "All done, talk amongst yourselves. Kochansky, did you get me that 'jacked handroid?"

After a tense twenty minutes, during which she ran the samples through her nanoscope and studied the results on her arhud, she started chuckling. The effect of someone just sitting, immobile, and laughing to themselves was a common enough sight since the inception of avtog, but never failed to solicit an initial reaction that it was a little disconcerting.

"Okay, I've got something here. I could carry on looking, probably find a whole lot more, but I think this is convincing enough for our purposes." She projected her findings onto a virtual screen, inviting them all to LANport to her handroid to view her stream. Six digitally rendered representations of their genetic sequences were displayed vertically, side by side. Pasqualé manipulated them gesturally, the long lines of bio-code scrolling up or down in response to her direction. "Here. And here. Look at the conformity."

Four of the lines showed the same long sequence of code, identical from one sample to the next. Evagora asked "What are we looking at here, Pasqualé?"

Deactivating the display and her 'jacked 'droid so they could speak freely, she replied "I can't say for sure without some original samples to compare with, but my best edu-guess is they were probably imported directly from one of the Super Trooper programmes without modification," Pasqualé reasoned. "Aside from the human performance augmentations conferred, this particular section functions as a Special Forces tag. Sir, everything your contact told you about genetic re-sequencing to avoid gene-screen detection was a lie. Those four sequences belong to each of you operatives. Only Kochansky and I are clean."

Victor hissed through his teeth, a sound like escaping steam. "Let me get this straight: so the Colonel, Major Leonard, Martinez and me – we'd show up as Colonial Special Forces at a check point?"

Kochansky nodded, elucidating Victor's concern. "The data flag would be enough for a Security Agent to keep tabs on your movements, without warranting on-the-spot detention by the GUNEs carrying out the screening."

"I bet that's why port security's so fucking polite and respectful to me, when they give all the other maintenance workers so much shit: I get screened every time I start a shift. They probably all think I'm ex-Delta squad, or something!" Victor and Leonard couldn't help but laugh at the evoked scene of the port's security guards talking amongst themselves in hushed tones about Martinez being some dishonourably discharged colonial super-veteran. "They probably think I have a Wackie ear necklace, or some shit!" Martinez had to hold his sides at the thought, restraining his laughter.

"It's a crude operation, by UNESA standards," Evagora was quick to point out. "They *have* been known to bend their moral code whenever it suits them, but genetic augmentation is still against UNE federal law. You might find Super Troopers in some of the rogue colonial marine outfits, but they're banned from UNE task forces, including UNESA."

"So, this guy's a rogue agent, using unorthodox means to boost his career? Or are we talking about a black op'?" asked Martinez.

"It's gotta be a black op': it's nothing groundbreaking, but the genetic re-sequencing *does* take a technical expertise that's beyond your typical GUNE's capacity. He must have at least one technician working with him, a specialist from the rogue colonies. And there're always two squaddies to every tech'. No offence, guys," Pasqualé placated.

"If that's meant to be a techie insult, then it's a little over my head," said Victor dismissively.

"No, sounds to me like you got her meaning exactly," Kochansky giggled, skipping quickly aside when Victor snapped a punch at his shoulder.

Evagora continued without bothering to call them to order "Either way, it's to our advantage. Assuming worst case scenario: we're dealing with a small group of S.A.s who know about this Op. As far as everyone else is concerned, we are who we say we are. Their need for secrecy about us, about what they've *done* to us, is something we can use against them. We need to be mindful that he might have a partner to provide backup, and a controller that knows our intimate details at HQ. I say we bring him in."

Looking around at her team mates, Leonard saw them all nod their agreement. "What's the bait?"

"Kochansky, we're gonna need a flexi-drive with some falsified data on it: identities for four targets, corresponding to each field operative. Leonard, since you've had the only success with your recogrithms, help him out to make the data look convincing, and distractingly complicated. When he accesses the file, I want him to get such a hard-on that the blood drains from his brain. Questions?"

"Yeah," Leonard responded. "Can I have a gun now, please?"

∞

The kafe was on the equatorial radial route running west through the mega block district, a three level walkway structure crossing the plaza-width gap between the mid-levels of *Elysian Fields* and *Fortunate Isles* blocks. Travelators and escalators occupied centre aisles, with enough room in the promenade zones to either side for the licensing of tables and chairs outside. Being close to the hov'train nexus, the kafe was enjoying a lively trade.

Evagora was the only one without a 'jacked 'droid, thanks to Kochansky. After sticking the flexi-drive to the underside of his table, he leisurely enjoyed the rest of his koffee, slipped out of his chair and made his way to his hov'train stop.

The benefit of continuing to play dumb was that his *contact* was required to adhere to his own rules of engagement, to continue playing the role of an O.A.C.I. spy undercover in UNESA. He'd specified no direct contact no maintain his anonymity, and no direct coms. If they'd been regular informants, and the contact were to drop the pretense, the data on the flexi-drive could easily have been transmitted to UNESA over the network, or the hardstore couriered or handed in to the Godsgood HQ security desk. The Security Agency operated out of a super block of federal office towers collectively known as *Little Geneva*, bordering the shipping district just a few blocks east along the Equatorial I.S.B. Connector. Instead, the agent was stuck with his spy game. Their advantage was that, as far as he knew, he was the only one playing.

Almost as soon as Evagora's hov'train departed, Leonard picked up the agent's movement in her peripheral vision, peeling away from the platform observation window then heading straight for the kafe and flexi-drive with a slow stride. '*...plucked his eyebrows, then he was a she...*' she nenned musically to herself. Obscure cultural references were a good defence against nen screens, and as soon as she recognised the agent she suspected that the whole area was being screened. It was *Curly* – the agent had identified herself as *Dunn*, during the port interview – and Leonard knew to switch to sign-language before nenning her moniker. She'd been watching Evagora in the reflective surface of a shoe store window, and if Leonard's experience at the port authority offices was any indication, probably monitoring environmental nen chatter from a vehicle-based nen screen transceiver moored somewhere nearby.

She looked over at Victor. After a few seconds of staring, his head twitched, and he looked around, quickly making eye contact. He didn't need a nen screen to know when someone was watching him, just honed instincts. She made the sign for *nen screen*, placing her flat left palm horizontally along her forehead, index finger resting on her brow, with her thumb extended back towards her left ear. Victor immediately turned his attention to Martinez, and a short while later he repeated the same warning motion in his direction.

Curly's presence here was certainly no coincidence. Leonard abruptly understood why her genetic augmentation hadn't raised comment during her visa renewal interview with Curly: she'd made sure she'd been the agent administering the gene screen in order to clear Leonard through the process without the Super Trooper genetic marker attracting unwanted attention from other UNESA agents. This suggested she was either Evagora's contact all along, or more likely a junior partner sent to do the dirty work, and assume all the risk of making a pickup.

Being a main transit structure, hi-def security cam's covered every square centimetre of the concourse. Leonard and Victor were keeping their heads down at a couple of vending kiosks. Martinez wore janitorial overalls and a hi-viz vest, the brim of his cap covering his down-turned face. He scoured the floor for litter, transferring any he found to the waste receptacles located at intervals along the sides of the travelators, making him appear so much that he belonged that he was easily overlooked, as if he were part of the scenery instead of another person in the crowd. She admired the way he hid in plain sight, blending in to his environment to the extent that his presence aroused no suspicion.

Leonard was back in a corporate disguise, a new outfit to replace the one hopelessly stained and damaged during her encounter with Watson, hoping to accomplish a similar feat. Knowing now that UNESA, or at least those agents running the black op', had a record of their likenesses and could identify them with simple facial recogrithms, the three field agents all wore silicone masks to alter the mathematical maps of their faces. Unfortunately, after a significant time under security cam surveillance, *not* being recognised by the security algorithms was almost as dangerous as *being* recognised: the security D.A.I. would flag anyone that couldn't be positively identified facially or by gait after twenty minutes, and notify local law enforcement of the suspect's G-PIP. Patrolling militia would be on the lookout for them, and would stop them for gene screening to confirm their identities for the security system. Normally, it was a routine process and the detained person would be on their way within a few minutes with a polite apology for the inconvenience. But only if everything matched up. Throw in a falsified G-PIP identity, and you'd find yourself heading down to the nearest Sector House for interrogation. And of course, with the genetic augmentation markers in their sequences, their gene screen results would inform the very people they were trying to tail that they were in the vicinity, and up to no good.

Curly was taking her time, waiting for a gap in the rush-hour foot traffic to cross the travelator lanes. Leonard was careful to avoid looking directly at her, something Curly would certainly be monitoring for on the sensory streams broadcast to her from those in the vicinity. She was being wary, checking everyone that had a stray nen concerning her.

She finally reached the table, took a seat. And then just sat there, zoning out like anyone streaming an entertainment or news site, until the kafe's *barista* approached her. Leonard would have loved to have lip-read their conversation, but the degree of scrutiny would certainly have been noticeable by her mark. She settled for the overall impression that she'd placed an order, then returned her full attention to the nen screen feed until it arrived.

Leonard suppressed the relief she felt when she saw it was a to-go cup, knowing how close they were to the twenty minute loiter-limit. Apparently satisfied by the absence of sinister nen chatter around her, Curly reached under the table and peeled the transparent film of the flexi-drive from Evagora's hiding place, pulling out her handroid and applying the sticker to its interface surface.

She stood up and started walking, heading east towards the UNESA office as she sipped at her drink. If she didn't head for the vehicle hosting the nen screen it would mean she had a partner to drive it back. Instead of taking the travelators, she walked along the promenade, showing interest in the store front displays probably as a cover to use their reflective surfaces to watch out for anyone following her. With this level of precaution, it was unlikely she was accessing the data on the flexi-drive at this point, especially if she was still streaming feeds from the nen screen: there was a limit to the amount of data one person could process at a time. But she certainly could have transmitted it to a partner for review.

Leonard waited. Martinez followed, confident in his ability to move unseen. He thwarted Curly's attempts to spot him tailing her, making frequent stops and scanning behind her, by being constantly in motion, pushing his cart, spot cleaning stains or gum deposits on the paved surface, sweeping and binning litter. She would only be on the lookout for people stopping when she stopped, and relying on her nen-screen proficiency to recognise if anyone was watching her.

With as little forethought as possible, Leonard left her hiding kiosk, and slowly followed Martinez, keeping him as far away as she could see. His hi-viz vest made it easy to keep track of him even when Curly blended in to the crowd. The inverse should also be the case: Curly wouldn't be able to see Leonard at this distance.

When Martinez and the agent he was stalking had almost reached the end of the walkway she saw Martinez abruptly remove and fold up his hi-viz vest. It was the pre-arranged signal for the target doubling back. She turned to a vending kiosk selling *kawaii* stuffed toys, engaging the proprietor in small talk, removing and folding her jacket over her arm to reveal an emerald green turtleneck, signalling Victor behind her.

A minute later, she saw Curly's reflection pass behind her on the travelator. The moment of attention was enough to alert the agent: she stared at Leonard's back, stopping and turning on the travelator's conveyor belt to watch her suspiciously.

"What's that one?" she asked the kiosk proprietor, pointing at a plump, yellow squirrel-like creature about seventy-five centimetres tall.

"Huh? Oh, that one's my display piece. It's not for sale."

"Not for sale? Why would you keep something that big in such a small kiosk without it being for sale? Go on, how much is it?"

"It attracts customers. Brings me good luck. You have a very good eye, but it's not for sale. Besides, it's an antique, you couldn't afford it, and even if you could you wouldn't want to let a child play with it. How about this one – does your daughter like *Sentai Centauri*?"

'My daughter!' The thought welled up beyond her capacity to restrain, from a completely surprising direction. Of course, she'd started the conversation by mentioning she was looking for a present for her daughter, but she was thinking at such a superficial level, giving the conversation such a small part of her attention that she barely remembered the wording. Now she found that she couldn't help but imagine her, what she might look like, what she might *be* like. What she could become. The place she would grow up in, under UNE rule or emancipated by O.A.C.I. efforts. A visual cascade, like a *.psy* download, rushed through her consciousness before she could regulate her thoughts through meditation. Calmly she reviewed her thoughts. There'd been nothing to flag a nen screen. This time, her wayward mind had stayed off the forbidden neural paths.

Her arhud blinked a text: it was from Victor: *I'm by the HT stop. Meet you upstairs.*

Also innocent enough. But the intent behind it was clear to her: Victor spotted Curly heading to the upper level above the hov'train stop. That's where the transit police mooring bays were located.

"I'll take that one!" She pointed at random. The kiosk proprietor handed her a pink octopus with elephant ears and an expression of genial excitement sewn permanently onto its face, cordially waving as she hastened towards the nearest escalator, mounting the metallic steps two at a time. At the top she sustained her pace whilst donning and buttoning her jacket to the throat, covering the green fabric beneath. She also ruffled her hair, changing the style for better urban camouflage.

There was Curly up ahead, approaching the enforcement bays. The section of corridor was otherwise deserted, with no reason for anyone other than authorised personnel to go there. Facing the enforcement bays was a cubicle for transit police use, a multi-purpose room they could use for interrogations, to incarcerate detainees, or just somewhere to sit and have a koffee on a break. A second text from Victor read: *Hurry up: we're all waiting for you.*

There were two black-and-whites and one unmarked flyer moored there. Leonard got close enough to determine that all the vehicles were empty, as Victor had hinted, then switched her attention firmly to Curly. Undoubtedly alerted by her nen screen interface she span around, right hand reaching inside her jacket for a holstered weapon, without drawing it.

"Excuse me, madam, I think you dropped this!" she called, waving the stuffed toy above her head.

"This is a restricted area, miss. Stop where you are!"

Leonard slowed her pace, but continued to close the gap. "Don't you want your...." She gave a carefree laugh. "Actually, I don't know what it's supposed to be, but I saw you drop it downstairs."

"It's not mine. You must have seen someone else drop it and got confused. Stay where you are, and keep your hands where I can see them!" She drew her pistol, at this, pointing it at Leonard. Feigning fear and surprise, Leonard complied, holding the toy in both hands above her head. With her free hand, Curly knocked on the cubicle window without taking her eyes off Leonard. A man in transit officers' uniform opened the door. "Agent Coulthard, officer." She streamed her e-badge on her empty hand. "I'm on urgent business. Please detain this woman and find out what she's doing here. Use extreme caution, she may be armed."

"No shit? Okay, ma'am, you go ahead, I'll take it from here." He drew his shockgun and turned towards Leonard. She kept her attention on the agent. Getting nothing from her nen screen, and eyeing the dumbo octopus warily, Agent Coulthard made a break for her flyer. At the receding click of her heels on the paved floor, the officer spun around and fired his shockgun, the wide spread of tiny piezo-electric crystals carrying just enough kinetic energy each to tear through the back of the agents jacket and into her skin, causing minor lacerations. The electrical discharge, however, was considerably more debilitating: Coulthard was unconscious before she hit the floor.

"Excellent job, officer."

"*To serve and to protect*, miss," Victor said as he took off the officer's hat. Entering the cubicle, Victor retrieved a folded pile of his own clothes from the floor beside an unconscious man in underwear, pushed up against the front wall of the cubicle beneath the window.

"Looks like you tucked him in nicely."

"Well – he's a civilian, isn't he? You nen the doors, and I'll carry her." Slipping Coulthard's handroid from her pocket, she began to hack the device as Victor scooped the inert agent onto his broad shoulder. By the time he reached the flyer, she was able to command the doors to open. In one movement, Victor hurriedly dove headfirst with Coulthard into the back seat row, pushing his way in beside her.

Slipping into the pilot's seat, Leonard addressed Victor in the back. "You sure you want me to take stick? This is only the second time I've flown since squelching."

"When you put it like that, I'm not so sure. How did it go the first time?"

PRIMED

"It came back to me pretty fast. I don't think my passenger thought much of it, though."

CHAPTER SIXTEEN: OPERATION WIPEOUT

"*What shall we do with the drunken sailor*, Colonel?" Martinez poked the slack face of Agent Coulthard, meeting with no response.

"Normally I'd cut her loose with her handroid in *Little Greece*, but we can't have her showing up on the network before extraction. *I'll* kill her."

Their initial decision was to get off world, head for the frontier, away from any GUNEs, and try to make contact with O.A.C.I., or whatever was really left of it.

"Wait, Sir, I have another idea." Everyone looked at Leonard. Her mind was racing, trying to put together everything they'd discovered from dry-cleaning Agent Coulthard. Kochansky was still combing through the residuals at the far end of the storage container, trying to glean any extra useful intel from the woman's long term memories.

"Let's go over what we know: Coulthard's working alone on some nasty Black Op's shit. She has a senior controller in the agency, the only other person who knows what she's up to."

"As far as *she* knows. This kind of shit rolled all the way down from the top of the hill, if you ask me," said Victor.

"Mmm. With maximum deniability, of course." Evagora had a firm grasp of the operating methods of a chain of command in such situations, and how it could easily be broken at any link to protect those higher up.

"Still, Director Chin's the only other S.A. incriminated. The only one we might tangle with, locally."

"You lookin' to tangle, Leonard?" Martinez asked.

"*Yeah*, I'm lookin' to tangle! These fuckers have been playing us for two years! Had us running around, chasing our own tails like a pack of hounds while they back-pat themselves all the way up to their four-stars for getting us to do the dirty work *for* them."

"What's your plan, Major," Evagora asked, forcing her back on topic. Leonard took a deep breath, assembling her thoughts.

"Now we know how they've been supplying us with the genetic material and *.psy* files for cloning: they have hardstores right here on A.C.P. For all we know, the only complete hardstores in the *galaxy* since UNE raided our corporate HQs." Pasqualé and Kochansky were nodding in silent concurrence. "What would that mean to O.A.C.I., if we could recover the samples *and* data?"

"Assuming we could establish a secure cloning facility, we could rebuild the entire fighting force from scratch, with sufficient time," Evagora speculated.

"Whoa, we're talking close to a million clones. That would have to be *some* facility," Pasqualé interjected.

"My plan is we go in to the UNESA building, get the samples and the files and *then* get off planet."

Martinez, arms folded, wondered aloud "How are you gonna get into the building? It's got the tightest security on the planet, *and* it's crawling with S.A.s." He sounded professionally curious, rather than discouraging.

Leonard looked over at the immobile, sedated body of Agent Coulthard. Kochansky had electronically extracted her memories via remote stimulation of her nano-plant, streaming the retrieved memories to the UNESA equivalent of a *.psy* file. It was a much cruder process than that used to create a *.psy* file save point for an O.A.C.I. operative's lifetime of accumulated experience and knowledge. The S.A.s called it *dry-cleaning* because it left the hyper-stimulated neural pathways relating to episodic memory in a damaged state, but left implicit and even semantic memory functions intact. On rare occasions, dream-like fragments of autobiographical knowledge might return over time, but most often a person would recover no memory of their former life.

"*She* could get me in."

"She's not in any shape to get anyone in anywhere. Even herself!" Martinez protested.

"Not yet. But if you put me *inside* her...."

"Leonard, if you're suggesting what I think then the answer is no. It goes against the Indoctrinal Trust Pact to subject your psyche to another person's body," Evagora ruled.

"Look at me, Colonel. It's already been done: this is *not my body*! UNE trashed the Pact when they cloned us."

"Okay, I take your point. But Kochansky just finished frying Coulthard's memories out of her brain: I don't think there's much grey matter left in there to use. What makes you think we could fit your *.psy* file in there without some serious spillage? We can't count on you being functional in that body."

"She couldn't do it, Colonel. She's not really prepared for the neural shock of trying to think through a brain with a completely different set of wiring," Kochansky called back to the group from his seat.

"There, our expert has spoken."

"But *I* could." They all stared at Kochansky in surprise.

"I've already gone through that process, when I was revived in *this* body. The neural pathways in this brain were radically different. It was a bit like trying to recover from a stroke, finding new ways to navigate thoughts through unfamiliar pathways. I can do it again. Plus, I just spent the last hour going through this woman's long term memories. I know most of what she knew, at least the good stuff."

"There's a big difference between what you went through during revival and transferring your psyche into another person's body, Kochansky. It's never been done before." Evagora's cool demeanor was slipping, responsibility for his subordinates showing through.

"I really don't see it that way, Sir. And actually, the first *.psy* file transfer ever made *was* to another person's body." This gave Evagora pause for thought.

"You're talking ancient history, Kochansky. And that guy was psychotic."

"He was like that *before* the transfer. And he *did* go on to become one of the leading philosophers and civil rights advocates of the last century."

"Wouldn't it bother you?" Victor asked. "Being inside a woman's body?"

"No, Victor. Unlike you, I *do* have some experience in the matter."

"What!? I get *plenty* of action, you dorky piece of –"

"Cool it, *Maverick*, I just meant it'll be like streaming a woman's avtog feed. What's the difference? You sense what she senses, feel what she feels."

"The difference is you can terminate the feed any time you want to," Pasqualé pointed out.

"I've spent as much as forty-eight hours straight streaming female feeds from weekend *tog-a party* sites with full immersion. Well, maybe *straight* isn't the right word to use. But my point is, I can handle it."

"Fucking nerd perverts," said Victor, shaking his head judgmentally.

"Most of the time, yes," retorted Kochansky, with a cheeky grin.

"Man, you are fucked up."

"*Different strokes*, Victor. *Lots* of different strokes!"

"If we do this," Evagora took charge of the conversation, "what... *arrangements* do you want to make for your current body."

Kochansky stared at him blankly for a moment. "Are you still talking about the Doctrine? With all due respect, Sir, Leonard's right: it's out the window. Don't terminate *me* just 'cause I download my *.psy* file to a second body. You need me as I am if we're gonna get out of this shit heap alive. Besides, there's already two of each of you running around A.C.P., why not a second *me*?"

"'Cause no sorority would ever be safe again? Colonel, he's right. We could definitely use an extra pair of hands. And if you want my professional medical opinion, I think he's good to go," Pasqualé said to Evagora. "But what about the brain damage and potential conflict with the residual personality?" she asked Kochansky.

"Multiple inscription passes. I'll out-write her. With live control, I can try to work around some of the fried synapses, get as much of the necessary data into her brain as possible. Keep any spillage on the handroid as a virtual neural network simulation, and maintain the interface to sustain a consolidated identity."

"That is the most fucked up shit I ever heard, Kochansky. Are you really talking about keeping half your brain on a computer?" Victor asked.

Kochansky shrugged. "I've had my *whole* brain stored on a computer already. We all have. What did you think a *.psy* file *was?* I really don't see the problem."

"I would have to see it to believe it, Kochansky. We've got no way of knowing if what you propose will really work, and how..." Evagora looked awkward for a moment as he sought the right word: "*functional* you might be in this agent's body. Leonard, if you're going to persuade me to go with this plan then now is the time. Let's hear what you have in mind," Evagora insisted.

"With Kochansky going in? Uh – he's not a field agent, he's a technician. And like you said, we don't know until he tries the download whether it'll work, or if Agent Coulthard here will become a vegetable! *Assuming* it works, I'll get his back in case he needs help to the E.P. The rest of you get to the port, get us all transit passes and go through the security checks. Don't wait for us. Get into orbit, split up and head for the frontiers. Try to make contact with the *real* O.A.C.I. and notify the rest of us if you're successful. Post a book review on StillGoodReads, uh... Star Wars, The Last Jedi. Use the word *prime* in the text."

"Colonel? Major?" Everyone turned to look at Victor, whose quiet call for attention was very much out of character. "There's no way we'd get a million distinct genetic samples through customs, let alone that amount of hardstored data. And don't forget that four of us are tagged as augments. Only Kochansky and Pasqualé have any chance of getting off this rock. I have another suggestion. A modification of Major Leonard's plan, really. These UNE motherfuckers have us chasing ourselves, right?" Everyone nodded at Victor. "Leonard here even found her... *self.* That means there's a version of me out there, or UNE wouldn't have revived *me.* And there's an original Martinez, and an Evagora, too. Maybe even a Kochansky and a Pasqualé, we dunno. Maybe others, all right here in Godsgood.

"I say we go with Major Leonard's plan, everyone make a break for it at the port, but only as a smoke screen to cover Kochansky and Pasqualé. Except for me. You get the genetic storage medium and the *.psy* file hardstore to me, and I'll do what I was revived to do: I'll find myself, make contact with the O.A.C.I. operatives we *know* are *here already*! Give *them* the genes and the *.psy*'s. If they've gone this long without getting caught – if UNE have to pull a stunt like *us* to catch them – then I'm betting their still connected, that they can keep the goods *safer* than us, use it *better* than us. What do you think?"

There was a long pause as everyone mulled over the proposal. Leonard finally made the call: "I think that's better than chocolate, Victor. Guys?" Looking from one to another, each nodded their approval. Evagora listened with his head lowered, deep in thought.

"Martinez, what happens to the waste from the port?"

"Sir? It goes the same place as the trash from the rest of the city: the automated disposal conduits convey bagged garbage through the undercity to the municipal waste treatment facility east of the port. Then it gets sorted for recyc', pedosynthesis or incineration. Why?"

Turning from Martinez, Evagora put an arm around Victor's shoulder, pulling him close. "Victor, you're going to need a little detour...."

∞

Her grey eyes fluttered open, pupils contracting in the light from the adhesive fluorescent panel stuck to the metallic ceiling above.

"Hey there, soul sister, how're ya doin'?" Kochansky leant over her, showing gentle concern. The woman smiled, facial muscles twitching erratically before settling into the unaccustomed expression.

"Not too bad, all things considered. Thanks for askin', handsome. Should I try to sit up?"

"Here, I'll help you. You'd better take it slowly." Kochansky slid a hand under the arm of whatever had become of Agent Coulthard, and guided her to a safe sitting position.

"Whoa. Thanks, Aaron."

"You're welcome, *Aaron*," Kochansky said, with a faint smile on his lips.

"Huh. That's sweet. But I don't *feel* like an *Aaron*: almost, but not quite. Besides, it would get kinda confusing if everyone calls *me* Kochansky, and *you* Kochansky.... Why don't you keep calling me *Curly*?"

"Okay, Curly, you're the man. Well, er... you know. D'you think you can stand?"

"Only one way to find out, loverboy. Help an old lady up, would ya?" Moments later, Curly was on her feet, politely declining further support. She didn't look the same as she had during Leonard's interview at the port, when she'd claimed her name was *Dunn*, nor at the radial connector. All the features were the same, but the expression, the mannerisms, were different. More *Kochansky*. She started to shuffle around, limbs jerking like a marionette's. "This might take a while."

With everyone staring at her, Curly Kochansky evidently couldn't resist putting on a show, abruptly striking a broken robot pose before pulling off a rather rusty-looking moon-walk across the steel floor of the storage container. "Oops, that was reverse. Ha ha! Just let me get back in gear, here." Curly took a few tentative steps forward again, looking considerably more natural, and within a few minutes had her limbs mostly under conscious control, if moving a little stiffly. Pacing over to Evagora, who had been following the progress with a critical eye, he snapped a smart salute and announced "Information Technology Specialist, Curly Kochansky reporting for duty, Sir!"

"At ease, Specialist Kochansky. I don't recall a *Curly* Kochansky ever enlisting."

"I'm a new recruit. Volunteering for active duty now, Sir."

"I see. I hope you don't mind submitting to Specialist Pasqualé for a medical evaluation?"

"Not at all, Sir."

"Okay, Curly, let's take a look at you." Pasqualé called her over to her improvised med' station, where she proceeded to hold up fingers for Curly to count, tested her reflexes, sensitivity to sensory stimuli, pupil dilation responses and long term memory recall.

Evagora signed for the operatives to gather around him. In hushed tones, he addressed them: "It looks like we have a mission. A *real* one, this time. I know a lot's changed, that normal operational protocols might not seem to apply, but I want to stress that one thing stays the same: the mission is more important than our lives. Our success here could be decisive in reviving the O.A.C.I. war effort. For that reason, everyone carries their Blue Option on their person at all times. I've also taken the liberty of breaking out our stock of EDs." He indicated crates of remote detonators and plastic explosives beside the container door. "Use them to create maximum disruption and distraction, cover our tracks as we make a pretend break for orbit. If we're not coming back, we may as well go out with a bang. Or twelve. Cover your apartments, vehicles... be creative.

"Before anyone goes anywhere, report to Kochansky and get your *.psy* files uploaded. Even if we don't *survive* this mission, I don't want to *lose* anyone. If we can pull this off, I give you my *personal assurance* that anyone losing life in the line of duty *will... be... revived.*

"Leonard, you take good care of Curly. I don't pretend to know exactly who or *what* she is, but she's one of us, now. Don't let UNESA get their hands on her." Leonard nodded. "Martinez, if our technicians are going to make it into orbit, we need you to take rearguard at the port undercover. I've asked Victor to support you. Get yourselves in position, and wait for the shit to hit the fan. Leonard, before they go, give Victor some pointers on how you found your double: anything you think might help him find his man." Raising his head from the huddle he called out "Kochansky." Both Aaron and Curly turned to look at him. Evagora diplomatically resolved the dilemma: "The earlier version. You're with me. I need you to take care of everyone in the field; get their *.psy* files updated now. We go to the port together, and wait for Leonard and Curly. You too, Pasqualé."

In unison, Kochansky and Pasqualé responded "Yes, Sir."

Evagora looked around at the assembled team for a moment in silence. "You are, without a doubt, the most cunning, ingenious and truculent bunch of bad-ass motherfuckers I've had the *good fortune* to serve alongside. Well, what are you standing around for, you've got your orders!?"

They broke up, Martinez heading for Kochansky and the recording of his long term memories, Victor and Leonard taking seats around the folding table to discuss her success in tracking Watson.

"Leonard, can I ask you something?" Victor leant in, intimately.

"Sure."

"Am I really *truculent*?"

CHAPTER SEVENTEEN: OPERATION THIN AIR

The body-heat drizzle was starting up again, beading on the hydrophilic treatment of her wicking layer and heralding the close of the day on Alpha Centauri Prime. Soon it would build to its typical torrent, and proceed into the evening, making the day's third shift change particularly harrowing.

The chronometer continued counting well beyond the agreed time on her arhud. If Curly didn't emerge soon, they risked losing the advantages of waning light and the covering rush of workers heading to and from their central workplaces, eyes down and umbrellas up in the rain.

Dressed as a non-descript plaza courier, carrying the backpack Kochansky had given her to house the device she'd constructed from the two dismantled hovertrunks, she made another random jogging circuit away from the plaza around the UNESA HQ to further defer the interest of the authorities. She noted the build-up of foot traffic from the outskirts of the tower district where the building was located, as workers headed into the low level shipping district in advance of their shifts. For now, current shift workers were still contractually bound inside their workplaces, but soon they would be released in a torrent of their own, rivers of humanity pouring homeward, to loved ones, or to bars and clubs to salvage the remains of the day from periodic productivity.

Her route had taken her a few blocks into the shipping district, beyond the perimeter of the UNESA nen screen, when she got the text, a pulsing, warning light on her arhud: *Problem at work, stuck in the office – can u order 4 me?*

'Shit. Okay, Curly, one main course coming right up.' An instant later, she'd nenned a text to Pasqualé: *Hey, P, can I borrow ur flike while ur out of town?*

She was already running for the port mooring lots when she received the affirmative reply, the authorising transfer and key codes to activate the flike with her own 'jacked handroid.

PRIMED

As the rain grew heavier, she found herself splashing through deepening puddles as the water accumulating on her garment ran and joined into rivulets, driven up her forearms and around her torso by the wind of her own passage. Following the indicator to Pasqualé's flike, she nenned it into operation even as she straddled the spartan padding that passed for a flight seat.

With only two sets of Casimirs, positioned fore and aft, the flike relied on the gyroscopic effect of side-oriented intake fans for the manoeuvring thrusters to improve its vertical stability. Forcing the vehicle into flight before it was fully spun-up made for a wobbly take-off, but Leonard was soon speeding towards the UNESA tower block, negating traffic control flight path demands as they popped up every few seconds on her arhud while struggling one-handed to don the flike goggles and facemask Pasqualé had left in the lockbox. Pasqualé's retro flike tastes meant this vehicle offered no virtual interface options: mechanical controls only. The only use for a handroid on *this* flike was to get flight permission from the traffic control D.A.I. so the plates and turbine could be charged, and receive the traffic signals and flight path stream.

Eventually she was forced to enter a destination at the threat of remote vehicle deactivation, with the designated flight path circling two blocks to the south of the no-fly zone surrounding the building where Curly had let cry for help.

"Okay, Curly, where are you." Only her op's terminal could locate Curly's G-PIP in the tower's mid-levels, on the west side. It also revealed thousands of handroid presences throughout the building.

Negotiating with the D.A.I. for altitude, she was soon well above the height of the tower, and reaching the closest approach when Curly streamed her a full avtog feed from her op's terminal, military-grade encryption protecting the content of the communication but starting the countdown to triangulation as the Internal Communications Security D.A.I. identified a foreign encryption algorithm on the network, and began processing location indicators. It was strange to hear Aaron Kochansky's voice sound in her mind when she knew the source was Curly. Evidently, that's how she imagined her own voice.

"Are you getting this?" Curly streamed a full panoramic view of her location. She was in a partitioned section on the twenty-third floor. Leonard quickly assessed the situation: heavily reinforced security walls to either side isolated the floor segment, and laminated bombproof transparencies thirty centimetres thick replaced the normal glazing separating the archive room from the atrium. The only access point was via an electro-magnetically floated footplate conveyor traversing a high-security conduit extruded from the same material that comprised the atrium glazing. The anachronistic use of magnetic repulsion justified the laying of exposed high voltage wiring along the length of the floor: any attempt to cross the conduit without using the footplate would result in contact with the wiring and electrocution. It was an archive room: a vault. It looked very much as though the room and its contents would survive the destruction of the rest of the building.

Focussing on her hands, Curly showed Leonard she clutched an alumalloy case. The *Biological Material* indicator suggested she'd retrieved the O.A.C.I. Operatives Matrix. Dozens of flexi-drives were stuck to the lid of the case, indicating that with Kochansky's memories and I.T. skills partly downloaded into her damaged brain, and the simulated remainder of his persona residing in virtual limbo on her active handroid, Curly had successfully obtained the data files they sought, and neatly combined the two items into one.

Agent Coulthard's biometrics had allowed Curly easy access to the building and archive room. Her D.N.A., fingerprints, retinal scans, D.A.I. monitored nen screening: everything had checked out, where even a clone would have failed due to minor variations accrued during cellular growth. Getting in hadn't been the problem. Getting the *.psy* mainframe and OACIOM hadn't been the problem. Getting out of the room *with* them was the problem. The OACIOM would trigger the bioscanners in the conduit, and that amount of data would trip the File Size Evaluator D.A.I.

Victor had been right: if Curly couldn't even get the material out of the archive room, there was little chance of any of them sneaking it through spaceport security checks, which used the same technology and methods for counter-terrorism.

'I've got a plan. I just need you to take the case at the other end of the security conduit' Curly nenned.

'How are you going to get through without raising the flags?'

'I'm not. I'm kinda counting on causing a bit of a commotion. I need you to get here as fast as you can, grab the case and get out of here.'

'Okay. What about you?'

Curly's ears picked up the sound of a klaxon from the lobby beneath, the avtog stream conveying the sound to Leonard. Both heard the

PRIMED

I.C.S.D.A.I. announcing "Unknown communications encryption detected. Tactical Security Personnel, deploy to twenty-third level atrium."

Curly looked at her own reflection in the thick, light-distorting glazing, and beamed a poignant smile at herself. 'Don't worry about me. I have my own way out.' The effect endowed the scene an otherworldly quality, as though she saw Curly in a dream. 'Hurry, Leonard: they're coming.'

Curly opened the airlock door into the security conduit. Stepping out onto the floating conveyor plate, waited for the door to close and the platform to slide her through the numerous scanners lining the walls of the conduit.

"Unauthorised bio-material detected. Tactical Security Personnel, deploy to twenty-third level atrium, Archive Room security conduit airlock." Inside the conduit, Curly shook her head and laughed.

"That was a boring flight path, anyway," Leonard announced as she twisted the flike's controls to veer through the prohibited air-space, gunning for full throttle.

Within seconds, the Traffic Control D.A.I. flagged her. Its synthetic tones, preternaturally calm and soothing, informed her: "Warning, you are entering a no-fly zone: turn back to the designated flight path immediately, or you may be subject to enforcement action." As it crooned, Leonard took the time to stick her 'jacked handroid to the flike's fairing. Without skipping a beat, the D.A.I. continued its scripted monologue: "Warning, you are in violation of traffic control regulations: your vehicle's flight controls will be overridden and commandeered by this intelligence in: three..." Leonard primed the detonator on the explosive device Pasqualé had planted inside the flike, selecting the proximity detector activation setting, still steering and throttling in the direction of the UNESA tower. "Two..." She popped up to stand on the seat of the flike as if it were a surfboard, eyeing the roof of the tower beneath her. "One..."

Without waiting for the end of the countdown, Leonard ran along the front of the flike, jumping forward with all her strength just before the Casimir plates in the nose. The anti-gravity updraft above the plates gave her a vertical boost, and she sailed forwards, angling her body to reduce drag. Behind and beneath she heard the D.A.I. conclude its threat: "Zero." As she started to freefall, she could hear the dying whine of the flikes plates and turbine as the D.A.I. appropriated control of the vehicle, throttling down and turning it away from the Security offices. "Please remain calm. You are being escorted to the nearest enforcement checkpoint, where you will be...." The soothing voice was lost in the rising sound of rushing air as Leonard accelerated downwards in A.C.P.'s gravity well.

Curly's avtog stream continued to feed. Leonard heard the building's security D.A.I. make another announcement, as Curly's viewpoint continued to move along the security conduit. "Unauthorised hardstorage of data exceeding file size restrictions. Tactical Security Personnel, deploy to twenty-third level atrium, Archive Room security conduit airlock." Curly joined in with the second sentence in a mocking tone. By now, armed responders in helmets and anti-ballistic vests were beginning to gather at the airlock door at the far end of the conduit.

Leonard watched the rooftop beneath her grow larger in her field of vision as the silently falling raindrops around her seemed to slow, then hang in relative motionlessness around her for an instant before completing the miraculous illusion of falling upwards, raindrops that had passed her by but moments ago on their downward journeys being passed in turn, slowly at first, then faster and faster as her downward acceleration took her beyond their terminal velocity.

Reaching her hands behind her back, she thrust them into the circular shell of her backpack through incisions she'd made in its seams, feeling for the grip points she'd welded into place. With a downward jerk, the device inside tore free of the backpack, the two hovertrunk sections pivoting out behind her, their connecting crossbar locking into place as she extended her arms, simultaneously pulling the tether cables taught, activating the Casimir plates within the two disk sections at either end of the crossbar. Sparking blue light reflected back at her from thousands of slowing raindrops as she drew the crossbar under her buttocks, along the back of her thighs and calves until she could clear the bar with her heels, and plant her feet squarely onto the auto-sealing stomp pads on the crossbar.

Still diving head first towards the rooftop, she felt the strain of deceleration pushing up through her limbs as she locked them over her head, the improvised hoverboard pushing back against A.C.P.'s gravity at full power, shifting her fall forward, over the rooftop perimeter towards the central atrium. Levelling off her descent, she was able to stand up with the board beneath her, quickly locating and connecting with the LANlinks wired into the Casimir plate controls. The board's rudimentary controls sprang into virtual existence on her arhud, and she deftly used them to reduce the anti-gravitational uplift, preventing her from bobbing upwards again. Pressing down with her toes, she tilted the board so that she slid

PRIMED

forwards through the air, clearing the atrium's anti-scale wall, and peered down through the heart of the tower at the downwards-spiralling web of walkways crossing the central void. Security lights were springing on throughout the atrium. From Curly's feed, competing for attention with her own perceptions, she was able to determine that Curly had reached the outer airlock door. A team of eight T.S.P.'s, looking extremely disgruntled, waited for the airlock door to open, levelling their weapons at Curly through the bullet-proof window.

As the airlock door opened, the senior guard started barking commands at Curly: "Agent Coulthard, put the case down slowly, put your hands behind your head and lie face down on the floor!"

She heard Curly's nen command, recognising it immediately as the one she had just given to the flike bomb. Curly stepped out of the conduit through the outer airlock door, a pulse of red light surrounding her as the D.A.I. announced the results of its latest discovery: "Warning! Explosive device activations detected. All personnel, evacuate, level twenty-three archive room and atrium priority."

The confusion on the guards' faces, many of whom had just arrived after being repeatedly told to go there, was visible even through their anti-ballistic face-plates. Drawn weapons faltered, and as Curly's feed streamed her hugging the case to her chest and bending down to lie on the floor, Curly and Leonard heard the first cry of the guard:

"It's on her back! Fall back, fall –"

With a bright flash of light, a roaring boom and the briefest sensation of an impact from above, like something heavy falling on her where she lay on the floor of the walkway, the sensory stream from Curly abruptly ceased. Her op's terminal futilely tried to re-establish the link before finally announcing *connection lost* on her arhud

Her own top-down view was obscured by the intervening walkways, but she saw the double flash of the explosions reflected around the glass walls bounding the atrium, windows around and above the detonation points blown in, lights extinguished, a rising ripple passing through the rest of the building's quartztic facade, bringing the sound of the distant blast to her ears seconds later.

When active, the hoverboard had a minimum anti-gravitational force output that would slow her descent, so instead of dropping down through the atrium on the board with the falling leaf technique, she equalised the plate-perpendicular force vectors and brought her feet up under her to sit on the crossbar, lining up the Casimir plates with A.C.P.'s mass attraction. 'Twelve-point-two-four metres per second squared....' she reminded herself, setting the right and left plates to accelerate her forwards at slightly different rates by a series of rough calculations. As she fell, picking up speed, she tweaked the outputs to match the spiral of the walkways, corkscrewing down through the tower with quartztic and metal railings whipping by her faster and faster, counting down each as another floor descended. At the twenty sixth floor, she snapped her legs straight out at forty-five degrees, feeling the kick-back as vertical force vectors came back into opposition, horizontal and angular vectors countering her helter-skelter ride.

Beneath her, the scene of Curly's self-sacrifice span into view around the central elevator shaft. Guards were down, most still moving weakly on the rain-soaked surface. The two closest to Curly's body were smoking from their knees up, chest armour and face plates charred. Clearing the top of the walkway's side rail, she disengaged the bond on the stomp pads and dropped lightly down, grabbing the floating board by its crossbar.

Kicking weapons away from the wounded, scattering them off the walkway through the drainage gap beneath the alumalloy and quartztic railings, she approached Curly. One guard more dedicated to duty than his colleagues made a lunge to grab for her ankle, which she side-slipped away from, chambering the leg he'd reached for to deliver a side-kick to his helmet; the guard's head whip-lashed as he collapsed.

Through the archive room's window she could see the destruction caused by the detonation of Curly's second explosive. The confinement of the blast by the thick walls had concentrated the device's damage potential in the small space, obliterating traces of evidence of her theft along with terabytes of hard-stored informant reports on the mainframe there, which had been presumed safe inside the armoured vault.

Turning her attention to Curly, Leonard noted that her body was un-burnt, like the lower legs of the nearby guards. The explosive device she'd detonated from her back had been a directional one, the thermal discharge occurring over a slightly-less-than-hemispherical arc. It wasn't likely Curly expected to survive the blast, given Kochansky's technical knowledge. The recoil and point-blank concussive force of the blast had killed her almost instantly. But it wasn't her *body* she was trying to preserve.

PRIMED

Turning Curly over revealed a flow of blood from her nose and mouth from massive internal bleeding. Her eyes were bloodshot, the compression wave radiating from the blast travelling through the gel of her tissues, bursting the finest of blood vessels there. It was an indicator of similar, fatal damage to the brain, synapses and avtog scaffolding alike torn apart, resulting in the abrupt feed disconnection she'd experienced. Her arms were still wrapped loosely around the metal case, the object of preservation. A mess of flexi-drives, presumably stuffed with data Curly had hacked out of the mainframe before its destruction, had been plastered across the lid. Leonard stood, the handle of the case in her left hand.

A fist-sized piece of quartztic railing panel beside her was suddenly punched out, accompanied by a flat cracking sound. She heard the sound wave from the gun an instant later, then its echoes reverberating around what was left of the atrium walls, confusing the direction of the shot. Rather than wait for a second shot to place her attacker, she ran. There was only one place to go: the central elevator shaft.

A second round struck the walkway ahead of her. Resisting the instinct to draw back, flinch, she threw herself through the line of fire and slid into the open elevator locked off by the guards now lying in various states of consciousness on the walkway behind her. The structurally reinforced quartztic of the elevator shafts provided good protection against inclined fire, several bullets ricocheting off the wall behind her, chipping off chunks but failing to penetrate. Through the transparent wall at the back of the elevator car, she could see two other cars converging on her level from below, each carrying six more armed responders. Rolling over, she saw a third elevator approaching from above, its opaque floor concealing any occupants. A muzzle flash from a walkway three floors up accompanied another smashed chunk of wall, pinpointing her would-be assassin.

By now, Curly's handroid would have been locked out of building activation systems by the D.A.I., and the elevator certainly wouldn't respond to any command she gave it. Climbing back atop her board, she punched out the emergency access panel in the ceiling and boosted herself up through it with the board, angling it to fit through the narrow square opening.

She slipped a detonator from her utility belt, jammed it into a block of explosive clay from her jacket and slapped it against the inside surface of the elevator shaft wall, where it stuck, before cranking the board's plates all the way up, feeling the smooth acceleration of the board as it pushed her up through the core of the elevator shaft.

She nenned the proximity detector activation code to the detonator, closely followed by the D.A.I.'s announcement: "Warning! Explosive device activation detected. Overriding elevator cars bound for level twenty-three atrium."

Drawing her handgun from the small of her back, she rotated the board to present her right side towards the shooter and extended the gun in her right hand at eye level, mimicking the ancient duellists' pose to present the narrowest target profile.

She counted down the floors: 'two...' another bullet from the shooter tearing a chunk from the outside of the wall, 'one...' the next round fired at such a shallow angle that it succeeded in smashing a piece of the wall inwards, but was so badly deflected, and its kinetics so dispersed, that it had no further capacity to cause injury, then 'zero!' As her head and shoulders cleared the new floor she squeezed off three rapid shots in a tight spread through the bottom of the closed doors directly to her right, the rounds coursing the length of the walkway that extended from the elevator to the far side of the building. The material of the doors was thinner than the walls, and didn't stand up nearly so well against flat trajectory fire, her bullets punching small, neat holes in a rising diagonal line through the quartztic. At the end of the walkway, a blue-suited figure ducked and dived sideways against the railing, evading the scattered volley but breaking his aim.

Spinning to face the descending elevator car, she opened up through the floor, her arhud bullet count needlessly reminding her of the remaining rounds: *7;6;5;4;3;2;1;0.*

She was already ejecting the empty clip, letting it fall down the shaft beneath her, and replacing it with a fresh magazine when the elevator slid past, six armed responders still sliding down the blood-sprayed walls of the car, either dead, dying or too concerned with their own injuries to respond to the sight of their assailant streaking past them towards the roof. Even the two wearing body armour and helmets hadn't fared well against the onslaught, the steep angle effectively negating the head-on threat protection it was designed for, as Leonard's shots tore up through lower abdominal entry wounds and under the armour into vital organs.

Muzzles flashed all around her from Security Agents manning the walkways of the upper levels, a spiral of light panning around her, accompanied by the staccato cracks of bullets smashing against the wall of the elevator shaft, like hail on a tiled roof. But she was moving too fast by now for anyone to take aim, and the structural quartztic was still serving her well for bullet resistance. She cleared the open top of the shaft, rocketing skyward, flipping her board out in front of her to push her backwards over the perimeter of the building and towards the shipping district side. It gave her a good view of the roof as she left it, so she saw the two agents burst out from the emergency stair hatch carrying rifles.

"Shit!" She had to keep the board active for a few more seconds to get enough horizontal velocity to clear the lip of the tower, at this parabola. The blue-white emissions from the plates presented a highly visible target in the darkening sky, and she saw them taking aim. To buy her the time she needed she squeezed off four rounds, more to put them off their aim than with any hope of hitting them under these conditions, but she saw one of the snipers spin away with her fourth shot striking his shoulder, and let off a fifth hastily in the direction of the remaining gunwoman, with no apparent effect.

Judging that she could clear the side of the building, she cut the power to the plates and they whined down to inactivity, their characteristic glow and electrostatic displays dimming to nothing in short order.

She saw the flash from the barrel of the rifle, felt the board buck against her left foot then heard the retort just as she tumbled below the roof of the tower. She was spinning slightly, pitching her over to fall head first, adrenalin coursing too much for her to tell yet if she'd been wounded.

In the city's shipping distance, stretching out beneath her towards the port, she picked out red flames licking at a low level warehouse building a few blocks away to the south-east. The Traffic Control D.A.I., true to its word, had brought Pasqualé's flike to a nearby enforcement checkpoint in the shipping district, to facilitate the apprehension of its operator. The explosive device had been detonated as soon as the flike reached ten metres from the ground, raining burning fragments down on the warehouse rooves beneath, further plunging the neighbourhood into chaos and hopefully helping to cover her tracks.

Quickly examining her legs and having received no pain indicators, she realised she hadn't been hit by the sniper after all. But there was a thumb-sized hole through the plastic disk covering the top of the left plate set, just a few centimetres away from her foot. She didn't dare reactivate her board yet, since the surviving shooter could easily run to the railing and fire down at her again, with much-improved chances of hitting a lit-up target straight-lining away from her. Instead, she returned her gun to its holster at the small of her back and angled her body in the air, taking advantage of aerodynamics to move her laterally, away from the sniper's expected aim-line, and stay close to the tower's external facade to prevent the use of the rifle's sights, unless the sniper was prepared to lean right out over the railing.

Only seconds later she was out of time. The plaza was already rushing up to meet her, and she had to reactivate the board to decelerate. Only the right plates lit up, the dark energy compressed between the punctured left plates having dissipated quickly, judging by the size of the hole. The sudden torque on the crossbar flipped her upright, and she had to disengage her right foot, wrapping that leg around the bar to pull herself down over the top of the functioning disks, gripping its rim two handed as its repulsive output buffeted her along with the rush of air through which she still plummeted. The case still flapped from its handle in her left hand.

There wasn't much hope of steering the damaged device, and any attempt to do so would reduce the device's decelerational capacity. So she hung on, watching the ground swell, angling for the plaza's central water feature. At the last moment she let go of the board along with her attachment to the last stomp pad, letting the anti-gravity updraft from the top of the plates give her an extra fraction of deceleration before the board, closely followed by her, splashed into the shallow pool around a sculpted fountain.

She must have blacked out, at least for a few seconds, because the case was floating a few metres away from her. The rushing sound of cascading water from the fountain matched the roar of her blood pumping. Stumbling through the chest-deep water, she grabbed the case and splashed inefficiently to the edge of the pool. She was barely able to claw her way over the molded concrete bund around it. Everything hurt. Flopping down onto the plaza floor like a wet fish in the bottom of a boat, she struggled to stand, staggering and clutching at plaza furniture to maintain balance. Gradually, her blurred vision re-focussed and her inner ear stopped spinning. She was able to recover her poise in time to make out the blue berets heading her way from the tower side of the plaza, signature headgear bobbing above the press of workers heading for the shipping district.

The impact with the pool had driven water into her flike goggles, and saturated the cloth covering her face, making it tortuous to breathe through. They had both served their purpose, and would now do more to aid UNESA in identifying her than continue to anonymize her, so she scraped them off her face and thrust them into her jacket pocket.

Quickly reorienting herself, she shuffled as fast as she could manage towards the shipping district, roughly shouldering aside startled pedestrians. The first line of low level buildings closest to the towers, known as *The Strip*, still provided novelty dining and retail services to the tower district. The Strip gave way to the inventory warehouses and packing facilities from which the hoverbarges and couriers loaded supplies meant for delivery amongst the superblocks and out to the 'burbs. These finally gave way to services centred on the port: the port's own mooring bays, flyer rental lots, and the bulk container storage yards and warehouses used in the import and export of goods via the Ladder.

Her op's terminal didn't have a single civilian G-PIP for the S.A.s to pinpoint, and wouldn't emit a *real* GP/t signal, either. Instead, it progressively hacked into an ever-shifting network of surrounding handroids, LANverts, info'casts and even traffic signals within range, using them to bounce-board encrypted and fragmented data packages that could only be decrypted and reassembled within her device upon receipt of the bounced, multiple signals. The only way they could track her remotely would be by isolating and triangulating her transmission requests.

Right now, though, they'd had line of sight and security camera footage, so it was a safe bet that they knew roughly where she was. Her identity should still be uncertain. UNESA should be struggling to piece together that puzzle, assuming they even connected the 'jacked droid from the flike to the aerial assault on their office.

The first tier of assumption would be that she'd abandoned her handroid on the flike, and was now ghosting. From UNESA's perspective this would continue to seem true as long as she maintained com silence, as any attempt at direct long range communication would shatter the illusion by providing a clear, traceable signal source, no matter how many different bounce-boards she scattered it to.

So the blueberries would be hunting a ghost. The safest place to hide would be in a crowd: every one of the rush-hour travellers pressing around her yielded a GP/t signal, and picking out the only one who didn't would be a time consuming process for even the most precise of D.A.I.'s, involving the correlation of each signal with a visually confirmed I.D. using facial and gait recogrithms. Each confirmation took time, especially under less-than-ideal lighting and weather conditions. In a shifting crowd like this, with new faces appearing as quickly as identified faces arrived at their destinations, dropping out of the crowd, the attrition rate of identities to be confirmed around her should be matched by fresh replacements, maintaining the low probability of her being identified. For as long as the two-way rush lasted. She just had to follow some simple rules to minimise her personal exposure to risk: no eye-balling cameras, and no recognisable walking pattern. UNESA probably had a pretty decent file size on *Angel Leonard*, by now, and could identify *her*. Since Leonard was bound by *.psy* file inscription to that body, it was effectively the same as being identified for who she *really* was (and even Leonard wasn't able to do *that*), with the same end result: identification, leading to dry-cleaning and/or death.

Leonard couldn't be sure *exactly* how long it would take Director Chin to make the connection between Agent Coulthard and her little Black Op's assignment, to pull the file identifying each and every one of her team members. But she was sure that sooner or later he would.

'Time for one last acting gig for Angel.' She joined a queue of workers heading through the perimeter gate of a nearby warehouse, pressing up against the man in front as he pushed through the turnstile so that she made it through on the same turn. She made sure to meet his suspicious, over-the-shoulder glare with a warm smile and an apology. When he saw there was no alarm from the gate, which detected no unauthorised G-PIPs on that turn, the worker relaxed and left her unchallenged.

The line of workers crossed a paved strip to the warehouse entrance. A security camera covered the door. This was as good a time as any. As she passed through the doorway, she affected a nervous backward glance, looking for the UNE militia trying to track her. She did spot three blue berets in the crowd outside the perimeter fence, but more importantly she presented a nice profile to the camera as she went through the well-lit and sheltered doorway.

Interfacing with her op's terminal, she put the finishing touches to a goose-chase program, using her current location, and unleashed the tethered G-PIP of Angel's handroid, which she'd left at her apartment in Marcus' keeping. The tether had dragged the handroid's allocated G-PIP around with her op's terminal, never more than a few hundred metres away. The pre-programmed goose-chase would cause the G-PIP to return along the relevant transit routes and interior corridors to the actual device, throwing a simulated auto-cab ride into the traffic control system for added realism. It was a misdirection to divert some part of UNESA and militia attention away from her real position, make them think she (the aerial attacker) may have handed off the stolen materials to an accomplice (Angel), tilting the odds of reaching the port in her favour.

She gave the S.A. D.A.I.'s an edu-guessed fifteen seconds to put the flags together for Director Chin. The flike shouldn't have been identifiable after its detonation, but there would be a network record connecting Pasqualé with Leonard's 'jacked handroid identity when she transferred the authorisation code for that flike. 'Not a great leap required to connect *those* dots. At least Pasqualé herself would be safe, at the port using another fake I.D.' If they were going to swoop on her, they'd go to her apartment: just like Leonard, she'd left her real handroid at her apartment with a nasty surprise for unwelcome visitors.

'So, what would Chin have? A dead Agent Coulthard, apparently somehow coerced into stealing classified former O.A.C.I. material instrumental in the implementation of a successful, top-secret but illegal and therefore politically sensitive counter-intelligence programme; a second infiltrator gaining access to said material moments after a flike, owned by a known participant in that programme, was turned back from the building's no-fly zone only to explode before its rider, if any by that time, could be apprehended; another known programme participant whose GP/t placed her in the vicinity of the incident detected in a workplace for which she was not authorised, making a sudden break for her apartment.'

She could only hope Chin believed they were all that stupid. That he'd order teams of GUNE's to all their known addresses, instead of determining their real objective and marshalling his forces to successfully lock-down and prevent their passage through the port.

And right now she needed to run. Peering through a window at the throng outside as she mulled over her situation, her keen military instincts piqued when she saw the laurels on the bobbing, blue berets turn about, their wearers animatedly yelling to each other and gesturing towards the warehouse she stood in.

Her arhud displayed *Angel Leonard's* GP/t heading out of the exit on the far side of the warehouse, directly away from the three GUNE's currently shoving their way through the people outside towards her. A line of workers finishing the previous shift filed out.

There were no other doors, but an alumalloy stairwell lead to an installed office platform above the warehouse work floor. 'Maybe a window...?' Walking briskly along the wall towards the stairs, she heard the commotion as the three GUNE's burst through the employees' entrance and raced across the work floor in pursuit of the virtual goose. With all eyes on their spectacle she was able to pass the uniformed shift supervisor un-noticed, and make her way up the stairs. The railings curved around the back of the manager's office, now on her left, with a series of doors on the right for janitorial storage and wetcubes.

Walking the length of the corridor, checking the wetcubes, she'd expected to find a window but the warehouse walls were unbroken. A sign on the janitors' closet suggested an exit, which turned out to be a ladder and hatch leading to the roof, presumably for maintenance purposes.

Entering the closet, closing the door behind her, she grabbed a set of navy-blue overalls, pulling them on over her shoes and covering her jacket. She was able to clip the OACIOM case onto a carabiner on her utility belt and zip the overalls up around it. It made a noticeably angular bulge at the crotch, but was no longer quite so obvious. It also left both hands free, and the overalls changed her appearance from that which was probably being circulated by UNESA and the local militia they directed. She shifted her pistol from the small of her back to the waistband of her pants at the front to make it more accessible, all the time taking inventory of the items around her – the usual cleaning supplies and equipment, tools for mechanical and electrical repair together with lengths of industrial electrical conduit and cable reels with a range of wiring gauges – before clambering up onto the roof using the rungs set into the wall.

'Well, I'm out. Now what?' She was close to a low lip which ran around the edge of the building, containing the precipitation that fell upon it. Somewhere, unseen, a drainage pipe carried the water from the flat roof to the under-city treatment system. She visualised the water's path, envied its ease of flow and escape from confinement. 'Huh. *Water treatment system*. No-one ever says *sewer* anymore. Just like no-one ever says *arm-pit*, except to describe any place other *than* an actual arm-pit. Now it's always *under-arm*. Just another sanitisation of our language, sterilisation of our thoughts.' It was the kind of realisation she'd usually find amusing, enough to make her issue a snorting laugh which she hoped people around her would dismiss as the result of her streaming some amusing avtog segment. But by the time the end of that train of thought rolled in to the station, she didn't feel like laughing anymore.

She peered over the roof. Nearly a six metre drop to the same narrow strip of concrete paving she'd crossed earlier, on the building's right hand side. She did a quick mental calculation: 'roughly two-and-a-half seconds air-time, at the end of which I'd be doing nearly five-and-a-half metres per second.' Nothing compared to her earlier feat in the plaza fountain. But then she'd still be inside the three metre fence, topped with a forbidding coil of razor-wire, facing security cameras, turnstiles and at least three GUNEs, probably more converging. Less than ideal. She ran her eyes around the fence, looking for her way out. 'There! A *lache*.'

Street furniture was a traditional accessory for parkour training. The sport encouraged its practitioners to look at their environment in a novel way. Where one of the many pedestrians below would see a simple pole supporting two street lights and security cameras, Leonard saw a way out. It was at the corner of the building, just outside the fence, where she wanted to be. The pole rose above the height of the fence by a couple of metres, with a horizontal crossbar on top forming a *T* shape, lights and cameras suspended from it. Getting to it was the problem. It was slightly lower than the rooftop, but not enough for her to jump the horizontal distance to it, and still catch the bar. Instead, she'd hit the razor wire and tear her hands, possibly even get tangled up in it. And still be on the inside of the fence.

'Anchor point – there!' A five centimetre hole passed through the bund, allowing water to drain through from the roof to a downpipe at the near corner of the building.

She went back to the janitors' closet, pulled out and snipped a suitable length of high voltage wiring from the largest cable reel, tied a graspable knot on one end, climbed back out and lowered the knotted end of the cable down the outside wall until it looked the right height from the ground. Then she pushed the other end of the wire through the drainage hole until it emerged from the near side of the bund. She bent it upwards with her other hand, looped it over the top of the bund and tied it securely together with the hanging section, using plenty of the spare metre of wire.

She walked away from the anchor point along the side wall, the ridged coating of the wire sliding through her hand until the knot stopped at her finger and thumb. Gripping the wire above the knot firmly with both hands, she leant back on the wire with her body weight, testing the stretch in the cable.

She sidestepped away from the edge of the roof until she was level with the street pole, just a couple of paces, and took a deep breath, holding it. 'Not too fast,' she cautioned herself. Holding the knot at full arms' length, leaning back a little on the wire to keep it taut, she slowly skipped sideways towards the edge of the roof. Her leisurely pace carried her off the edge, and she let herself fall. She'd imagined the pendulous path of that knot, *XYZTing* it, and her hanging off it as it swung through the air, two-and-a-half seconds down, two-and-a-half seconds up, then two-and-a-half seconds back down to crash into the bottom of the warehouse wall around the corner on the backswing. She didn't want to be on the end of that knot when that happened.

As she fell, the tension in the wire busily converted her vertical acceleration due to gravity into a horizontal acceleration vector, turning the dropping movement into a forward swing. After two-and-a-half seconds, the downward fall was complete, and she was whipping through the air level with the corner of the wall towards the perimeter fence. She began to swing up again, as she continued to move closer to the fence and razor-wire coil hanging on the outside of it. Needing to gain a few metres to the right before starting the backswing she threw a variation into the system of forces, pulling on the wire. When she eased off, the tension-equalising action in the stretched cable was enough to bounce her upwards a little, a relatively slight, whip-cracking effect on her trajectory so that she spent a fraction of a second more in the air, flicking her towards the street pole at the very end of her outward swing. Pumping her legs up beneath her, she released the cable, which started to fall back towards the warehouse wall. She continued to move forwards through the air, and sideways, her legs snapping out behind her to further propel her centre of gravity towards its objective, and at the last moment snapping her arms out to complete the *lache*, grabbing the crossbar at the top of the street pole with both hands.

The metal of the bar flexed under the force of her landing, like the arm of a bow bent to loose an arrow, springing up a moment later like a wild horse trying to throw her, the metal creaking and fixtures clanking conspicuously as lights and cameras were jarred out of alignment. Passersby looked up in alarm, the sudden, close clamour triggering their primordial survival instincts. She hung there, swinging and bouncing until the reverberations of her impact subsided enough for her to risk moving hand over hand to the central pole and slid down, wrapping her legs around the metal pole to slow her descent.

"Sorry, I was just fixing the camera when I slipped," she excused herself to the crowd. Several people gave her disbelieving looks, but they carried on about their business.

Through the air above the crowd she could see a troop transport floating ahead of her position, perhaps bringing reinforcements to cordon off the area until they found her. Switching her thoughts to sign language, she nenned to herself 'and maybe a nen screen'.

Quickly joining the self-assembled line of people heading away from the tower district, she kept her head down to avoid providing further detection opportunities for her adversaries. The going was slow, but a nen screen would certainly pick up the thoughts of the people around her if she started pushing her way through, and GUNEs would be despatched to investigate the disturbance and determine exactly why she was in such a hurry. So instead she shuffled along with the civilians, head down in the rain like everyone else.

Several minutes later, she received the incoming audio signal from her apartment door cam, shunted to her op's terminal by the handroid in Marcus' keeping. Quickly opening the stream, she caught the end of the address: "...ten seconds to open the door!"

She opened up the video stream, which revealed a standard five-person compliment militia squad, two backed up to her apartment wall, two flanking the corridor to either side and one standing in front of the door to make the address, all carrying assault rifles. The GUNE making the address had his weapon shouldered and aimed straight at the door's spy hole, a long suppressor screwed on to the end of the rifle's barrel. She eyed the togglicon for the speaker, and asked "Hello? Who is it?"

The marine in the hallway slid his eyes to the right for orders, and at the edge of the cam's fisheye view she discerned the nod from the squad's corporal. "Ma'am, this is P.F.C. Keller, Alpha Centauri Militia. We have a UNESA-issued warrant to search your property. Open up, in the name of the law."

'*Warrant*, my ass. What do you need the suppressor for if you're conducting a search?' she sign-asked herself, rhetorically. Marcus followed his programming, approaching the door with her handroid to give their G-PIP and motion detectors something to fix on. A second later, she swept her eye-point over the light admitter togglicon, darkening the spy hole to the outside.

The marine facing her twitched his finger reflexively, and she lost the feed as the bullet from his rifle tore through the spyhole. She had to guess the rest: the bullet, striking Marcus, made the android recoil enough for the marines to pick up his movement using their Doppler device. Their G-PIP locator would confirm the corresponding movement of her handroid, adhered to Marcus' leg. Noting their target injured, but not downed, they would smash down the door and storm the apartment, hoping to overwhelm the target with the element of surprise, superior numbers and firepower. Unfortunately for the militia squad, they wouldn't find the target of their assassination attempt, just a superficially damaged android butler. Perhaps one of them would check the wetcube. Perhaps one would even open the refrigerator to make sure she hadn't taken out the shelves to make a hiding space. Perhaps one would even ask "Hey, what's this cut in the android's gut? Looks like there's something in there –" But that's about all they'd have time for before Marcus detonated the explosive device she'd inserted into his abdominal gel.

With the hit squad down, it wouldn't take long for Director Chin to figure out he'd been played. Maybe they'd already paid a visit to Pasqualé's, following up the flike lead, getting a similar reception there. Each of them had taken two packs of plastic explosive and two detonators. Hers and Pasqualé's were accounted for. Evagora and Kochansky had similarly rigged their apartments aswell as the group's last safe-house storage container. Victor and Martinez had set their explosives according to their plan to thwart UNESA's efforts to reacquire the OACIOM and *.psy* database. For *that* plan to work, she had to get the case to the port.

The further she walked, the thinner the crowd grew, and the rain abated to a warm drizzle. Beyond the shade of the towers, the primary was sinking over the horizon, the salmon-pink bellies of the tropical storm clouds losing their hue as the sky darkened to full night. As the pedestrian numbers dwindled so too did the safety and cover they provided. Ahead, she spotted a bottle-neck, a throng of people building up at the next intersection. She raised her eyes without raising her head, scanning for the cause. It was difficult to see through the press of people, but there was a lot of extra light. Glimpses of a banded barrier and a flash of a helmeted soldier beyond soon told her what she needed to know: UNESA had set up a cordon, either around where they suspected she was or around the port, depending on how much of their plan Director Chin had managed to infer.

'The only thing this changes is the tempo' she reassured herself as she felt her adrenaline start to surge. She shuffled into the line along with the other pedestrians, allowing herself a normal degree of curiosity to evaluate the situation. Everyone would be doing the same, it would be out of place if she avoided looking at the hold-up. And they were sure to be operating a nen-screen.

Two blue-suited Security Agents were gene screening a line of grumbling workers they'd delayed on their way to work, in the direction of the spaceport. They had no interest in anyone travelling from the port outwards, allowing them to pass. They'd moored their flyer across the walkway to block it and buoycasted a luminous, orange and white chevron-striped virtual barrier, scrolling towards the inspection point to the right. Working her way over to the left hand side of the group, she spotted a greater threat over the top of the flyer: a squad of five Colonial Marines, wearing state-of-the-art anti-ballistic armour. They were well equipped, like Hardys, but they eschewed the use of UNE's blue headgear markings. This indicated they weren't working with the garrisoned militia, which was a UNE taskforce. They were part of A.C.P.'s own distinct military force, which weathered the controversy and official disapproval from Earth to genetically augment its personnel. They were also certainly trained to be more aggressive than their peacekeeper counterparts.

Their troop transport was moored across the plaza beyond the agents' vehicle, and the marines formed a casual-looking, but deadly, firing line. The transport's floodlights and active denial dish were trained on the plaza behind the agents. Their purpose was clear: to establish a kill zone in the plaza, and in the event of any loss of crowd control by the S.A.s to eliminate potential security threats, *A.K.A.* shoot anything that moved.

Without the added line of troops, her course of action would have been simple: crawl through the barrier and under the moored flyer, sneak away without being seen. Most people wouldn't do it because of the narrow clearance and fear of the CPs failing, the flyer falling and crushing them at any moment. Anti-gravity wasn't a new technology, but most people still preferred to see something visible and solid holding a heavy object up before they lay down under it. Most people *trying* to do it would get busted by their nenning: the agents would certainly pick up on the sensory stream of someone crawling under a flyer. That's where the nen discipline training came in, internal control over what your senses informed your consciousness. The most obvious thing to do would be to close your eyes before ducking down and make the crawl blind. This could be supplemented by any rich visualisation or internal thought process to so occupy the mind that the sensations would scarcely register, the mental equivalent of rubbing above an injury to confuse the pain signal to the brain.

She could certainly get past the Security Agents, only to be shot by the marines. This situation called for a lot more creativity. She edged her way back into the middle of the crowd, closing her eyes with her head lowered, allowing the press of bodies around her to slowly nudge her towards the front of the line, but used her op's terminal to scan the area for hardware interfaces. The flyer, a civilian vehicle at its core, showed up but the transport and terminals used by the marines were military-grade encrypted, as she would have expected. Even the Security Agents would have found them inscrutable, since their helmets incorporated nen-muting technology to prevent nen screens picking up their thoughts. She filtered out the dozens of handroids within her search radius, until she could identify the two carried by the agents via their GP/t signals.

She didn't need a full 'droid 'jack, just a very specific authorisation code. One of them would have it. The best way in was through the nen screen uplink they were both using, since she knew it was right there in the moored flyer, its G-PIP plain to see. She couldn't access its function, not without the authorisation code, but that wasn't even what she needed. Tracking back along the comlink, she investigated first one agent's handroid, then the other. There were a number of possible codes, so she copied them all before pulling out.

When she looked up, the agents had stopped the line with just one person between them and her, and were trying to locate the source of the stream she'd just generated. Her closed eyes had separated any recognisable visual perspective from her arhud activities, so while they had sensed someone within the range of the nen screen involved in what looked increasingly like some sort of hacking activity they weren't able to locate her position.

Staring hard at the back of the person in front of her, she ran through the codes she'd extracted, trying them one by one. Some would have been personal access codes for residences, lockers, privately owned vehicles. Some would have been the right class of code, but for other flyers in the pool, since S.A.s were only designated vehicles when needed.

The bland coat in front of her swept aside as the closest agent pulled its wearer out of the way, staring at her accusingly. She returned his glare innocently, as she tried the next code.

The agent drew his pistol, the civilian throng around the scene freezing instantly in well-practiced servility, and without taking his eyes off her turned his head slightly aside, opened his mouth to call his partner. At that instant the code was accepted and the moored flyer beside him thrummed to life, headlights dazzling, and lurched forwards as its turbines pulsed. It was certainly startling enough to make him look, and as soon as he did, Leonard ducked forward under his gun arm, catching his wrist with her left hand above her shoulder, planted her right foot behind the agent's legs and right-hooked a *shikan-ken*, a narrow profile, second knuckle punch, horizontally into his throat, flowing forwards with her shoulder into his ribcage, using her body weight and momentum to tip him over her leg.

As he fell backwards, the lunging flyer's front impact-rail struck his shocked partner in the knees, flipping him over the front of the vehicle and slamming his head into the windscreen. The flyer reversed thrust, gliding to a stop between Leonard and the marines, blocking their line of fire.

She slammed the agent she was grappling downwards. Unable to get his left arm back quickly enough to break his fall his head hit the floor hard. He was momentarily stunned, and almost certainly going to suffocate with a collapsed windpipe. But at that instant, he was still alive and conscious, a continued threat.

His stricken partner, sliding forwards off the curved fairing of the braking flyer, was caught in the updraft from the surging Casimir plates at the front edge, flipping him, legs first, into the air. Pin-wheeling, stunned and helpless, he sailed a few metres upwards, coming down to land heavily on the walkway in front of the flyer on the left hand side of his neck and shoulder, his head forced sideways with a sickening crack.

The glazed look was already clearing from the eyes of her sparring partner. Placing her knee against his shoulder and controlling the arm to fully extend, locking the elbow, she leant back and wrenched his arm out of its socket. The fingers clutching the gun spasmed, the agent's eyes bulging as much in muted agony as oxygen deprivation, and she easily wrested it from his grip.

The gull-wing door nearest her opened upwards at her nenned command. She vaulted into the flyer's front seats, with the door hissing shut behind her.

Through the flyer's far side window she could see the marines levelling weapons and advancing cautiously. They hadn't seen anything other than an inexplicable accident, but it didn't look like they were going to let that stop them from opening up. Without the militia training, which necessitated sensitivity towards civilians, the marines were left with the purer, undiluted military protocol of *shoot first, ask questions later*.

Behind her, the gathered crowd held up by the gene screen checkpoint started screaming and clawing, trampling over each other to get away. It was more than fear alone could have sparked: the marines had activated the transport's active denial system, the roof-mounted dish emitting low frequency microwaves over the targeted area of the checkpoint. Leonard was protected by the flyer's alumalloy plates, but the unshielded pedestrians were in excruciating pain, the microwaves penetrating just far enough into their skin to convince their nerve-endings that they were actually on fire.

"*Fuckers!*" It was a non-lethal weapon, but excruciatingly painful in application. Engaging the flyer's virtual manual interface, she slewed it sideways, watching with amusement the split second of indecision on the face of the marine she was surging towards, as he tried to decide whether to shoot or dive out of the way. Self preservation sensibly won out, and he scrambled aside.

The rear window was punched by several rounds from his colleagues, but she kept accelerating sideways. She hadn't been aiming for the marine, but that would have been a bonus if he'd decided to try out-chickening her.

The commandeered flyer slammed into the side of the marines' moored transport, knocking it sideways. She kept going until it came to rest, tangled up in the perimeter fence on the far side of the plaza. The targeted area of the transport's microwave dish moved with it, and now played over the firing line of marines to her right. It was their turn to howl with pain, the squad leader calling, shrilly, "Turn it off! Turn it *off*!"

She gunned the turbine, her dented and bullet-riddled flyer thrusting away from the scene, staying low as she banked around the nearest building for the cover of its wall.

She made it to the next intersection, where a sudden explosion erupted beneath her, with a tinny rattle of shrapnel peppering the underside of the flyer as it bucked up into the air. 'Twice in one day. Lucky, *lucky* me.' The marines had laid rows of surface-to-air micro-missiles around the checkpoint in a one block radius, a smart precaution against just this eventuality. They called them *stingers*, and their function was to target and rupture an overhead vehicle's Casimir plates, the only things maintaining the compression on the store of dark energy upon which the flyer, and any vehicle like it, relied for anti-gravity. At least this time she didn't have so far to fall, and she had a nice soft crash seat to sit in while she did it.

She barely had time to brace her head with her limbs before the flyer hit the ground, nose first, flipping over to land on its roof as it slid along the ground, tearing through a fence before grinding to a halt.

The gull-wing doors wouldn't open with the whole weight of the flyer resting on their mechanisms, so she had to finish the job the marines' volley had started, kicking out the side window to escape. Every extra kick, every moment lost, brought the pursuing squad of marines closer to her position.

Finally, the quartztic half broke, half bent out of the way, and she pushed herself feet first through the gap. As she cleared her head, she pulled herself upright by gripping the underside of the flyer, arms crossed, and spinning around as she stood to scan the walkway for her pursuers. As she did so, the first marine rounded the corner, dropped to one knee and brought his rifle to his shoulder, aiming for her protruding head.

PRIMED

Ducking down, she scrambled across the flattened fencing into the commercial premises the downed flyer had broken into, abruptly coming up short before a corrugated, red-painted steel wall. Instead of the warehouse she'd expected to see, she found a shipping container, two other containers stacked on top of it, an uneven line of varicoloured clones extending to the end of the lot some eighty metres distant. Checking the firing line behind her for duration of exposure to fire, she sprinted left, finding the end of the container as a hastily-fired round sent sparks flying from the wall of the container behind her with a metallic *ping*. She heard the bullet ricochet inside the container as she scuttled sideways through the end gap between it and its neighbour. On the far side, a ninety centimetre strip of concrete had been left between the rows for container inspections and clearance for antiquated side-grabbing lifters.

Sprinting as far as she dared before slipping between another pair of container stacks, she worked her way across the lot as quickly as she could. She set her op's terminal scanning for accessible interfaces, finding two lifters operating on the lot, and assigned the device the task of hacking in to the interface. She wouldn't be able to take control of the lifters, but she could access their workload manifest, and get an overview of the site: ahead, she saw a container placed at right angles across the end of the third row, suggesting the lot had a labyrinthine layout.

As she turned into the fourth row she glanced quickly back along its length and saw a marine skid to a stop. The squad leader had sent a spotter along the perimeter of the containers to locate which row she was in. No doubt the other marines were working their way through the maze of containers behind her, and the spotter was most likely the best marksman. She was already bringing her rifle to bear when Leonard dived across the narrow gap between the two containers opposite.

The marine had more room to move across the ends of the rows than she did, squeezing between them, so it was safe to assume her rival would get there first, set up to take a shot as soon as she emerged. Leonard could duck back to the previous row, but there was also a good chance that a second marine would already be covering it. In the long run, it wasn't a sustainable strategy, because even if the other marines were all pursuing her amongst the containers, she would constantly be back-tracking towards them. They would gain ground and eventually catch up with her. Also, after the first feint the spotter would know to expect such a move, giving her no better than a fifty percent chance of it working each successive time.

These were not acceptable odds. Probability alone dictated she'd get no further than two more rows before the sniper would correctly guess which of the two rows she'd emerge between, and have a perfect opportunity to make a kill-shot: the narrow gap between containers would prevent any evasive weaving, and she'd be running directly away from the sniper, at relatively close range. Leonard could easily make that shot herself with a handgun, let alone an assault rifle with arhud-assisted targeting. They had her beaten in a two-dimensional game of cat-and-mouse.

'I know this game; time to change the rules.' The only other way was up. Bracing her hands and feet against the steel storage door, her back against the facing container, she worked her way up the narrow gap, chimney climbing, keeping an eye on the direction she expected the other marines to come from. Once she cleared the top with her head, she was able to boost herself onto the top of the containers by pushing hard with both feet, and throwing both arms up and back to grab the surface behind her, like a backwards butterfly stroke.

She slid across the smooth metal surface, looking up into the night sky. There was no trace of paint on the load-bearing faces of the containers: the bio-chemical solvents and adhesives applied to them as they rose and fell on the Ladder would have made a short life of any soluble coating applied there.

By the optical illusion created by its immense height, the vertical Ladder seemed to lean out, curving over and above her from its base nearby. Distant specks of passenger and cargo stock still caught and reflected the primary's light, even though it now lay well below the horizon from her perspective.

The scuff of a muffled footstep beneath her snapped her out of her sight-seeing. The arrival of the first marine, directed by the spotters who, hopefully, still thought she was hiding between the containers they'd seen her pass between.

Silently, she drew herself into a crouch, and padded across the top of two containers. Off in the distance, the two lifters she'd identified were transferring containers to and from hoverbarges that completed the relay to the Ladder. Behind her, she heard the plastic-on-steel clatter of body armour as the marine tried the climb to re-establish visual contact with their target. She smiled at the thought of the difficulty her adversaries would have trying to chimney climb in smooth, slippery armoured plating, compared with the ease she'd had in fabric. At least they'd take the pristine paint jobs off the formed nanopoxy spine protectors!

PRIMED

She dropped down behind the first of a series of rows lying perpendicular to the others, cutting off the line of sight to the spotters. From the ground, she started right, heading for the centre of the lot. Within a few seconds she received a notification from her op's terminal: it had hacked the lifter interfaces, streaming the site's data in a series of translucent windows popping up in her arhud.

From the visual display, she could see the lot had been divided into quarters by rotating the layout line of the containers in each section. Each uniquely identified container was designated a storage position by the lifters' four-dimensional site diagram and storage duration soft, with the cargo manifest appended to its location. The lifters were completely automated. She couldn't steer them in any conventional sense, as she had the S.A.s flyer at the check point. The only human interface came via their work orders, which were conveyed directly from the Ladder.

Reviewing the cargo manifests as she cut through the rows between containers again, anticipating the climbing marine's arrival, she scanned for the cargo she needed. The list became much more useful when she filtered the data for *perishables.* Above the clatter of the lifters, she heard another sound, growing louder every moment: a flyer, approaching slowly. It was sure to be the marine's transport, untangled from the fencing, or perhaps a second support vehicle with another squad called in to help conduct the search, providing an aerial spotter and reinforcements. That didn't leave her much time. Fortunately, she didn't need much: lifter *Castor* was dropping a delivery of industrial chemicals then heading for an outbound shipment of live nutri-vats. She could hide amongst the nutri-vats, the genetically engineered flesh covering her life signs from the marines' scanners. But it wasn't in this quarter, which was designated mostly for electronics, so she'd have to run.

'Electronics....' A better plan started to form in her mind, data from the lifters dropping into place like Tetris pieces. Scanning the vicinity ahead for G-PIPs yielded a handful of active signals, the nearest two belonging to the hoverbarge operators at the far edge of the compound. Lifter *Pollox* was on its way to pick up a container of oranges freshly harvested from A.C.P.'s agricultural belts.

She opened up the flexi-drive analysis soft in her arhud, and started partitioning the drive on her op's terminal. She set the drive for a ten percent nano-shear, specifying the duplication of normal handroid transceiver circuitry and independent power supply in the sheared portion: she needed it to have a comlink and a copy of the main terminal's encryption soft. It would take the terminal a while to re-configure the nano-circuitry pathways, copy the software and re-allocate the data stored in that portion to other areas. In the meantime, she had some ground to cover.

Avoiding the flying transport vehicle overhead, doing her best to maintain an accurate idea of its position, and wary of the foot soldiers tracking her through the maze, she wove through the rows of containers towards the nutri-vat load in the edible exports quarter. The multi-faceted surfaces of the containers reflected sound and radio waves both, confusing not only her ears but also the Doppler motion detectors the marines would be using to try to locate her. As long as she wasn't visually spotted in an open row, she should be safe.

By the time she reached the nutri-vat container, her op's terminal had completed the partition, the second device popping up on her arhud ready for use. The container was pressure sealed for the ride into orbit, with a double, reinforced hull and hand-wheel operated air-lock doors. Gripping the hand-wheel, she applied increasing pressure until, with a complaining squeal of metal-on-metal, it started to turn. Listening intently for any response to the noise she'd made, she continued swivelling the wheel, more quietly now, until it was fully turned. Pulling on the handle to open the door issued another metallic sound as the heavy hinge groaned open, but by now the approaching lifter was making all kinds of covering rattles, creaks, crackles and whines of its own.

Slipping in through the narrow crack she'd been able to make in the small space between containers, she peered into the interior, seeing lines of self-luminous panels that shed no real light on their surroundings. Tapping the back of her glove activated a bright, fluorescent panel on the palm, beneath the sticky silicone grip-layer that coated it, enabling her to survey the contents: a double row of nutri-vats, similar in appearance and function to the cloning bells she'd been pulled from, herself, more times than she cared to contemplate. Weak transmissions from each exhibited virtual display screens to advise technicians of the conditions within each cell-growth and gestation chamber. According to the readings, the huge balls of genetically-engineered animal protein floating in a soup of their own metabolic discharge were all being sustained under optimal conditions for their survival and continued growth. 'Mmm. Meat in piss soup: my favourite. Time to fuck things up.'

Slipping her op's terminal from her pocket, she pressed her thumb to the top of the device, fingers beneath, and applied a sliding pressure. With a click, snapping the few remaining polymer cross-bonds that persisted in the protective matrix housing the terminal's nano-circuitry, a thin sheet of the partitioned drive sheared away to finalise the physical separation of the two devices.

She nenned open the lid of the middle nutri-vat on the right, its display panel flashing a warning of breached hygiene conditions. Wrinkling her nose at the smell of warm urine that filled the shipping container, she pulled open the top of the liquefied feed container and thrust the second device down into it. Feeling for the mouth of the wide tube that led to the digestive intake valve of the mass of meat below the steaming liquid layer, she released the terminal into the gentle suction and withdrew her arm, wiping off as much of the brown soup as she could with her other hand.

She nenned the lid closed as she made for the door, wiping her hands on her clothes to clean off the rest of the gruel, then transmitted an intermittent comlink initiation soft to the second device, already nestled within the bowels of Doctor Frankenstein's Sunday roast before shutting the door.

The automated lifter, *Castor*, was already overhead, latching on to the lifting points at the sides of the container's roof. The electrostatic side-effect output from *Castor's* massive Casimir plate rows made her hair stand on end as she finished closing the door and resealing the air-lock with the hand-wheel, then sprinted for her second objective, the container of oranges that the sister lifter, *Pollox*, was picking up.

As she ran, she received the notification from the second device: it had begun its first transmission, an automated S.O.S., using the full military grade encryption softs she'd copied to it from her own device. The signal strength was weakened by all the steel surrounding it, but that would serve her purposes, too, suggest to her pursuers that she believed her signal would be too muffled for them to trace. They'd congratulate themselves on their skill in locating her.

As she turned into the next row, she saw *Pollox* was ahead, already latched on to its load and, judging by the extent of electrostatic discharge from its perimeter plates, about to lift. With only seconds to spare, she started widening her steps, swinging right to left as far as she could in the narrow pathway between the container rows. Her next step landed half on the concrete slab that formed the ground of the lot, and half on the steel lip at the base of the container on her left, turning her foot to contact both surfaces. From here she pushed more upwards than forwards, landing her right foot flat against the wall of the container to her right, then lurching upwards and sideways to the opposite container wall, working her way up their sides as she continued her forward motion towards the lifter.

With a creak of redistributed stresses, the lifter rose slowly, centimetre by centimetre, into the air. Sparks from its plates jumped the gap to the walls of the container, rippling across its surfaces in a blue-white cascade. Her last step of the right side left her stretching for the lip running around the base of the rising container, grateful that the height of the container placed her outside the macro-Planck range of the lifter's antigravity downdraft, fields of force spontaneously re-entering the brane from which they'd been coaxed.

Clinging on by her fingertips, she swung her second hand to the steel lip and pumped her elbows to her waist, bringing her knees out and up, then straightened her arms beneath her to land her feet on the lip. With all points of contact aligned, she wobbled about the turning point they formed, trying to maintain her balance as the lifter's aged load handling softs reacted poorly to the relatively small changes her arrival had imparted to the system of forces it was managing, the container rocking slowly in her grip. She switched her hands to grip the underside of the lip with her fingers, pinching with her thumbs, so that she could press down through her toes on the top of the lip, enhance the perpendicular resistance preventing her from sliding off the narrow ledge of steel as it pivoted below the horizontal, the friction acting on the silicone grips of her gloves and shoes. She felt like a deadlifter, struggling to raise a weight that was not only too great but that she was also standing on top of, but somehow she was able to hang on until the container rocked back to horizontal, her shoulders burning and forearm muscles tearing with the effort.

Once gravity was again her ally, she released her pinch-hold and pumped upwards with her legs, throwing her arms wide and above her head, catching the top of the container and hauling herself up. Ripples of static from the lifter washed over her, making her muscles twitch during the movement, and she felt the extra pull pass through her upper body, then her legs as she slipped through the gap between the lifter's container-length starboard Casimir plates and the side of the container, briefly passing through the periphery of its anti-gravity effect zone.

Behind her, the marines' transport was slowly drifting sideways across the top of the metallic canyons towards the nutri-vats, allowing the side-door gunner to train a mounted thirty millimetre chain-gun on the suspect container. Hoping that her decoy would keep all eyes, and guns, averted from her she crawled across the bared steel roof using the little cover afforded by the lifter's long, parallel Casimirs and the structural alumalloy scaffolding that rose from them, connecting them to the small, weather-proof cabinet housing the lifter's CPU, comlink and power source.

At the far end of the container, she lowered herself over the edge into better cover, and opened the weathered door one-handed with its rusted bar handle. Dropping down, she pulled herself into the container by the second door, still barred shut, and used her other hand to draw the door almost shut behind her. There was little room within: the container had been stacked to the roof with crates of locally harvested oranges, their sweet, citric smell filling her nostrils, so she pressed up against the crates and pulled the door against her body as closely as she could.

The thought of the Marines surrounding the nutri-vats and her phony distress beacon made her smile in the dark, aromatic, confined space. It stayed on her face almost for the whole journey to the port, as the shipping container was loaded onto the hoverbarge and borne to the Ladder. The hoverbarge deposited the container onto an anti-gravity conveyor, queued for insertion into the stream of cargo and passengers heading into orbit.

The Ladder had its own D.A.I. traffic control system, co-ordinating with inbound passenger and cargo loads from orbit. It would select from the multitude of queued containers to minimise localised strain between containers and improve the system efficiency. After radioactive decay, it was considered by lay-observers to be one of the most random events in the universe, and a sub-culture community of black market, online gamblers had sprung up centred on predictions as to which container the D.A.I. would select next, or when a certain container would be selected in the loading sequence. During the nearly one-hundred years of its operation, no-one had been able to successfully duplicate the D.A.I.'s selection algorithms better than chance or statistical significance would suggest, and the system was a commonly cited example of Chaos Theory in academic resource materials across the Arm.

Unlike the nutri-vats, the oranges were not being shipped in a pressurised container. If she rode with them into orbit the falling air pressure and availability of oxygen would kill her. Besides, their plan wasn't to get the OACIOM off world, just to make UNESA think that *was* what they were attempting. She needed to get into the port complex, deliver the case to her comrades.

As she widened the door she could see dozens of other, similar shipping containers floating around her. The low structure of the port's passenger complex lay a few hundred metres away, across the cargo area.

She squatted down in the doorway, hanging onto the metal doorframe with one hand then leant forward until her body was parallel to the ground beneath her. CP panels crackled and hummed less than two metres below. Stretching out her free hand, she felt the buoyancy at the field terminus, and pushed off gently with her feet, floating across the top of the repulsion field to the container in front. Grabbing the lip at the bottom of the container in her outstretched hands, she dragged herself onto it, drawing her legs in with her arms and abdominal muscles, since there was nothing but thin air for her legs to work against, until her feet found purchase.

Abruptly, the container she clung to started to rise into the air, accompanied by the usual elevated electrostatic activity in the CP panel beneath it. Against all odds, it had been selected for the Ladder, and was about to be shunted into a loading lane which would carry the container through the ground-based SpinnerET, smothering it with organic adhesives and tying it into the rising sequence of containers on the Ladder into orbit. 'Too bad I didn't place a bet in *The Laddery*,' she mused, scuttling sideways along the narrow steel lip before jumping to the safety of a metal gantry between rows.

After climbing up over its railing, she looked towards the passenger terminal. Off to the side, she spotted a cluster of uniformed, armed port security guards heading her way from the security station, guns drawn. The port's nen-screen had probably raised a flag alerting them to an unauthorised presence in the cargo area as soon as she opened the door on the container of oranges. Maybe even the strong smell of oranges alone was enough to make someone suspicious, as soon as she passed within range. There was nothing else for it: she un-seamed the front of her overalls and drew her handgun, holding it behind her back. The case containing the OACIOM, clipped to her belt, still bumped against her thighs as she ran in a low crouch towards the security team.

She instinctively ducked even lower when a bullet twanged off the railing ahead of her, kicking up sparks. She seemed to have worn out any benefit-of-the-doubt port security may have had regarding her intentions. 'Too bad.' Skidding to a stop with her right foot forward, she brought her pistol around from behind her, raised it level with her eyes, extending her arm straight out from her shoulder to her right side, pointing directly towards the shooter. He'd lifted his head after his first shot, wondering from her sudden dropping motion if he'd hit her on a lucky ricochet.

Crack. The gun in her hand bucked as she squeezed the trigger, managing the recoil with an upward motion from the elbow. She returned the weapon to level with her triceps an instant later, ready to fire again. It wasn't necessary: her bullet had hit the top of her target's head, bending him backwards as he slumped to his knees, so that his feet lay trapped beneath his arched back, his cap flying away with a handful of liquefied brain, blood, scalp and skull fragments.

The other four guards dropped to the deck, their cries of horror and anger reaching her faintly across the humming lot. 'So, it's OK for you to shoot at me, but not for me to shoot back? That's a little hypocritical, don't you think?' Taking advantage of their heightened caution, she sprinted for the far end of the gantry, the metal mesh panels clanging and bouncing with every stride. Ahead, the gantry ended at an upper-storey door leading into the terminal through the luggage area, according to the site map provided by Martinez. Somewhere, another Security Agent would be picking up her every thought, streaming her sensory data, providing feedback to the officers in the field to help them manage the security breach.

She allowed herself to drop backwards as she slid forward, feet-first, sensing her run was at an end, and a split second later heard the retort of another shot aimed her way. The mesh floor of the gantry provided a good surface for grip and water drainage, but tore through her overalls like a cheese grater. The aramid weave in her couriers' outfit beneath fared better. Scrambling on hands and knees across the rest of the gantry, her cover from the metal grating actually improving as the officers ran closer to her position across the ground below her, she made it to the door, Martinez's codes unlocking it even as she slapped her hand down on the opening bar.

The humid air inside the building from the combined perspiration and respiration of its human occupants hit her like a blast of steam: sweat sprang from the pores of her forehead, neck and scalp within a few paces of the door, which was wet with condensation on the inside, as it swung shut behind her. Her op's terminal scrambled the door's security interface at the eye-point of a togglicon, preventing the officers outside from following directly behind her.

A.C.P.'s equatorial region was humid enough at the best of times, but its buildings were usually well climate-controlled for the comfort of their occupants. Looking around the corrugated, metal-walled space, she concluded that most of the port air conditioning exhaust must feed into the baggage area, which is where she now stood. Old fashioned, mechanical conveyor belts hauled regular luggage from check-in desks beyond the far wall to designated containers scheduled for departure along with their pressurised and radiation-shielded passenger compartments for the Ladder.

Other belts brought in bags from arrivals to the carousels on the upper floor. Alongside this bulky and noisy, low-tech', antique system, hovertrunks were conveyed elegantly by overhead rails with retractable hooks drawing them along by their tethers. Leonard couldn't help but envision it as a miniature replica of the traffic control system that governed flight paths in the city beyond the port.

Ripping off the tattered overalls, wiping her forehead on the cloth before discarding it, she proceeded along the gantry, looking for a way down as she unclipped the flexi-drive-festooned OACIOM case from her belt.

She cracked open a door on her left. After some distance, the gantry beyond led to a set of metal steps to ground level, and a behind-the-scenes service area for passengers in the departure lounge. At the far end of the building, hatches for A.C.P.'s automated garbage disposal system lined the service corridor behind fast food establishments whose fronts opened out into the enclosed section of the terminal where Kochansky and Pasqualé waited with their e-passes to board the Ladder, overseen by Evagora. She avoided visualising her colleagues, or trying to locate their G-PIPs, since she was almost certainly under the closest nen-screen scrutiny and didn't wish to incriminate any of them.

She made her way down the steps, which led towards a double set of sliding security doors opening to the Departures Lounge. Around the doors, a large floor-to-ceiling quartztic window divided the passengers from the service area. On the far side, civilians passed by on their way to and from the food court, and beyond she could make out a seating area where passengers waited for official notifications about their compartments prior to departure.

This close to her objective she felt the first surge of relief and accomplishment. She rounded the bottom of the stairs into a produce delivery area, doubling back towards the corner of the corridor leading along the building's back wall behind the fast-food outlets, but before she reached the turn the door behind her hissed open, the sudden rush of noise from the terminal alerting her. Turning, she saw five uniformed port security guards falling with pseudo-military imprecision into firing positions around the opening, two propping open the doors in kneeling positions to allow the three behind to level their weapons overhead. The overweight, bearded officer in the middle of the back row yelled "Don't move, or we'll open fire!" They looked twitchy and terrified, no doubt aware of what she'd done to their colleague outside.

PRIMED

As she called their bluff, backing slowly towards the corner, the sound of clicking heels and scuffle of footfalls drew her attention in that direction. A cordon of five navy-blue suited S.A.s reached the corner, stopping out of the line of crossfire from the port guards, barring the turning. They appeared casual, unthreatened, not even bothering to raise their weapons. She held her own handgun low, loosely, with the case still gripped tightly in her other hand.

The five agents parted to allow a shorter man to pass between them. His cropped, black hair was turning to grey, his long-sleeved shirt cuffs, where they emerged from his jacket, sporting jewelled gold cufflinks.

"Stand down, we've got this," he called to the port guards, not even bothering to stream his unquestionable Security Agency e-badge. "The case, please, Miss Leonard." His voice was brusque, his accent clipping the words. She stared at him blankly. "Come, now, *Angel*... you've had a good run, but the run is now *over*. Give me the case, and I'll make sure everything else goes... *smoothly*."

Aware that she had only four remaining bullets followed by her bare hands to take out or evade eleven armed assailants over various ranges, she approached the line of agents slowly, distracting with bluster: "What makes you think I want things to go smoothly?"

The man gave a small, derisive snort, muttering something she couldn't quite identify in a Chinese language she didn't know well enough, perhaps Taiwanese. His expression hardened as he turned his head almost imperceptibly toward the agent at the corridor's inside corner to his left. An instant later, the agent lifted his oversized, black *SIG P226* in his right hand and shot her unhesitatingly and unerringly in her left thigh, then kept the gun trained on her.

Staggering backwards to a stack of boxes beneath the stairwell for support, she cried out in pain.

"And now, without any further bullshit, drop your gun and give me the case."

For an older man, he was quick. His entourage was even quicker. The agent with the already levelled gun fired again before she'd raised her Heckler and Koch more than ten centimetres, the high calibre round hitting her in the left side of her chest. Startled, the guards still barring the doorway to her right released a volley. As she was partially obscured by the stairs, they mostly missed, ricocheting off the steps and railings or kicking chips out of the building's external wall beyond her, but one did clip her right calf and another sliced across the underside of her right forearm even as the chest shot drove her backwards into the stack of boxes. Her head struck a crate and she slid to the ground as the older man jumped back for cover, his subordinates closing around him, raising their weapons and shielding him. When she didn't try to shoot again, another agent peeled away from the group, stepped in cautiously with her gun trained continuously at Leonard's head and, with one pointed-toed shoe, flipped the HK out of Leonard's stunned fingers to skitter across the floor towards the port guards. With Leonard's apparent threat level reduced, she relaxed and lowered her own weapon, stepping back.

Yelling "Hold your fire, we need that case undamaged!" at the guards, the senior agent approached her again. "It's still not too late to co-operate. We can get you the medical attention you need. Just give me the case."

With her right hand, she covered her mouth as she coughed blood into it from a punctured and collapsing lung. The blood and the movement disguised the Blue Option she'd been carrying in her mouth, which now lay in the palm of her right hand. The last two fingers were unresponsive, tendons damaged by the grazing shot to her forearm, but her thumb and first two fingers still felt strong. Strong enough.

"Are you... Chin?" she managed to ask, through gritted teeth. Every gunshot wound burned fiercely.

"*Director* Chin, yes. Perhaps under different circumstances I might have been pleased to meet you." He held out his hand for the case, which she still clutched in her left hand. If Chin was still trying to keep his dirty little black op' secret – which would explain why he was so keen on retrieving the case undamaged – perhaps he hadn't told his entourage about the others in her team, or at least not enough to identify or locate them within the port. She could improve their chances, and those for the success of their mission, by eliminating Chin.

Exaggerating the difficulty of the movement by wincing and reaching with her right hand to support its moderate weight, she lifted the case for Chin with her best feigned look of submission. The Security Agency Director extended his hand towards her to hasten the exchange of her burden. 'Ooh, he wants it *bad*.' As soon as his fingers closed around the handle she'd turned towards him, she jerked the case back towards her with her left hand, pulling Chin off balance with her floor-level body-weight as she ground and grated the Blue Option in her right palm across the back of his exposed hand. The smear of blood it left was as much his as her own, but this would not be immediately apparent, a mild anaesthetic in solution with the poison inhibiting awareness of any injury.

She still wore her gloves, so the lacerating pad didn't reach her own skin. This gave her a moment of satisfaction during which she watched Chin's initial looks of surprise and confusion grow slack, his eyes glazing over and rolling upwards in their sockets, eyelids fluttering in chemical shock as the potent poison from the gel-encapsulated Blue Option travelled system-wide through his bloodstream in a matter of seconds, plunging him into coma. He would have fallen on her if his bodyguards hadn't dived in to grab him, pull him away from her. They were too late to help him: the poison, binding irreversibly to his haemoglobin, completely blocked his bloodstream's ability to take up oxygen from his lungs. He would be brain dead in just a few minutes.

The same agent that had put bullets through her leg and chest stepped towards her, raising his pistol to point it straight at her head. Leonard smiled at him shakily, already struggling to retain consciousness herself. Behind his inscrutable sunglasses, the agent's forehead furrowed in irritation as his finger squeezed the automatic's trigger, lip curling up in disdain at the same time.

She saw the first flash from the barrel, but never heard the sound. She was already dead before the front of the wave of compressed air reached her lifeless ears.

CHAPTER EIGHTEEN: OPERATION MUSKETEERS

There was a moment of vertiginous distortion as the perspective shifted. Small differences in eye height, spacing and focal ability, combined with the effects of a new, unique neural resonance took a moment of reorientation, acclimatisation, like when trying on a pair of prescription glasses: a brief and unfamiliar effort to adjust and restore normal perception.

Evagora heard every gunshot, including the muffled, flat crack that sounded the end of Angel Leonard's life. It came from beyond the quartztic partition keeping passengers out of the service area, and as the panicked crowd parted he saw the cluster of port security guards blocking the doorway. At the first hint of a disturbance near the food court, he'd started walking in that direction, visualising a doner kebab for the benefit of the spaceport's nen-screen. By the end of the incident, he had line of sight through the double doors, and could see enough of the action between the petrified guards to be certain of Leonard's termination.

He allowed himself the genuine feeling of horror that filled him, with the knowledge of Leonard's death: it would be a normal, civilian reaction. The GUNEs nen-dropping via the spaceport's protective anti-terror nen-screen wouldn't find anything suspicious or out of place about it. What he *did* have to control were any coherent thoughts that might hint at his intent, or his involvement with Leonard.

As casually as he could manage, he looked around at the other passengers that had been waiting to use the Ladder. Many had expressions that married well with the clenched-gut feeling he experienced himself, but a few wore expressions of condemning scorn, perhaps born of an assumption that Leonard must have done something exceedingly wrong to deserve such harsh justice, and that everyone was now safer thanks to the swift and decisive action of the men and women who'd administered it. Playing a similar role, Evagora nenned with mustered conviction 'They're right, she *did* deserve it. Another threat to quadrant security eliminated.'

PRIMED

As he was throwing the nen-screen that curve-ball, he allowed his eyes to pass over Kochansky. His glazed expression could have been interpreted as shock, but Evagora knew his I.T. tech' better than that: right under the watchful scrutiny of the port's security personnel, Kochansky was dispassionately finalising and encrypting the upload of Leonard's *.psy* file, preserving their colleague's memories and character that she might be revived to fight alongside them again. He'd witnessed Leonard's death, but the Doctrine he recited daily informed him everything essentially *her* yet lived, residing in latent form in the stream of data she'd generated in life, the sum of her experiences, her thoughts, words and deeds.

Leonard's op's terminal was scattering the high volume of the data stream off every bounce-board in the vicinity as Kochansky reconstructed the final moments of her life from the device's recording of her *.stm* feed, his fellow passengers unknowingly aiding and abetting his operations simply by being connected to the network of handroids and servers which formed Kochansky's element, his medium of specialisation.

Walking towards the barred doorway, Evagora bumped into one of the guards as he inquired gruffly "Detective Sergeant Callahan, South Central Homicide: what's going on here, officers?" Guards usually got a kick out of being called officers, giving them the official credit they often felt they deserved. He flashed a faked e-badge from his op's terminal, a convincing display hovering by his pleather-gloved right palm.

The group turned around, managing to look both startled and guilty. The leader in the middle spoke for the group: "Sorry, Detective, we –"

"Detective *Sergeant*," Evagora corrected him. The senior guard blinked twice before proceeding.

"Detective Sergeant, we didn't really get a good look at what happened. It was so fast."

"Are you trying to tell me that five trained port security officers couldn't see how two people died right in front of them?" Shaking his head and frowning fiercely, Evagora barked "Let me through!"

The guards parted, allowing him to press past them through the door. The agent he'd seen unload a round into Leonard's head was making himself scarce, heading for an external door with the OACIOM case in his hand. Two other agents were lifting their fallen colleague, an older man, carrying him towards the same exit in an attempt to get him into medical care as soon as possible, perhaps having commed for an ambulance to meet them outside the terminal building. They were wasting their energy, on that score: unless someone was hit by a Blue Option while they were actually *in* an intensive care unit, there was absolutely no chance of survival.

The female agent in the pointed shoes approached him, raising her hands. "Thank you, D.S. Callahan, we have the situation under control."

Turning to the senior guard, he ordered him in a low voice to "Get your men out of here, and get this door sealed shut, zero entry, zero override. You've got about five minutes to get this whole area sealed off *completely,* by which I mean *airtight.* There's a high possibility of airborne contaminants in here. Cover every exit, every window, and get that E-CU shut down *yesterday.* Do you understand?"

Growing visibly pale, he nodded, pulling the other officers hastily out of the doorway, allowing it to close. Turning back to greet the advancing agent, he challenged her: "Under control, my ass! That agent just shot that woman in cold blood. Step aside."

"I don't know what you think you saw, but we have an Agency Director down in need of immediate evacuation."

"We'll see *exactly* what I think I saw when we review the avtog stream I'm recording right now, Agent. For your sake, I'm warning you, do not fuck with this investigation unless you *want* to spend the rest of your career in Archives." He'd pushed past her, by this point, and was starting to jog towards Leonard's shooter. "You! Agent! Hold it right there!"

The fifth agent, bringing up the rear of the departing group, turned back to apprehend him. As Evagora drew within a few metres, the agent hailed him: "Aren't you a little outside your jurisdiction, D.S. Callahan? We have an agent down –"

"I know you have an agent down, you fucking idiot, and unless you know what killed him and what's in and *on* the outside of that case I suggest you get the fuck out of my way. We may have a bio-terrorism incident on our hands, and I'm not, in good conscience, going to allow that man to be carried out of this enclosed, quarantinable environment into the open air and expose thirty million people in Godsgood city to God-knows-what until it's been nano-scoped by C.D.C. Now, are you going to stop those men from ending their careers, and make a pay grade jump of your own while you're at it, or am I? 'Cause, Agent, I don't mind tellin' ya, I'm happy to be the hero if it means I can pay my ex-wife's alimony *and* afford rent for my own apartment.

Fortunately, the agent wasn't waiting for Evagora to stop talking before he started thinking about the potential damage a biological weapon might cause if it was allowed to get outside. "Agent Lowe, wait!" Surprised to hear his name, the agent with the case stopped and turned, placing a hand inside his jacket on the grip of the same black handgun he'd used to kill Leonard.

"Thank you, Agent...?"

"Lamar. Special Agent Lamar."

"Special Agent Lamar, I'll be sure to commend your insightfulness in my report." Evagora advanced towards the case-carrying agent Lamar had identified as Lowe.

"Agent Lowe, we have a potential bio-terrorism incident on our hands. There's no way you and your colleagues can leave this space until the C.D.C. bio-tech's clear quarantine. Set the case on the ground."

Lowe sneered at him, his eyes concealed behind reflective glasses. "I don't have time for this. My orders are to return the case to HQ, and Director Chin needs immediate medical attention – there's an ambulance landing outside in less than a minute, and he's going to be on it."

"I have no doubt about your orders or the E.T.A. for the ambulance, Agent. But as I said before, none of us are going anywhere until C.D.C. gives us a green light."

"C.D.C.? This isn't a bio-terrorism incident, Director Chin's been poisoned!"

"Are you willing to stake your life on that, Agent Lowe? Or the lives of thirty million civilians?" Lowe's adam's apple started bobbing above the knotted tie at his shirt collar. "Open your eyes, Lowe: *look* at that thing." Lowe's face tilted down, and he raised the case from his left side, tilting it with his wrist. The warning *Bio-material* label was clearly visible under the veneer of slap-dash, stuck-on flexi-drives giving the case the appearance of a potentially A.I.-controlled, improvised bio-bomb. "Did Director Chin tell you what's inside? Or was he behaving strangely, secretively, when he ordered you and your colleagues to accompany him here?"

"I...." Lowe's jaw worked, but despite a lot of chewing he had nothing else to add.

"That's what I thought. Put the case down, Lowe."

Lowe's jaw muscles hardened. "No, I have my orders. I'll wait here for C.D.C., but the case stays with me."

"You're a brave man, Lowe. A credit to the Agency. Thank you for understanding the situation." Evagora reached out his gloved, right hand. Lowe's mirrored lenses revealed no response from the agent, but after a moment of hesitation, during which Evagora made an encouraging second profferance, Lowe took his hand and shook it. "Good man. Good man." Evagora met the agent's forceful grip, adding extra gratitude with his second hand in a clapping motion. When he let go, and turned to walk away, Lowe lifted the hand that had been double-shaken, looking at the back of it. Evagora began announcing to the other agents: "Okay, people, thank you for your co-operation. I'm sorry to inform you that we appear to be in the middle of a bio-terrorist attack. But as long as we all stay cool –"

Lowe began talking quietly. "Why is your glove wet?"

Evagora pretended not to have heard, continuing his address: "and work together, there's a good chance we'll make it through alive. Better than that, we'll be hailed as heroes!"

Lowe wiped the back of his hand with his index finger, where Evagora had slapped him left-handed with his palmed Blue Option. Under pressure, tiny punctures in his skin oozed blood, colouring the wet patch of poison solution a translucent red. Evagora stared at him, expecting him to to incriminate him, but Lowe was already losing bodily control as a series of convulsions shuddered through his limbs. The narrow window during which Lowe could have pointed an accusing finger or found some other way to alert his colleagues to his realisation had already passed. Only his eyes twitched accusingly in Evagora's direction, a silent curse shared between them. His attempts to speak coughed forth only a froth of saliva, which ran down his chin, dribbling onto his dark suit jacket. His closest colleagues, still holding Director Chin under one arm, called out "Lowe?" in concerned unison before his legs buckled, dropping him to his knees on the floor. Falling forward onto his hands, his torso shook from the involuntary twitching of his limbs as the agent fought against the shutdown of his body, gradually inching towards Evagora.

'Fuck, he's still trying to crawl at me!' To appear the innocent, Evagora darted towards him, a look of shock and concern applied to his face. "Stand back, we have a second case! Bio-terrorist attack confirmed," he spoke, for the benefit of his alleged case-file avtog recording, "Contaminant appears to be spreading by initial contact with a metallic case marked with a bio-hazard warning label." Dropping to his knees, he drew Agent Lowe into his lap as he finally collapsed into coma, rolling him over and opening his dilating eyes to examine them with his still-gloved hand.

Behind him, Special Agent Lamar called out "Callahan?" Evagora ignored him, lowering Lowe's head gently to the floor, spread open the navy blue jacket and placed his hands on the agent's chest to begin C.P.R.

"Cardiac arrest! A little help, here, please?" he called to the two agents holding Chin. Glancing at each other, they slowly lowered Chin to the floor.

Again, behind him, Lamar called out more stridently: "Detective Sergeant Callahan! South Central Homicide?"

'Sounds like *Pointy-toes* blew my cover. Maybe I should've been a bit nicer to her.' Sliding his hands around Lowe's chest, Evagora reached into the navy jacket for the black grip in his underarm holster as he flicked his gaze up at the other two agents in front of him. They were still occupied with the task of setting their superior gently on the ground, but alerted by Lamar's tone they were raising their heads to see what was going on. Just behind him, a door clicked open and the sudden sound of a busy kitchen spilled into the service corridor. Lamar and his female colleague started yelling "Get out of the way!" at the person now blocking their line of fire.

Trusting to his team mates and providence, Evagora drew Lowe's pistol and fired at the agents in front of him, his first shot hitting the agent on the left, punching through her abdomen, the force of the impact keeping her from rising, the second piercing downwards through the left side of her neck, behind her collarbone and into her chest where she was bent forwards. The second agent, foregoing any further concern for Director Chin's well-being in light of the turn of events, released the poisoned man to drop to the floor and began to stand, reaching for his own weapon. Without any room in the corridor to dive aside, Evagora aimed his third shot carefully, allowing the agent to stand up into the line of his headshot. Blood flowered behind him as Lowe's *SIG P226*, this time in Evagora's hands, re-visited an instantly fatal head wound; vengeance and justice for Leonard.

Behind him, multiple shots rang out in quick succession, as the female agent Evagora had shot first, fallen forward, was still struggling to draw her own gun from beneath her arm on her wounded left side. From his kneeling position, Evagora dived forwards over Lowe's body to lie flat on the ground, pistol extended in both hands ahead of him. At less than three metres from the stricken agent, he delivered another shot to the top of the woman's head, the cavitation wave from the bullet causing a backsplash of blood that reached his gloves.

Rolling over onto his back, he flipped the gun towards his feet as he raised his head. The kitchen door swung shut, revealing Martinez, moving weakly, slumped over a black garbage bag full of kitchen waste. A spray of blood on the wall beside him looked the right height for an abdominal gunshot wound. Beyond him, Lamar was stretched out, motionless. As Martinez lifted himself, a soft spitting sound came from the suppressor on his handgun, and a spray of blood burst from the left thigh of the female agent with the pointed shoes. Her gun was already up and firing again, Martinez twitching as her shot hit him again somewhere mid-mass.

Lining up the heavy *SIG P226* between his feet, Evagora squeezed twice on the short trigger, both shots hitting her in the middle of her chest and toppling her backwards as the slide on the handgun locked back, depleted of its high calibre ammunition. Her feet churned for a few seconds, and her back arched once before she lay still.

In the suddenly quieted corridor, Evagora could hear Martinez's laboured breathing. Grabbing the case from Lowe, Evagora crawled over to him.

"Martinez?"

Through a haze of pain, Martinez warned him, hissing: "They're coming! Complete the mission; I'll buy us some time."

From the far end of the corridor, the clatter of armoured marines bursting through the double doors from the Departure Lounge around the corner reached them. Martinez waved Evagora towards the automated garbage disposal units, as the Spaceport Security D.A.I. began to buoycast: "Warning: explosive device activation nen de –"

A ball of flame erupted from the set of boxes stacked beneath the metal stairs leading to the upper level gantry. The heat and noise of the blast rolled across Evagora, as he instinctively dived away along the floor of the corridor.

"Fire detected in Service Corridor Eight B. Warning: fire suppression system activating. Evacuate Service Corridor Eight B immediately. Access restricted to authorised fire-fighters with full Rebreath-O supplies." The kitchen doors along the length of the corridor clunked in quick succession as their auto-locking mechanisms sealed them shut, expanding silicone diaphragms filling out from the door jambs, sills and lintels to form airtight and fire-resistant seals.

Above the crackle of burning boxes and catering supplies, overhead conduits hissed with the release of fire suppression gases from their nozzles, positioned at intervals along the length of the corridor. Evagora took a deep breath and ran for the garbage hatches. Closing his eyes to confuse the nen screeners, working by feel alone, he lifted the locking handle, and pivoted the door open on its heavy, metal hinge. He felt around the cylindrical space inside, made by a grease-smeared tube, stinking of old food. He set the OACIOM case down inside the compartment, testing the resistance of the trapdoor in the base to make sure it was functional.

He slammed the door shut, and cranked the locking handle with a pumping motion, clicking it into its down position. The air was thickly fogged, by now, both with smoke from the fire and the fire suppression gases themselves. The last flames were sputtering out on the cardboard fragments littering the floor, and dying down on the debris beneath the stairs at the far end of the corridor.

Over the sound of his own blood pumping, his circulatory system responding to his held breath and physical exertion, Evagora again heard the approach of heavily-equipped hostiles. 'Too bad these units are too small for people', Evagora sign-lamented, resigning himself once more to death in the line of duty.

The lights on the garbage disposal unit shone diffusely through the fumes, and were all he could see. Guided by them, he hit the activation button, heard the rattle of the case falling down through the trapdoor into the tube below and the accompanying rush of air that the system used to force garbage through the underground ducts to the central disposal facility eight blocks away to the west. Martinez had formulated the final stage of their plan, using his knowledge of the spaceport and attendant service systems: Victor lay in wait at the disposal facility to retrieve the OACIOM case during the manual recycling stage, and would be long gone before the S.A.s figured out what had happened. For now, they would still be certain the case was at the port, that Evagora and his team were still trying to get it off world via the Ladder. Kochansky had ruled out that possibility early on, realising there was simply no way to get a million distinct genetic samples through the spaceports bio-scanners, along with the same number of *.psy* files on flexi-drives through the data volume evaluators.

Satisfied with the completion of his assigned role in the mission, Evagora slid down the front of the disposal unit's hatch to sit on the floor. Scattered light from the red sighting lasers used by the Colonial Marines marked their positions as they rounded the corner by the stairs, proceeding cautiously towards him. Evagora blew out whatever oxygen he had left in his lungs, and waited, motionless. His vision was beginning to tunnel around the edges, a dark circle closing slowly inwards.

The soldiers' suit-mounted flashlights did little to improve the range of their vision, scattering back from the smoke particles as badly as their red sighting lasers. He could make out the dimmer lights from their respirator-equipped facemasks as they reached the faint shadow cast by Martinez. They'd come back with Rebreath-O. There was a muffled thud, and a small shift in Martinez's shadow, as one of the Marines kicked a heavy, armoured boot into his torso.

"He's dead. No sign of the parcel."

"Keep looking. What's down there?"

"Sealed fire doors... external door, also sealed."

"What are those lights?"

"Uh... not sure. Hang on... I think they're just the panels on the disposal units."

They were getting closer.

"There's another thermal, over there, on the floor."

The red and white lights and dark shape of a Marine loomed above him. Evagora anticipated, and then felt the blow as the Marine sank a forceful kick into his midriff. He'd blown everything out of his lings, but the impact with his diaphragm caused an involuntary suck of the fumes surrounding him. The smoke, more than the halogenic fire suppression gases, burned and irritated his throat and lungs, and although he resisted the instinct as long as he good, eventually the mounting strength of the instinct won out over his self-control, and he released a first sputtering cough, quickly followed by convulsive, wracking coughs that made white lights go off in his pin-holing vision.

"He's alive! Get me a respirator, *now*!"

Gauntleted hands grabbed at his jacket, began hauling him up. With as much co-ordination as he could manage, Evagora slid his hands up inside the Marine's grip and clawed at the space beneath his facemask. He found something that felt tube-shaped, and started to pull down. The Marine release his jacket, allowing Evagora to drop to the floor, using his whole body weight against the facemask's Rebreath-O supply tube. He felt it break away from its seal, then saw another flare of light in what remained of his vision as a weighted left hook broke his jaw. He clung on as long as he could, the Marine echoing his hacking coughs while pounding down on his forearms until every bone there was broken, too. His sight was already gone when he felt his fingers slip from the marine's life-supporting tube, slipping and falling.

Slipping and falling into blackness.

∞

Another shift, a distortion of the senses to receive another perception. A port security officer was looking over Kochansky.

"What's wrong with him?"

"There's nothing *wrong* with him: he has Autism Spectrum Disorder. His nano-plant's mitigating most of the symptoms, but he's still a little... eccentric, that's all. Gentle as a lamb, though," Pasqualé assured him.

"Sorry, ma'am, I didn't mean *wrong* wrong, just... his behaviour's a little unusual."

"Yes, everyone says that. He doesn't take it personally."

"I just have to ask... he's carrying a lot of data, you see?"

"Yes, of course. He's an avtog editor: *lives* for his work. I paid the *Data Limit Exception* license fee for him, already, it's all there in his e-pass." As the security officer reviewed their e-doc's, Pasqualé continued on with distracting small talk: "You're sure to have streamed some of his material: most of the *big celebrity* names don't let anyone else *near* their feeds."

"Is that right?" the officer asked, credulously.

"The A.S.D. doesn't hold him back at all, when it comes to sensory data augmentation. In fact, he's uniquely gifted at it."

"You work with him?"

"*For* him, actually. I'm his personal assistant, nurse, spokesperson...."

"*Spokesperson?*"

Pasqualé smiled at him warmly: "Yes, he prefers the term to *translator*, which is probably the more accurate job description. He prefers not to interact verbally with people, and he pays me to do the talking for him. He's the boss, after all."

"That's very interesting." The security officer appraised Kochansky anew. "How do you know what he wants you to say? Does he use sign language, or something?"

"Sometimes. He has his own unique language, though: I was already a certified American sign language translator before I came to work for him, but I had to learn his dialect from scratch, pretty much. Mostly I just say whatever I think he would say, and if I'm wrong he'll correct me."

"I see. But he does speak English?" Pasqualé nodded, smiling even more widely. The officer waved at Kochansky, trying to attract his attention. "Excuse me, Sir? I just need to ask you a few questions before I can let you board the Ladder: did you pack this carry-on bag yourself?"

Slowly, Kochansky turned towards him. His expression was glazed from the intense concentration he needed to manage the thousands of bounce-boards, parallel streaming the data chunks from Martinez and Evagora, and scrambling the comlinks on the fly to avoid detection by the port's D.A.I.s. His normal set of ticks and fidgets were all evident, but subsumed beneath a whole new barrage of micro-gestures associated with his virtual interface interactions. Leonard's discovery that SPITS wasn't a functional D.A.I. running recogrithms was good news for all of them, but especially so for Kochansky, who had never truly succeeded in eliminating what she had termed his *SPITS tells*.

"Yes...?" From Pasqualé's perspective, Kochansky was clearly struggling to combine comprehension of the officer's question with the level of operations per second he was attempting. The officer pointed at the bag again. "Yes! My bag!" Kochansky enthused.

"Did... you... pack... it?"

Ironically, the officer's condescension actually worked in Kochansky's favour, since speaking slowly and clearly was exactly what he needed to follow the question in parallel with his terminal handling.

"Yes!"

"Are you carrying any prohibited items?"

Kochansky was still nodding from his previous answer throughout the whole question, but successfully switched the direction of his head movement at the end, with a firm "Nooo-*ooo!*"

"Thank you, sir. You, too, ma'am. Now I just need to check –"

"Thank you. You've been *very* patient and understanding; my employer's condition, unfortunately, makes him *very* sensitive to unexpected requests. Would you mind if I contacted your boss to let him know how appreciative we are of your delicate handling and support for disabled passengers?"

The man's shirt swelled as he pushed out his chest with pride. "Not at all! That's Captain Ferris. And I'm –"

"Officer Stolojan, yes, thank you *very* much," said Pasqualé, as she scooped Kochansky's backpack up from the baggage scanner's exit belt.

"You're welcome, very welcome. Thank you, enjoy your ride." He called after them as she nudged Kochansky into the conduit leading to the waiting passenger compartment. She found their seats, and guided him into his by an elbow before sitting beside him. After a few moments he grew still, and bowed his head in silence.

"I got them," he murmured. Pasqualé nodded, somberly. Reaching for his hand, she gave it a reassuring squeeze.

"Great work, Aaron. *Really* great work. I'm so proud of you."

She didn't let go of his hand again until they reached the orbital docking ring at the top of the Ladder, where their ship waited to carry them to the jump gate, and from there to the remote frontier beyond UNE-controlled space and the reach of UNESA.

EPILOGUE

His eyes flickered open, the dim lights in the room helpful in restoring him gently to reality. The memories of pain left a residual ache, a psychosomatic response that faded quickly in the absence of ongoing sensory input. He took a few moments to re-centre, remind himself where he was; *who* he was. Looking over at Marsden, he croaked "Well? Was it real?"

"As far as I can tell. There's no indication of simulation, tampering, barely even any editing. Looks like a pure stream, recorded start to finish on the main uploader's field op's terminal. The subsidiary entries made after she was shot at the port obviously come from her colleagues. The *Evagora* entry showed an unusually high neural resonance conformity with your own activity pattern; statistically speaking, there's a ninety-six percent likelihood you actually generated that stream yourself. And there's one more file entry which *definitely* belongs to this guy," Marsden gestured to the man tied to the chair with a bag over his head in the centre of the otherwise bare, concrete-walled room, "but we already know *his* story. I've checked that entry myself, and the neural resonance is a hundred percent match."

Dmitri calmly took in his technician's report. 'There are lies, damned lies, and then there are statistics....' he nenned to himself, a phrase he'd heard in another life. "Any of that could be faked."

"Not by any technician UNE has to offer."

Colonel Dmitri shook his head slowly. "The best lies are the ones that are true but for one small point. This avlog confirms they had one of our best technicians working *for t*hem. What did you call him?" He directed his question at the man in the bag, but there was no answer.

Kosoko, looming behind the chair, slapped him on the head, and barked "Answer the Colonel! What did you call your IT technician?"

The bound man answered, his voice muffled by the heavy material over his face, and hoarse from dehydration. "Kochansky. Aaron Kochansky."

"Right. Any luck figuring out who he used to be before UNE revived him?" he asked Marsden.

"There weren't many I.T. tech's *on* A.C.P. when the assassinations started. From the description he gave, it had to be Hyam Berkow. Also, I can't think of anyone else who could upload a whole squad's *.psy* files while sitting *inside* a spaceport nen screen, and *then* pass through security carrying exabytes of data without raising a single flag. The guy's a fuckin' legend!"

"Exactly my point: *he* could have faked the neural resonance conformities. This whole record could be nothing more than very clever avtog machinematics. Why should we trust him, when he's given us no solid reason to believe him? The only fact we can be certain of is he gene-screens as a Colonial Special Forcer." He stared hard at the bag, as if it would help to penetrate into the mind of the man beneath it, get to the truth. "This could be a ruse to get us to accept a Super Trooper as one of our own, allow him to infiltrate our operations. What do you think, Berrisford?"

Kosoko held up the metal case, branded with its *Biological Material* label and covered all over its lid with adhered flexi-drives. It looked tiny in his huge, dark hand. "He *did* bring *this*. Says it's important."

"What is it?" Again, the bagged man, unaware it was he being addressed, remained silent. Dmitri made a flicking gesture with his head towards Kosoko, who pulled the bag off the man's head. Victor, his lips cracked and face bruised, sat bound to the chair, blinking in the harsh light from the overhead panels.

"What's in the case?" Kosoko rephrased Dmitri's question.

Clearing his throat, Victor did his best to answer: "I told you before: it's the OACIOM. And the *.psy* database contents are stuck all over the lid, there."

Bringing his face level with Victor's, Kosoko asked him "How are we supposed to know it isn't a bomb? Or a bio-warfare device? It certainly looks like a bio-warfare device, with the label and everything."

"Why would I bring you a bio-bomb that *looked* like a bio-bomb? Let me open it for you, brother, and you'll see –"

Kosoko jerked his hand back to his shoulder, prepared to cuff the bound man across the face. "I *told* you *before*: I'm *not your brother!*"

Dmitri raised his palm in a calming gesture meant for Kosoko before addressing Victor "We can't just let you open it. We don't know what it is. And you could be perfectly prepared to die, as long as you kill all of us along with you."

"Then evacuate the room. Seal the doors. Put me in quarantine, if it makes you feel better, until you're sure there's no risk. I'll open the case, leave it by the door and sit over in the far corner. You can watch the whole thing on a camera, I'll film it for you. You'll see if I blow up, or get sick. If you still don't trust me then keep me sealed in here until I die from dehydration. That won't take much longer anyway. Open the doors after six months, a year, whatever your bio-tech' says is a safe quarantine period. Just consider reviving me when you *do* find out I'm telling you the truth."

Stepping from the shadows behind Dmitri, Berrisford, Dmitri's infiltrations expert and, if Victor's elaborate story were to be believed, the former incarnation of his comrade, Martinez, spoke out in an impeccable English accent: "This raises an interesting question, 'though, Colonel: clearly our prisoner is prepared to die for whatever he believes in, but aren't we, too?" His three comrades stared at him, as Victor nodded slowly in comprehension. Berrisford elaborated his point: "So, what if it *is* a lethal device? Marsden does a *.psy* backup for us all, you notify Central to warm up some fresh clones for us, and we go ahead and open the case."

"Our lives aren't the only thing at stake, 'though, Berrisford: we've dedicated the last two years to building up the credibility of these identities; healing from cosmetic surgery; evading UNESA the whole time. We're all well placed in secure positions on A.C.P. to strike decisively when the right time comes. We shouldn't jeopardise that advantage lightly, since it wasn't easily gained."

"What if this *is* the right time, Sir? And so what if it *isn't*? That just means there'll be another time. But if this *is* the right time, then that's *it*, right? If we don't seize the moment it'll just slip by, and we'll never even know we blew it." Berrisford stared intently at Dmitri until he came to a decision.

"Marsden...?"

"Not meaning to be presumptuous, Sir, but I already started the updates when Kosoko got here with the prisoner: it's not often that we all get together, these days. Also, I've bounce-boarded the data to one of our secure, external transmitters to deal with any possible local jamming attempts, and set an automated, prescheduled transmission back to Central in case anything unpleasant happens here. We're all set, Sir."

Dmitri nodded appreciatively at the technician's efficiency and initiative. Looking at Kosoko, he ordered him to "Open it."

Popping open the tiny latches with his big fingers, he cracked open the lid with a wincing expression before opening it wide, peering inside. "Well?" Dmitri asked him after several seconds.

"Is this a joke?" Kosoko asked Victor. He pulled a small box of chocolates out of the case, rattling it experimentally.

"What?" Victor craned his neck to see what Kosoko was referring to, a look of concern passing across his face "If it is, then it's not one of *mine*."

Marsden, sighing, took the box from Kosoko's fingers, and opened it. Inside the box, in the six-by-six recesses in the two cushioning plastic trays lay a set of clear quartztic cubes, two centimetres to a side. Marsden took one from the top at random, carrying it over to the nano-scope set up in its case in one corner of the bare room. He inserted the cube into a designated slot, and nenned the device to transmit to everyone in the room. "You wanna see this, too, Victor? It's your balls on the line...."

Together, they accessed the stream. A virtual screen sprang up above the device, displaying its findings: at low magnification, the cube could be seen to contain a three dimensional matrix, twenty-four dots per row of reddish-brown material encapsulated in quartztic. "Fits the format." Marsden reached his hand towards the display, manipulating the virtual zoom control to close in on one of the dots. The display identified *Organic material, animal cellular nature*, as the device continued to scan.

A few seconds later, the nano-scope pinged and displayed a series of text confirmations on their arhuds, with a softly-nenned voice-over:

Human cellular sample identified

Haematopoietic stem cells extracted from medulla ossium rubra

Viable genetic sequences detected in seventy-eight percent of available nuclei.

Marsden whispered urgently into Dmitri's ear: "We need to get these samples to the bio-tech's at Central for further analysis *right away*, Sir!"

Kosoko sounded out the calculation: "So that's twenty four cubed samples, in seventy-two matrix cubes: I make that nine hundred and ninety-five thousand three hundred and twenty-eight. Fuck, that's *everyone!*"

"*If* those are really O.A.C.I. operatives' donor samples, then yes." Dmitri cautioned Kosoko to curb his enthusiasm until all the facts were ascertained, but for once he felt like throwing his own habitual caution aside.

Victor let out his held-breath with an explosive laugh of relief: "Curly Kochansky, you fucker, you had me worried for a second."

Kosoko looked at him questioningly, so Victor explained the source of his amusement, Curly's subtle, light-hearted reassurance that everything had gone according to plan: "*Better than chocolate!*"

THE END

PRIMED

GLOSSARY

NB: this glossary includes only place names and terms unique to the story setting, or which differ in meaning from their real-world usage. Real-world terms with currently understood meanings are not included.

A.C.P.: acronym for *Alpha Centauri Prime*, an Earth-like planet with slightly higher gravity, longer days and years than Earth; located in the habitable zone and second orbital position around *Alpha Centauri α*; the first extra-solar-system planet colonised by humanity following the eighty-five year Jump Gate delivery mission of the nuclear pulse propelled, interstellar pioneer, *The Centaur*; largest extra-terrestrial population

Alumalloy: nano-formed alloy with high aluminium content, striking an optimal balance between light weight and mechanical strength, both stronger and lighter than structural steel

Anti-gravity: the strong matter-repulsive force generated by dark energy, amplified when condensed, stored and variably compressed via adjustable Casimir plates, and subjected to electro-magnetic excitation; widely used for levitation and propulsion in vehicles, but also finds application in tractor beam and force field projectors as well as the expansion of quantum flux wormholes used to enable instantaneous space transitions by space-faring vessels; in keeping with brane cosmology, anti-gravitational forces emerge from a higher dimension of the *bulk* usually not interacting with the four-dimensional brane we inhabit, the lines of force extending from their point of origin only over a limited distance before exiting our brane and returning to the higher dimensional bulk where their effects are no longer felt within our brane. In practice, this means a device can project lines of matter-repulsive force comparable to a planetary or even stellar mass, enabling them to hover over or move away from such masses, without the force exerted conforming to the inverse square law and so without having any detectable interaction with more distant objects, e.g. another planet in the same star system

PRIMED

A.O.D.: acronym for *Anticipated Operative Demise*, an OACI operational contract clause allowing for the waiving of usual operative revival fees in cases where the parameters of an operation require, or can be reasonably expected to result in, the death of participating operatives; popularised reversal of the acronym *D.O.A.* for *Dead On Arrival*

Arhud: acronym for *Augmented Reality Head-Up Display*, a display of virtual imagery blended into a streamer's actual field of vision, offering a human-terminal interface by eye-point icon selections and activations: replaces screen-based technology

Arm: the Orion Arm, a region in the Milky Way galaxy within which Sol and its neighbouring systems reside: still largely unexplored beyond a relatively small radius of light years from Sol

Autho-stamp: an uniquely identifying e-signature used for authorising official and legal e-documentation

Autoseal: a nano-technology adhesion system allowing for a variety of prepared surfaces to join to each other at a molecular level by electronic activation, forming a superior chemical bond strength. Electronic deactivation releases the re-usable bond

Autoseam: a similar nano-technology to *autoseal*, but with particular application to seaming and fastening fabric and/or garments, allowing for prepared surfaces to join to each other at a molecular level by electronic activation, forming a superior chemical bond strength. Electronic deactivation releases the re-usable bond

Avblog: recorded sensory streams posted publically on the network, usually limited to audio-visual content, but aspiring and professional actors record full sensory streams for home-made-styleentertainment purposes, lacking the professional editing and augmented reality quality of studio made avtog products

Avlog: a private, sensory diary or journal filed in a data storage device such as a handroid. Content can be purely text based, but more often mixed with still images, audio and audio-visual clips

Avtog: popularly uncapitalised acronym for *Aural Visual Tactile Olfactory Gustatory*: the stream of sensory data generated by human senses when recorded from or induced artificially within a living human brain; *verb:* to stream sensory data

Bell: a clone gestation chamber, named for its bell-like shape, i.e. dome topped cylinder with flat base, often suspended in an inertial dampening frame for improved sensory deprivation

Blueberry: slang derogatory term for a UNE peacekeeper contributed by a poorer nation-state, referencing their older issue equipment, notably the blue beret formerly associated with UNE's parent organisation, the United Nations (since disbanded)

Blue Option: euphemism for a *suicide pill*, containing a virtually undetectable organic compound causing a rapid-onset of debilitation, coma and death by inoxia

BOHICA: military slang, acronym for "Bend Over, Here It Comes Again"

Bounce-board: a secure, chunked military-grade encrypted data routing technique, piggy-backing multiple civilian transmissions to avoid detection

Buoy-cast: a public information broadcast over a short range local area network by buoy transceiver device, using similar technology and methodology to LANverts, typically carried by emergency service providers and civic repair teams to notify affected persons regarding flight path diversions/closures, etc. Sirens and lights on emergency vehicles are buoy-cast, as are loud-hails

Casimir Plates: aka *Casimirs*, *plates* or *CPs*: a pair of parallel, metallic sheets separated by distances too small to permit the presence of atomic matter. Quantum flux effects between the interior surfaces result in a net output of pressure. With nano-technological refinements to responsively control the separation distance and containment, Casimir plates are routinely employed to store and compress dark energy for the purposes of generating and varying anti-gravitational effects following electro-magnetic excitation of the dark energy

C.I.N.: citizenship identification number; unique identifying code for all citizens of the United Nations of Earth and its colonies

Civ': military term, abbreviation for *Civilian*

Com: abbreviation for telecommunication

Com-drop: telecommunication eavesdropping, a routine intelligence and counter-intelligence activity utilising both live streaming Security Agents and Dedicated Artificial Intelligences with threat assessment algorithms triggered by specific nen phraseology or imagery

PRIMED

Commercial spire: a designated structure for commercial units, either free-standing or atop a mega block

Communiquétion: a method of stilted avtog communication utilising sensory instant-message clips edited by the sender prior to transmission to ensure the removal of inappropriate content, appropriate to professional and workplace settings

D.A.I.: acronym for *Dedicated Artificial Intelligence*, a computer generated entity assigned to a specific vocational task, usually involving data processing or analysis at a rate no human could match

Dark energy: a ubiquitous, directly undetectable energy believed to account for the increasing rate of expansion of the universe, making up close to seventy-three percent of the matter-energy constant; passive *dark energy condensers* are able to draw in and store dark energy from their surroundings, after which its negative pressure characteristics may be utilised in anti-gravity technology

Doctrine, the: a system of psychological and philosophical training in the private army of the O.A.C.I., intended to prepare service people for the shock of revival after death in action

Dry-clean: a crude process of long-term memory extraction utilised by UNESA technicians as a standard interrogation technique. Unlike the more sophisticated O.A.C.I. method of *.psy* file recording, UNESA dry-cleaning often results in irreparable brain damage and permanent memory loss in those subjected to the procedure

E.A.N.: acronym for *Encephalic Avtog Nano-plant*, a human-computer interface device constructed within the brain by non-self-replicating nano-bots injected through the back of the neck to the base of the brain, usually in infancy. Utilising colloidal gold nutritional supplements, the nano-bots manufacture four elements: nano-wire scaffolding surrounding the brain's own synaptic architecture both for detection and induction of neural pathway activation, weighing only several grams; a nanoprocessor translating between neuro-electrical impulses and virtual sensory data; an ultra-short-range radio-wave transceiver; a bioelectrical power supplier for the device, drawing on the body's own energy content. The nanoprocessor is able to store and run a handful of softs independent from a handroid, but lacks the greater power and memory storage of an external device

Edu-guess: contraction of *educated guess*

Eihog: acronym for *Echoic, Iconic, Haptic, Osmatic, Geusic,* subcategories of long term, sensory memory: the whole range of sensory memories produced by a person, the *in vivo* version of computer-recorded or generated *avtog*; eihog is monitored and recorded via the avtog nano-plant to create avtog streams, and by reversal streames avtog is converted into eihog by the brain, encoded into memories

Eye, or eye-point: updated term for *finger*, as in to identify by pointing: a visual selection and activation method for human-terminal interface via arhud

Feed: *noun*: a data transmission, synonymous with *stream*; *verb*: to transmit data, past tense *fed*

Field Operations Terminal: a military-grade portable computer similar in appearance to a handroid but noticeably thicker, rigid and light-absorbant due to the protective matrix that houses it; O.A.C.I. models are capable of a number of functions beyond the scope of a normal handroid: bounce-board data reception to prevent location of the device by data-tracking methods; server hacking, allowing the user access to surrounding G-PIP codes (enabling location of unencrypted terminals and their carriers, useful also when 'jacking data or entire e-identities), remotely access terminals and upload false GP/t data trails (*aka Goose chase*); military-grade comlink encryption, preventing comdropping by enemy agents (with the unfortunate problem that UNESA counter-intelligence D.A.I.s are constantly looking for such transmissions, and can quickly locate a transmission point by triangulation of the signal); active internal nano-bots capable of navigating across the porous membranes of the protective matrix and making useful modifications within the nano-circuitry on-the-fly, e.g. physical flexi-drive partitioning by breaking down molecular bonds between membranes, component duplication allowing the terminal to be divided into two separate, functional devices, and data destruction in the event of operative demise to prevent mission data falling into the hands of enemy agents.

Flexi-drive: a solid state, persistent memory/data storage device, consisting of integrated nano-circuitry in a protective, transparent quartztic matrix; the quartztic utilises auto-sealing nano-technology to create a molecular adhesive bond with handroids when applied to them (and other surfaces, if so instructed), facilitating rapid parallel data transfer across the connected surface, rather than discreet contact points or bottlenecked connection cables

PRIMED

Flike: a one to three externally seated private vehicle capable of atmospheric flight, typically requiring wind and water resistant clothing for comfort

Flike suit: weather resistant clothing for flike operation, typically insulated, water and wind resistant; silicone-impregnated aramid fibres are often used for strength, abrasion resistance and other properties

Flyer: a private vehicle with a pressurised, enclosed passenger cabin capable of atmospheric flight, often utilising anti-gravity for uplift, and sometimes or partially for propulsion, supplemented by alternative propulsion methods

Four-stars: a very senior ranking group of military leaders, as in *four-star Generals*

FUBAR: military acronym for "Fucked Up Beyond All Recognition/Reason"

Facial recognition: computer software capable of matching still images and security camera video footage of unaltered facial features to known subjects

Gait recognition: computer software able to match locomotory attributes of known subjects with security camera video footage

Gel-o'tine: a transparent gel patch delivering a payload of nicotine to a user's bloodstream by firm dermal application

Gene-screen: an on-the-spot DNA test administered by local police and UNESA Security Agents cross-referenced with a database of known subjects, used to unequivocally identify the subject in cases where false identification by G-PIP is suspected

Gene therapy program: a controversial *in vivo* genetic modification procedure utilised in the militaries of certain rogue UNE-loyal nation-states and extra-terrestrial colonies: genetic re-sequencing techniques affect gene activation and expression to enhance desirable traits in the subject, whilst also inserting and activating sequences obtained from donors found to have superior traits. Some question whether the donor sequences were really obtained from live subjects, or if they were artificially designed and constructed, others the ethics and morality of modifying a human's DNA

Ghosting: slang term for being in a public place without a handroid, declared a criminal act by the UNE martial law declaration, akin to jaywalking

Godsgood City: capital city of Alpha Centauri Prime; population of approximately thirty million; founded in 2143CE by the first Jump Gate survey team

Goose chase: a false set of GP/t data uploaded to servers to create a false record of a person's whereabouts

G-PIP: acronym for *Global/Galactic Positioning Internet Protocol*, the system by which every terminal or device wirelessly connected to the network is uniquely identified and its precise location determined: handroid terminals typically incorporate global

GP/t: data record of a handroid's precise location over time, used by law enforcement organisations to monitor people's movements. Even inactive handroids generate a GP/t signal and transmit it to the network

Grunts: derogatory term for rank-and-file law enforcement, para-military and military personnel regarded as minimally trained and of low intelligence

GUNE: derogatory for a representative of the government of the United Nations of Earth, especially when a member of federal law enforcement or military

Handroid: a portable, personal computer accessed via an avtog interface, especially an arhud; a transparent, quartztic matrix protects thousands of parallel nanoprocessors which provide incredible computing power, and solid-state flexi-drives with massive memory capacities, in a device with the size and flexibility of a credit card; UNE martial law finally made carrying a handroid mandatory in public places, assisting law-enforcement and counter-intelligence activities with GP/t data provided by global positioning systems in each device, originally intended to facilitate mobile connection to the internet through the G-PIP system. Handroids also contain

Hardstore: physical data storage device, such as a *flexi-drive* or mainframe computer

Hardy: slang term employed by Independentists for a UNE peacekeeper contributed by one of the wealthiest of Earth's nation-states, often better trained and equipped than their poorer counterparts. Used in conjunction with Laurels to denote slapstick comedic duo Laurel and Hardy, but also with reference to literary characters, the Hardy Boys, criticised as agents of the ruling classes controlled by propaganda

Helicorp: an O.A.C.I. member company specialising in genetic intellectual property and engineering, largely responsible for the successful development of human cloning technology, declared illegal by UNE: a counter-insurgency operation by UNE military forces seized the headquarters of Helicorp and obtained centralised storage of O.A.C.I. operative donors' D.N.A.

Hauler: an anti-gravity vehicle for conveying goods, analogous with a modern-day truck or lorry barge; also a remotely guided container for conveying goods, similar to a hov'train

Hind-nenning: reminiscence; introspective mental functions generated by the nature of mind in the absence of sensory stimuli, tending to draw upon associated chains of encoded memories; part of the *stream of consciousness*

Hover: in addition to its use as a verb, and a noun for the act of hovering, it is also a noun in the story-setting for a *person who hovers*, in the same way that a skater is a person who skates, making use of an anti-gravity device to eliminate surface friction between the *hover* and the ground, fulfilling a similar function to wheels on a skateboard or rollerblades

Hoverbarge: analogous to the canal barges of the Industrial Revolution, except that anti-gravity replaces water and buoyancy as the support for the load carried; large, sometimes automated cargo conveyors carrying shipping containers to and from the port, or bulk goods from the shipping district to tower district I.S.B. retail connectors and suburban retail premises

Hovertrunk: luggage employing anti-gravity technology to support its load

Hov'train: public passenger-carrying compartments utilising anti-gravity flotation and propulsion, conveyed along pre-determined routes and scheduled stops controlled by traffic control system guidance software, operating at mid to low block levels

Independentist: politically correct term for an activist, operative or supporter of O.A.C.I.; one agreeing or siding with the movement for independence from UNE legislation and governance

Indoctrinal Trust Pact: autho-stamped agreement between O.A.C.I. and its operatives, members of its private army, clarifying rights regarding their full-human-privilege status as revived clones, attribution of a persistent identity transcending personal death and solemn promises on the part of O.A.C.I. to make no deliberate alterations either to the donor's genetic sample or their electronically recorded digitised memory storage files, and of course to have only one version of each person active at any given time. Operatives, on their part, undertake to accept the risks that small variations may occur randomly, beyond the influence and control of O.A.C.I.s technicians, in their genetic sequence and its expression, and their memory retention during the cloning and revival processes

I.S.B.: acronym for *Inter-Super-Block*, designation for public travelators and hov'trains conveying passengers between super blocks, and also for the horizontal structures traversing super blocks, which tend to be multi-storied and mall-like, typically including hov'train stations, supermarkets and hoverbarge delivery bays and cash-and-carry distribution points from which the surrounding blocks' retail establishments receive their stock

I.S.R.: acronym for *Immune System Restorative*; a nano-processor regulated device for the administration of drugs, nutrients, antibodies and/or vaccines via an intravenous drip or dermal delivery system

'jack: slang term for *steal*, abbreviation of *hijack, carjack*, etc.

Jacob's Ladder: aka *the Ladder*, a space elevator conveying shipping containers and passenger compartments between the surface of A.C.P. and a geostationary orbiting docking ring for interstellar ships. The ground level terminal is located at Godsgood City Spaceport, on the shore of a large, equatorial, cometary impact crater. Containers and compartments are strung together by a matrix of recycled organic nano-tubes: powerful, adhesive mono-molecular strands connecting the containers together, extruded from and applied by extruded from a pair of devices, one at each terminal, called *SpinnerETs*, based on the techniques utilised by terrestrial web-building spiders. At each terminal, the cables are dissolved to remove the object from the Ladder, and the chemicals recycled into fresh cables for the next object added

Jordan Fleet: man-made river of surplus potable water released into a park to the north of Godsgood City centre from the under-city water treatment plants, named for Earth's (mainly subterranean London) Fleet and Jordan Rivers

Jordan Fleet Park: recreational area north of Godsgood City centre extensively planted with terrestrial plant species, surrounding a man-made reservoir fed by surplus potable water from the under-city water treatment plants

Jump: instantaneous point-to-point transition across space via a network of jump gates supporting permanently maintained wormholes

Jump gate: a permanent wormhole-maintaining-device capable of expanding the wormhole to enable the instantaneous transit of solid matter from one point in space to its similarly maintained *other end* at another, distant point in space

Krunked: badly incapacitated, as by an accident or severe illness, to the point of prolonged immobility

LANvert: *Local Area Network advertisement*: short range wireless connectivity establishes proximity based links with terminals in range, broadcasting pre-approved streams of usually audio-visual data, but sometimes including tactile, olfactory and gustatory elements

Laurel: as Blueberry, but referencing the same issued beret's laurel leaf emblazoning

Level: single storey of a residential tower or mega block and their interconnecting walkways and platforms, accessible without recourse to elevators or escalators/stairwells: in a block setting, a substitute for the word *local*

L.T.M.: acronym for *Long Term Memory*

Meg': abbreviation for *Mega block*, a super block hub surrounded by six lower level residential towers, often topped by architecturally diverse commercial spires or other unique, distinguishing features, fulfilling centralised needs within a super-block

Megaloblastocyt: a pseudo-scientific technical term for the preformed, cultured, roughly human-sized and shaped cluster of stem-cells used in the creation of human clones

Nanodaid: a wound dressing containing a dose of non-replicating nano-bots, sterilising and delivering nutrients to damaged tissues to promote rapid healing in an optimal micro-climate

Nanoprocessor: advance, miniaturised version of a modern microprocessor, with data processing speeds and capacities to volume ratios several orders of magnitude greater than contemporary computers;

much of the increase in operations per second is due to thousands of parallel processors and data chunking, rather than the size reduction

Neuromemetic Industries: an O.A.C.I. member company specialising in the technology required for digital duplication and inscription of encoded human long term memories *in vivo*, largely responsible for the successful transferral of human memories and personalities into cloned brains, declared illegal by UNE: a counter-insurgency operation by UNE military forces seized the headquarters of Neuromemetic Industries and obtained a hardstore of O.A.C.I. operative donors' *.psy* files

Nova gate: space transit technology responsible for the rapid expansion of human-occupied space; a similar operating principle to the skip drive, except that the gamma photons utilised in the expansion of the transit wormhole are derived from remote high energy gamma photon sources, i.e. recurrent novae from white dwarf binary systems. Due to light speed time dilation, nova gate travel involves not only instantaneous space transit to the gamma photon source point but also travelling back in time to the exact moment the photon was emitted, i.e. a number of years equal to the number of light years travelled, invariably arriving somewhere in the middle of a massive explosion of hydrogen gas surrounding a white dwarf star. Many of the unmanned probes do not survive the arrival conditions. Those that do are programmed to fly to a safe distance, if possible, and from there maintain a nova gate terminus to receive a series of standard jump gate delivery drones, spreading out from the nova gate in pre-determined directions to build up a massive jump gate network. Several are sent back by skip drive to the point of origin. Because they are travelling from the past, at near light speed, any surviving ship should arrive soon after being sent, relative to the sender, establishing a present-day link to the new network far sooner than could be achieved by sending out skip drive transiting ships from the point of origin alone.

Nano-form: the process of building macroscopic structures at a molecular level

Nano-plant: *noun:* a nano-tech' device assembled via nano-bot *in situ* and/or *in vivo*; *verb*: to so implant a nano-tech' device

Nanopoxy: a nano-fiber reinforced, thermoset plastic

Network: system of computer terminals and devices interconnected via the internet

Nen: coherent visualisations and internal voice or monologue, corresponding to *the mind's eye* and *the mind's ear*: derived from Zen

PRIMED

Buddhist phrase *Nen nen ju shin ki*, roughly translated as *thought following thought*, aka the *stream of consciousness*

Newscast: avtog news broadcast

Nutri-vat: a gestation chamber for insensate, genetically-engineered organisms cultivated for nutritional purposes, similar in appearance and function to a cloning bell

O.A.C.I.: acronym for *Orion Arm Conglomerate for Independence*, umbrella organisation for numerous corporations seeking from UNE legislation and taxation by means of armed resistance, giving rise to the declaration of martial law throughout the UNE jurisdiction

Oper': *abbrev*: operative, member of O.A.C.I. private army

Op's terminal: see *Field Operations Terminal*

P2P: acronym for *person to person*: terminal to terminal data exchange over the network or local area network (LAN)

P.I.B.: acronym for *Public Information Broadcast*, referring to a set of protocols that allow an agreed data content to be broadcast under license for the purposes of public information or commercial advertising, as with tourist attraction way-pointing or storefront and billboard advertising

Plasticrystal: a class of nano-formed, silicone-based compounds possessing both plastic and crystalline properties: variations can manifest optical clarity, electrical conductivity, photo-reactive/voltaic, thermo-reactive/voltaic, piezo-reactive/voltaic and/or electro-luminescent properties

Polysorb: a reusable, rapid-drying, highly absorbent sponge-like fabric with anti-microbial properties

.psy: file type used by O.A.C.I. for recording long term memories and synaptic pathway strengths of donor operatives, used in the clone revival process to impart the memories and character of a deceased operative into a fresh, cloned body

Psychitects: specialists in environmental psychology, the effect of environmental factors on the mind

Quartztic: a highly durable, recyclable, thermal shock and abrasion resistant, ceramicised and nano-formed plasticrystal compound used to manufacture a wide variety of consumer products from drinking bottles to kitchen countertops and even whole wetcubes

Rads: slang term, abbreviation of *radiation sickness* or other effects of damaging levels of radiation

Rebreathe-O: a device that electro-chemically recycles respired carbon dioxide to make breathable oxygen available to the user; the oxygen thus provided

Recogrithm: contracted form of *recogniser algorithm*, complex physical data comparisons carried out by D.A.I.s

Revive/revival: O.A.C.I. practice and processes of cloning – and reprogramming clones with the recorded memories of – operatives killed in the line of duty

S.A.: abbreviation for *Security Agent*, a federal agent for UNESA

Scrote: slang term, abbreviation of *scrotum*

Seconde: an industrialised, rocky and habitable planet orbiting *Alpha Centauri β*; surface temperatures are considerably colder than Earth equivalent latitudes, and the planet has a slightly smaller mass, day and orbital period; rich source of minerals, ores and isotopes, leading to extensive commercial mining operations

SeizULFem: a geological and seismological scanning device emitting and sensing ultra-low frequency electro-magnetic radiation

Server: cellular network coverage device connecting wireless terminals within its service area to the internet, responsible for G-PIP recognition and GP/T recording

Sham: a meat-substitute product grown from cultures in a nutri-vat

Sim-torial: an instructional program using sensory data streams to provide a repeatable simulation to improve simulated task performance, largely transferable to real world task performance ability gains

Sim-gram: simulator training programme, often utilising full immersion and participant immobilisation

Skip: transit instantaneously from point to point in space via skip drive; an arbitrary measurement of distance covered by one skip, often standardised by preset skip drive navigational computations, e.g. skipping every thirty-one point five-three-six seconds generates a wormhole transit covering a distance of five million eight-hundred and sixty-five thousand six-hundred and ninety six miles, approximately one twenty-fifth of the distance from Earth to the Sun, i.e. point zero-four Astronomical Units. A million such skips will convey a ship one light year

Skip drive: a space transit device utilising jump gate wormhole projection technology to extend the exit point of a wormhole in the desired direction of transit at the speed of light via focused, converging gamma photons , enabling a spaceship to transit instantaneously from one point in space to another. Between *skips*, a ship waits for the next wormhole exit point to be reached by the transmitted gamma photons responsible for converging interferometrically, exciting the dark energy residing in the quantum flux wormhole targeted. The theoretical speed limit is that of the gamma photons, i.e. light speed, but in practice some small efficiency losses due to computation and occasional skip point focal failure add up over time, reducing a skip drive's average journey time to slightly less than light speed

Soft: abbreviation for software; a computer program or application; sometimes pluralised as *softs*

S.O.P.: military term, acronym for *Standard Operating Procedure*

SpinnerET: a device that recycles organic chemicals based on spider silk, used in the form of spun strands of cable to adhere cargo and passenger containers together in an ascending and descending system to convey goods and people between a planetary surface and a geo-stationary orbiting space station serving as a docking ring for spaceships capable of interstellar travel

SPITS: acronym for *Subversive Personnel Identifiable Traits System*, an A.C.P.-based UNE initiative to identify undercover O.A.C.I. operatives in UNE jurisdiction population centres based on behavioural, postural and gesticulatory mannerisms derived from *.psy* files in a mainframe database seized during counter-insurgent operations

Squaddy: *noun:* member of a military squad, esp. rank-and-file; *adj*: of or relating to squad mentality

Squelch: slang term for the removal of a clone from its gestation chamber, or *cloning bell*

Stingers: a law enforcement device designed to disable low-flying anti-gravity vehicles in cases of traffic-law violations; the camouflaged, flat-packed device is laid on the ground, launching a payload of explosive micro-missiles which selectively target and rupture an over-flying vehicle's Casimir plates, allowing the store of dark energy therein to disperse back into the environment; the design circumvents anti-landmine treaties and legislature through non-lethal anti-vehicular, rather than anti-personnel, application

.stm: file type used by O.A.C.I. for recording and streaming live sensory data from operatives in the field; file contents are usually the last data streamed, in real time, to clones during the revival process, following *.psy* file inscription and ingraining, forming, as they do, the most recent living memories and experiences of the donor operative they are replacing. Field Operations Terminals routinely compile *.stms* into simulated *.psy* files to maximise data storage density and as a precaution against operative demise and loss of streamed *.stm* data. Both *Short Term Memories* and *stream* lend their connotations to the file name designation

S.T.M.: acronym for *Short Term Memory*

Stream: verb: to access and/or receive a transmission of data; noun: the data transmission itself, esp. when accessed, synonymous with *feed*

Streamer: an avtog user, a person sending or receiving a sensory data stream over the network

Super block: a self-contained group of six highly interconnected residential towers around a central mega block, arranged on a hexagonal grid system around the spaceport and shipping district of Alpha Centauri Prime; reachable from other super blocks by I.S.B. routes traversing the voids between super blocks, but with a much lesser degree of interconnectivity than that evidenced between blocks belonging to the same super block

Supiter: a hydrogen-rich gas giant in the Groombridge 1618 expeditionary staging system many times the size of Jupiter

Terminal: any computer device, e.g. static mainframe, field operations, handroid or on-board vehicular

Togless: old and antiquated systems of communication and entertainment lacking in tactile, olfactory and gustatory sensory data streams, e.g. audio-visual entertainment, telephones, video-phones, etc.: modern records or communications omitting those same sensory data streams for stylistic or privacy reasons

PRIMED

Togglicon: contracted term for *toggle icon*, an arhud button for activating and deactivating assigned functions via eye-point or virtual touch interaction

UNE: pronounced *YOON* (anglophonic variant) or *OON* (teuto-francophonic); acronym for *United Nations of Earth*, federal government of Earth and its controlled colonies: crony capitalism rose to dominance during the successive breakdown of Soviet, US and Chinese superpowers, contributing to the dissolution of the United Nations and the establishment of UNE as a unifying, federal government better serving the interests of transnational corporations. Martial law declaration during the O.A.C.I. movement has created a police state. Recent development and implementation of the Nova Gate program has led to the rapid expansion of UNE-controlled space from a relatively local, one-hundred light year expanse to a sparsely explored and impossible to govern ten thousand light year empire spanning the whole of the Orion Arm

UNERA: acronym for *United Nations of Earth Revenue Agency*, responsible for federal tax collection

UNESA: acronym for *United Nations of Earth Security Agency*, UNE's federal government counter-intelligence organisation

UNO: federal currency denomination valid throughout UNE space

Vegg: a molecularly engineered, high protein food-stuff encapsulated in a leathery ball; hypo-allergenic egg-substitute eliminating avian-borne disease vectors

Ver-assessment: analogous to a modern polygraph or so-called *lie-detector test*, wherein a subject's avtog stream is monitored via *nen-screening* for psycho-physiological stress responses to questions and answers

V-nano: a molecularly engineered food-stuff providing for a balanced diet, containing recommended daily amounts of vitamins and minerals in an easily digestible, hypo-allergenic carbohydrate base, resembling straight bananas

Voider: an O.A.C.I. veteran described by peers as having been *up against the void* one time too many, burning out from the psychological strain of multiple death experiences and revival via cloning and memory transference technologies.

Wackie: slang derogatory term employed by UNE federal law enforcement and military personnel for service persons of the O.A.C.I.

Wetcube: a prefabricated, roughly cube-shaped enclosure often nano-formed into a single piece of continuous *quartztic*, maximising hygiene, hooked up to hot and cold running water supplies and sewage outlet, replacing traditional washrooms, bathrooms, toilets, etc. with self-cleaning and water-conservation features standard

Witch Head: name of an O.A.C.I. outpost in the Witch Head Nebula; the main purpose of the outpost is to provide barracks for the privately contracted O.A.C.I. security force, comprised mainly of rookies, defending the dust cloud miners in the nebula from piracy. Its remoteness, apparent strategic insignificance and low intrinsic value to UNE make it an ideal, secret location for the O.A.C.I. Special Operatives Training Facility

XYZT: pronounced very much like *exist*; the sensor-based detection of a target object's precise three-dimensional position, and its extrapolated movement over time; used for intelligence gathering for artillery strikes and other tactical operations

AFTERWORD

I hope you enjoy reading *Primed* as much as I enjoyed writing it. This is my first novel-length work, and my first self-publication. If you'd like to encourage me to write more you can do so by spreading the word: tell your friends about how much you enjoyed the story; bring it to your local book club; post a review at Amazon, Goodreads or Shelfari; blog, tweet or post about it on Facebook, Google+ or Pinterest; contribute to my crowdfunding campaigns at Indiegogo; talk and nen about it wherever you go!

In this day and age of corporate hegemony, where consumer electronic media ownership rights are being steadily eroded, you find yourself in possession of something precious, something that can't be reclaimed or revoked: a book! Read it on buses and trains, stand on the street and read aloud, flaunt your lavish data-ownership rights publicly. When you've finished reading it, lend it to a friend, and thereby participate in one of the few data-sharing methods that haven't (yet!) been declared an act of piracy.

If you'd like to discuss any of the themes raised in *Primed* you can also contact me directly via e-mail through my publishing webpage:

http://gp4ancis.wix.com/dissidentpress

There you can sign up to receive an e-newsletter about my continuing work, as well as finding links to follow my posts on Goodreads.com, Google+ and Facebook. Phew! Hopefully, in between all the website maintenance, I'll still have time to actually write another novel.

Thank you *so much* for reading. All *I* did was *write* it (yes, and publish, and market, blah, blah, blah): *you* brought the story to its fullest potential. I'll always owe you a debt of gratitude for that.

PRIMED

ABOUT THE AUTHOR

I was born in Wales in 1973. My parents separated when I was eight, and my mother, sister, brother and I moved to England to stay with my grandfather in a two bedroom maisonette. We drove him crazy. He kicked us out.

Before he did, I remember there was just enough floor space to open our bedroom door in one corner, and the wardrobe opposite, but the rest of the floor was covered by our beds, touching side-by-side from wall to wall. In the winter, ice built up on the inside of the windows overnight, forming etched, crystalline patterns across the glass by morning.

After scraping through college I was fortunate to find my way into an Environmental Science degree programme and after an adventurous career path, including toxic waste disposal, fork-lift truck operating and motorcycle couriering, I landed a few Environment Department jobs with Central London authorities, where I met the love of my life and followed her back to Canada. We now live in Vancouver with our three beautiful daughters.

Made in the USA
Charleston, SC
28 March 2016